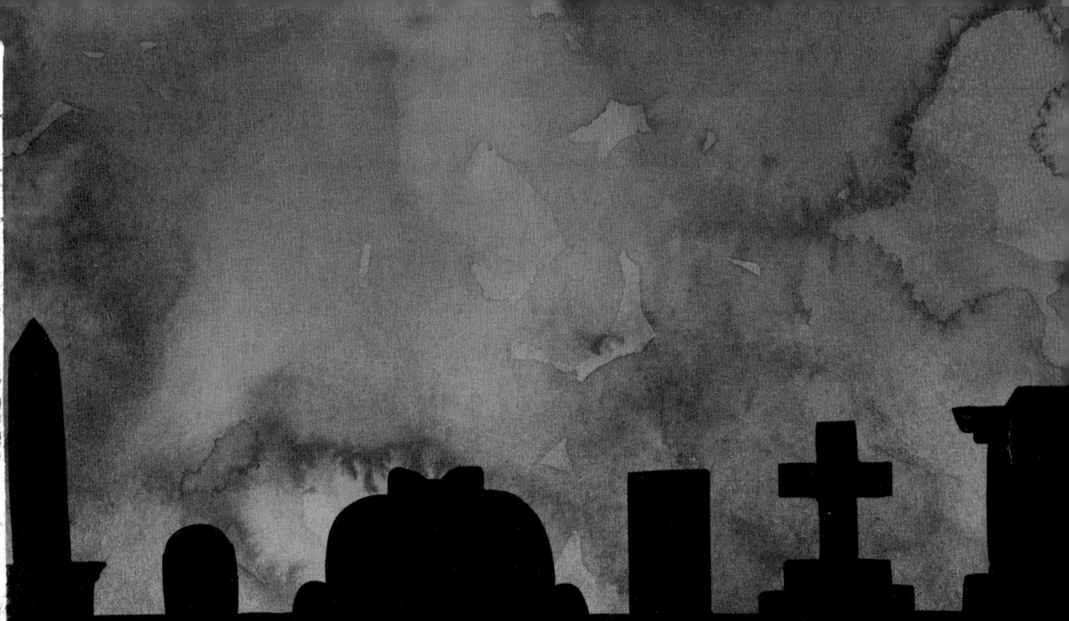

THE GHOUL NEXT DOOR

HarperAlley is an imprint of HarperCollins Publishers.

The Ghoul Next Door

For information address HarperCollins Children's Books, a division of HarperCollins Publishers, 195 Broadway, New York, NY 10007.
www.harperalley.com

Library of Congress Control Number: 2020949436
ISBN 978-0-06-289610-0 — ISBN 978-0-06-289609-4 (pbk.)

The artist used Clip Studio Paint, ink, watercolor, and mixed media paper to create the illustrations for this book.
Typography by Rick Farley
21 22 23 24 25 EP 10 9 8 7 6 5 4 3 2 1

First Edition

THE GHOUL NEXT DOOR

CULLEN BUNN & CAT FARRIS

LETTERING BY

ADITYA BIDIKAR

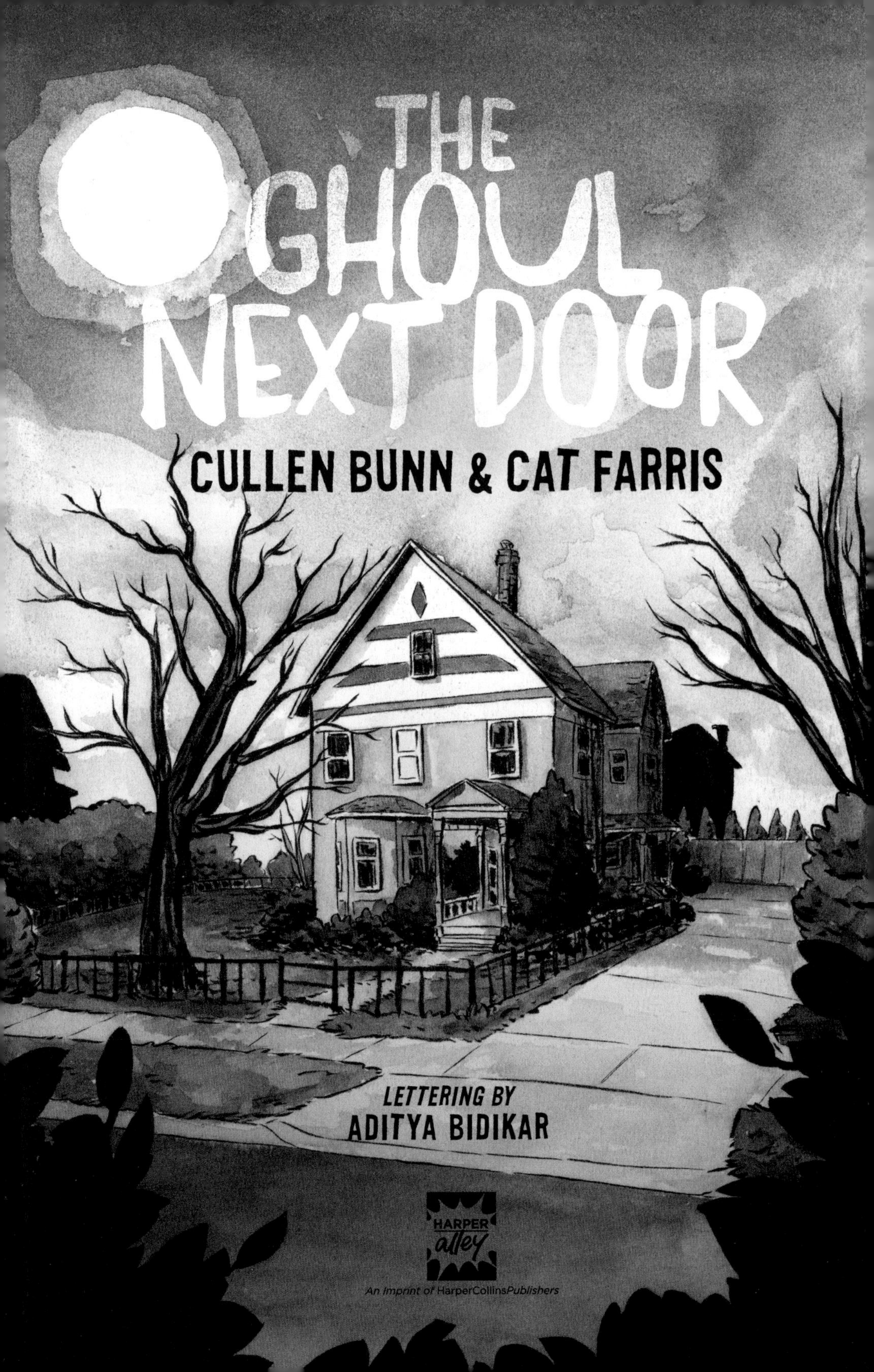

HARPER alley

An Imprint of HarperCollinsPublishers

To Cindy and Jackson, the best family—ghoul, human, or otherwise—a guy could hope for.

—C.B.

For Grandma Mayo, my biggest fan.

—C.F.

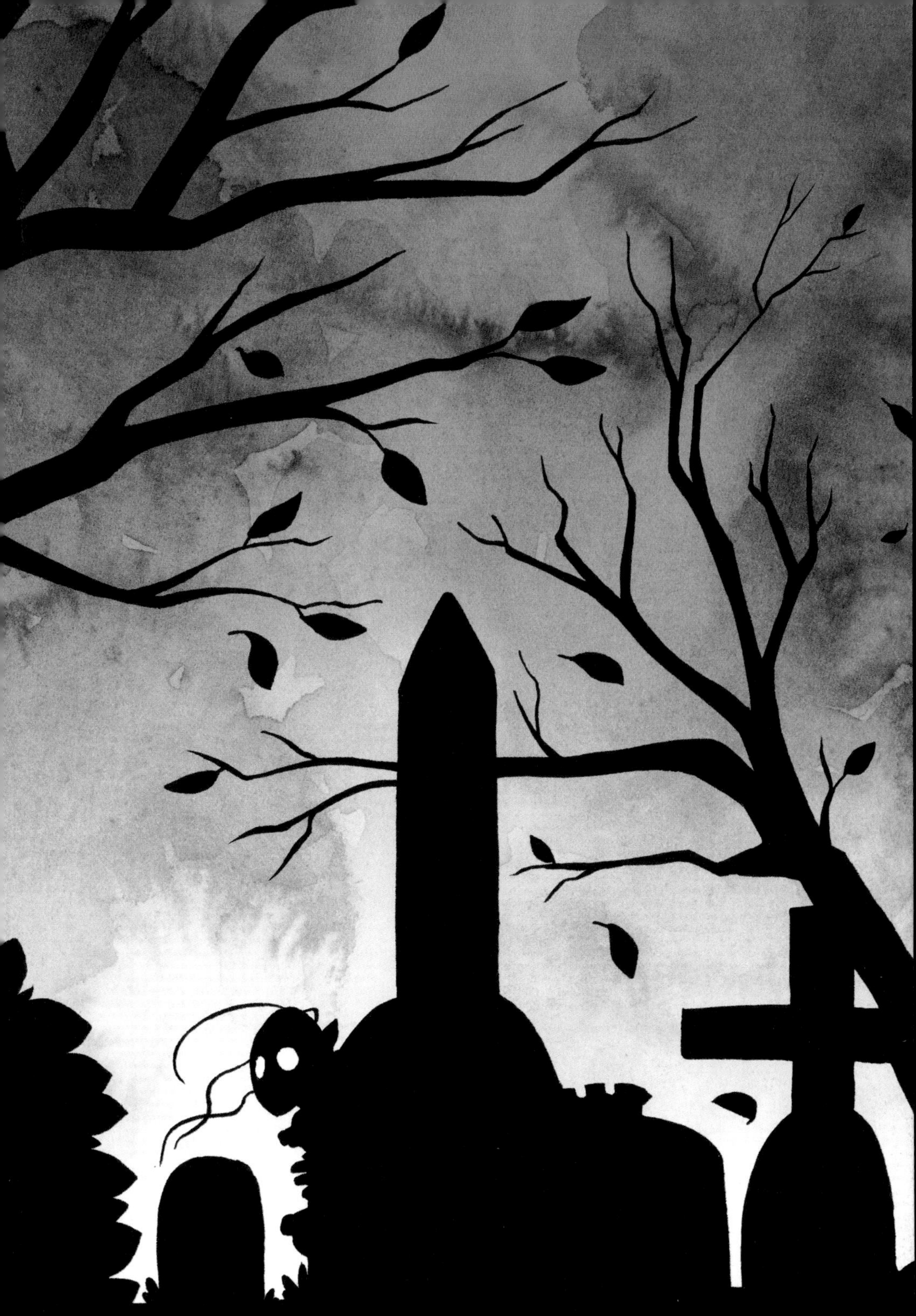

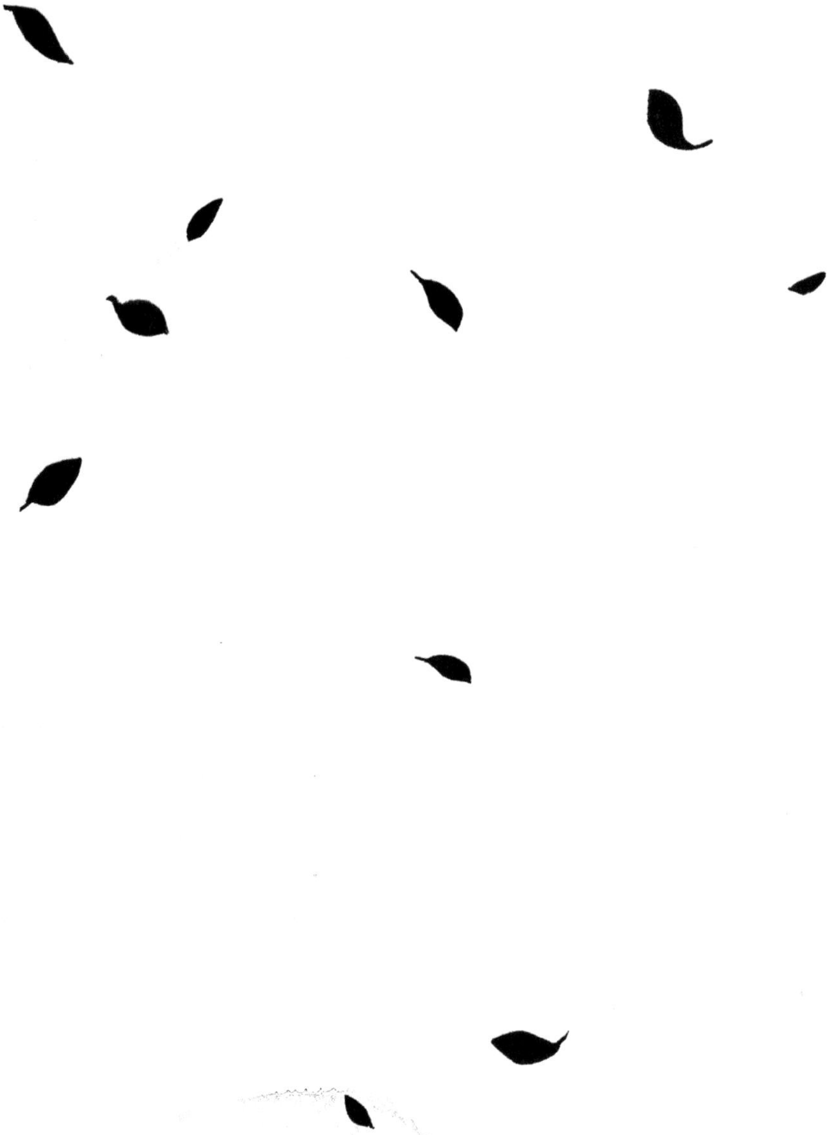

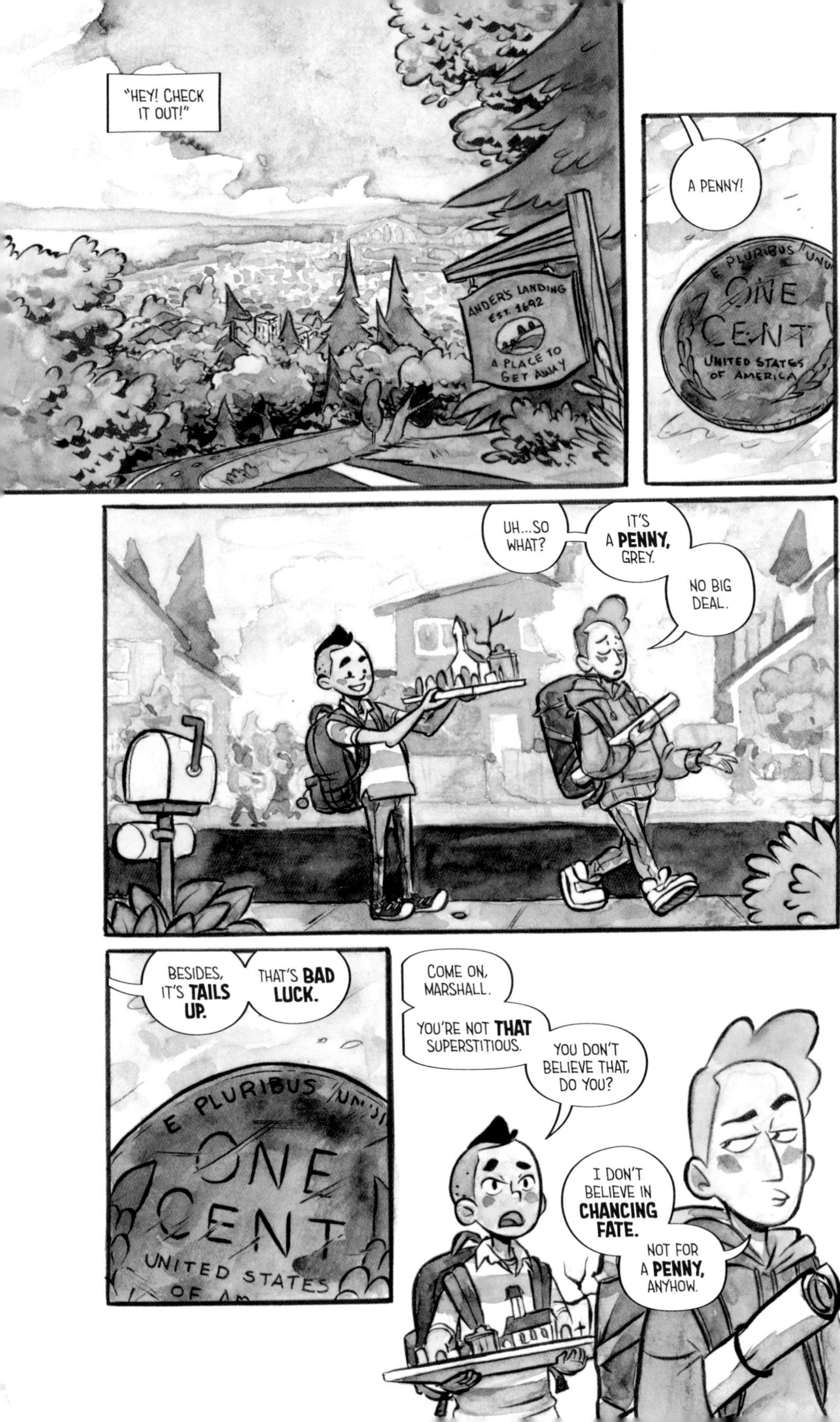
"HEY! CHECK IT OUT!"
ANDER'S LANDING EST. 1692 A PLACE TO GET AWAY
A PENNY!
E PLURIBUS UNUM ONE CENT UNITED STATES OF AMERICA
UH...SO WHAT?
IT'S A **PENNY,** GREY.
NO BIG DEAL.
BESIDES, IT'S **TAILS UP.**
THAT'S **BAD LUCK.**
E PLURIBUS ONE CENT UNITED STATES
COME ON, MARSHALL.
YOU'RE NOT **THAT** SUPERSTITIOUS.
YOU DON'T BELIEVE THAT, DO YOU?
I DON'T BELIEVE IN **CHANCING FATE.**
NOT FOR A **PENNY,** ANYHOW.

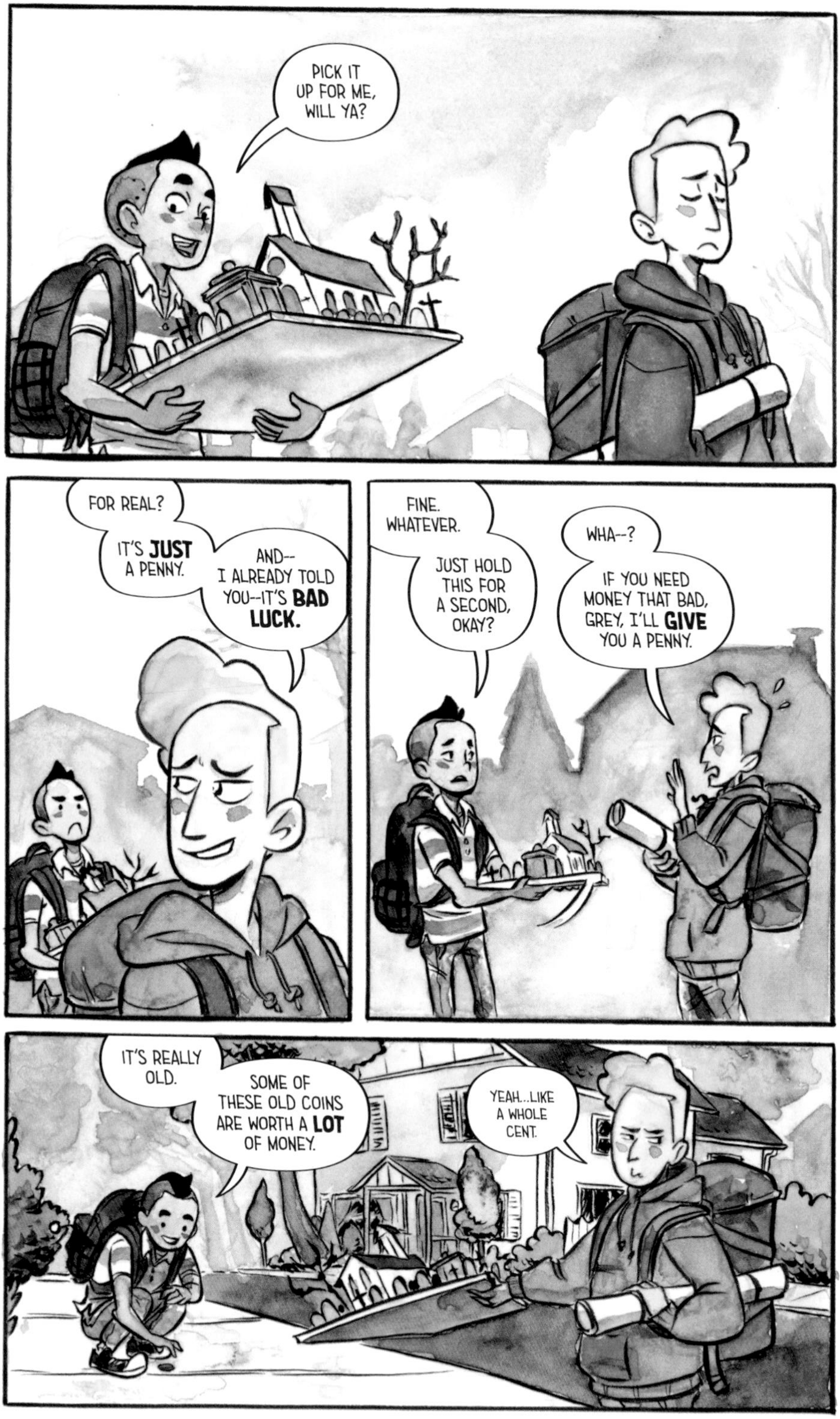
PICK IT UP FOR ME, WILL YA?
FOR REAL?
IT'S **JUST** A PENNY.
AND-- I ALREADY TOLD YOU--IT'S **BAD LUCK.**
FINE. WHATEVER.
JUST HOLD THIS FOR A SECOND, OKAY?
WHA--?
IF YOU NEED MONEY THAT BAD, GREY, I'LL **GIVE** YOU A PENNY.
IT'S REALLY OLD.
SOME OF THESE OLD COINS ARE WORTH A **LOT** OF MONEY.
YEAH...LIKE A WHOLE CENT.

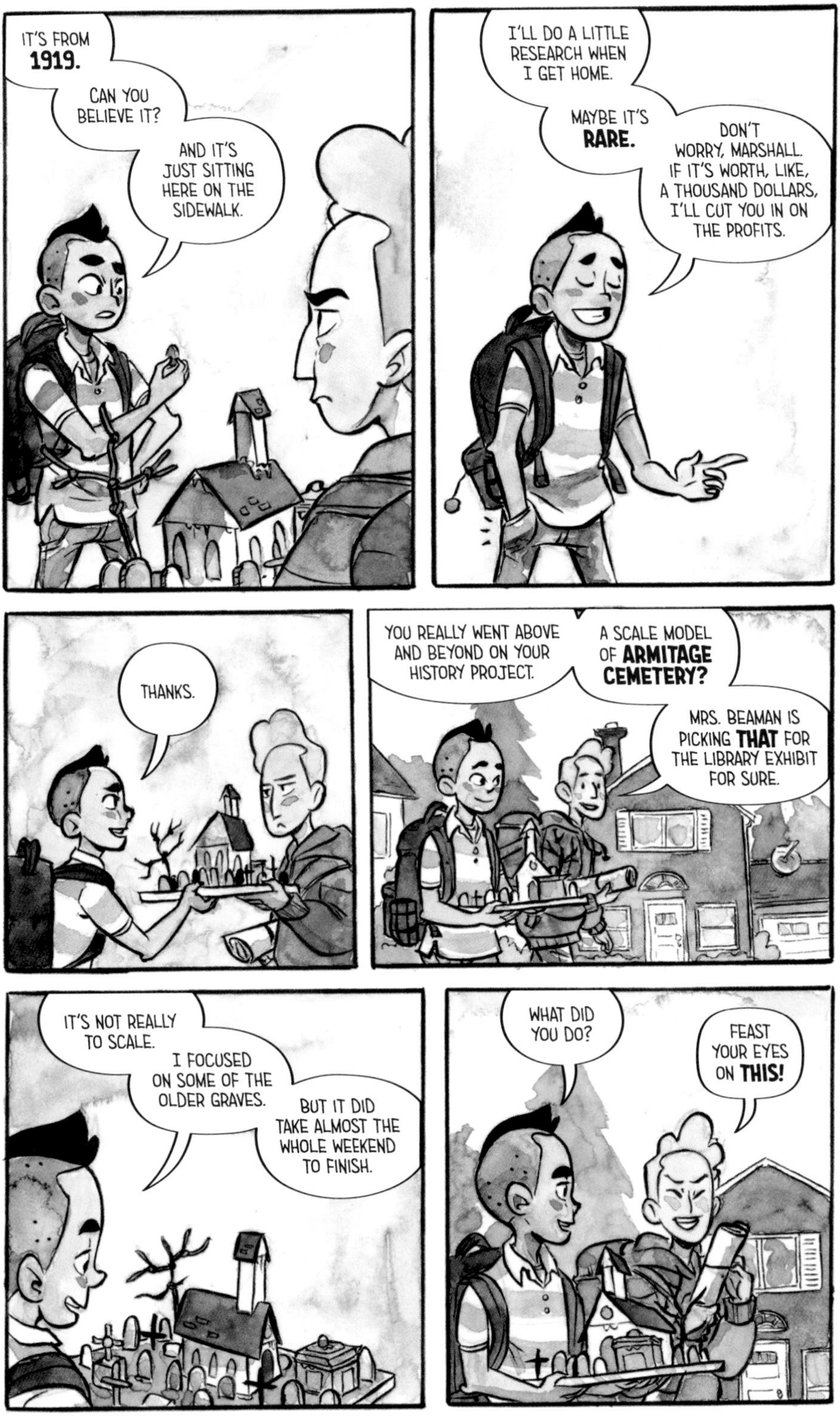
IT'S FROM **1919.**
CAN YOU BELIEVE IT?
AND IT'S JUST SITTING HERE ON THE SIDEWALK.
I'LL DO A LITTLE RESEARCH WHEN I GET HOME.
MAYBE IT'S **RARE.**
DON'T WORRY, MARSHALL. IF IT'S WORTH, LIKE, A THOUSAND DOLLARS, I'LL CUT YOU IN ON THE PROFITS.
THANKS.
YOU REALLY WENT ABOVE AND BEYOND ON YOUR HISTORY PROJECT.
A SCALE MODEL OF **ARMITAGE CEMETERY?**
MRS. BEAMAN IS PICKING **THAT** FOR THE LIBRARY EXHIBIT FOR SURE.
IT'S NOT REALLY TO SCALE.
I FOCUSED ON SOME OF THE OLDER GRAVES.
BUT IT DID TAKE ALMOST THE WHOLE WEEKEND TO FINISH.
WHAT DID YOU DO?
FEAST YOUR EYES ON **THIS!**

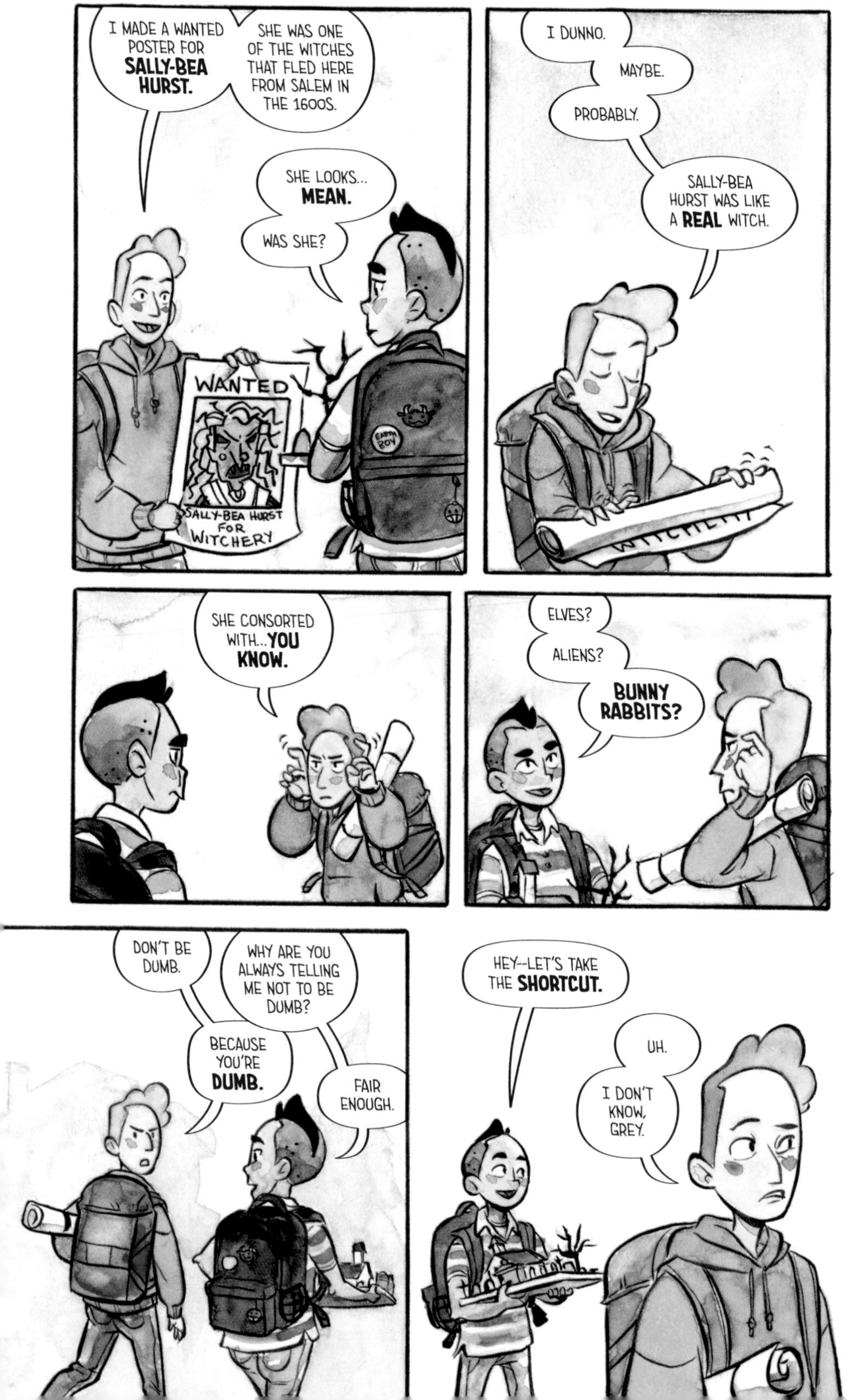

I MADE A WANTED POSTER FOR **SALLY-BEA HURST.**
SHE WAS ONE OF THE WITCHES THAT FLED HERE FROM SALEM IN THE 1600S.
WANTED
SALLY-BEA HURST FOR WITCHERY
SHE LOOKS... **MEAN.**
WAS SHE?
I DUNNO.
MAYBE.
PROBABLY.
SALLY-BEA HURST WAS LIKE A **REAL** WITCH.
SHE CONSORTED WITH...**YOU KNOW.**
ELVES?
ALIENS?
BUNNY RABBITS?
DON'T BE DUMB.
WHY ARE YOU ALWAYS TELLING ME NOT TO BE DUMB?
BECAUSE YOU'RE **DUMB.**
FAIR ENOUGH.
HEY--LET'S TAKE THE **SHORTCUT.**
UH.
I DON'T KNOW, GREY.

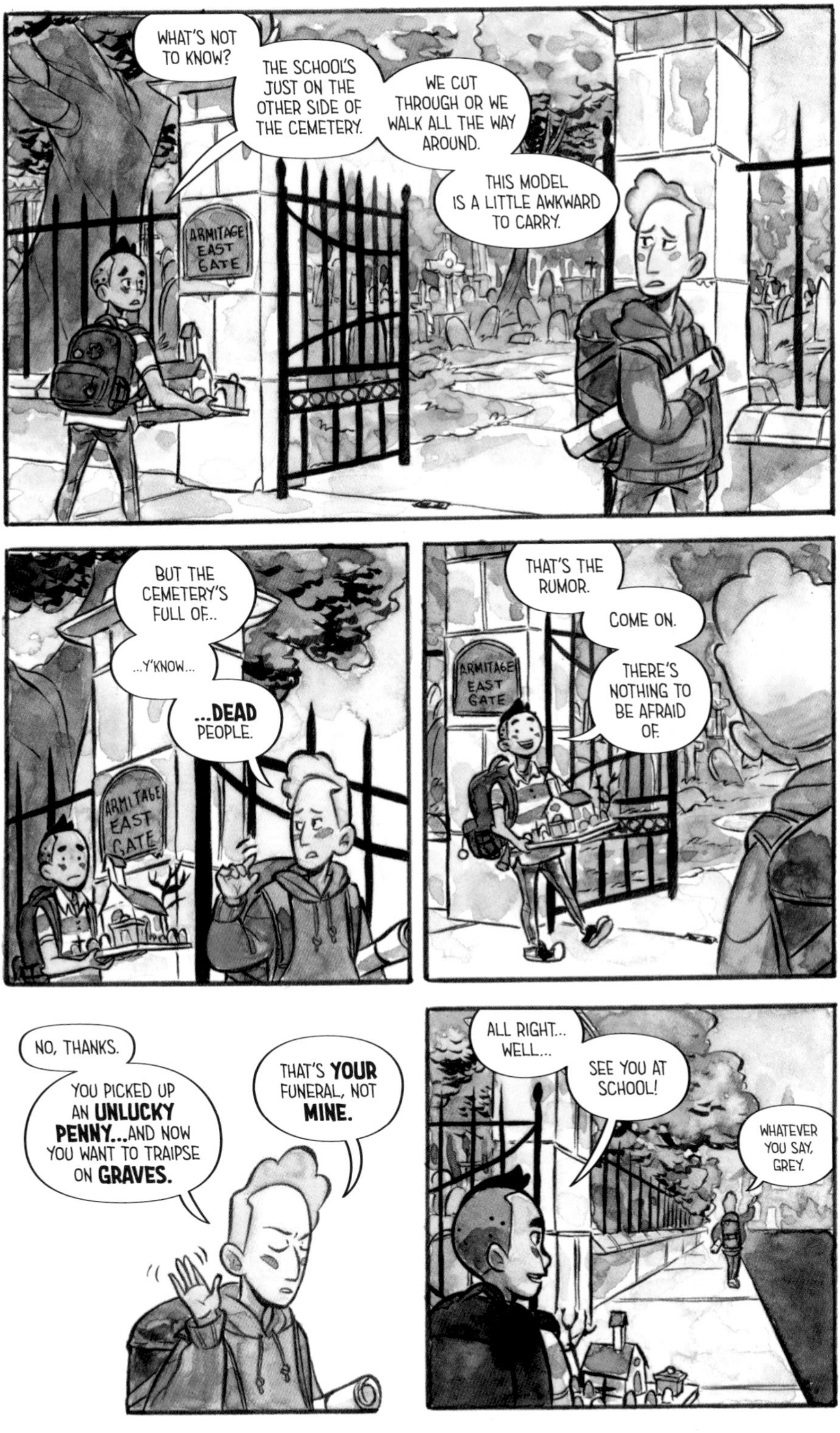
WHAT'S NOT TO KNOW?
THE SCHOOL'S JUST ON THE OTHER SIDE OF THE CEMETERY.
WE CUT THROUGH OR WE WALK ALL THE WAY AROUND.
THIS MODEL IS A LITTLE AWKWARD TO CARRY.
ARMITAGE EAST GATE
BUT THE CEMETERY'S FULL OF...
...Y'KNOW...
...DEAD PEOPLE.
ARMITAGE EAST GATE
THAT'S THE RUMOR.
COME ON.
THERE'S NOTHING TO BE AFRAID OF.
ARMITAGE EAST GATE
NO, THANKS.
YOU PICKED UP AN UNLUCKY PENNY...AND NOW YOU WANT TO TRAIPSE ON GRAVES.
THAT'S YOUR FUNERAL, NOT MINE.
ALL RIGHT... WELL...
SEE YOU AT SCHOOL!
WHATEVER YOU SAY, GREY.

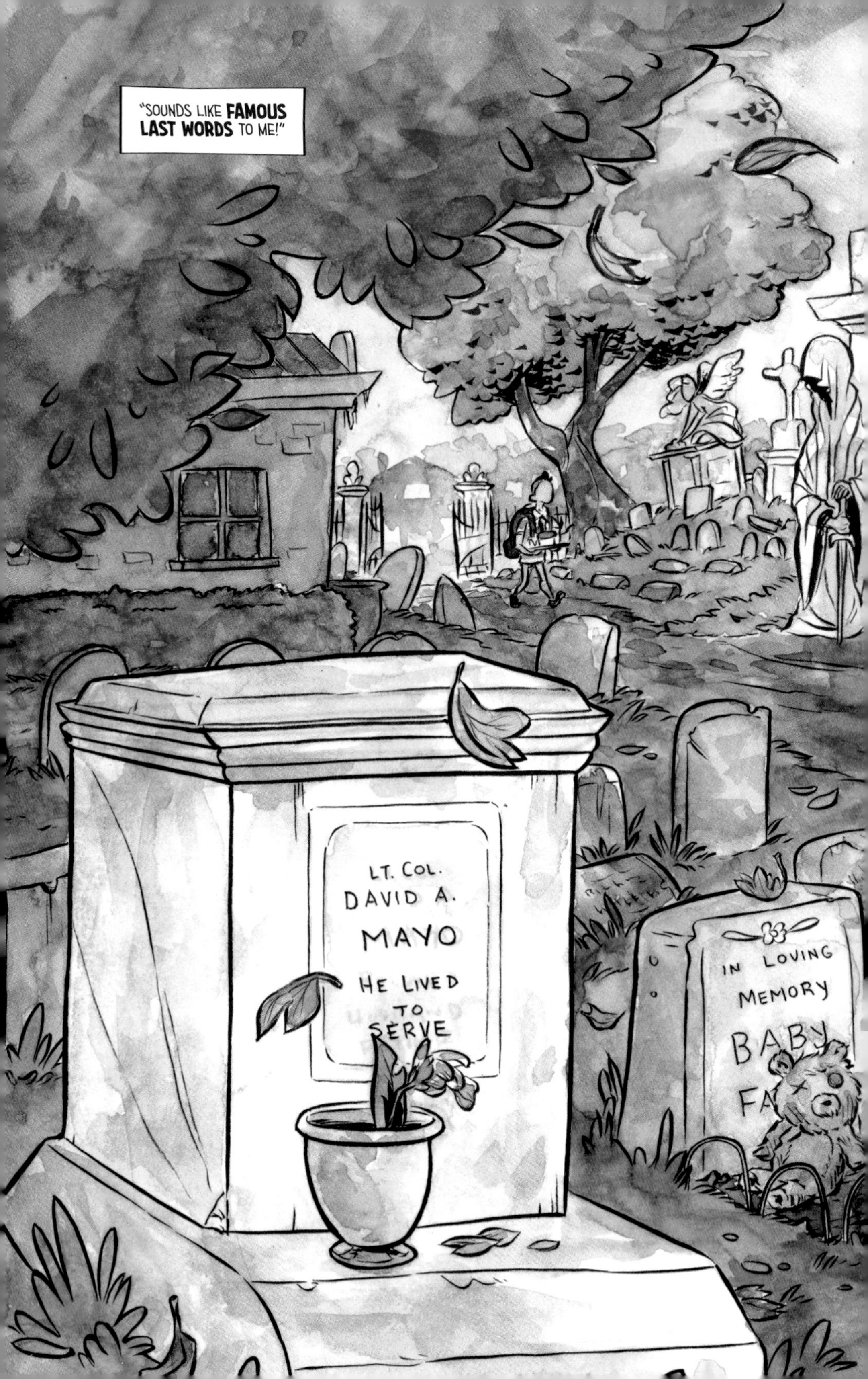
"SOUNDS LIKE FAMOUS LAST WORDS TO ME!"
LT. COL. DAVID A. MAYO HE LIVED TO SERVE
IN LOVING MEMORY BABY

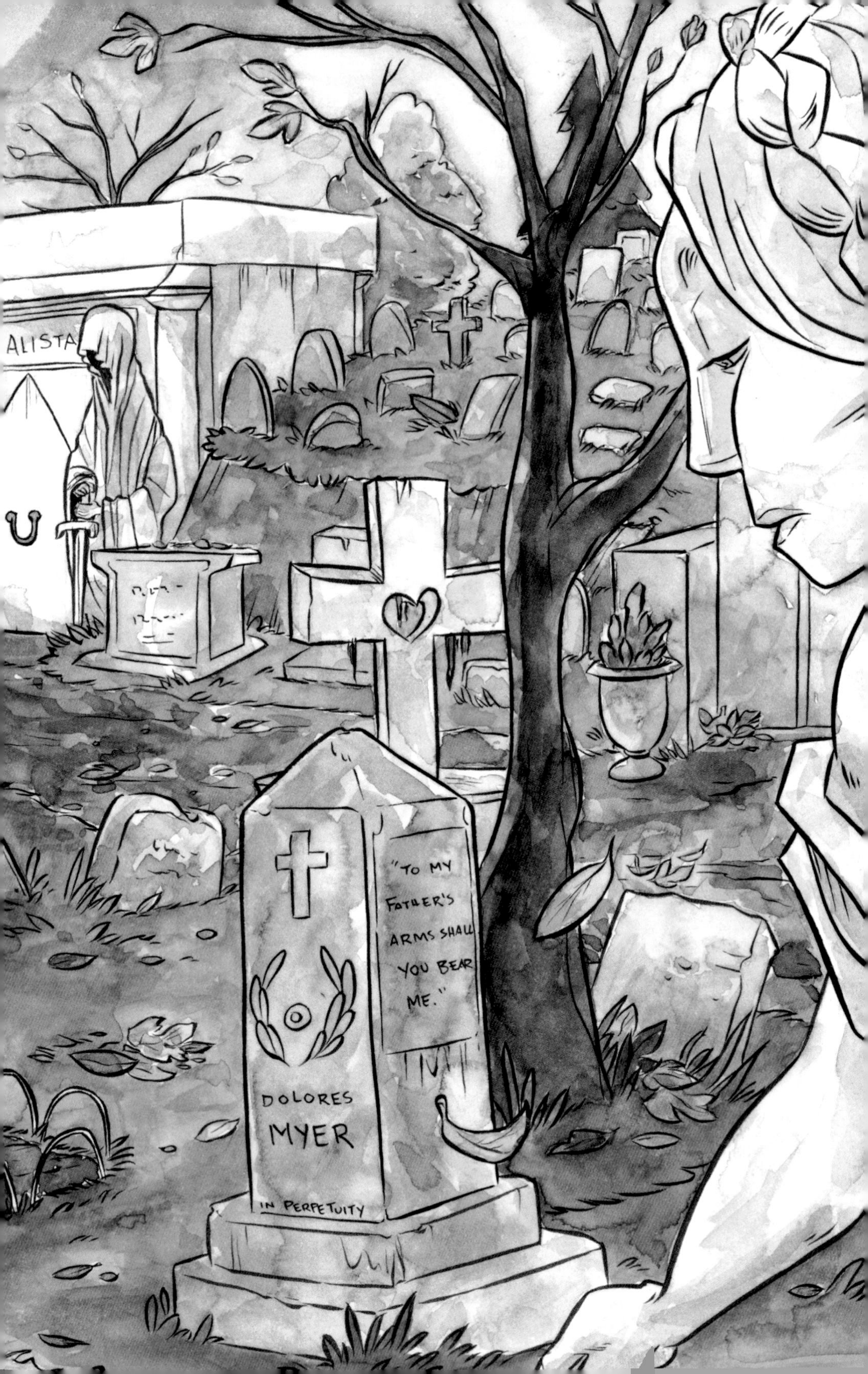
ALISTA
"TO MY FATHER'S ARMS SHALL YOU BEAR ME."
DOLORES MYER
IN PERPETUITY

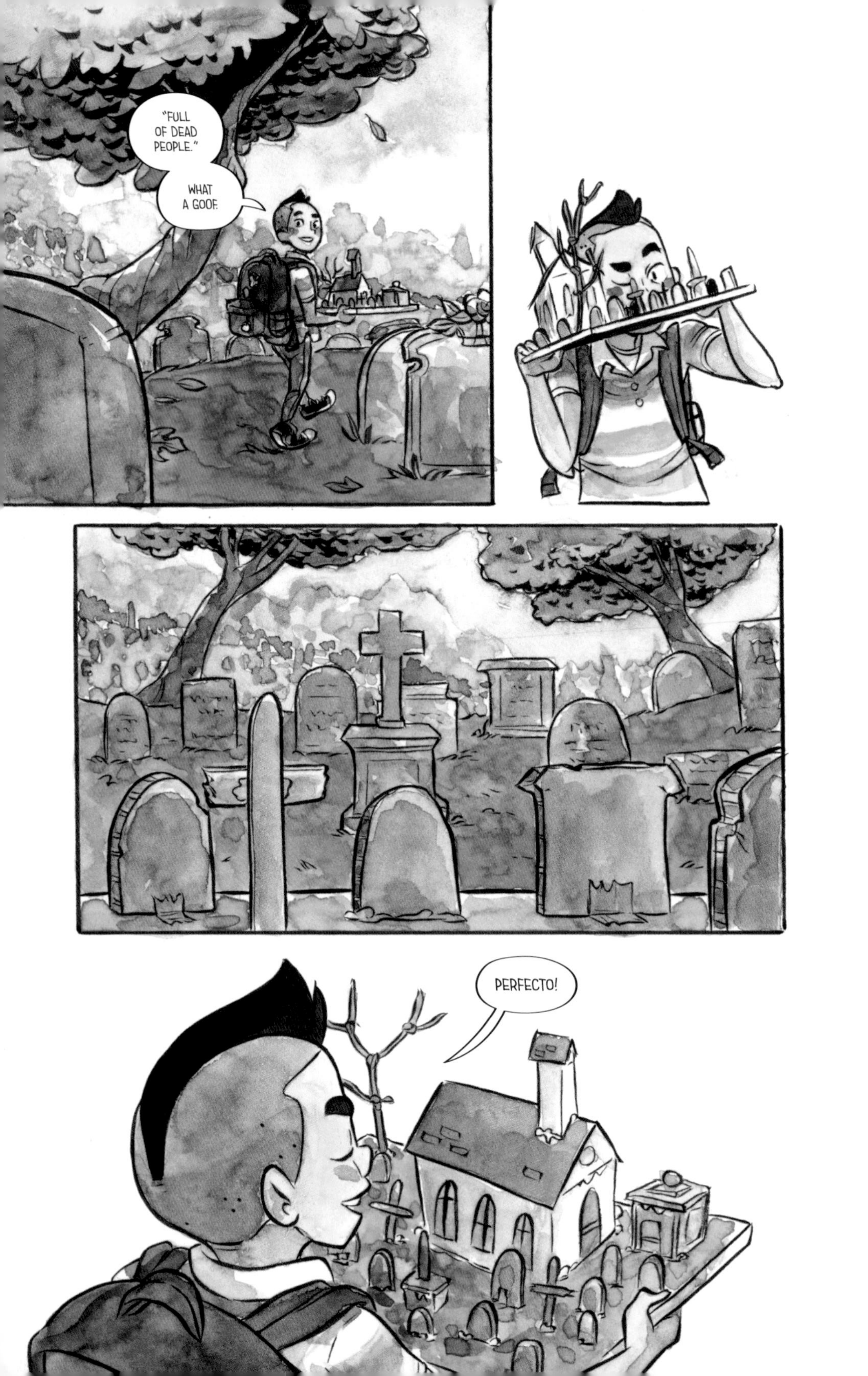
"FULL OF DEAD PEOPLE."
WHAT A GOOF.
PERFECTO!

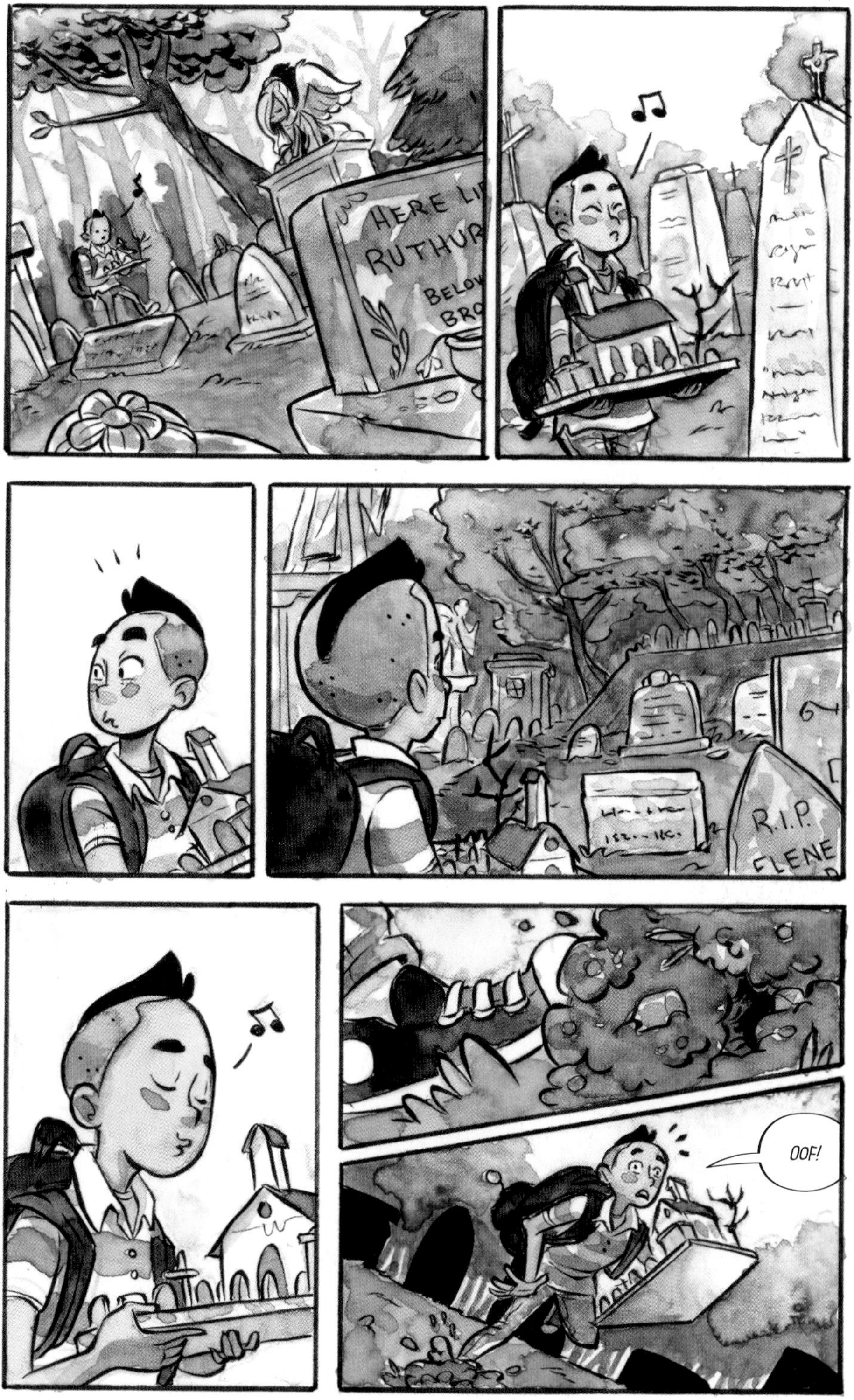
HERE LI
RUTHUR
BELOV
BRO
R.I.P.
ELENE
OOF!

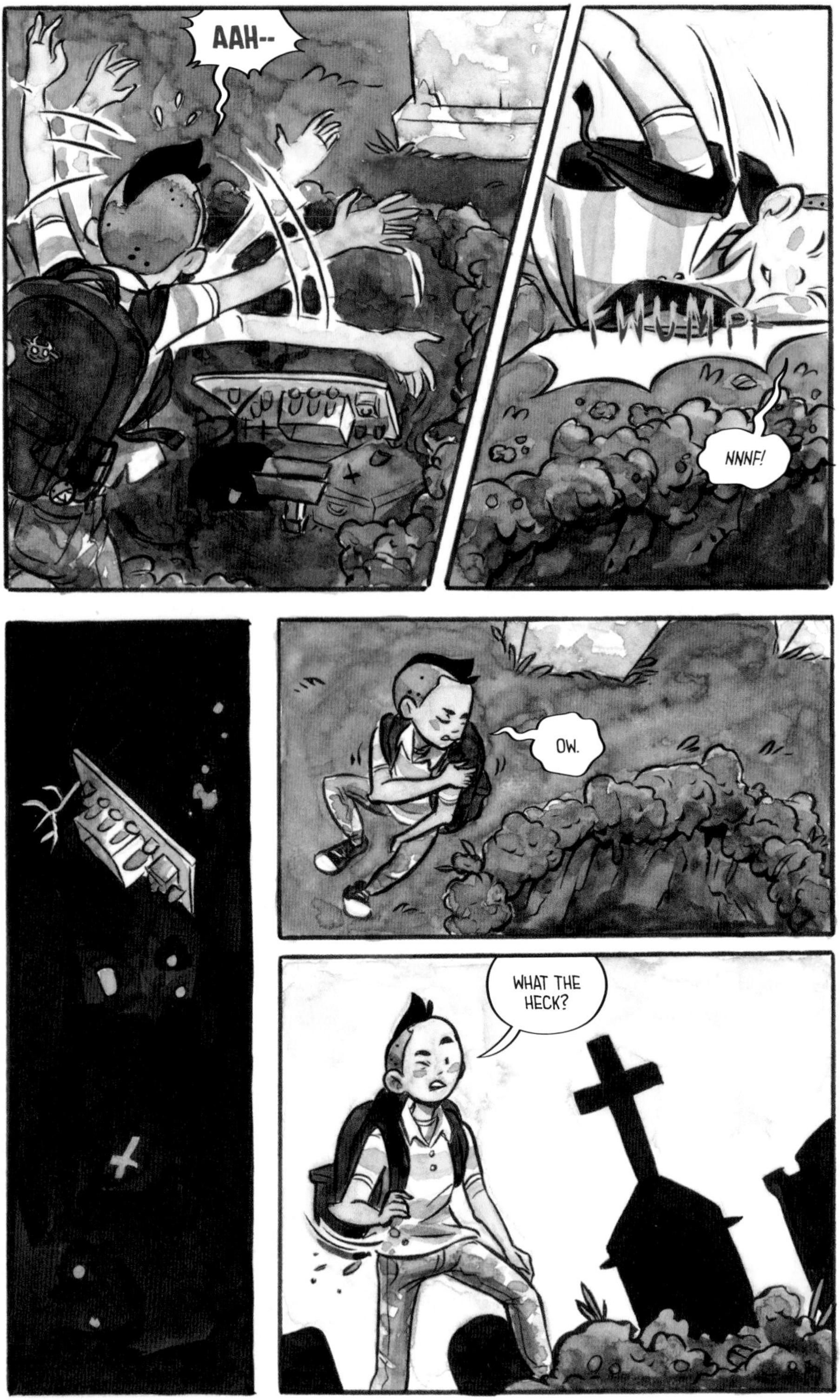
AAH--
FMUMP!
NNNF!
OW.
WHAT THE HECK?

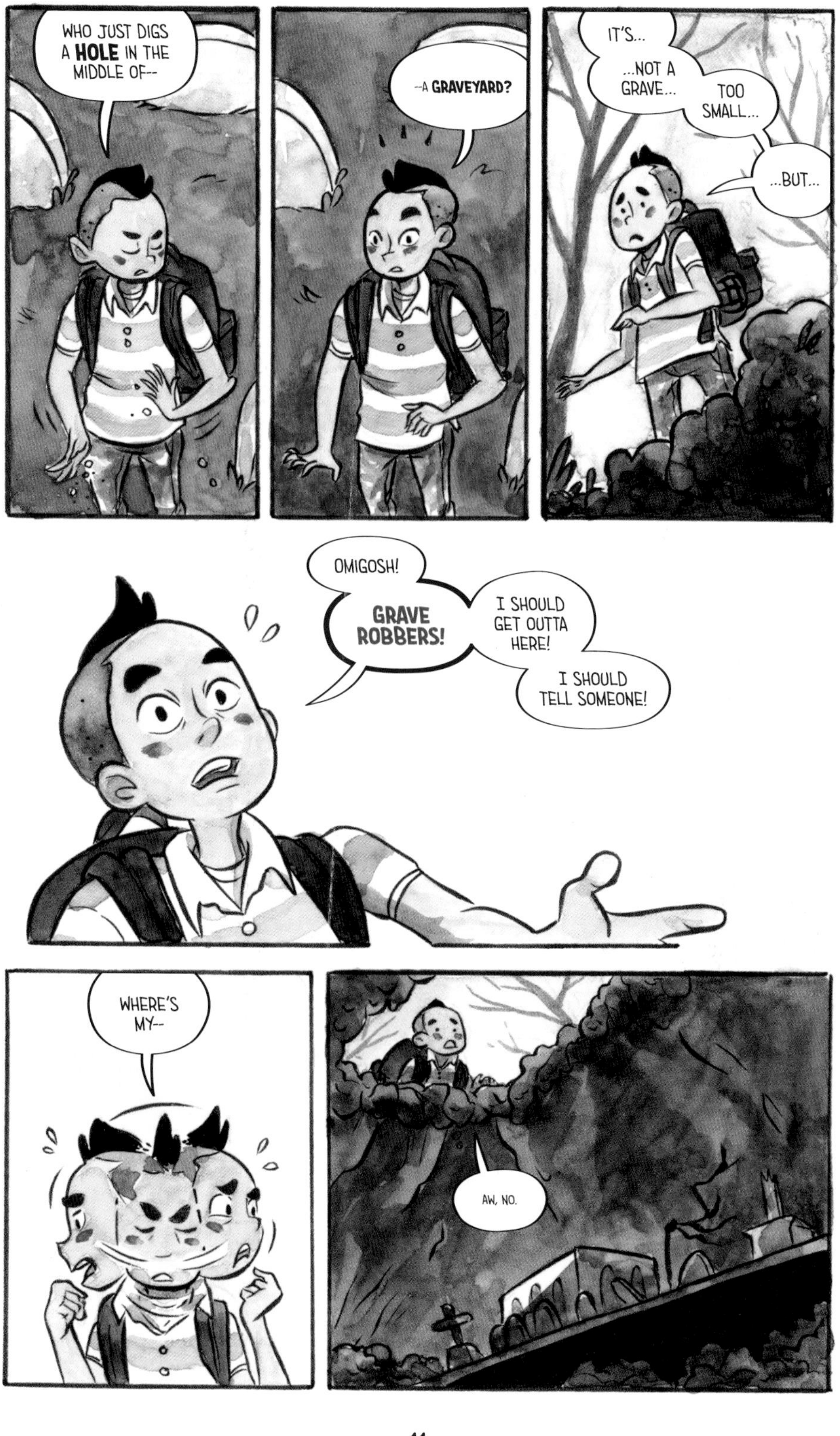
WHO JUST DIGS A **HOLE** IN THE MIDDLE OF--
--A **GRAVEYARD?**
IT'S...
...NOT A GRAVE...
TOO SMALL...
...BUT...
OMIGOSH!
GRAVE ROBBERS!
I SHOULD GET OUTTA HERE!
I SHOULD TELL SOMEONE!
WHERE'S MY--
AW, NO.

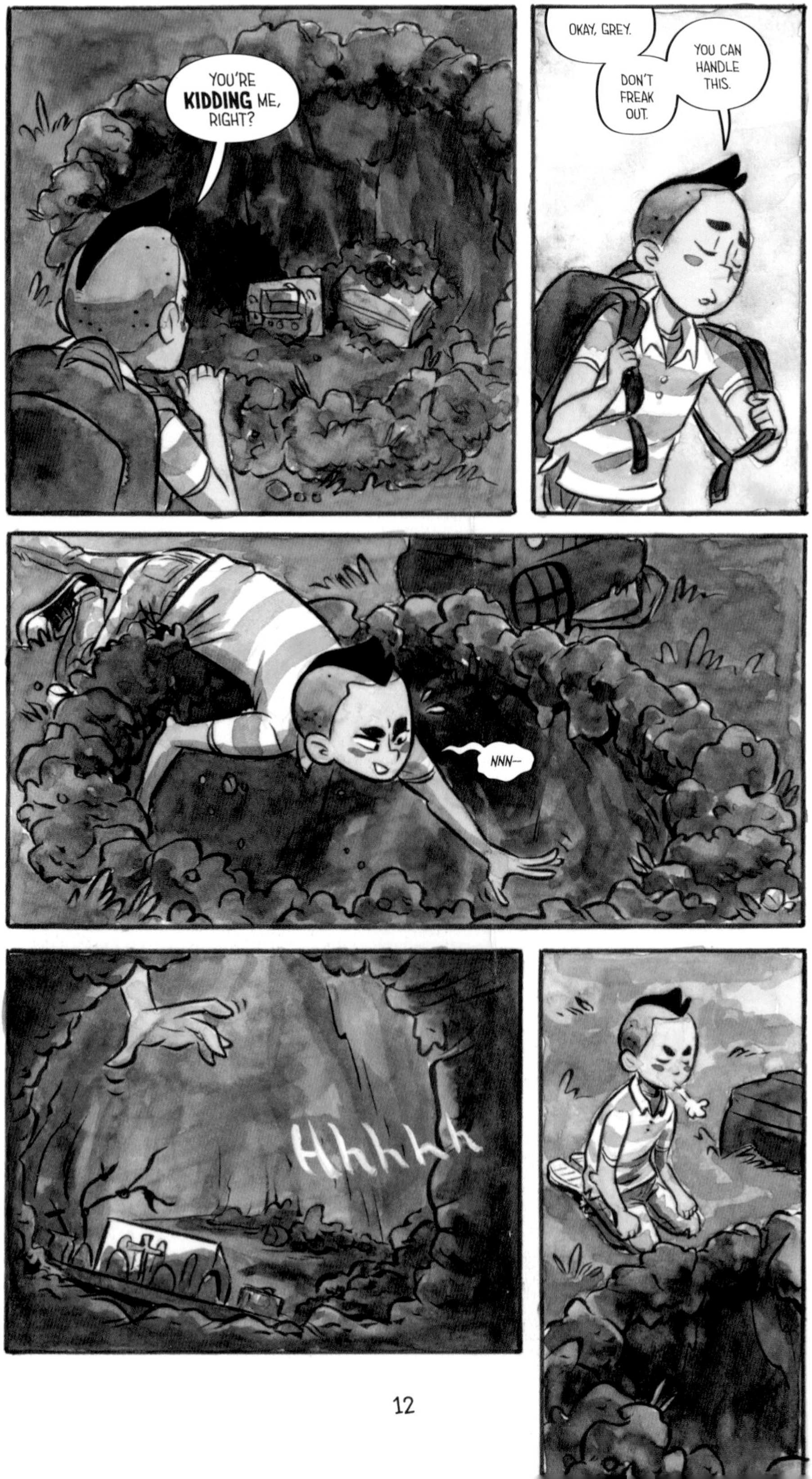
YOU'RE KIDDING ME, RIGHT?
OKAY, GREY.
DON'T FREAK OUT.
YOU CAN HANDLE THIS.
NNN--
Hhhhh

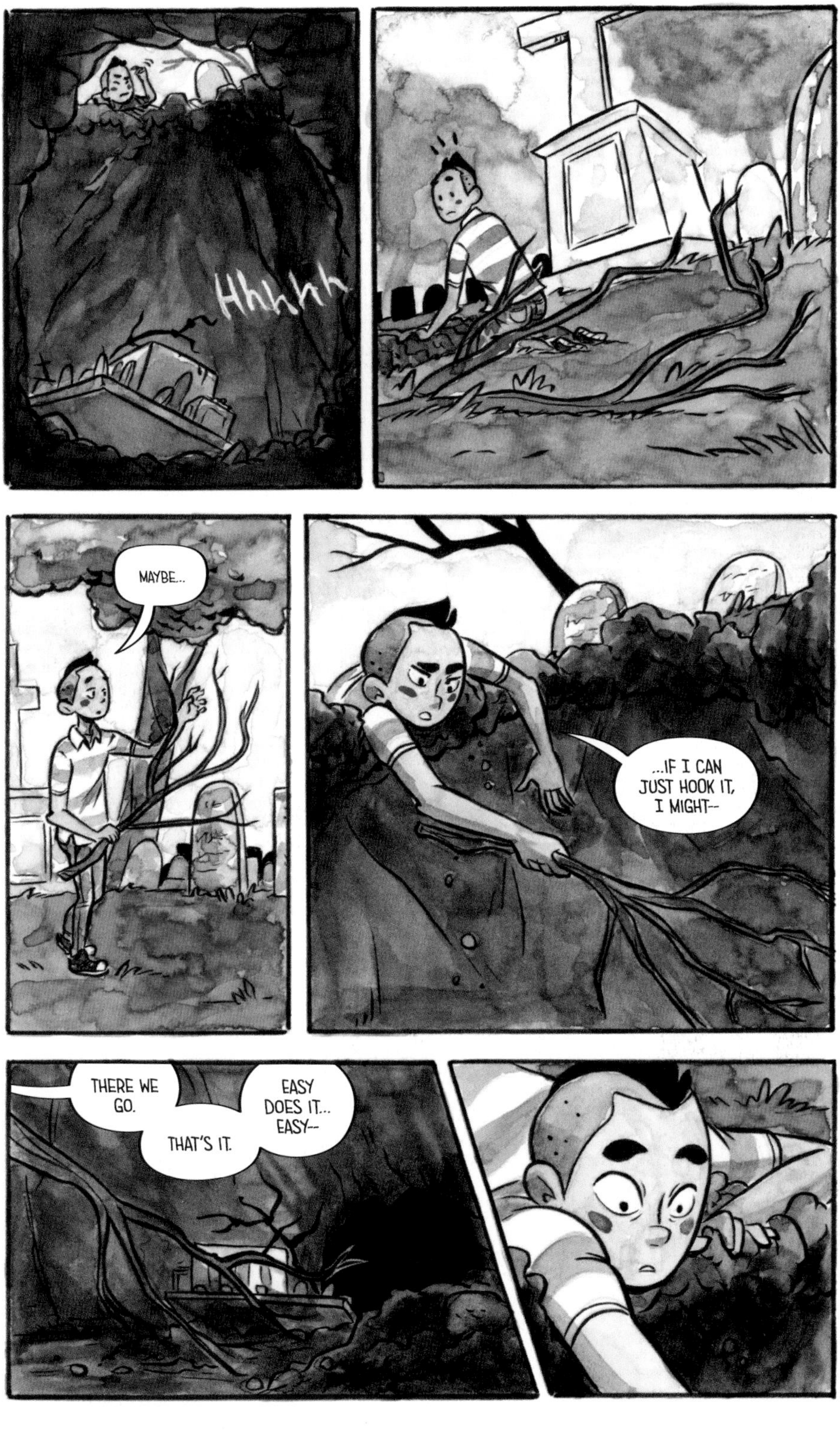
Hhhhh
MAYBE...
...IF I CAN JUST HOOK IT, I MIGHT--
THERE WE GO.
THAT'S IT.
EASY DOES IT... EASY--

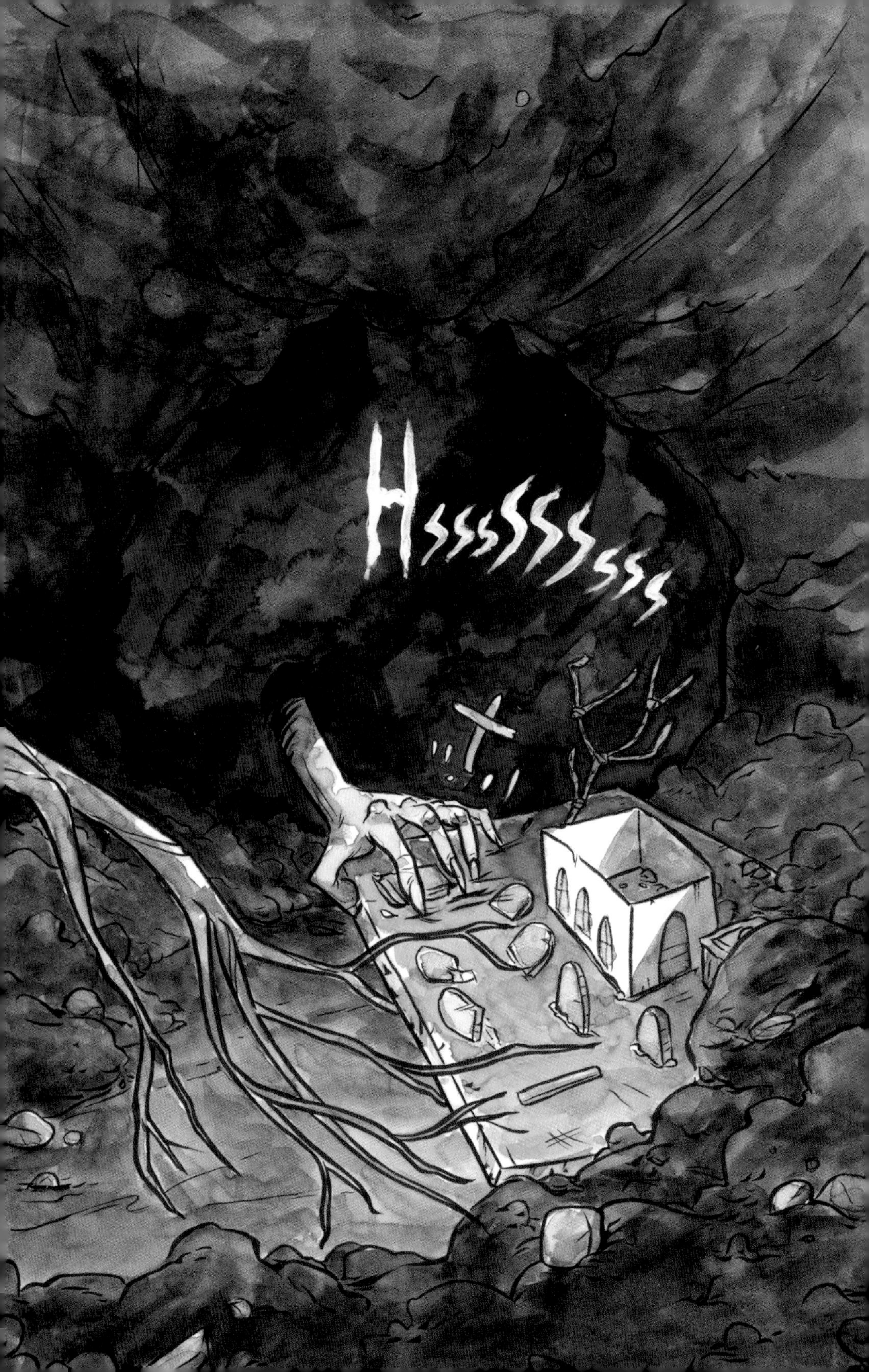
Hssssssss

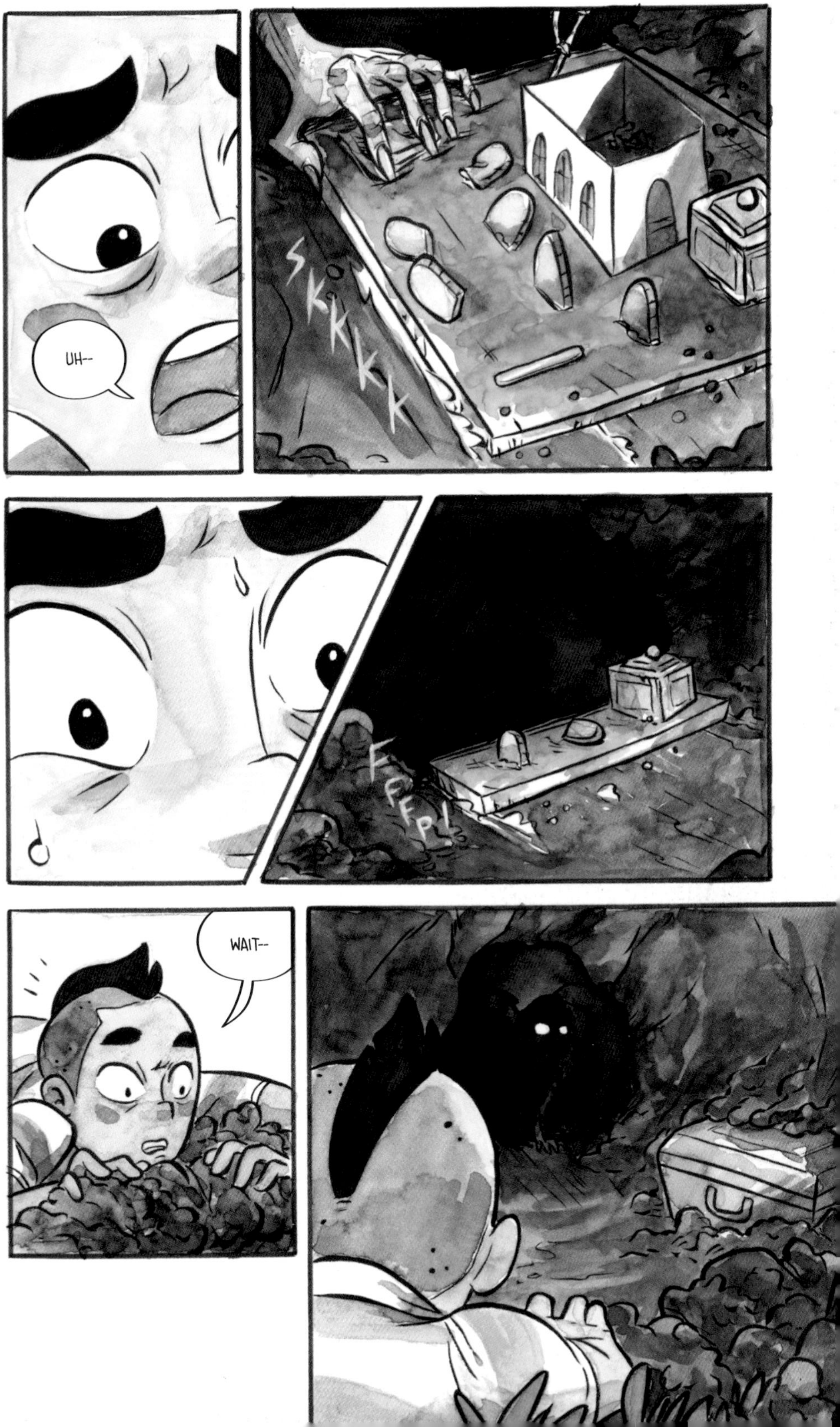
UH--
SKKKKK
FFFP!
WAIT--

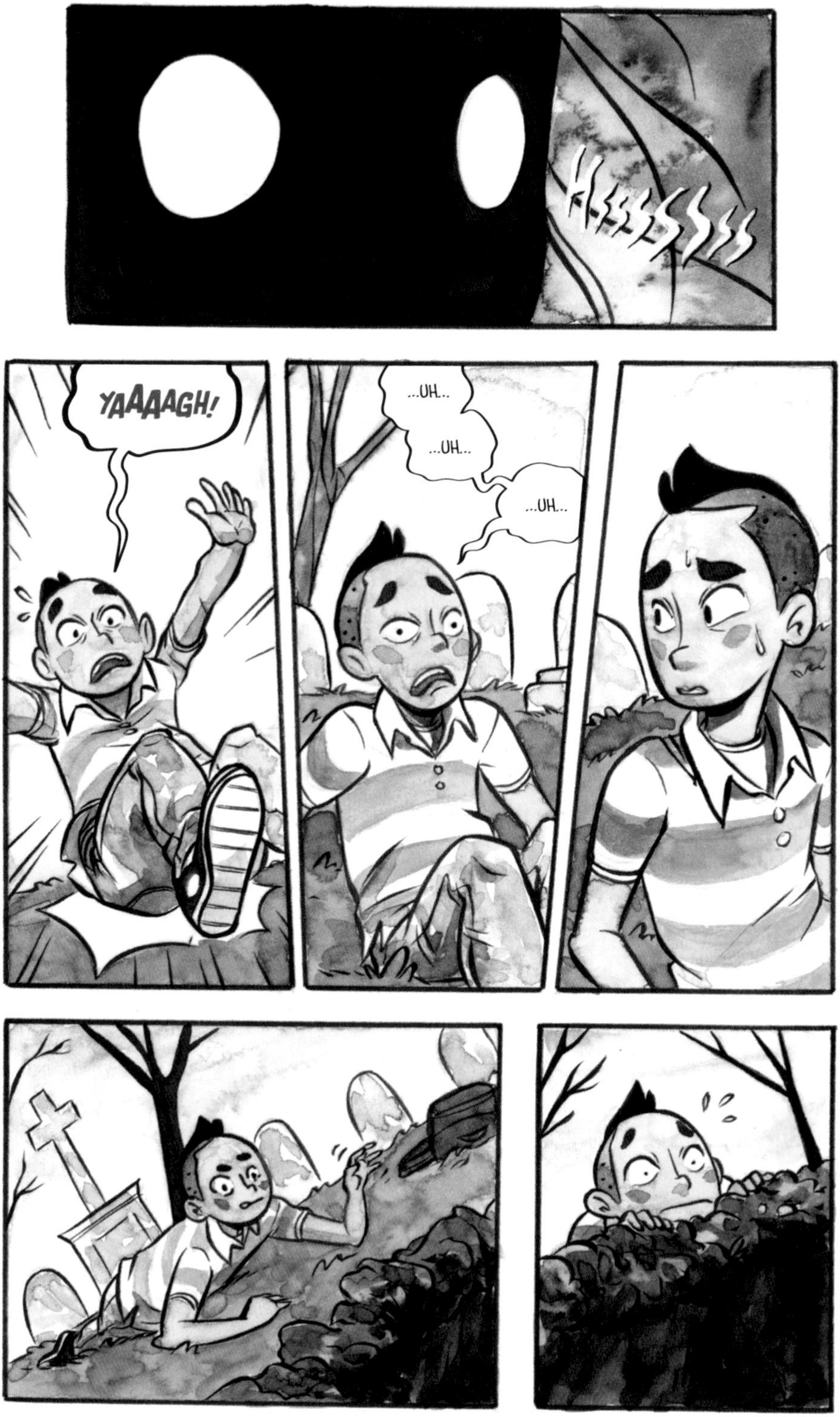
HSSSSSSS
YAAAAGH!
...UH...
...UH...
...UH...

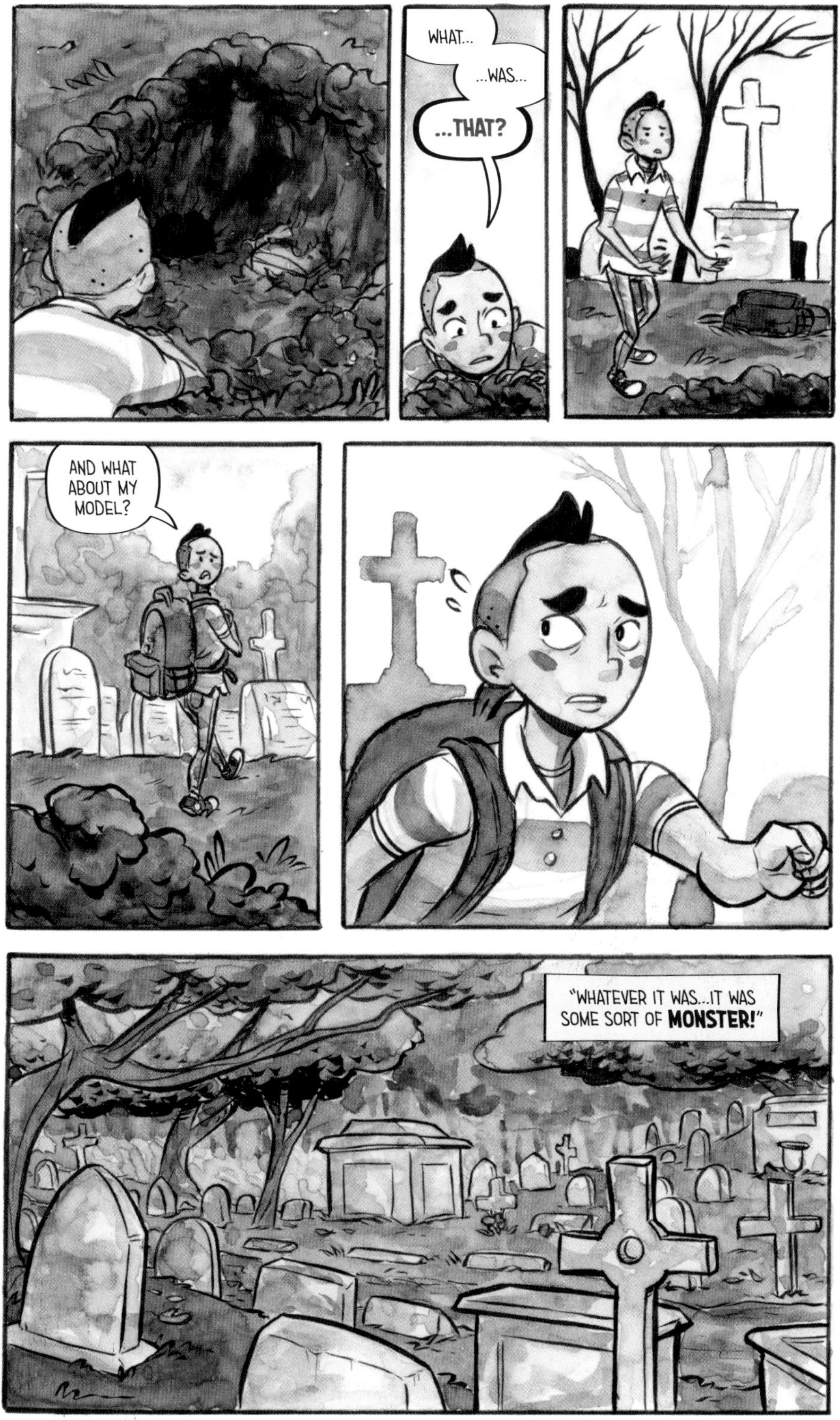
WHAT...
...WAS...
...THAT?
AND WHAT ABOUT MY MODEL?
"WHATEVER IT WAS...IT WAS SOME SORT OF **MONSTER!**"

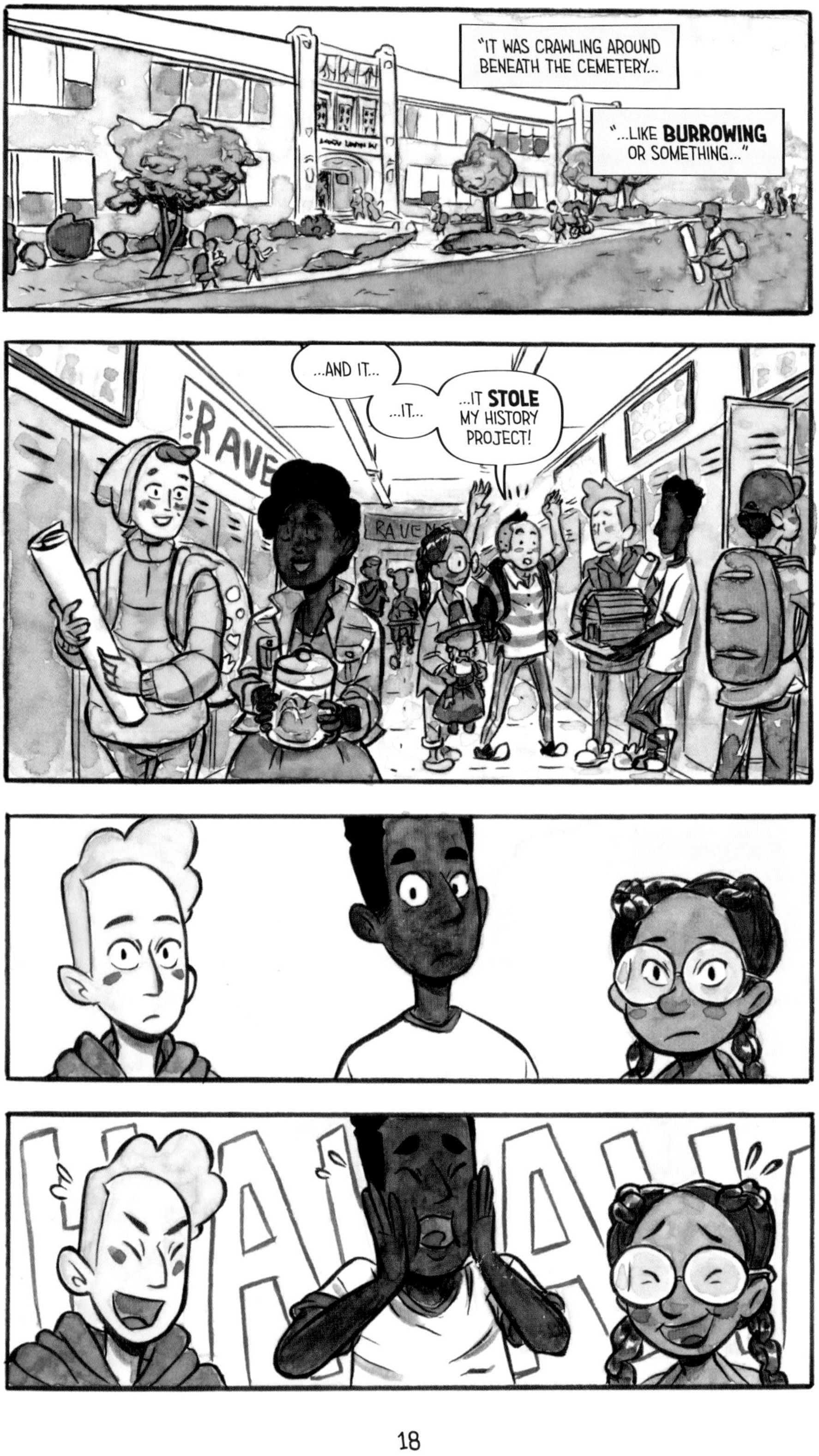
"IT WAS CRAWLING AROUND BENEATH THE CEMETERY...
"...LIKE **BURROWING** OR SOMETHING..."
...AND IT...
...IT...
...IT **STOLE** MY HISTORY PROJECT!

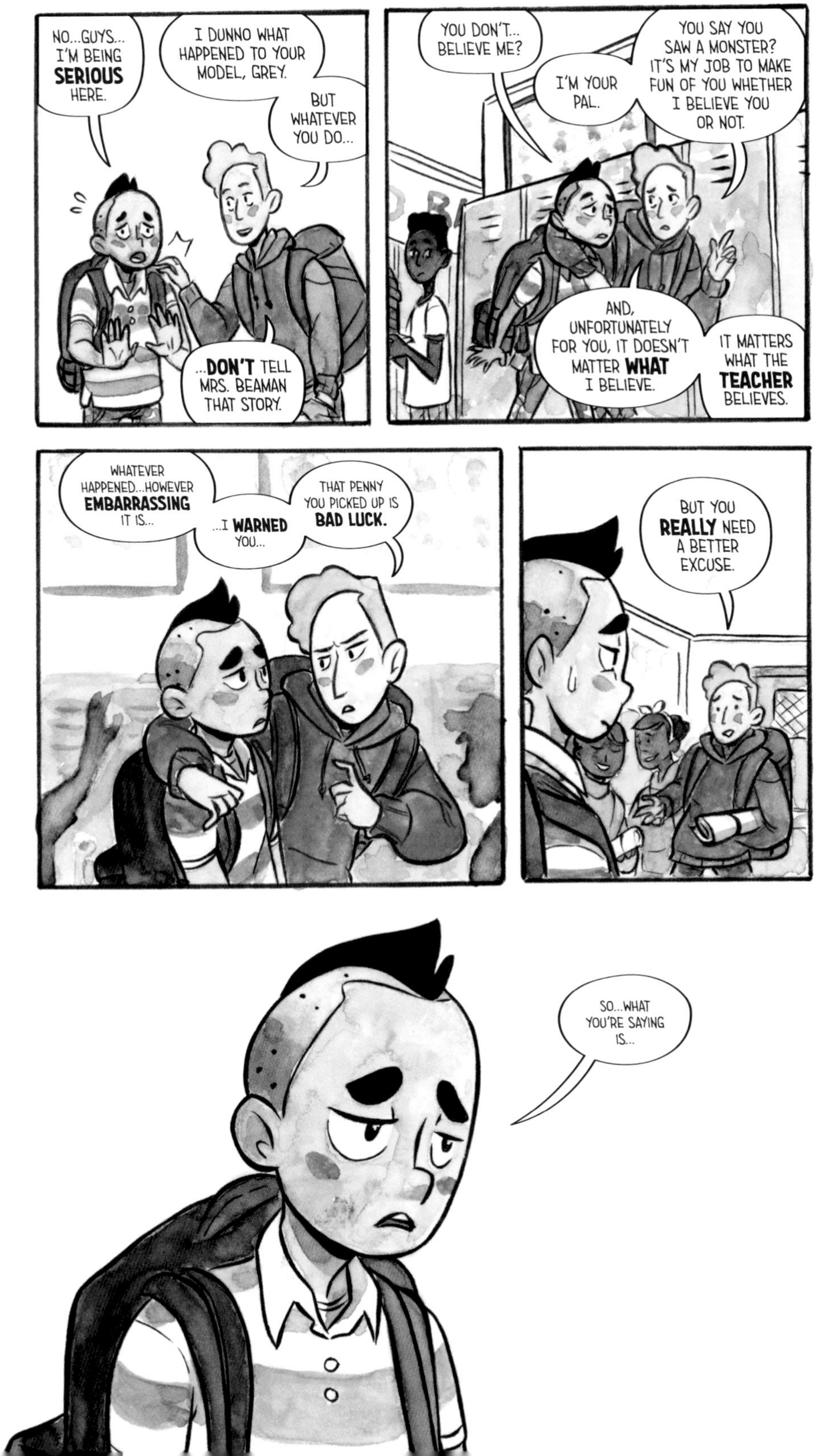
NO...GUYS... I'M BEING **SERIOUS** HERE.
I DUNNO WHAT HAPPENED TO YOUR MODEL, GREY.
BUT WHATEVER YOU DO...
...**DON'T** TELL MRS. BEAMAN THAT STORY.
YOU DON'T... BELIEVE ME?
I'M YOUR PAL.
YOU SAY YOU SAW A MONSTER? IT'S MY JOB TO MAKE FUN OF YOU WHETHER I BELIEVE YOU OR NOT.
AND, UNFORTUNATELY FOR YOU, IT DOESN'T MATTER **WHAT** I BELIEVE.
IT MATTERS WHAT THE **TEACHER** BELIEVES.
WHATEVER HAPPENED...HOWEVER **EMBARRASSING** IT IS...
...I **WARNED** YOU...
THAT PENNY YOU PICKED UP IS **BAD LUCK.**
BUT YOU **REALLY** NEED A BETTER EXCUSE.
SO...WHAT YOU'RE SAYING IS...

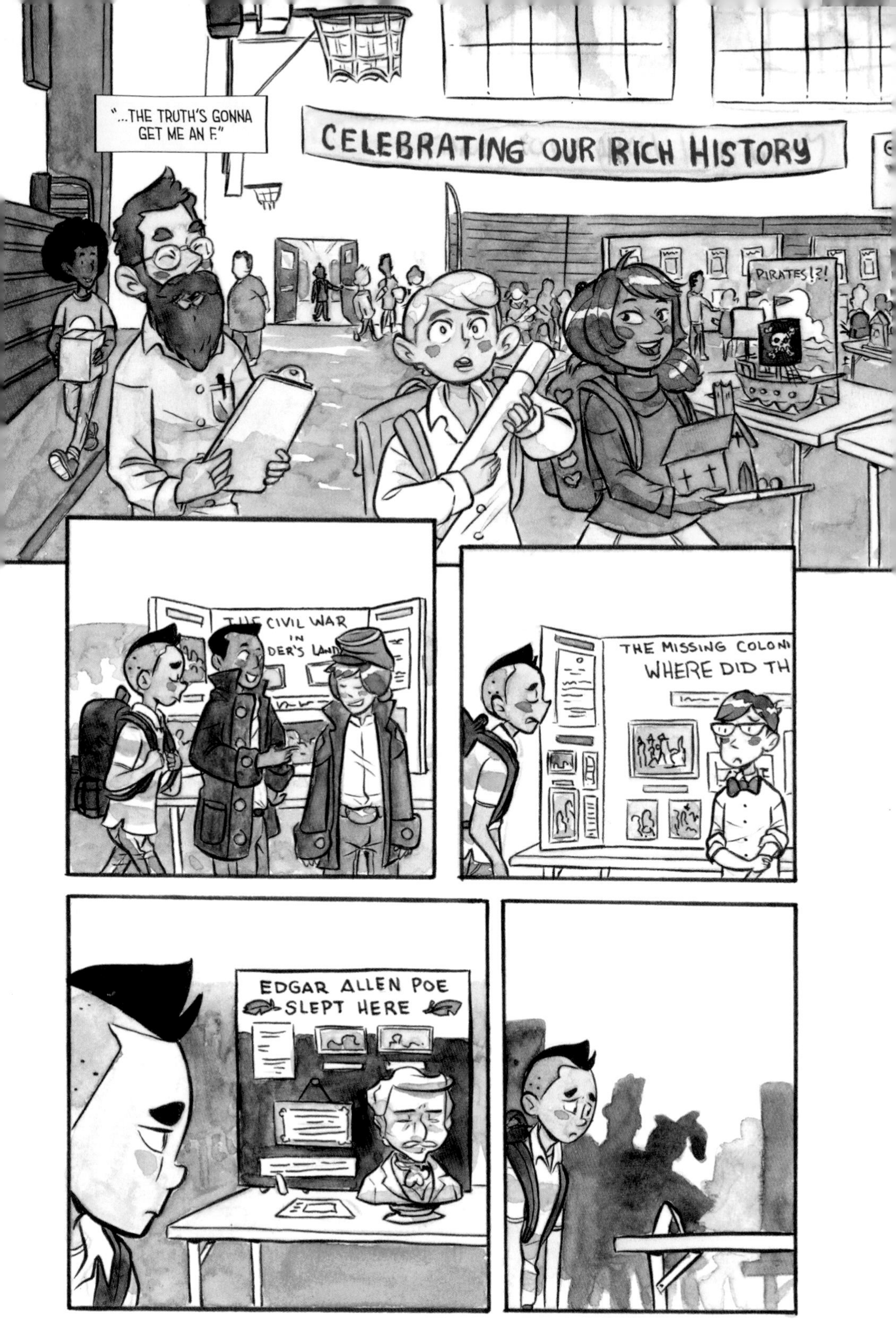
"...THE TRUTH'S GONNA GET ME AN F."
CELEBRATING OUR RICH HISTORY
PIRATES!?!
THE CIVIL WAR IN
DER'S LAND
THE MISSING COLONI
WHERE DID TH
EDGAR ALLEN POE SLEPT HERE

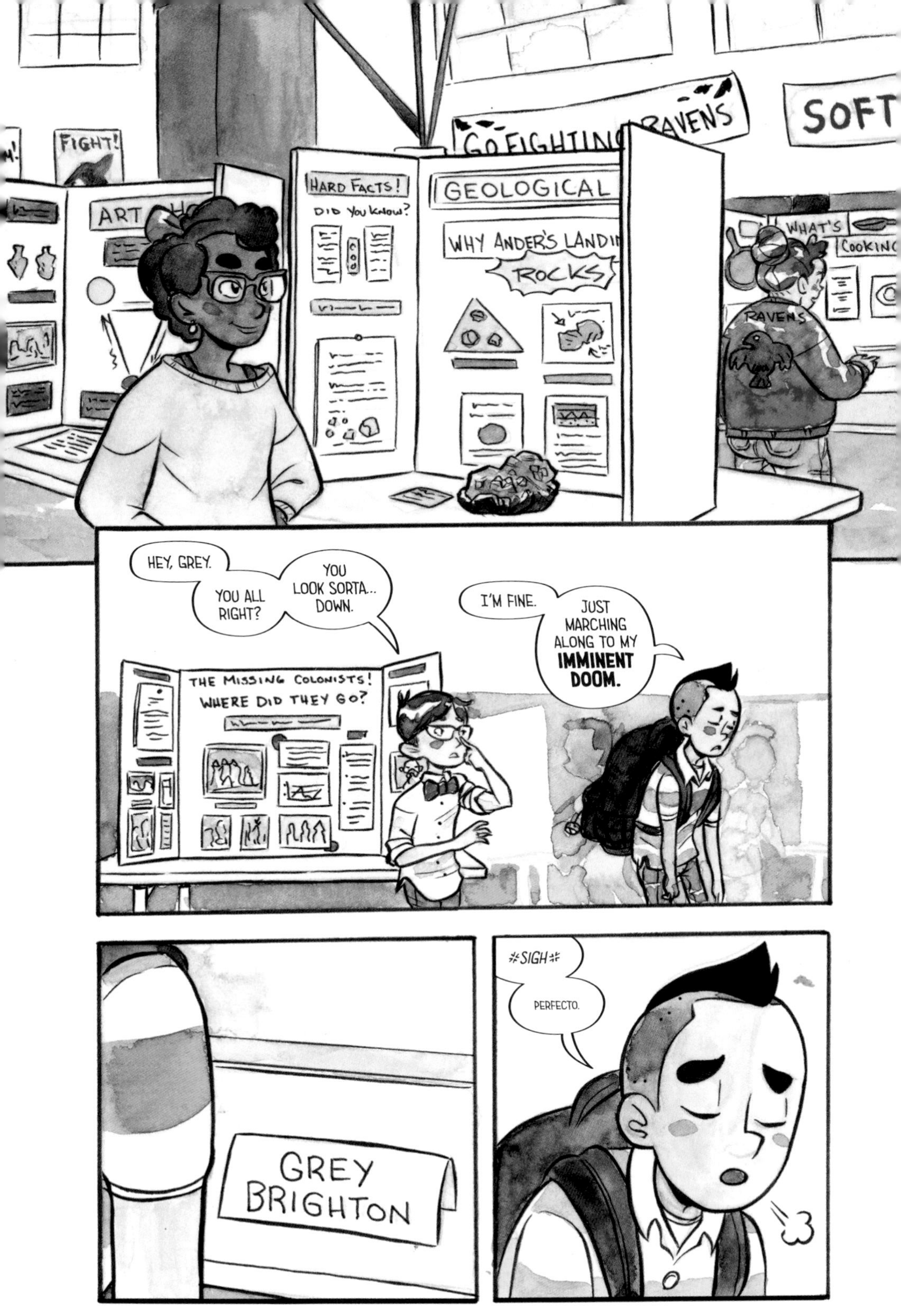
FIGHT!
GEOLOGICAL
HARD FACTS!
DID YOU KNOW?
WHY ANDER'S LANDI
ROCKS
WHAT'S
COOKIN
RAVENS
SOFT
HEY, GREY.
YOU ALL RIGHT?
YOU LOOK SORTA... DOWN.
I'M FINE.
JUST MARCHING ALONG TO MY **IMMINENT DOOM.**
THE MISSING COLONISTS! WHERE DID THEY GO?
GREY BRIGHTON
SIGH
PERFECTO.

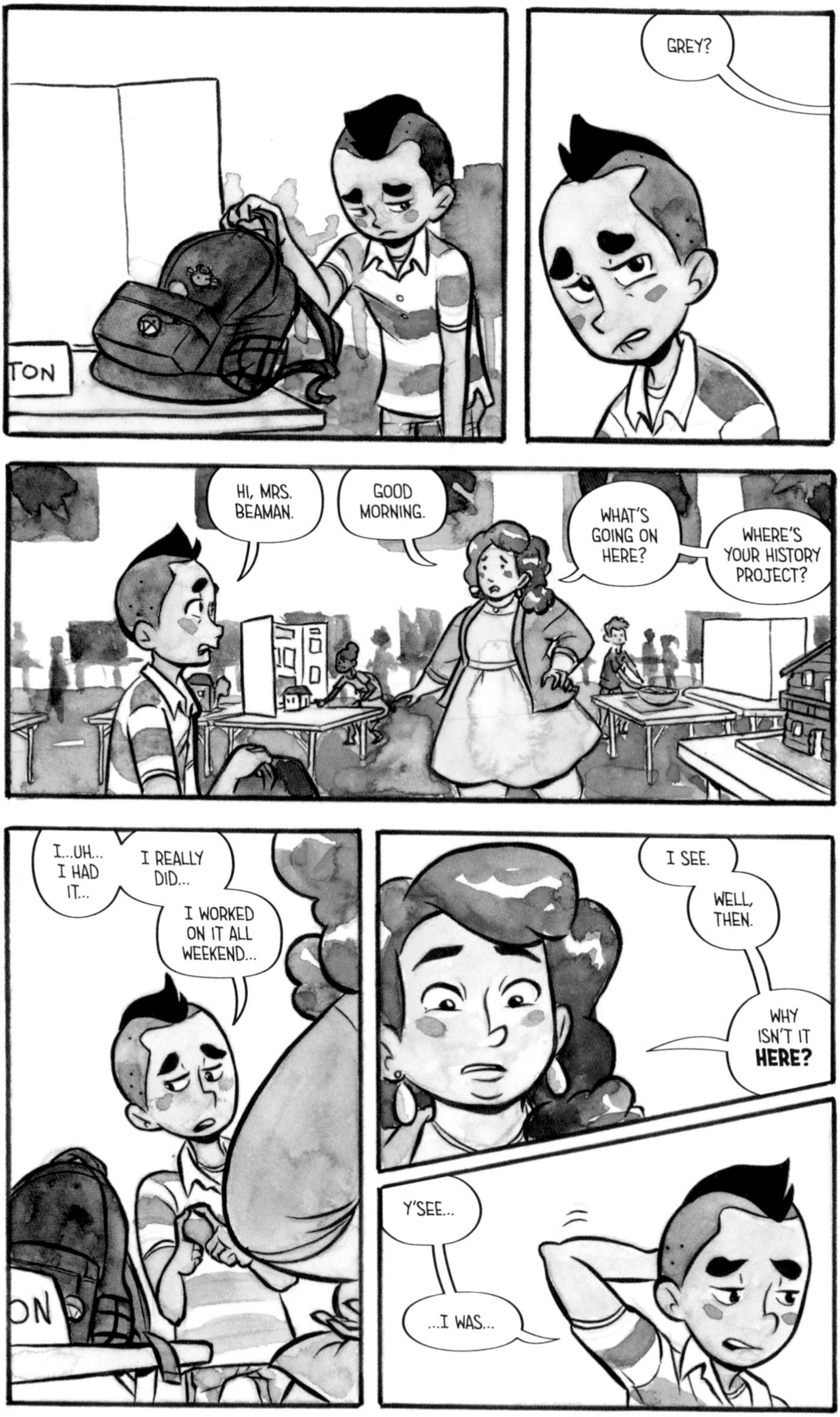
TON
GREY?
HI, MRS. BEAMAN.
GOOD MORNING.
WHAT'S GOING ON HERE?
WHERE'S YOUR HISTORY PROJECT?
I...UH... I HAD IT...
I REALLY DID...
I WORKED ON IT ALL WEEKEND...
ON
I SEE.
WELL, THEN.
WHY ISN'T IT **HERE?**
Y'SEE...
...I WAS...

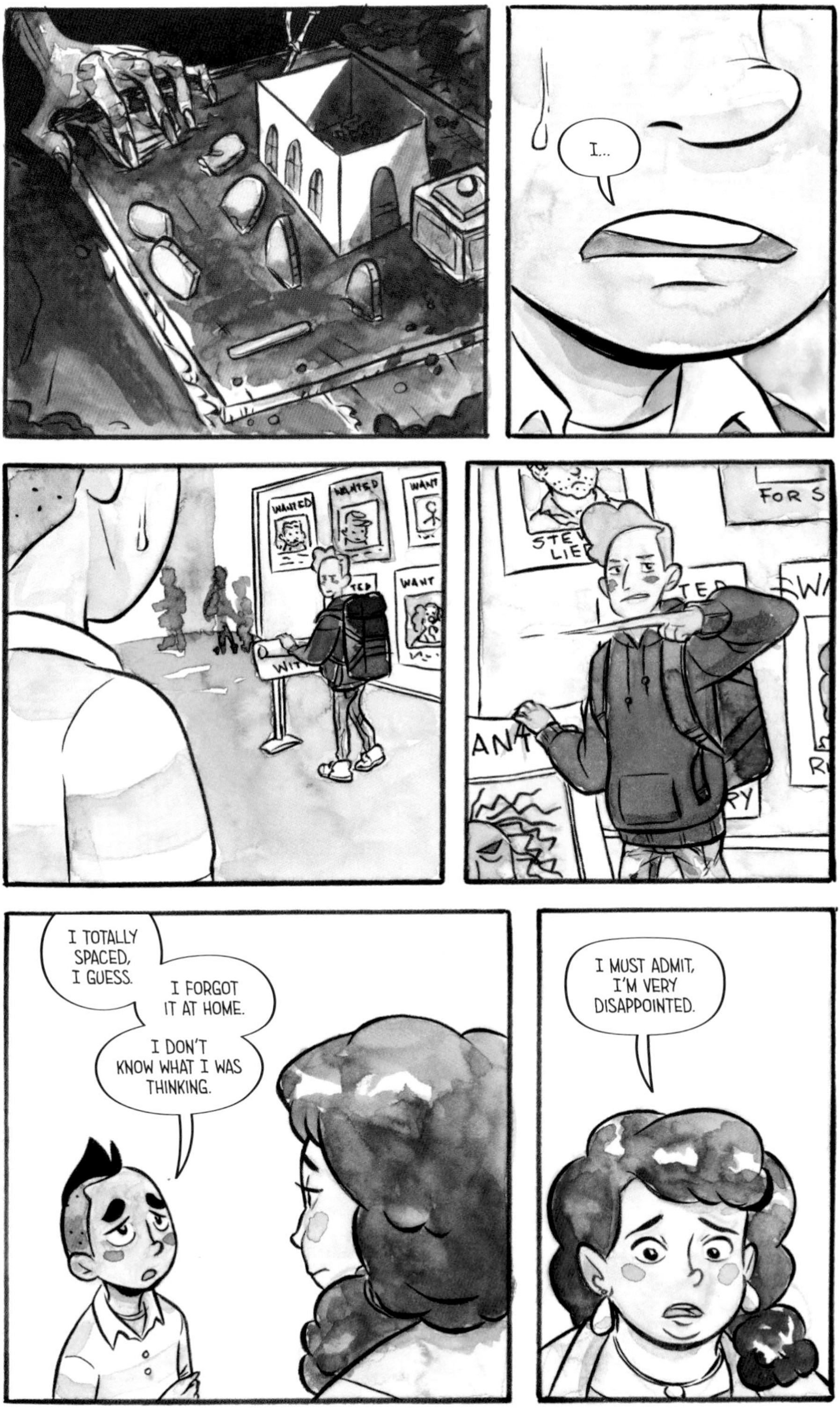
I...
WANTED
WANTED
I TOTALLY SPACED, I GUESS.
I FORGOT IT AT HOME.
I DON'T KNOW WHAT I WAS THINKING.
I MUST ADMIT, I'M VERY DISAPPOINTED.

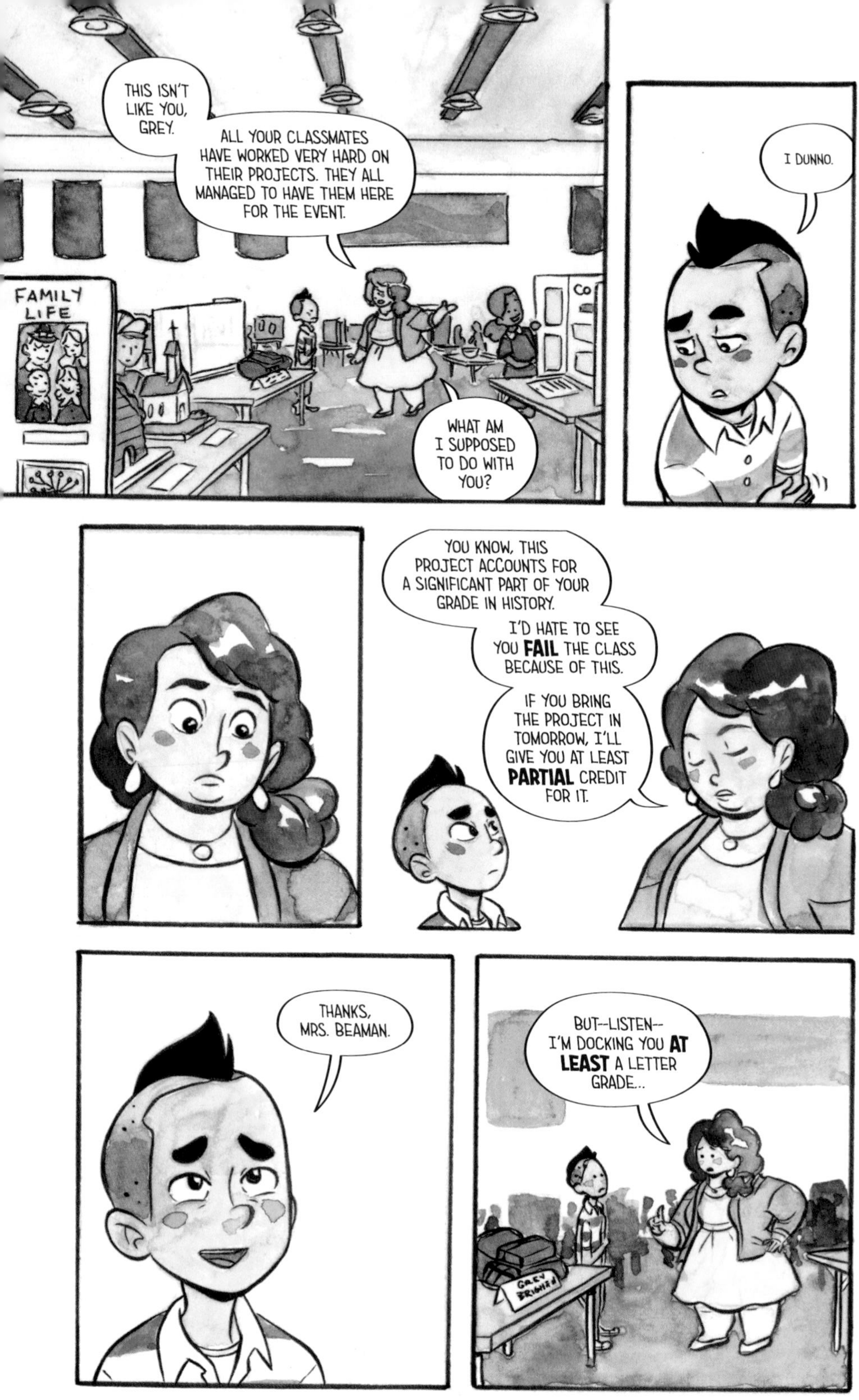
THIS ISN'T LIKE YOU, GREY.
ALL YOUR CLASSMATES HAVE WORKED VERY HARD ON THEIR PROJECTS. THEY ALL MANAGED TO HAVE THEM HERE FOR THE EVENT.
FAMILY LIFE
WHAT AM I SUPPOSED TO DO WITH YOU?
I DUNNO.
YOU KNOW, THIS PROJECT ACCOUNTS FOR A SIGNIFICANT PART OF YOUR GRADE IN HISTORY.
I'D HATE TO SEE YOU **FAIL** THE CLASS BECAUSE OF THIS.
IF YOU BRING THE PROJECT IN TOMORROW, I'LL GIVE YOU AT LEAST **PARTIAL** CREDIT FOR IT.
THANKS, MRS. BEAMAN.
BUT--LISTEN-- I'M DOCKING YOU **AT LEAST** A LETTER GRADE...

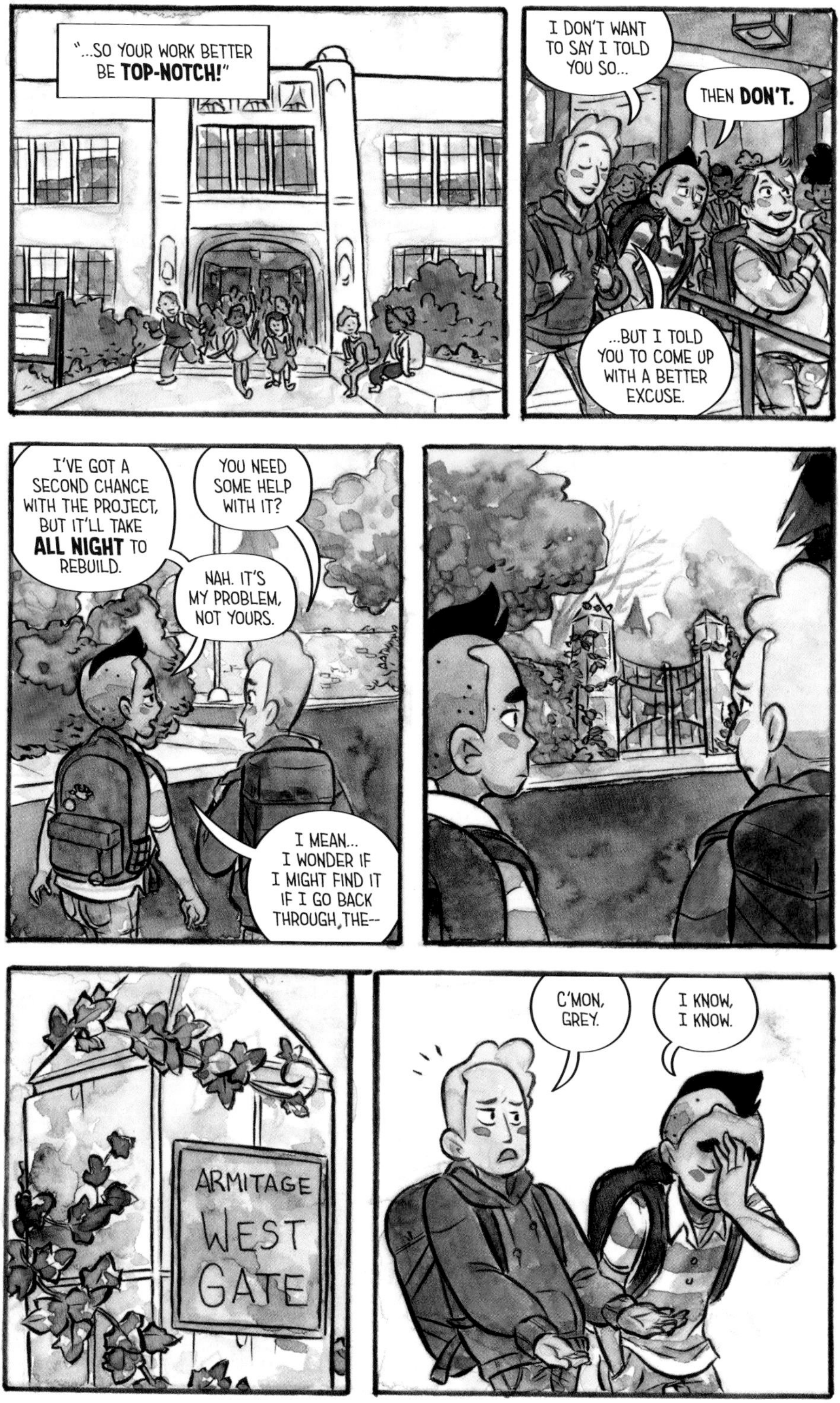
"...SO YOUR WORK BETTER BE **TOP-NOTCH!**"
I DON'T WANT TO SAY I TOLD YOU SO...
THEN **DON'T.**
...BUT I TOLD YOU TO COME UP WITH A BETTER EXCUSE.
I'VE GOT A SECOND CHANCE WITH THE PROJECT, BUT IT'LL TAKE **ALL NIGHT** TO REBUILD.
YOU NEED SOME HELP WITH IT?
NAH. IT'S MY PROBLEM, NOT YOURS.
I MEAN... I WONDER IF I MIGHT FIND IT IF I GO BACK THROUGH THE--
ARMITAGE WEST GATE
C'MON, GREY.
I KNOW, I KNOW.

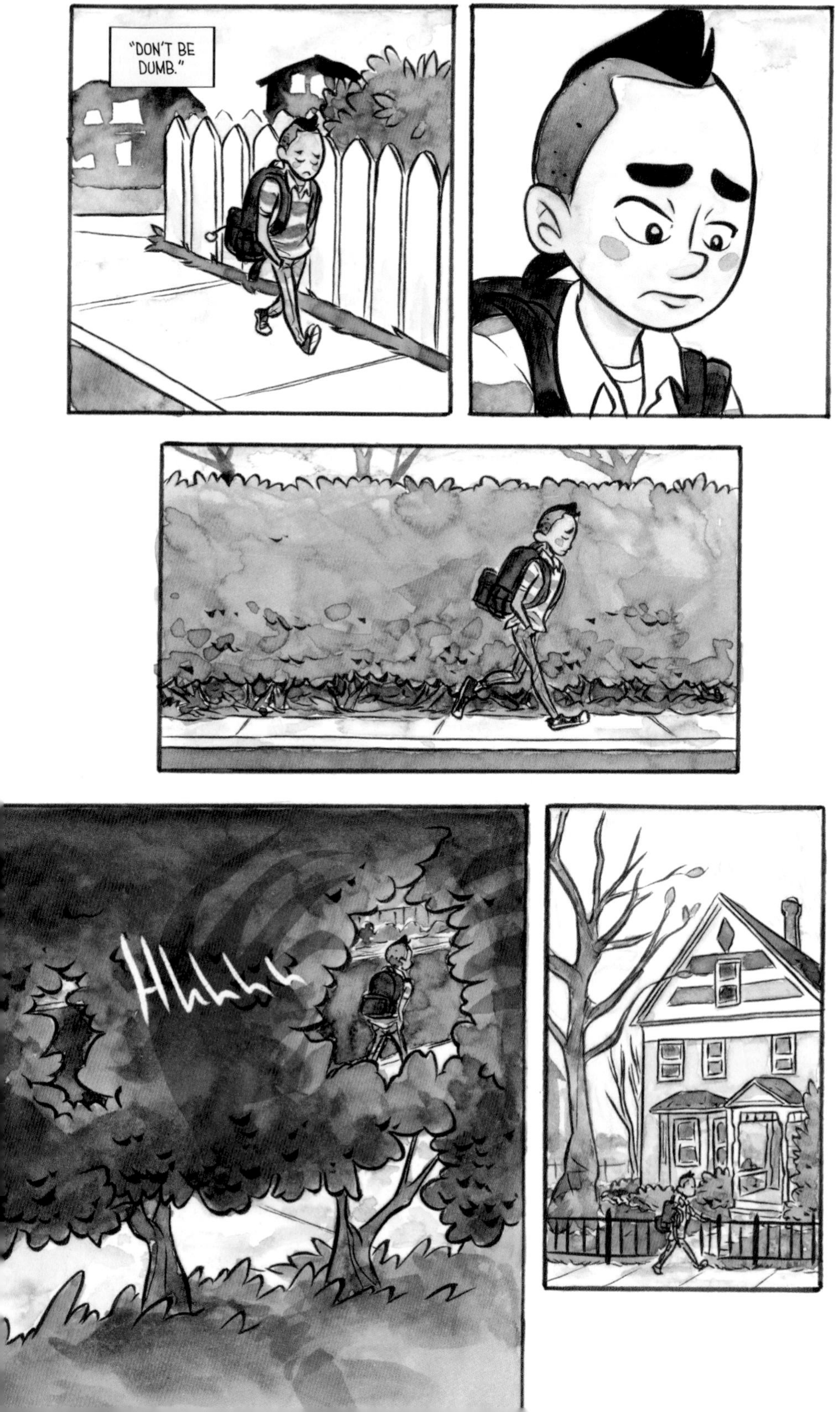
"DON'T BE DUMB."
Hhhhh

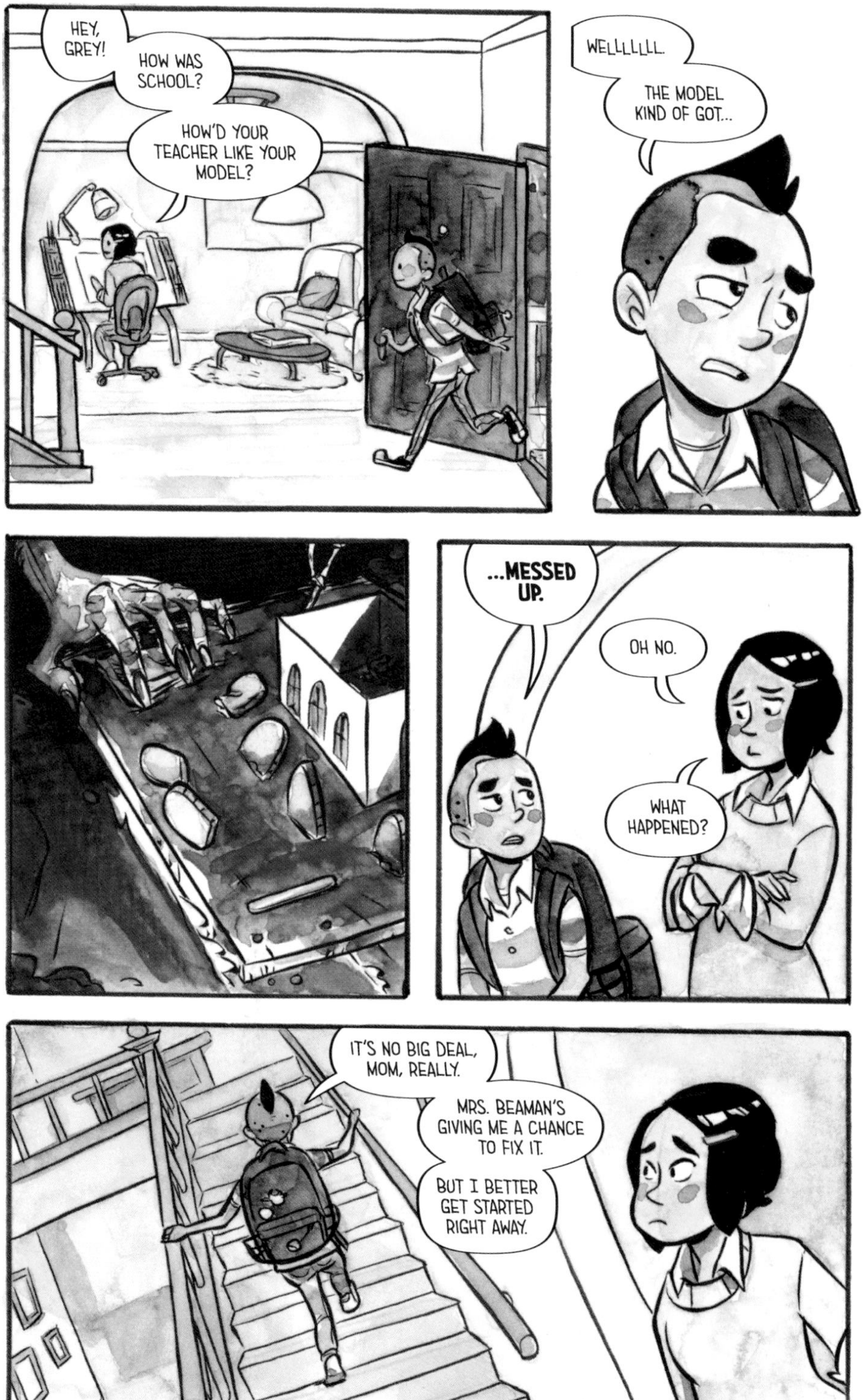
HEY, GREY!
HOW WAS SCHOOL?
HOW'D YOUR TEACHER LIKE YOUR MODEL?
WELLLLLLL.
THE MODEL KIND OF GOT...
...MESSED UP.
OH NO.
WHAT HAPPENED?
IT'S NO BIG DEAL, MOM, REALLY.
MRS. BEAMAN'S GIVING ME A CHANCE TO FIX IT.
BUT I BETTER GET STARTED RIGHT AWAY.

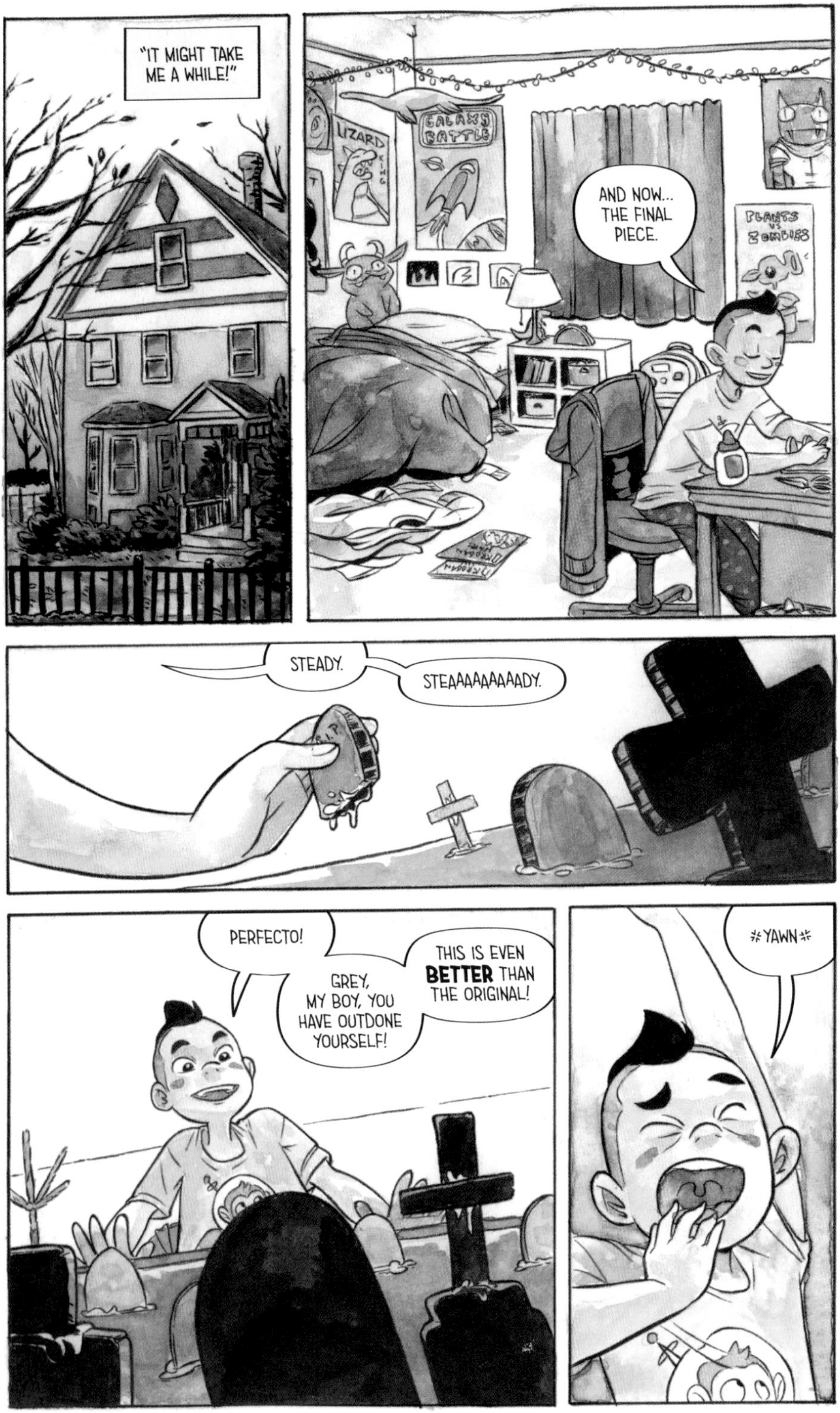

"IT MIGHT TAKE ME A WHILE!"
LIZARD KING
GALAXY BATTLE
PLANTS VS ZOMBIES
AND NOW... THE FINAL PIECE.
STEADY.
STEAAAAAAAAADY.
PERFECTO!
GREY, MY BOY, YOU HAVE OUTDONE YOURSELF!
THIS IS EVEN **BETTER** THAN THE ORIGINAL!
YAWN

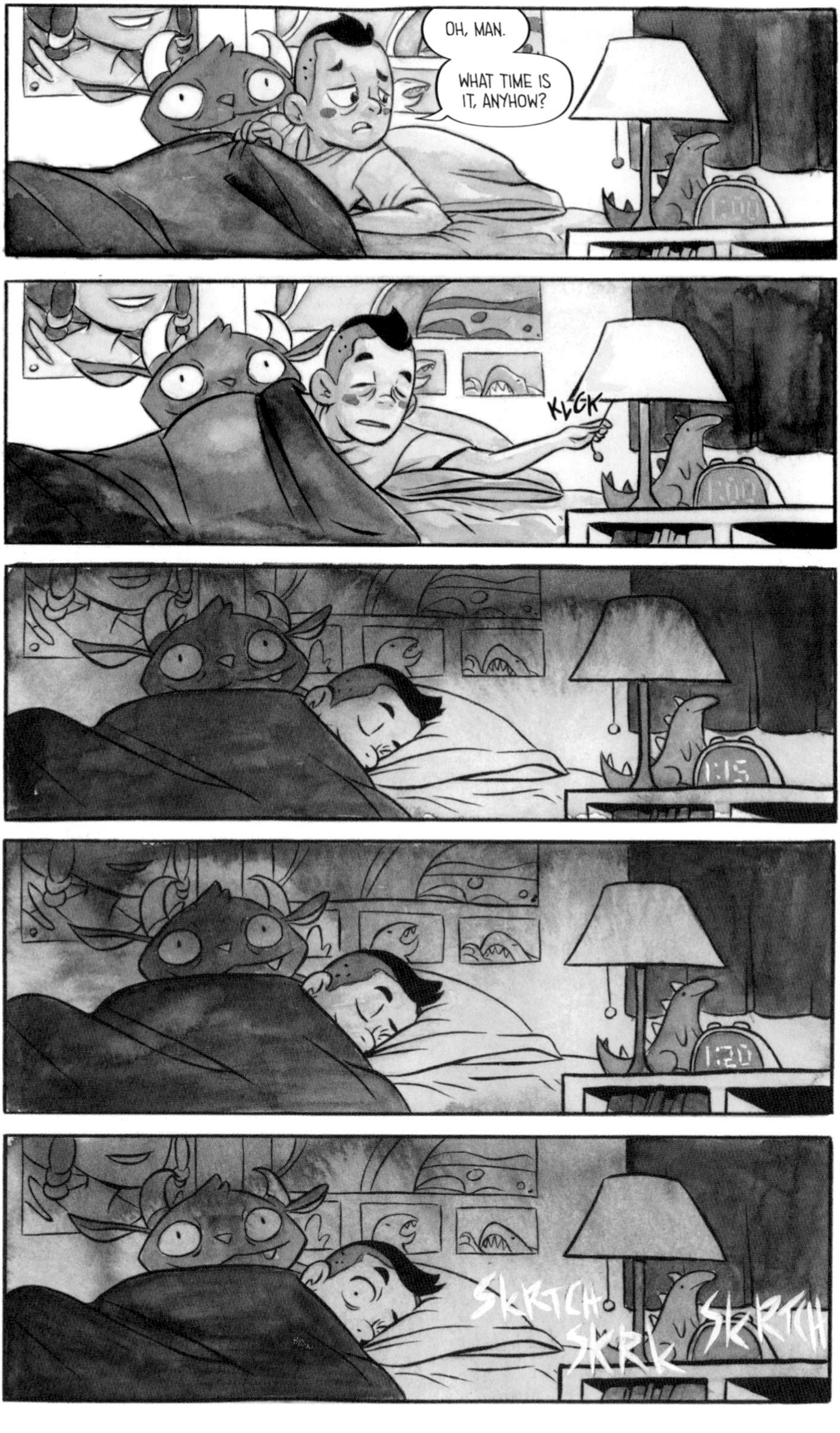
OH, MAN.
WHAT TIME IS IT, ANYHOW?
KLICK
1:15
1:20
SKRTCH
SKRK
SKRTCH

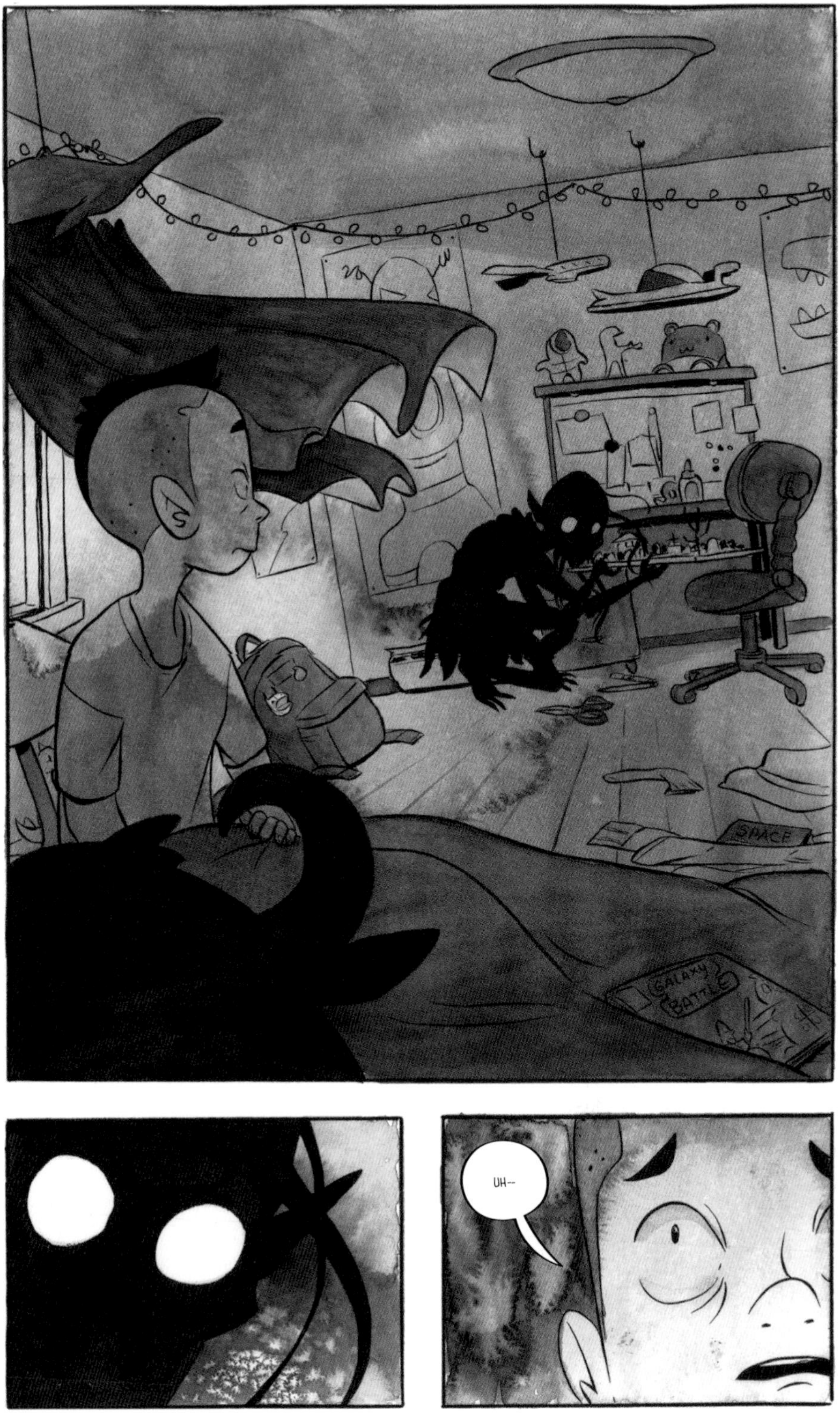
SPACE
GALAXY BATTLE
UH--

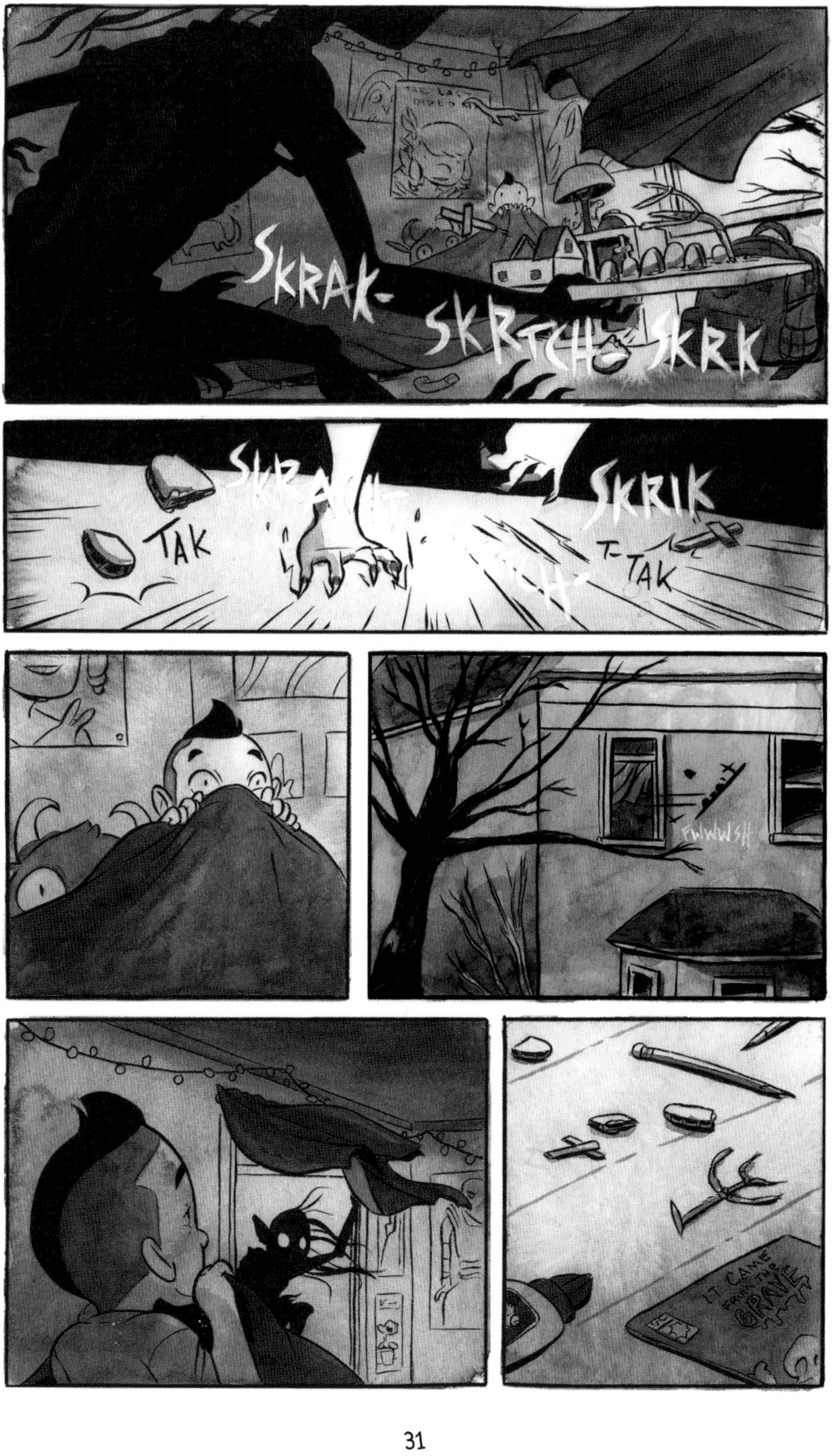
SKRAK-
SKRTCH-
SKRK
TAK
SKRIK
T-TAK
FWWWSH
IT CAME FROM THE GRAVE

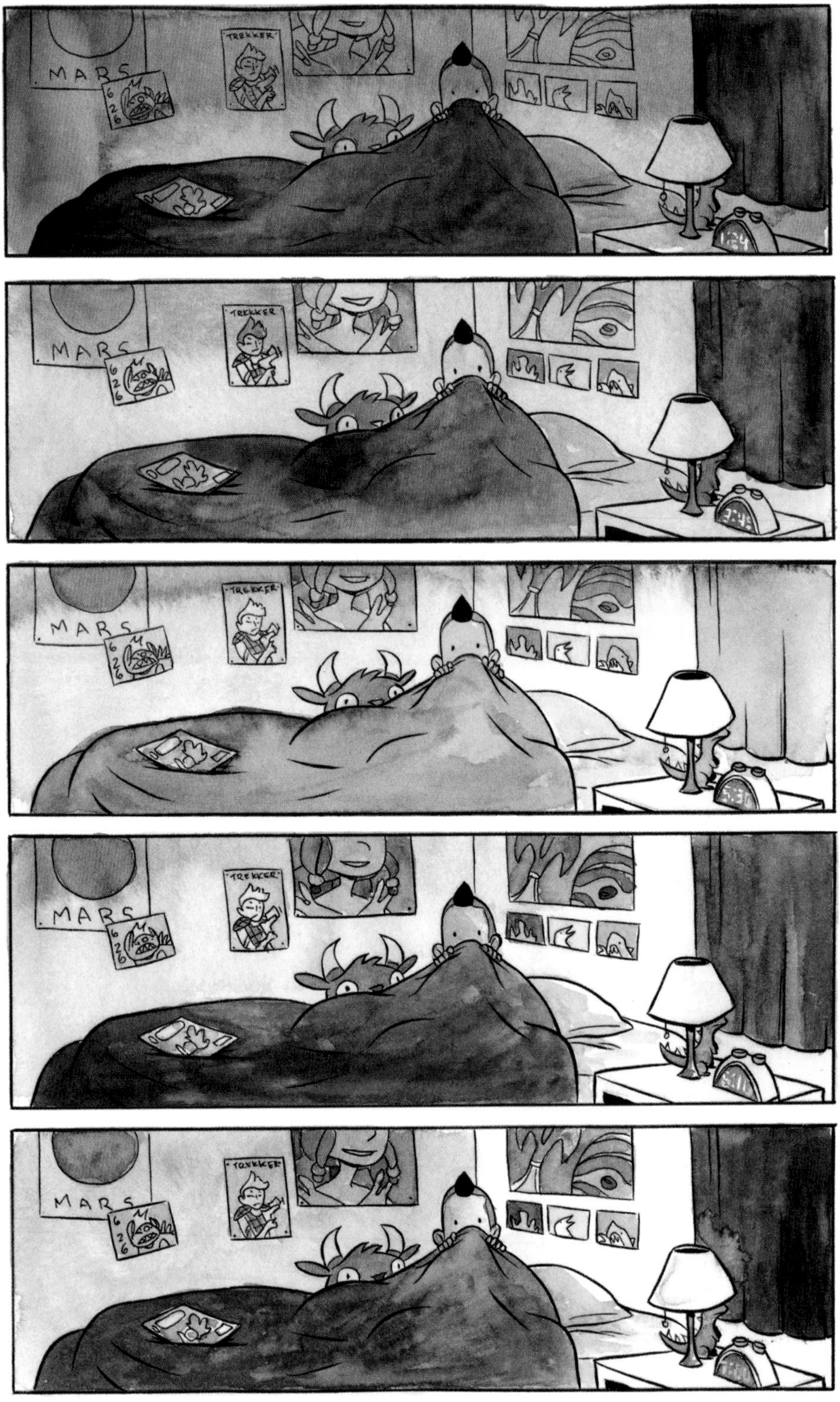
MARS
TREKKER
626

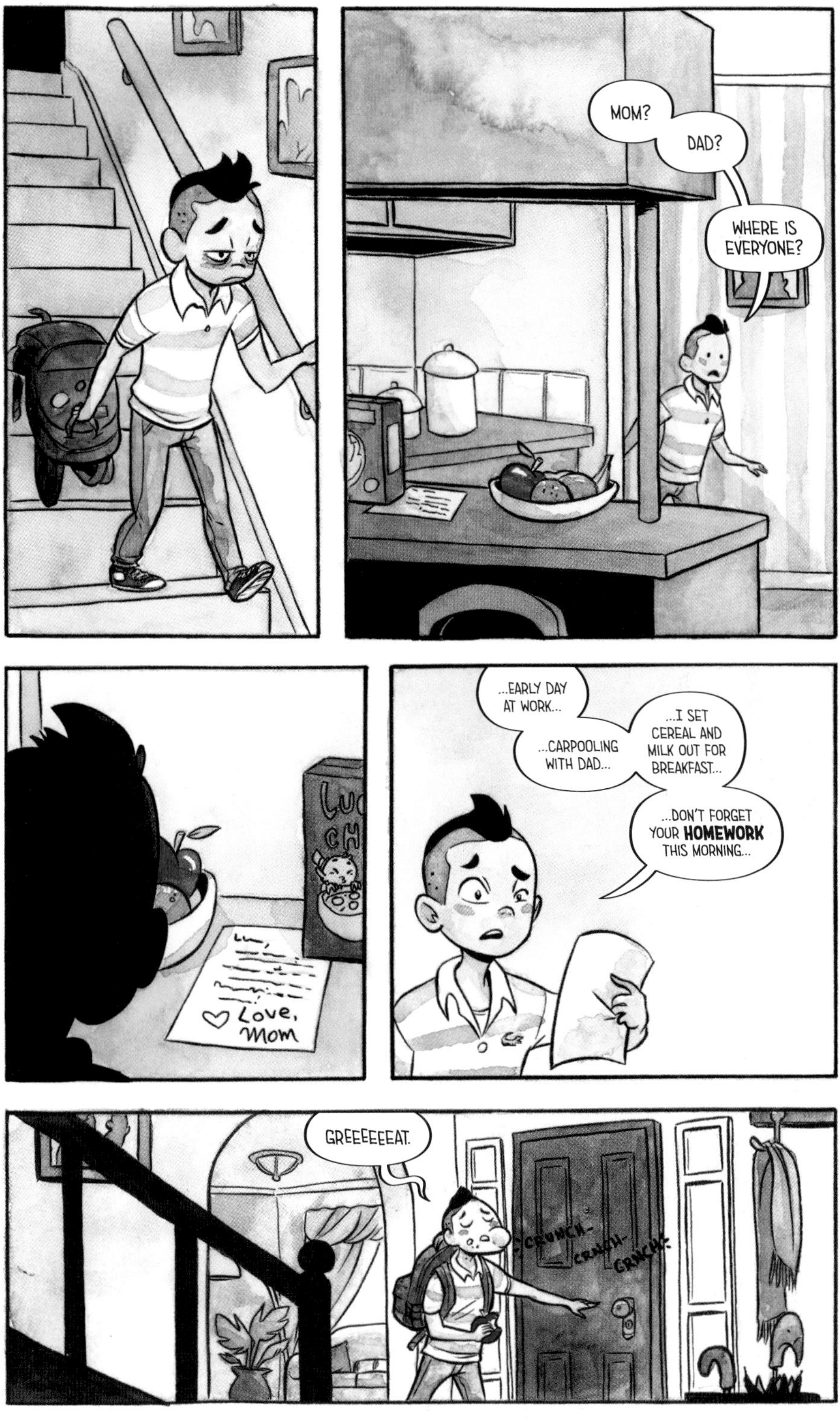
MOM?
DAD?
WHERE IS EVERYONE?
Love, Mom
...EARLY DAY AT WORK...
...CARPOOLING WITH DAD...
...I SET CEREAL AND MILK OUT FOR BREAKFAST...
...DON'T FORGET YOUR **HOMEWORK** THIS MORNING...
GREEEEEEAT.
CRUNCH-
CRUNCH-
CRUNCH-

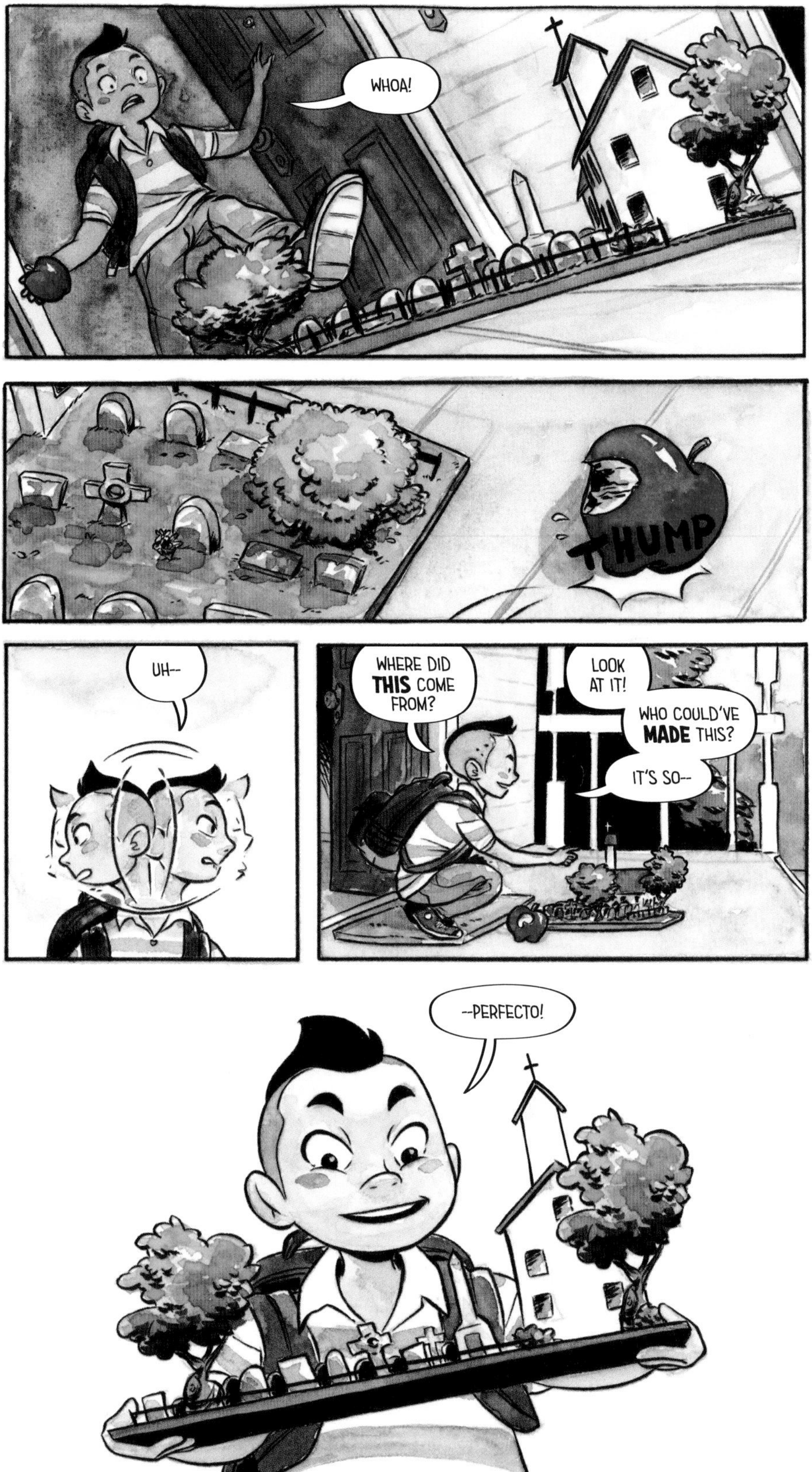
WHOA!
THUMP
UH--
WHERE DID THIS COME FROM?
LOOK AT IT!
WHO COULD'VE MADE THIS?
IT'S SO--
--PERFECTO!

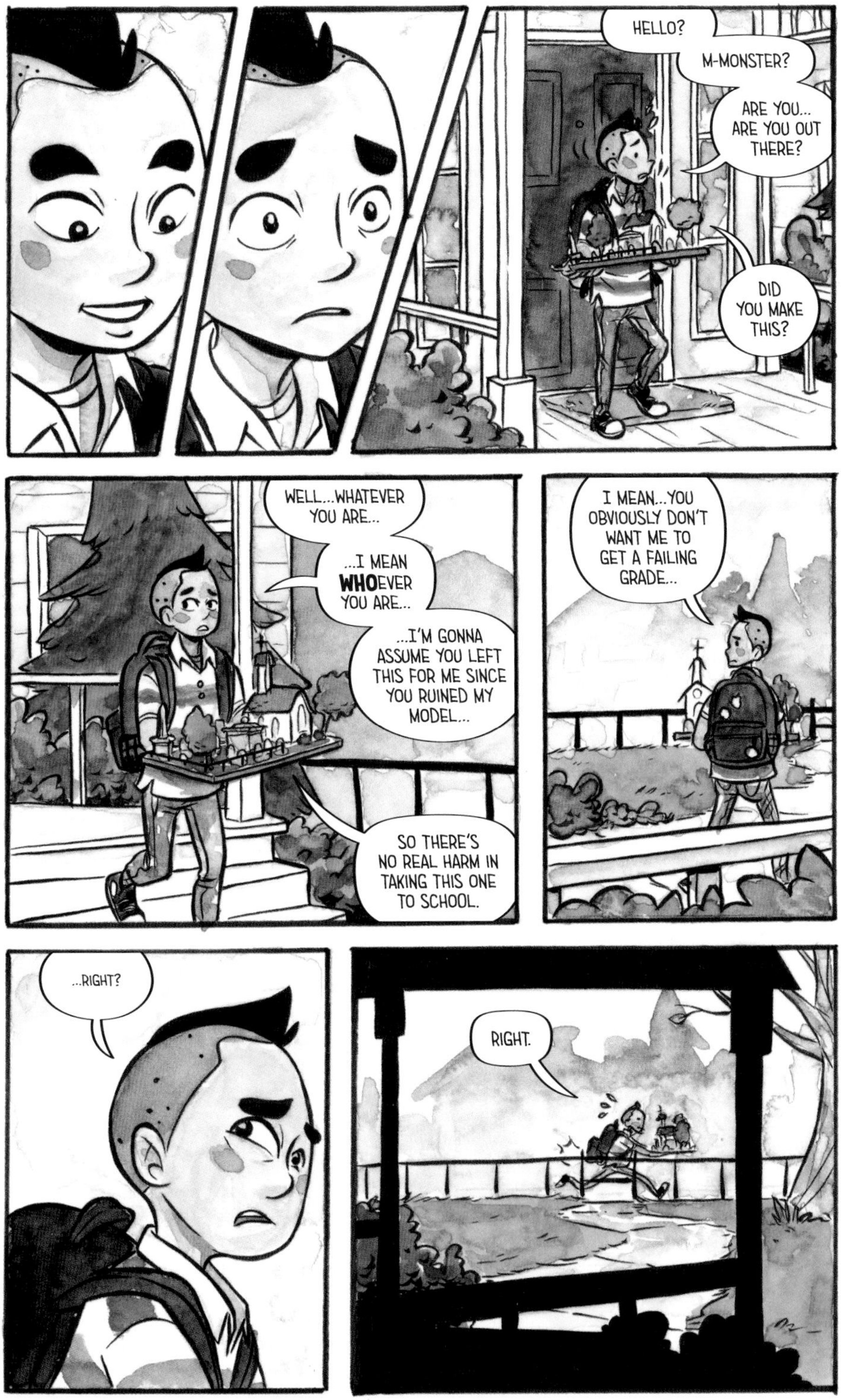
HELLO?
M-MONSTER?
ARE YOU... ARE YOU OUT THERE?
DID YOU MAKE THIS?
WELL...WHATEVER YOU ARE...
...I MEAN **WHO**EVER YOU ARE...
...I'M GONNA ASSUME YOU LEFT THIS FOR ME SINCE YOU RUINED MY MODEL...
SO THERE'S NO REAL HARM IN TAKING THIS ONE TO SCHOOL.
I MEAN...YOU OBVIOUSLY DON'T WANT ME TO GET A FAILING GRADE...
...RIGHT?
RIGHT.

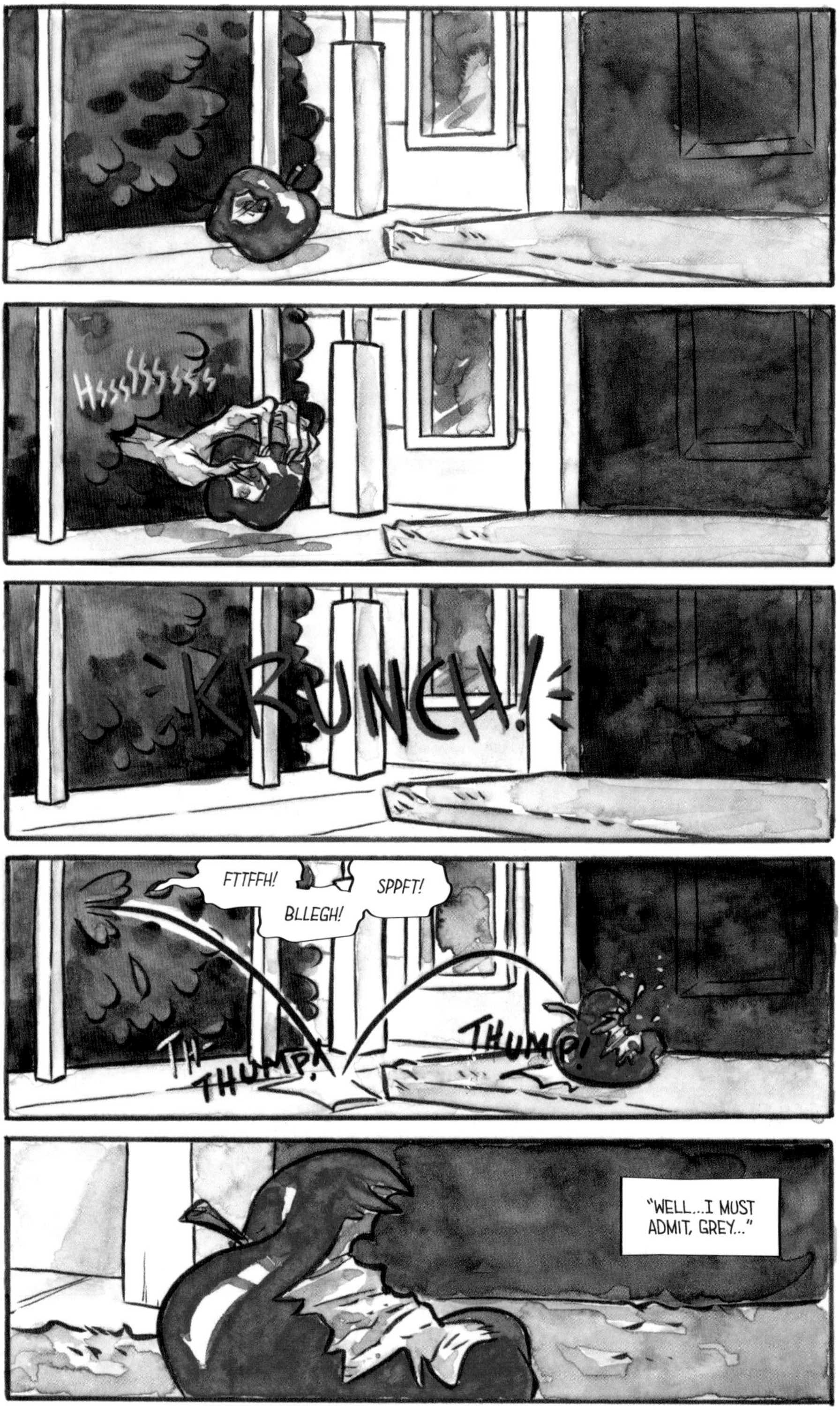
Hsssssssss
KRUNCH!
FTTFFH!
BLLEGH!
SPPFT!
TH THUMP!
THUMP!
"WELL...I MUST ADMIT, GREY..."

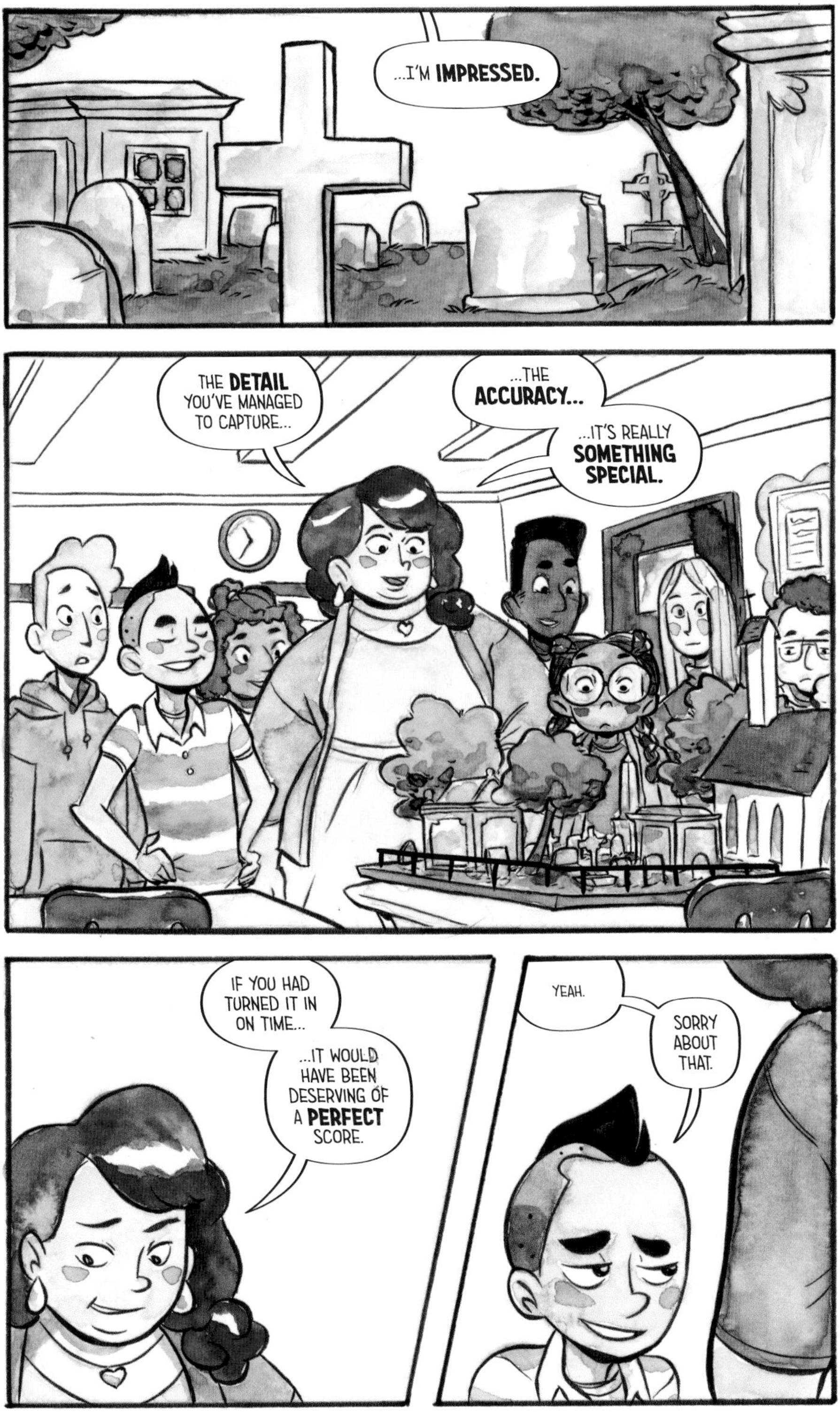
...I'M IMPRESSED.
THE DETAIL YOU'VE MANAGED TO CAPTURE...
...THE ACCURACY...
...IT'S REALLY SOMETHING SPECIAL.
IF YOU HAD TURNED IT IN ON TIME...
...IT WOULD HAVE BEEN DESERVING OF A PERFECT SCORE.
YEAH.
SORRY ABOUT THAT.

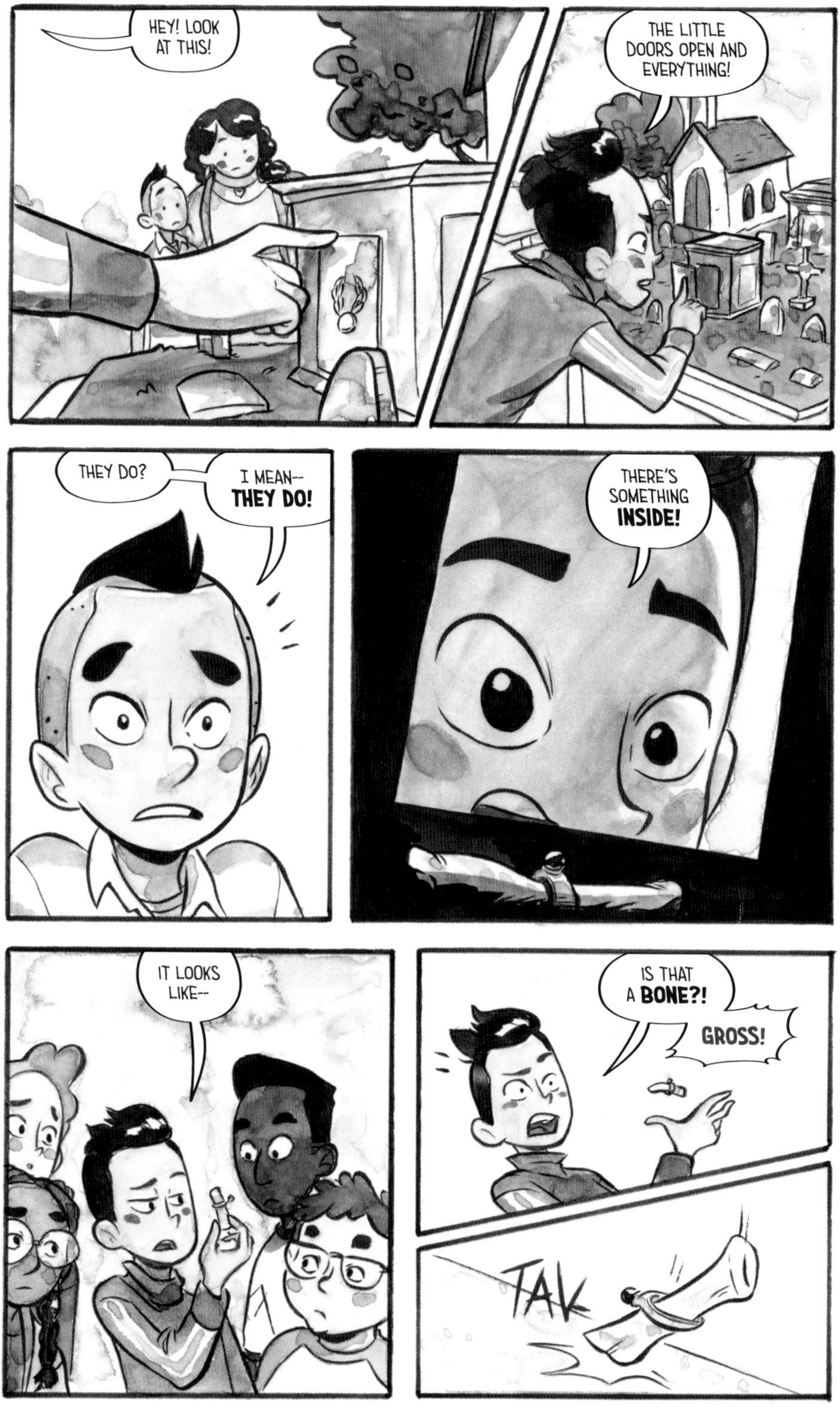
HEY! LOOK AT THIS!
THE LITTLE DOORS OPEN AND EVERYTHING!
THEY DO?
I MEAN-- THEY DO!
THERE'S SOMETHING INSIDE!
IT LOOKS LIKE--
IS THAT A BONE?!
GROSS!
TAK

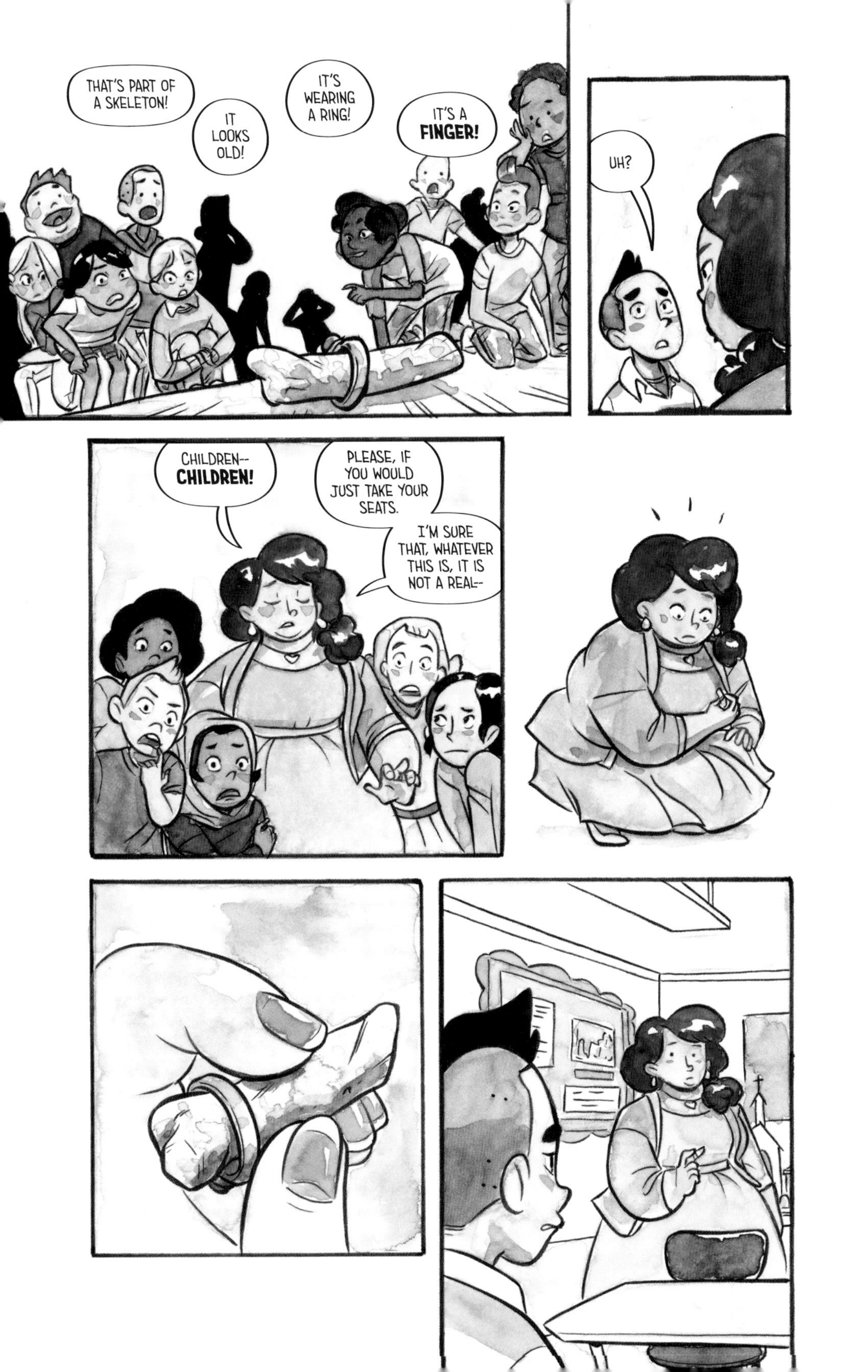
THAT'S PART OF A SKELETON!
IT LOOKS OLD!
IT'S WEARING A RING!
IT'S A **FINGER!**
UH?
CHILDREN-- **CHILDREN!**
PLEASE, IF YOU WOULD JUST TAKE YOUR SEATS.
I'M SURE THAT, WHATEVER THIS IS, IT IS NOT A REAL--

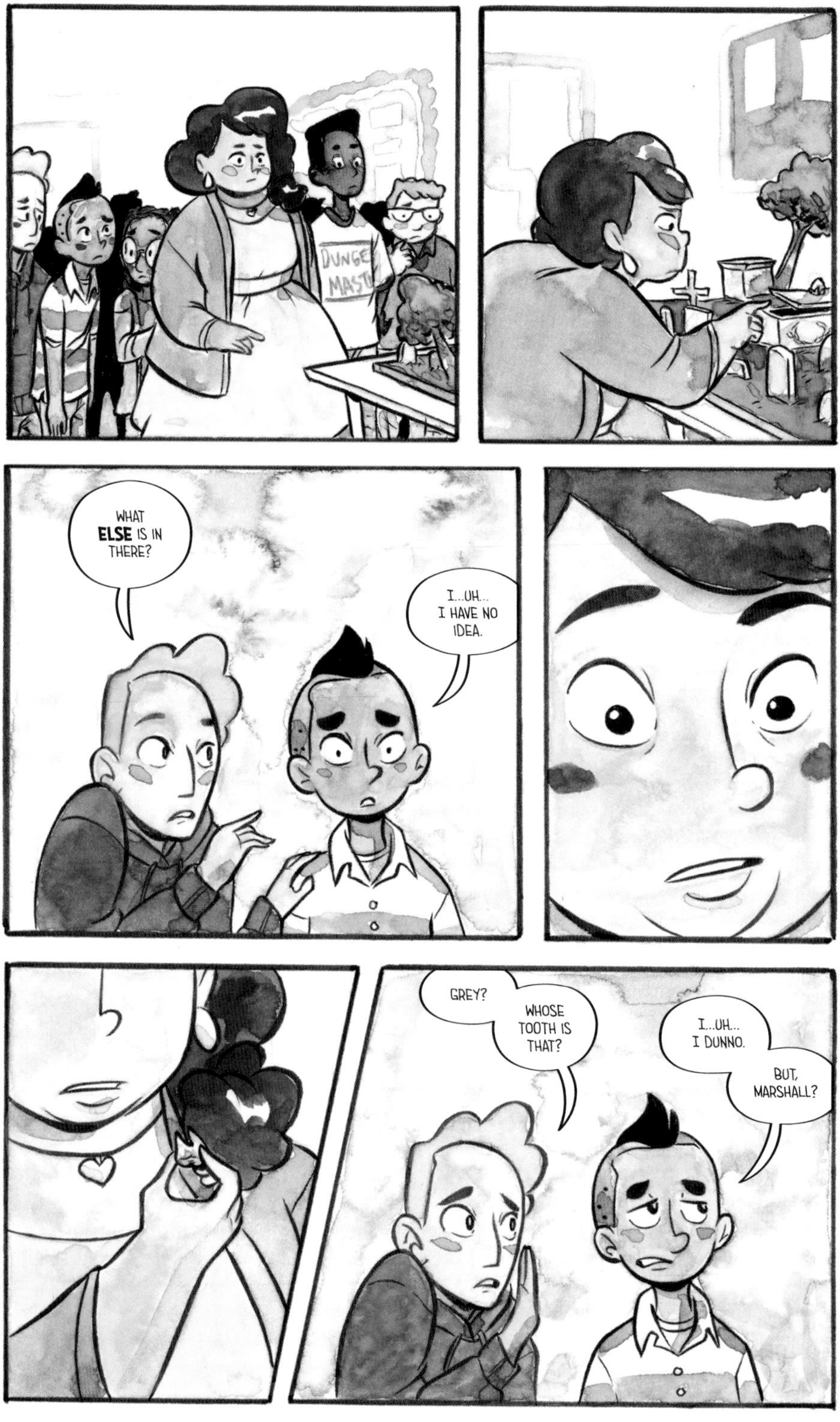
WHAT **ELSE** IS IN THERE?
I...UH... I HAVE NO IDEA.
GREY?
WHOSE TOOTH IS THAT?
I...UH... I DUNNO.
BUT, MARSHALL?

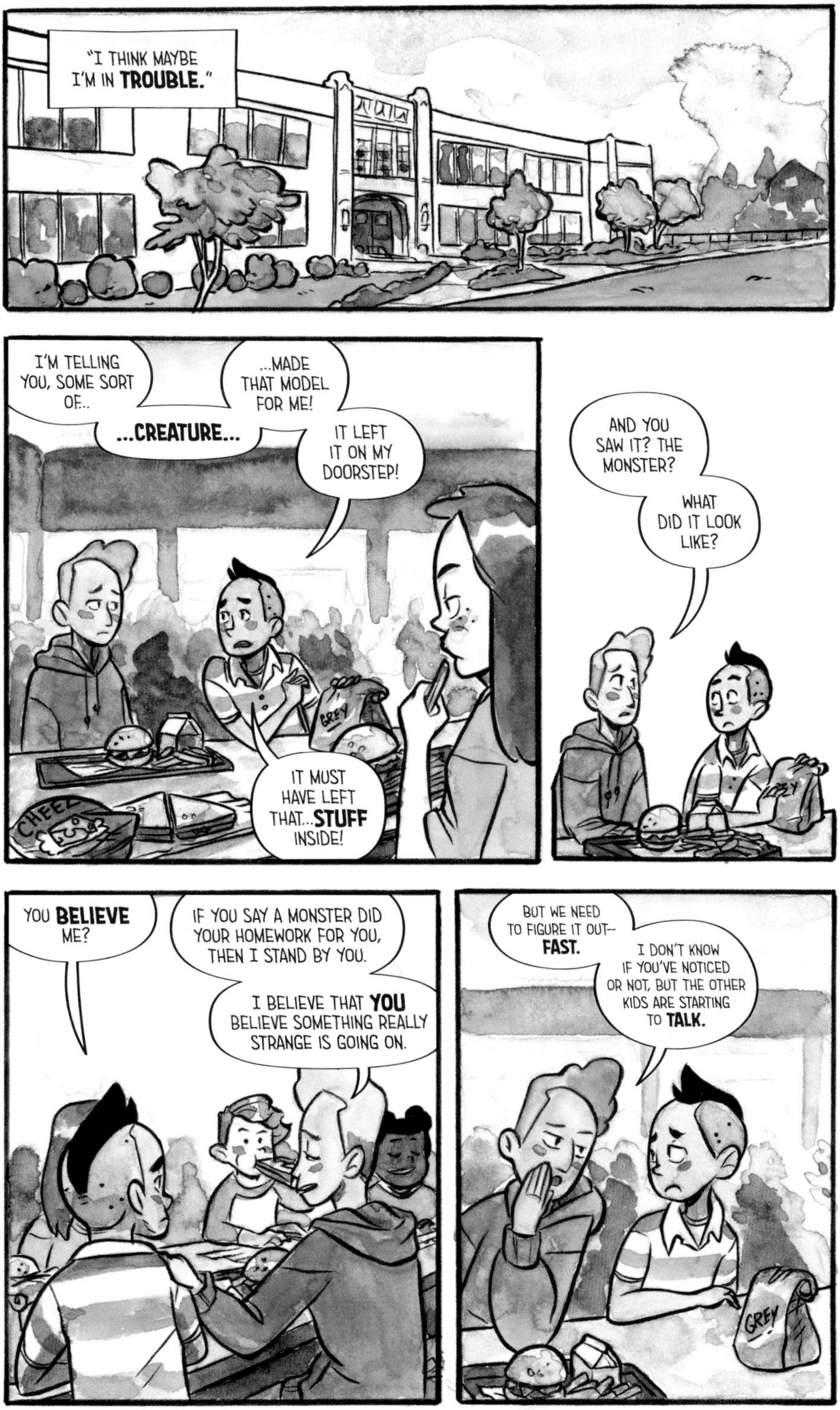
"I THINK MAYBE I'M IN **TROUBLE.**"
I'M TELLING YOU, SOME SORT OF...
...CREATURE...
...MADE THAT MODEL FOR ME!
IT LEFT IT ON MY DOORSTEP!
IT MUST HAVE LEFT THAT...**STUFF** INSIDE!
GREY
AND YOU SAW IT? THE MONSTER?
WHAT DID IT LOOK LIKE?
YOU **BELIEVE** ME?
IF YOU SAY A MONSTER DID YOUR HOMEWORK FOR YOU, THEN I STAND BY YOU.
I BELIEVE THAT **YOU** BELIEVE SOMETHING REALLY STRANGE IS GOING ON.
BUT WE NEED TO FIGURE IT OUT-- **FAST.**
I DON'T KNOW IF YOU'VE NOTICED OR NOT, BUT THE OTHER KIDS ARE STARTING TO **TALK.**
GREY

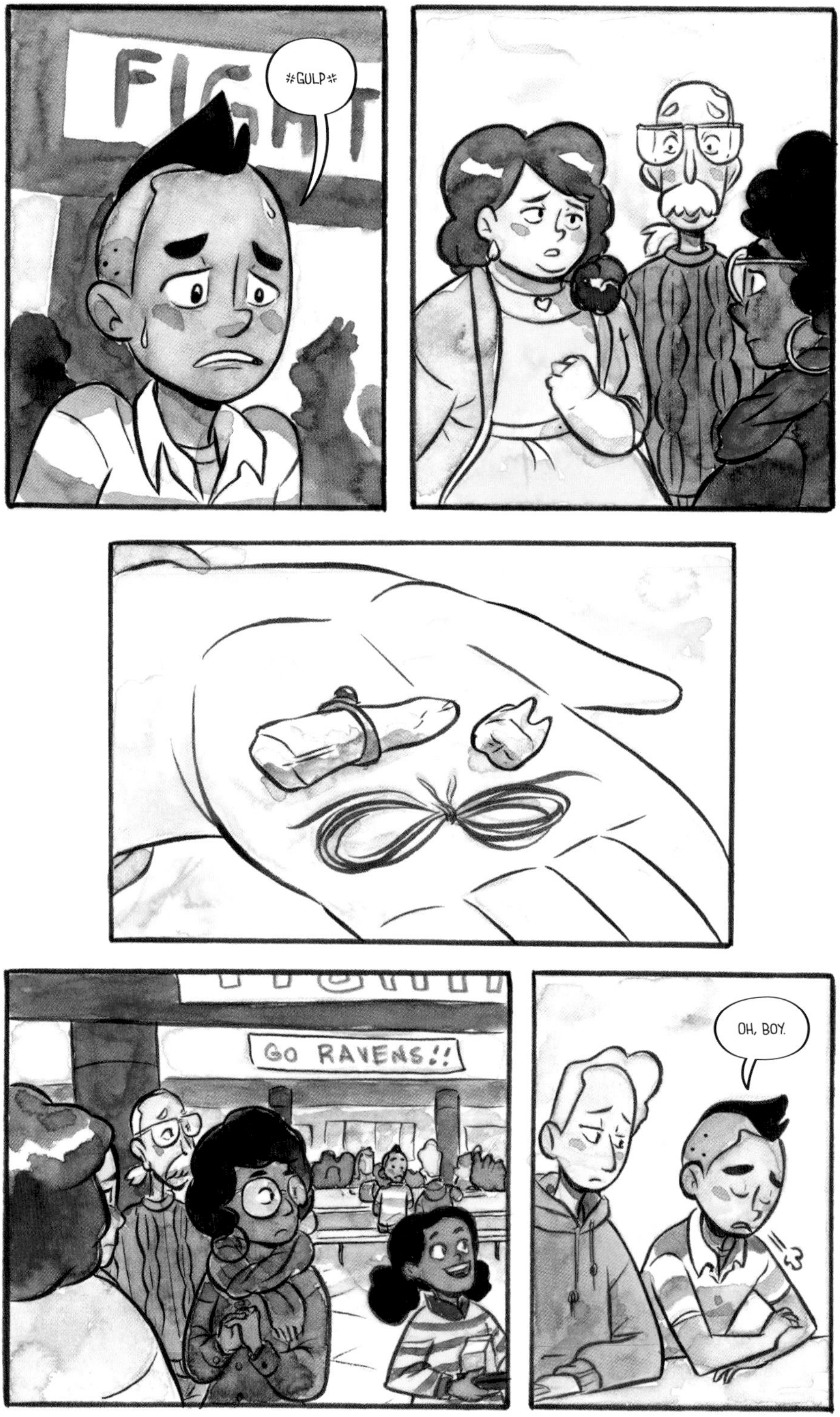
FIGHT
GULP
GO RAVENS!!
OH, BOY.

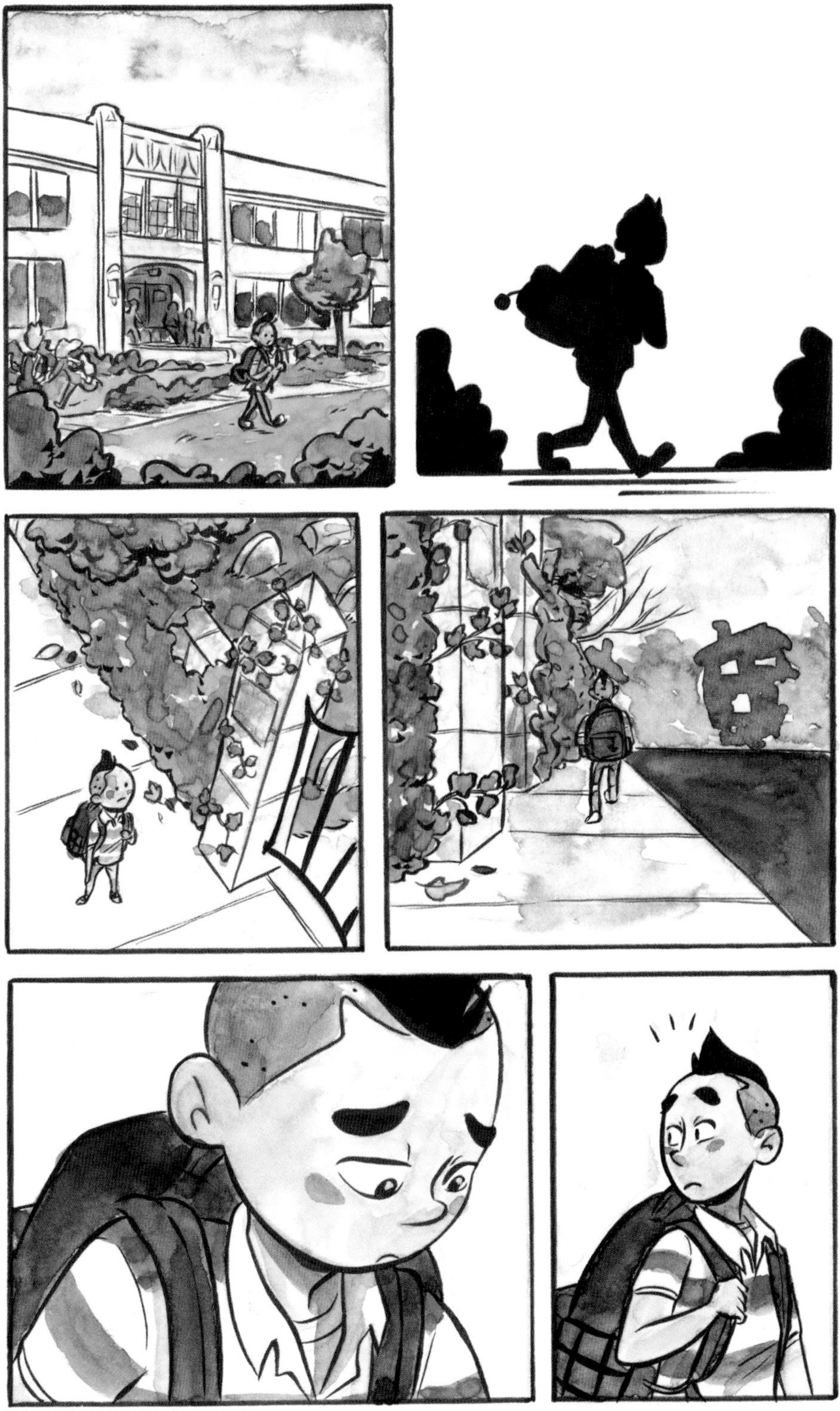

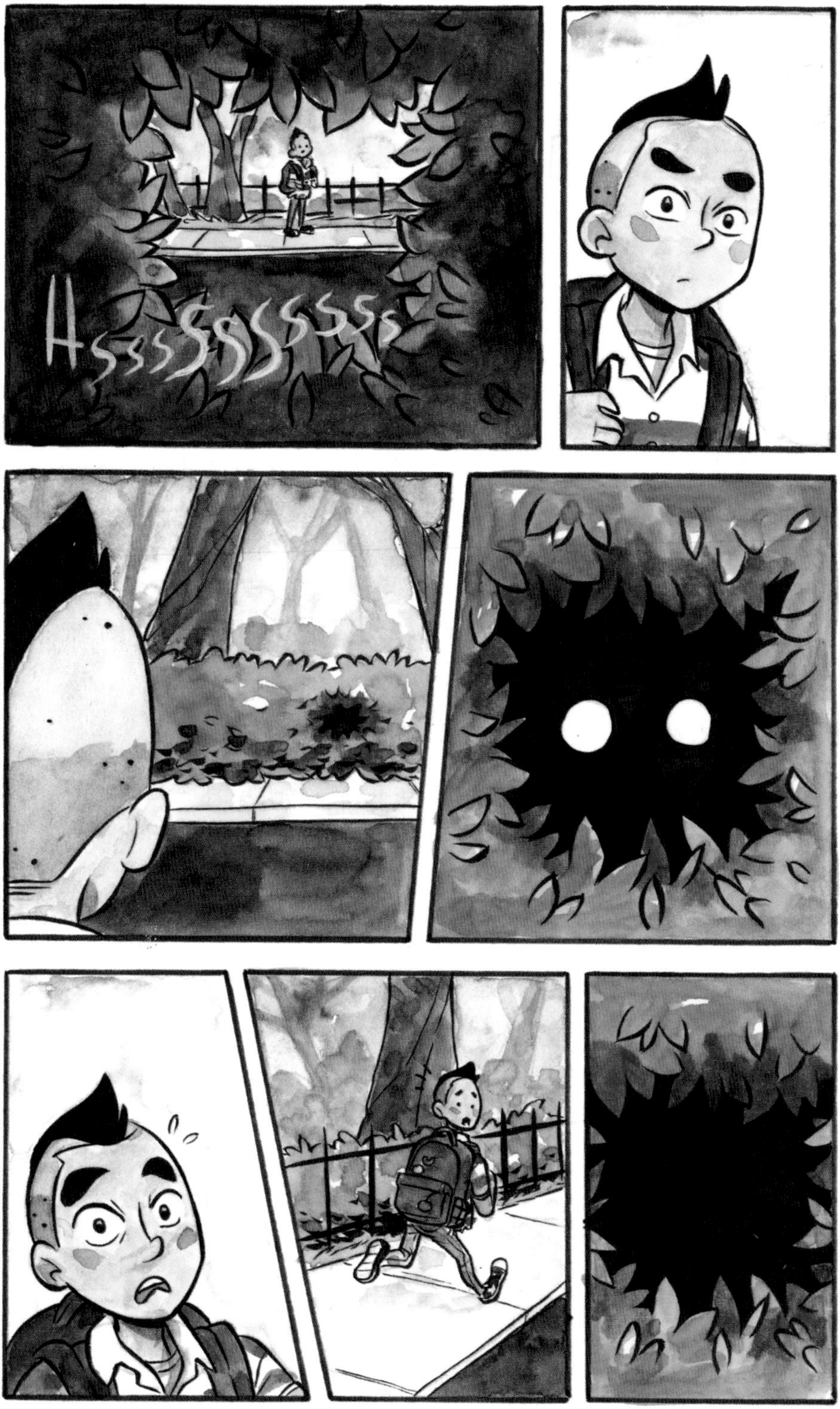
Hsssssssssss

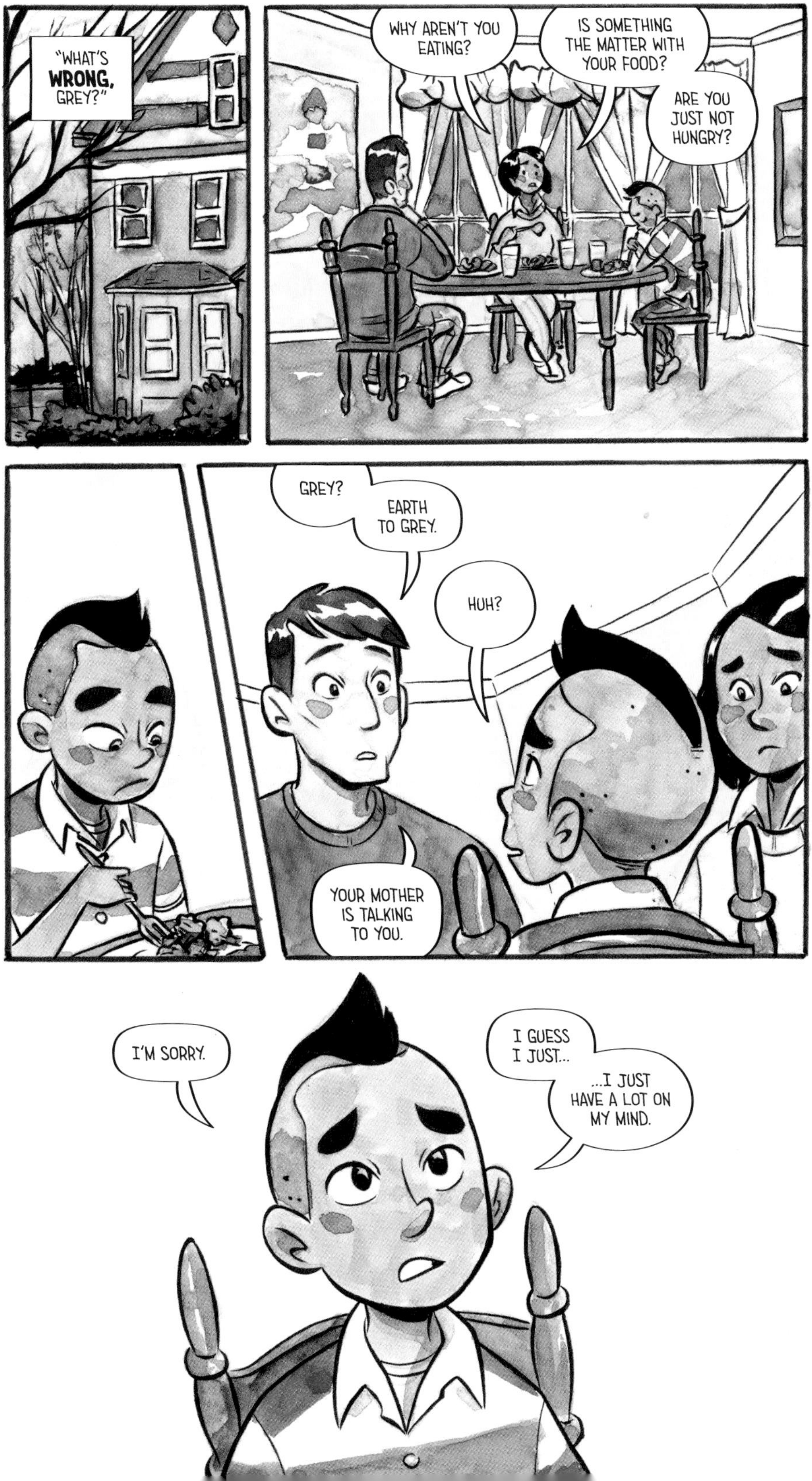
"WHAT'S WRONG, GREY?"
WHY AREN'T YOU EATING?
IS SOMETHING THE MATTER WITH YOUR FOOD?
ARE YOU JUST NOT HUNGRY?
GREY?
EARTH TO GREY.
HUH?
YOUR MOTHER IS TALKING TO YOU.
I'M SORRY.
I GUESS I JUST...
...I JUST HAVE A LOT ON MY MIND.

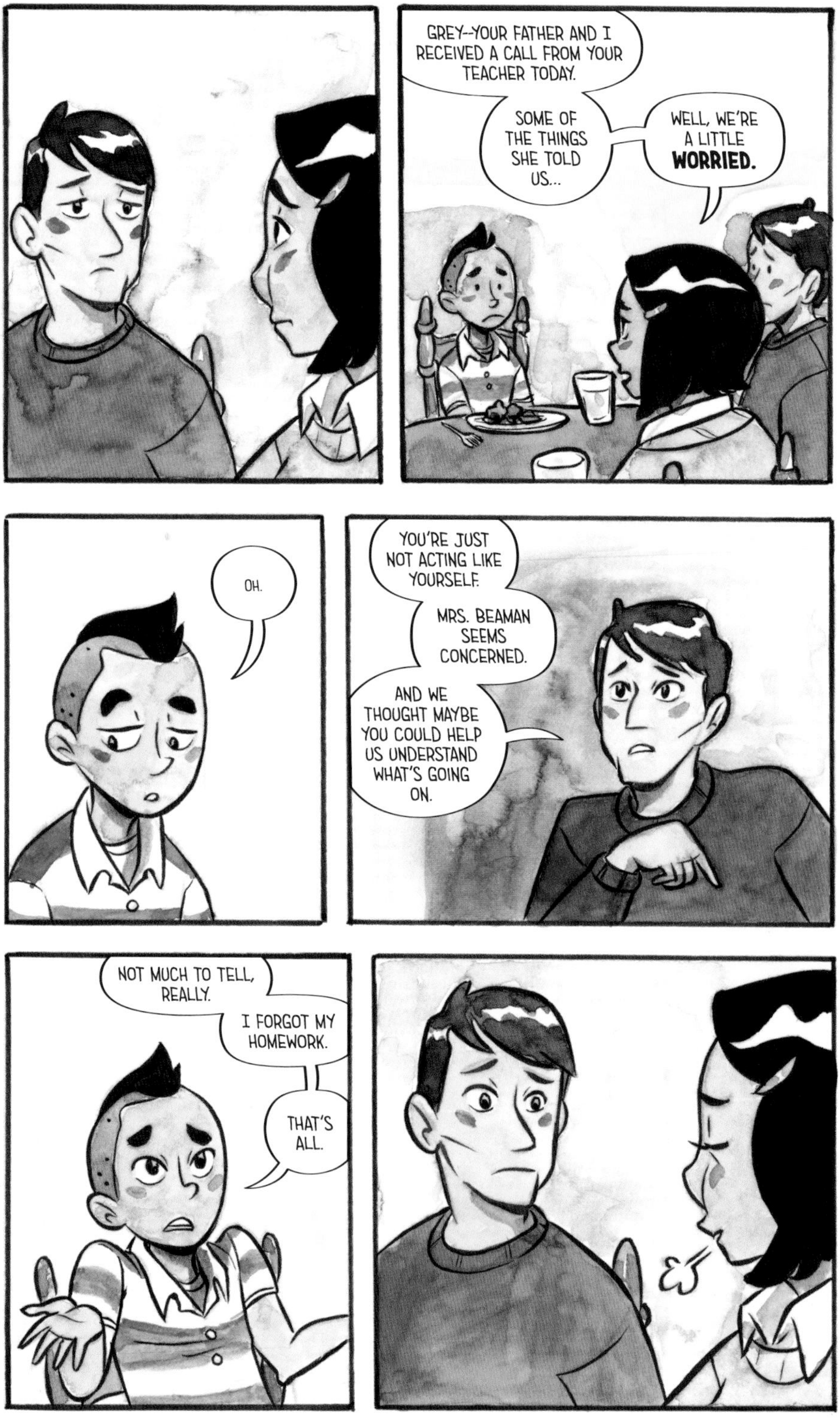
GREY--YOUR FATHER AND I RECEIVED A CALL FROM YOUR TEACHER TODAY.
SOME OF THE THINGS SHE TOLD US...
WELL, WE'RE A LITTLE **WORRIED.**
OH.
YOU'RE JUST NOT ACTING LIKE YOURSELF.
MRS. BEAMAN SEEMS CONCERNED.
AND WE THOUGHT MAYBE YOU COULD HELP US UNDERSTAND WHAT'S GOING ON.
NOT MUCH TO TELL, REALLY.
I FORGOT MY HOMEWORK.
THAT'S ALL.

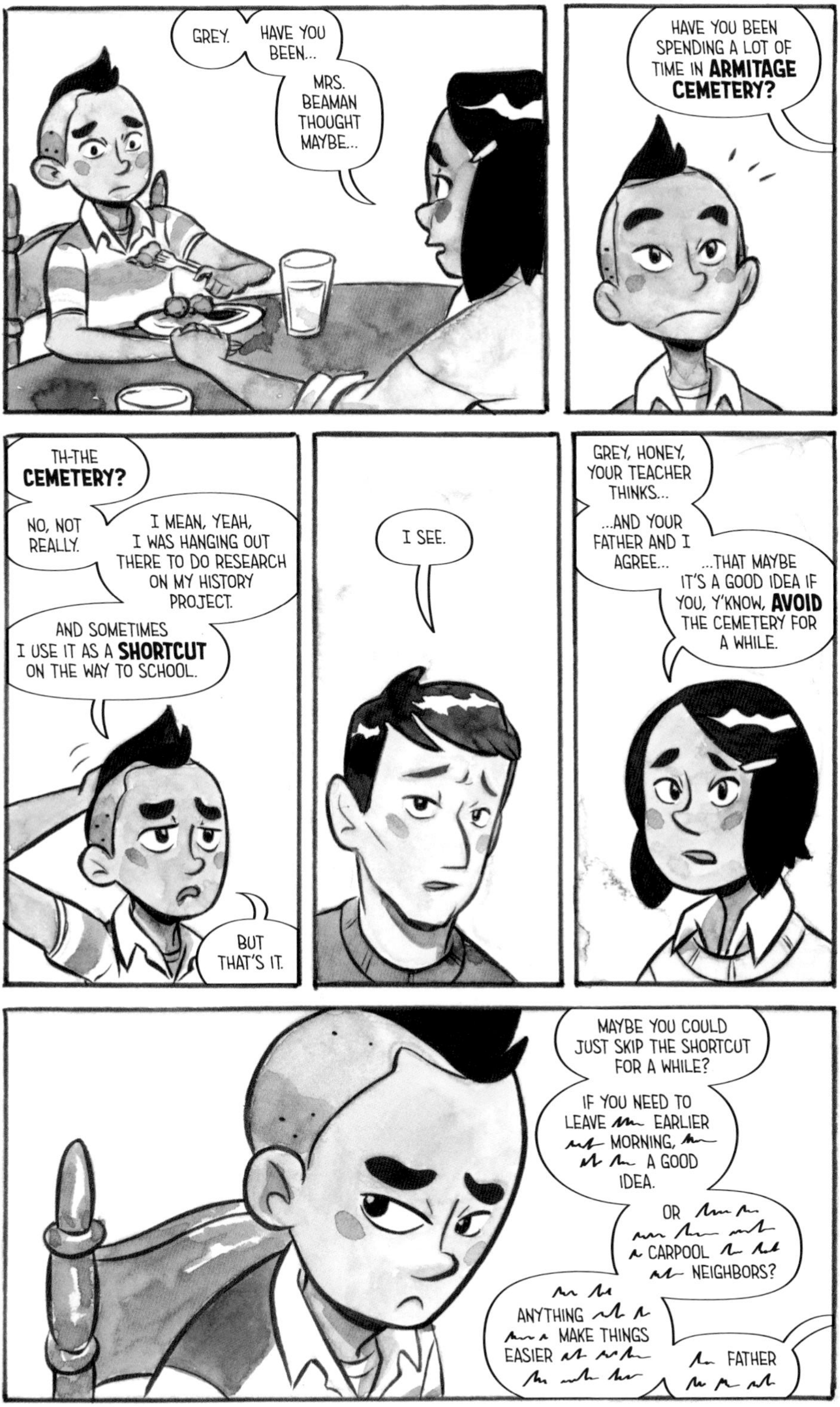
GREY.
HAVE YOU BEEN...
MRS. BEAMAN THOUGHT MAYBE...
HAVE YOU BEEN SPENDING A LOT OF TIME IN **ARMITAGE CEMETERY?**
TH-THE **CEMETERY?**
NO, NOT REALLY.
I MEAN, YEAH, I WAS HANGING OUT THERE TO DO RESEARCH ON MY HISTORY PROJECT.
AND SOMETIMES I USE IT AS A **SHORTCUT** ON THE WAY TO SCHOOL.
BUT THAT'S IT.
I SEE.
GREY, HONEY, YOUR TEACHER THINKS...
...AND YOUR FATHER AND I AGREE...
...THAT MAYBE IT'S A GOOD IDEA IF YOU, Y'KNOW, **AVOID** THE CEMETERY FOR A WHILE.
MAYBE YOU COULD JUST SKIP THE SHORTCUT FOR A WHILE?
IF YOU NEED TO LEAVE EARLIER MORNING, A GOOD IDEA.
OR CARPOOL NEIGHBORS?
ANYTHING MAKE THINGS EASIER
FATHER

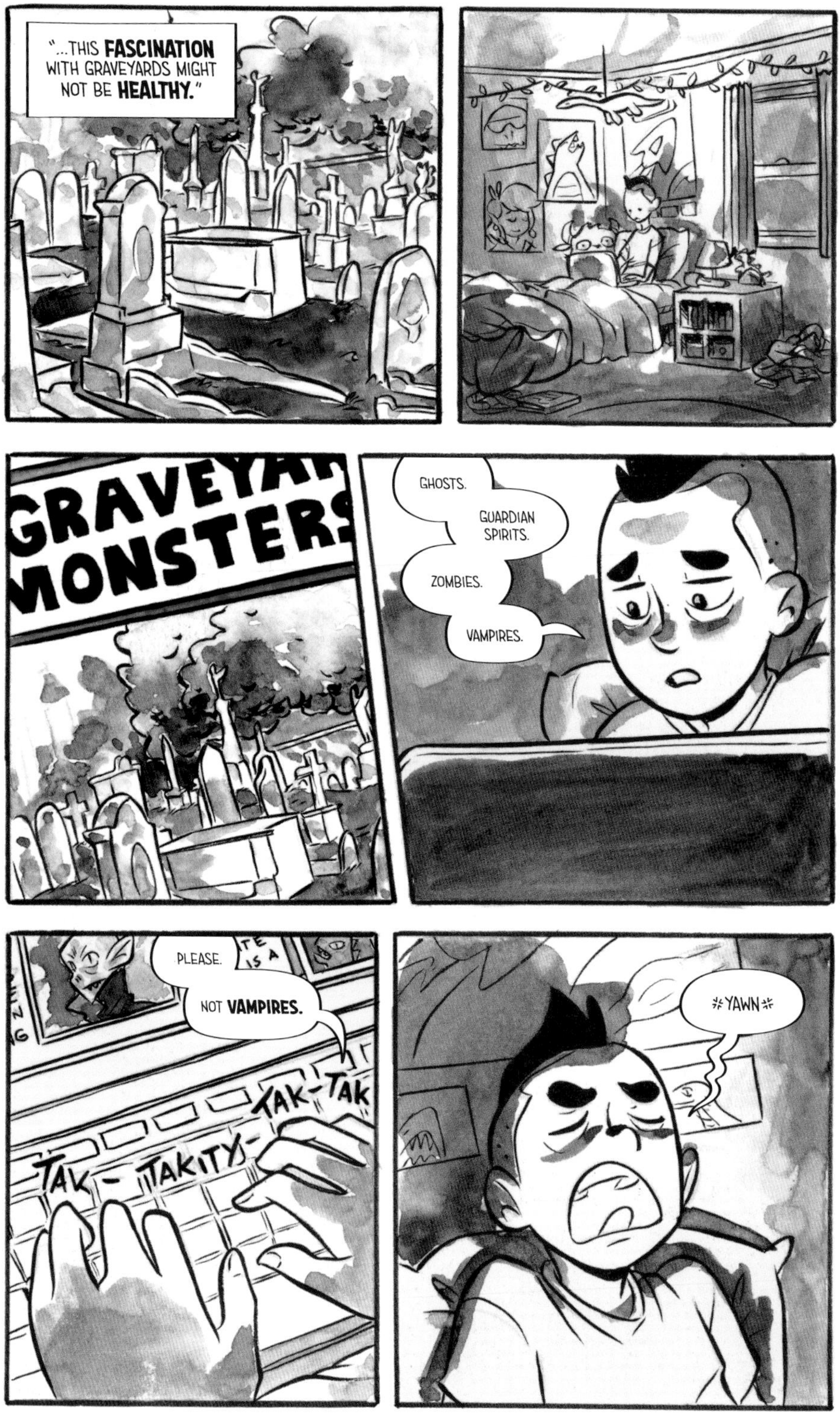
"...THIS **FASCINATION** WITH GRAVEYARDS MIGHT NOT BE **HEALTHY.**"
GRAVEYAR MONSTERS
GHOSTS.
GUARDIAN SPIRITS.
ZOMBIES.
VAMPIRES.
PLEASE.
NOT **VAMPIRES.**
TAK - TAKITY- TAK-TAK
YAWN

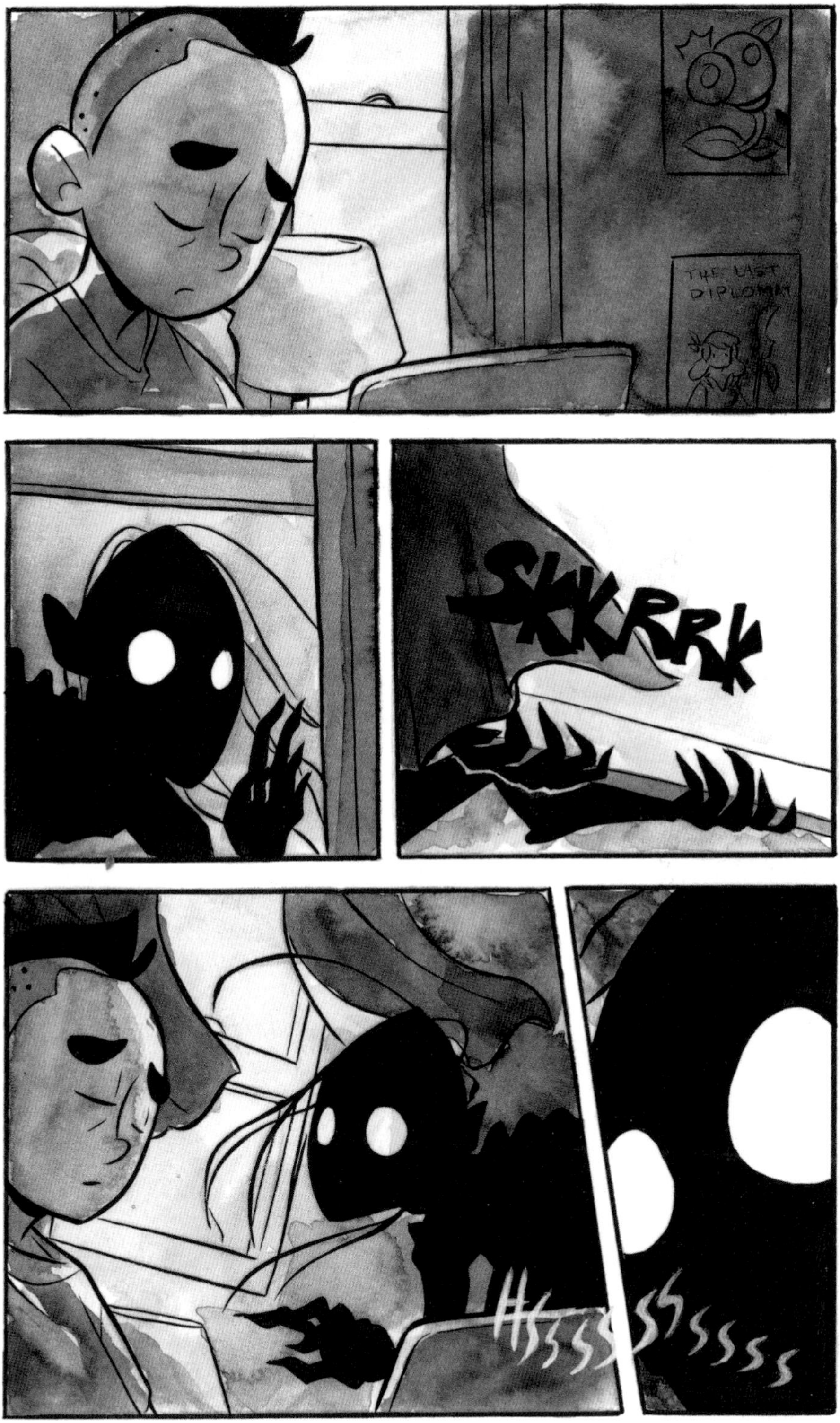
THE LAST DIPLOMAT
SKKRRK
HSSSSSSSSSSS

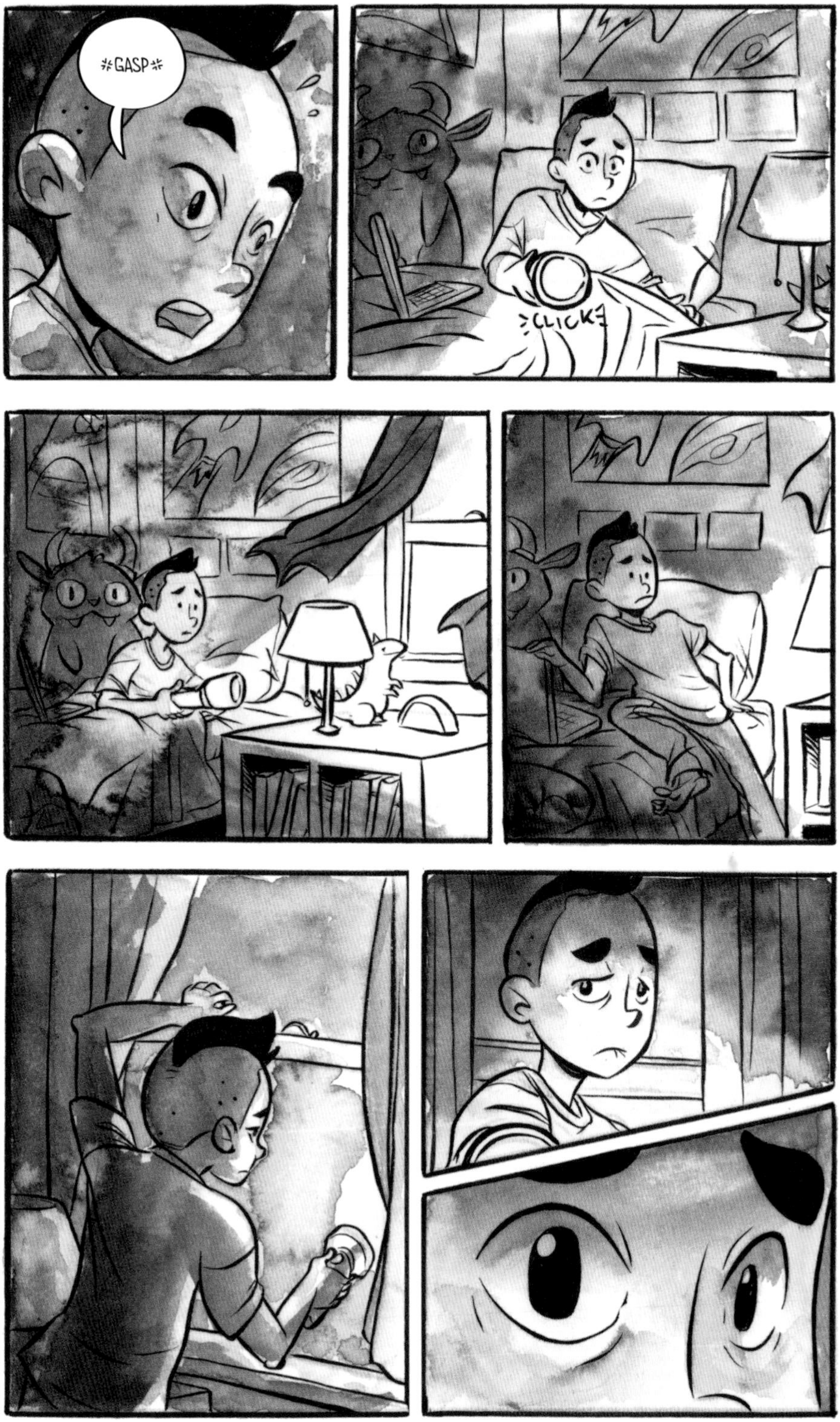
GASP
CLICK

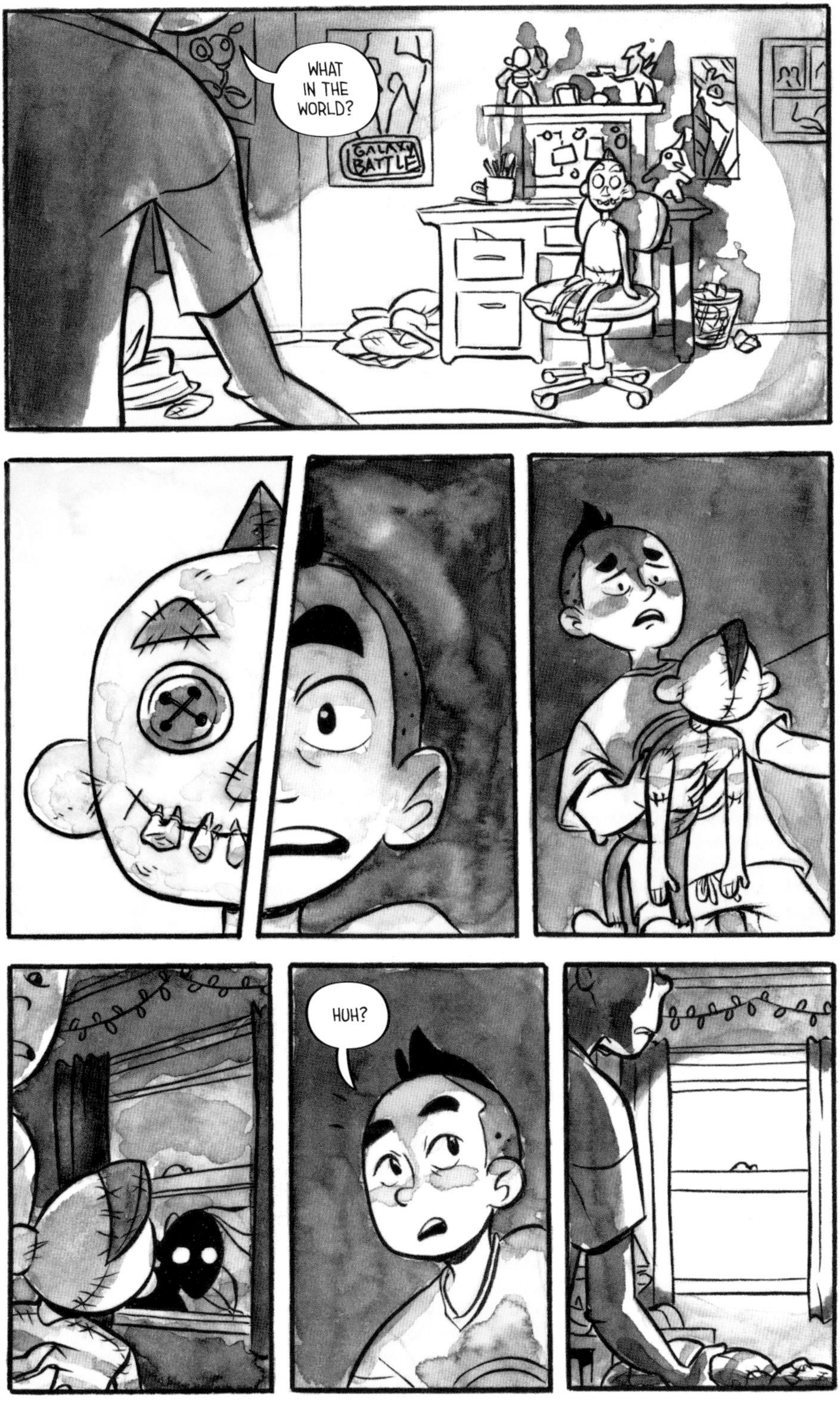
WHAT IN THE WORLD?
GALAXY BATTLE
HUH?

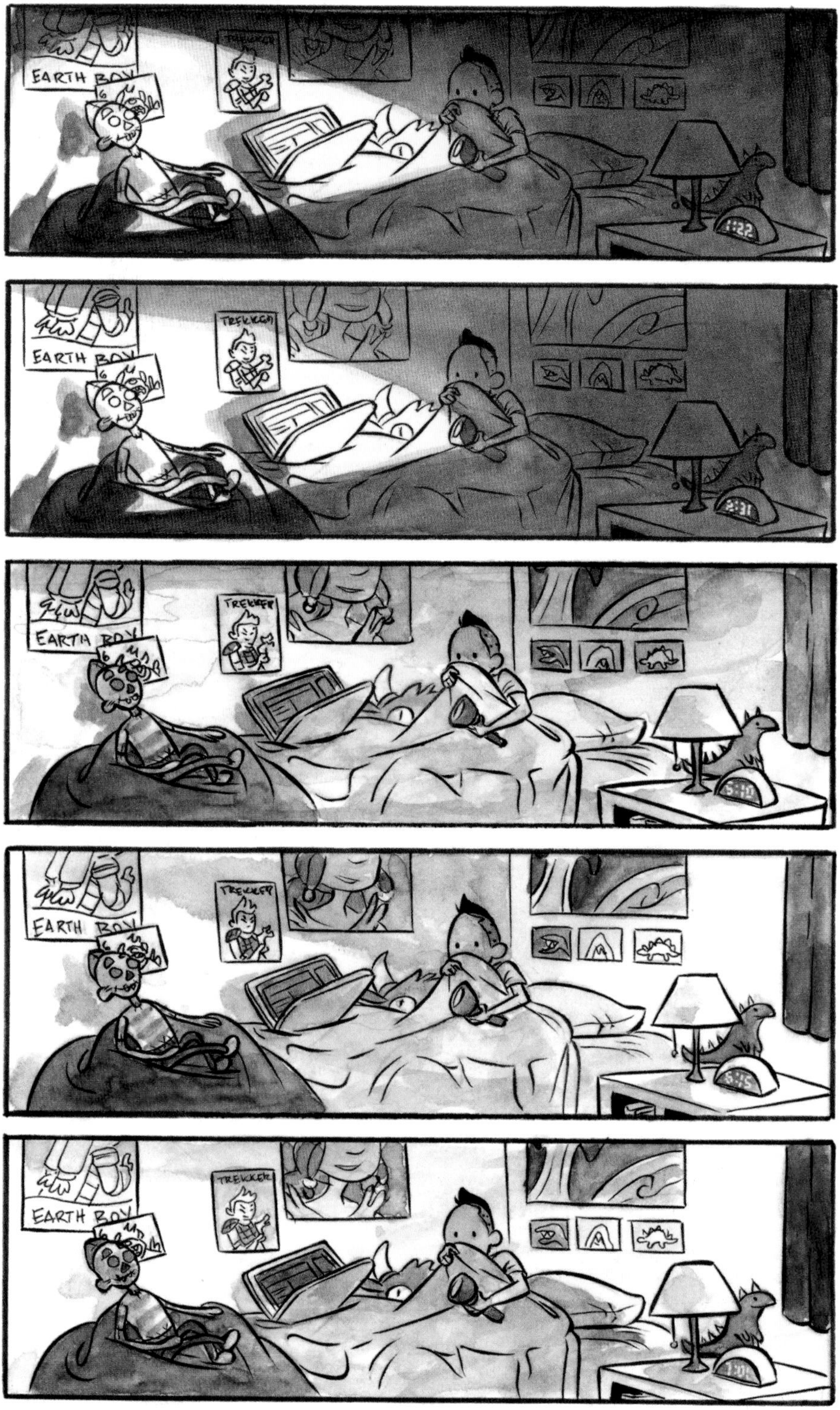
EARTH BOY
TREKKER

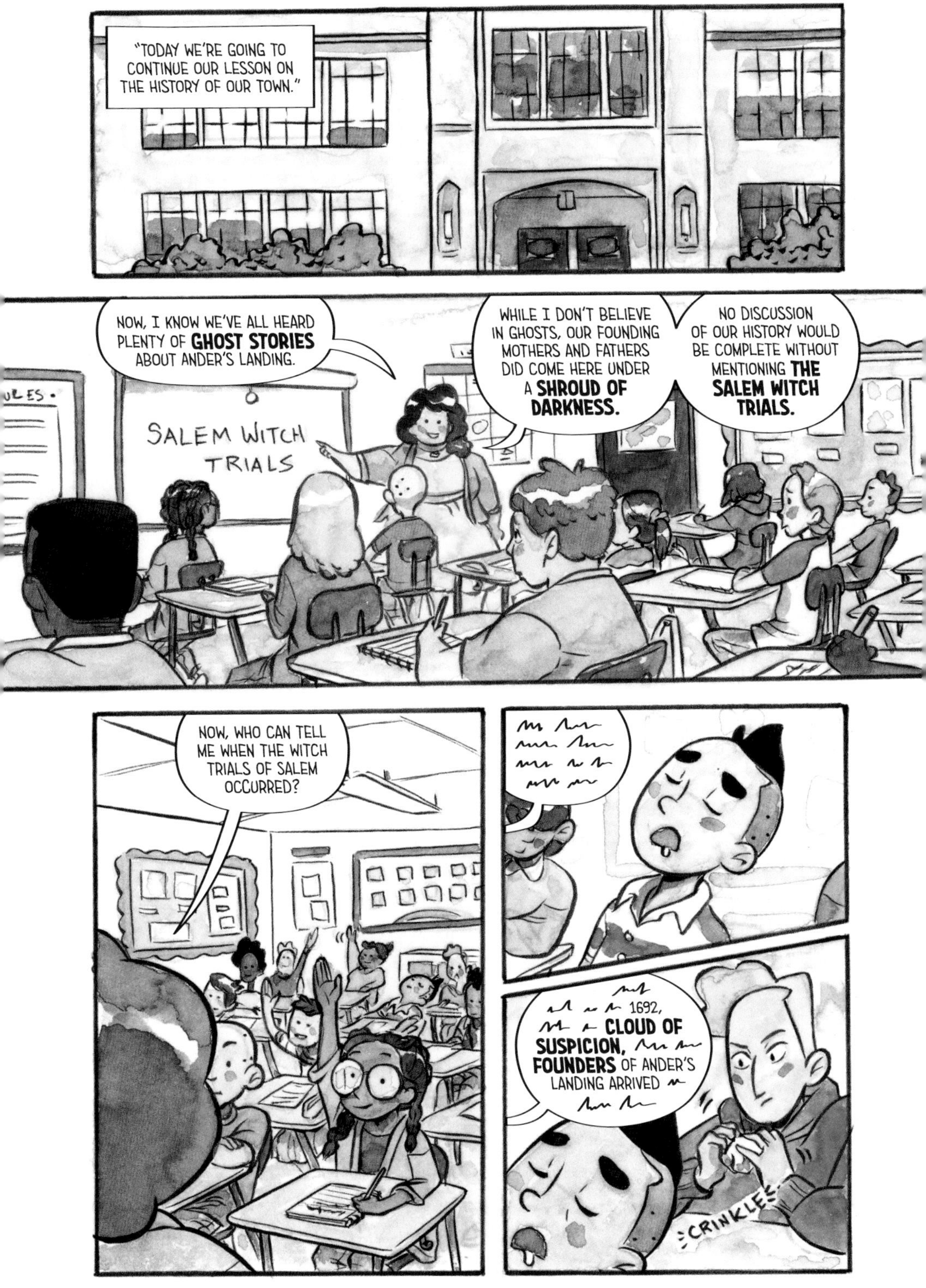
"TODAY WE'RE GOING TO CONTINUE OUR LESSON ON THE HISTORY OF OUR TOWN."
NOW, I KNOW WE'VE ALL HEARD PLENTY OF **GHOST STORIES** ABOUT ANDER'S LANDING.
SALEM WITCH TRIALS
WHILE I DON'T BELIEVE IN GHOSTS, OUR FOUNDING MOTHERS AND FATHERS DID COME HERE UNDER A **SHROUD OF DARKNESS.**
NO DISCUSSION OF OUR HISTORY WOULD BE COMPLETE WITHOUT MENTIONING **THE SALEM WITCH TRIALS.**
NOW, WHO CAN TELL ME WHEN THE WITCH TRIALS OF SALEM OCCURRED?
1692, **CLOUD OF SUSPICION, FOUNDERS** OF ANDER'S LANDING ARRIVED
CRINKLE

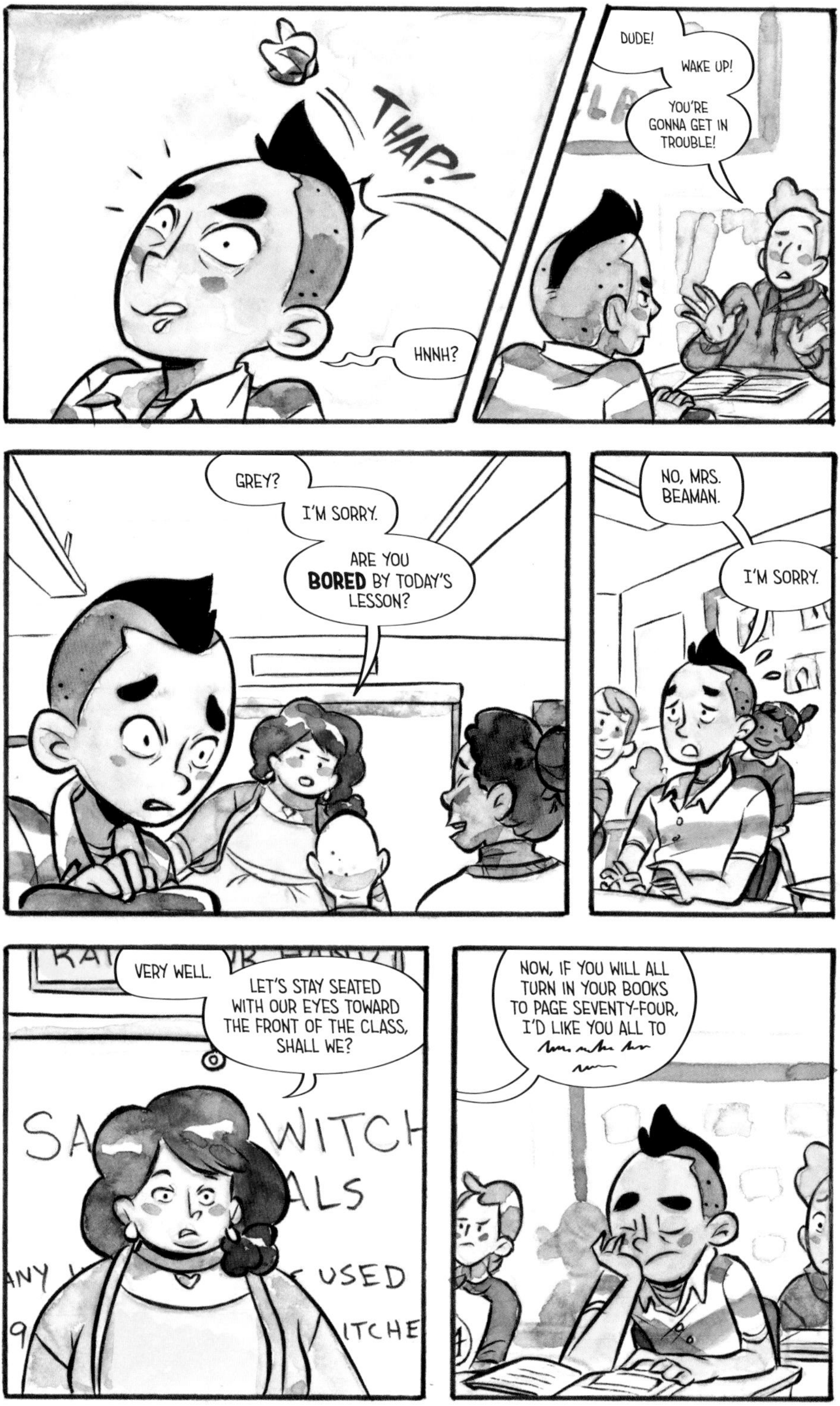
THAP!
HNNH?
DUDE!
WAKE UP!
YOU'RE GONNA GET IN TROUBLE!
GREY?
I'M SORRY.
ARE YOU **BORED** BY TODAY'S LESSON?
NO, MRS. BEAMAN.
I'M SORRY.
VERY WELL.
LET'S STAY SEATED WITH OUR EYES TOWARD THE FRONT OF THE CLASS, SHALL WE?
NOW, IF YOU WILL ALL TURN IN YOUR BOOKS TO PAGE SEVENTY-FOUR, I'D LIKE YOU ALL TO

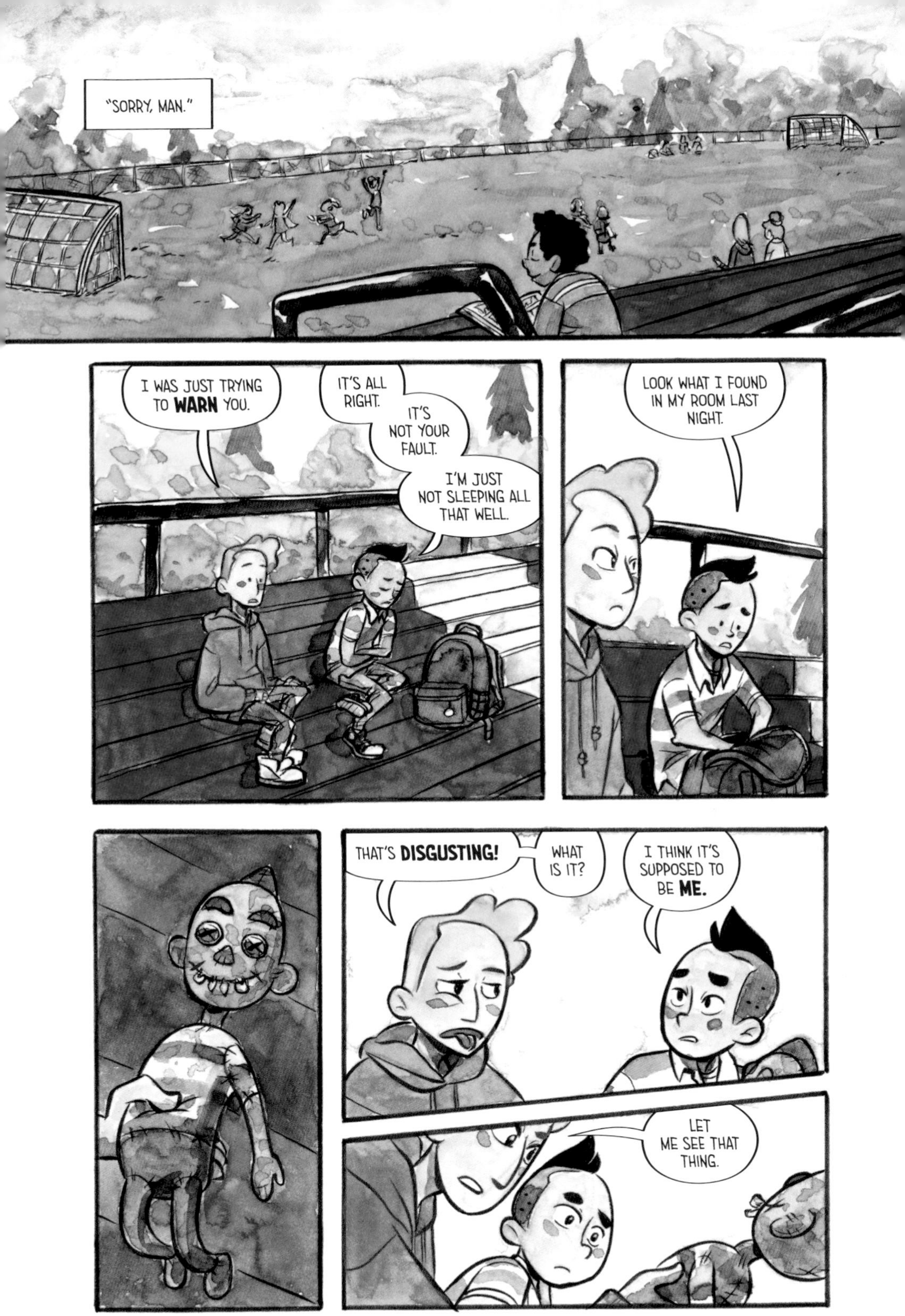
"SORRY, MAN."
I WAS JUST TRYING TO WARN YOU.
IT'S ALL RIGHT.
IT'S NOT YOUR FAULT.
I'M JUST NOT SLEEPING ALL THAT WELL.
LOOK WHAT I FOUND IN MY ROOM LAST NIGHT.
THAT'S DISGUSTING!
WHAT IS IT?
I THINK IT'S SUPPOSED TO BE ME.
LET ME SEE THAT THING.

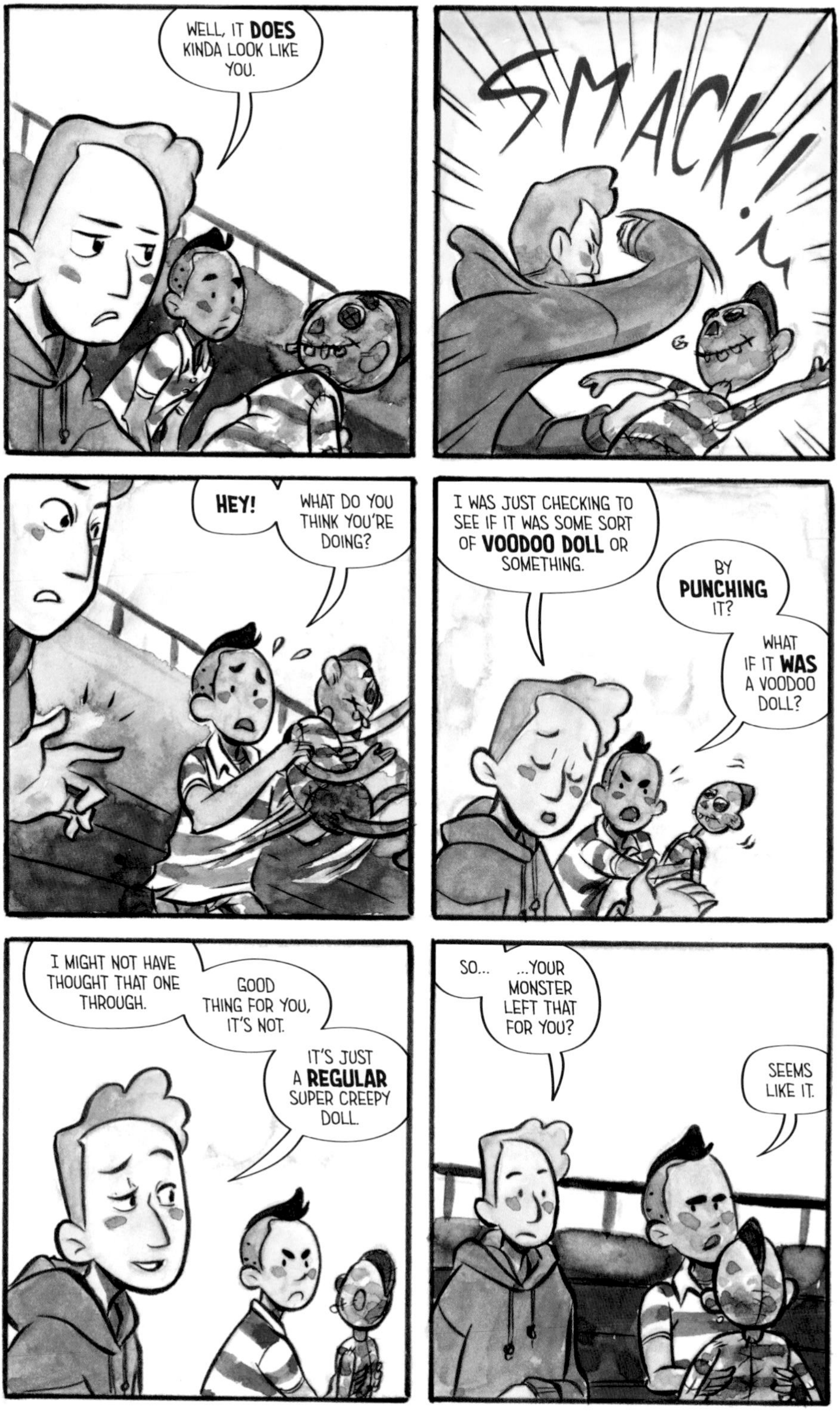
WELL, IT **DOES** KINDA LOOK LIKE YOU.
SMACK!
HEY!
WHAT DO YOU THINK YOU'RE DOING?
I WAS JUST CHECKING TO SEE IF IT WAS SOME SORT OF **VOODOO DOLL** OR SOMETHING.
BY **PUNCHING** IT?
WHAT IF IT **WAS** A VOODOO DOLL?
I MIGHT NOT HAVE THOUGHT THAT ONE THROUGH.
GOOD THING FOR YOU, IT'S NOT.
IT'S JUST A **REGULAR** SUPER CREEPY DOLL.
SO...
...YOUR MONSTER LEFT THAT FOR YOU?
SEEMS LIKE IT.

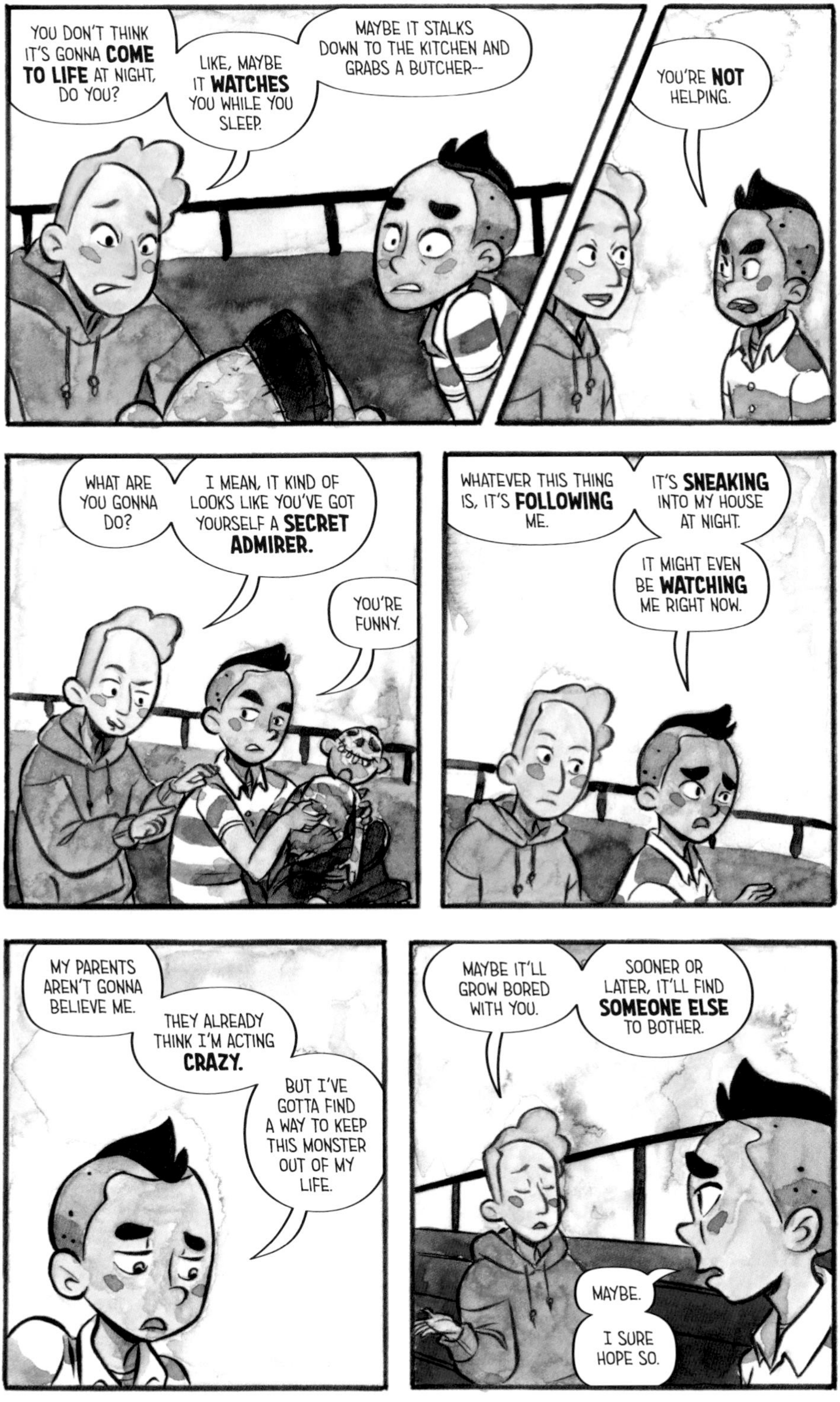
YOU DON'T THINK IT'S GONNA **COME TO LIFE** AT NIGHT, DO YOU?
LIKE, MAYBE IT **WATCHES** YOU WHILE YOU SLEEP.
MAYBE IT STALKS DOWN TO THE KITCHEN AND GRABS A BUTCHER--
YOU'RE **NOT** HELPING.
WHAT ARE YOU GONNA DO?
I MEAN, IT KIND OF LOOKS LIKE YOU'VE GOT YOURSELF A **SECRET ADMIRER.**
YOU'RE FUNNY.
WHATEVER THIS THING IS, IT'S **FOLLOWING** ME.
IT'S **SNEAKING** INTO MY HOUSE AT NIGHT.
IT MIGHT EVEN BE **WATCHING** ME RIGHT NOW.
MY PARENTS AREN'T GONNA BELIEVE ME.
THEY ALREADY THINK I'M ACTING **CRAZY.**
BUT I'VE GOTTA FIND A WAY TO KEEP THIS MONSTER OUT OF MY LIFE.
MAYBE IT'LL GROW BORED WITH YOU.
SOONER OR LATER, IT'LL FIND **SOMEONE ELSE** TO BOTHER.
MAYBE.
I SURE HOPE SO.

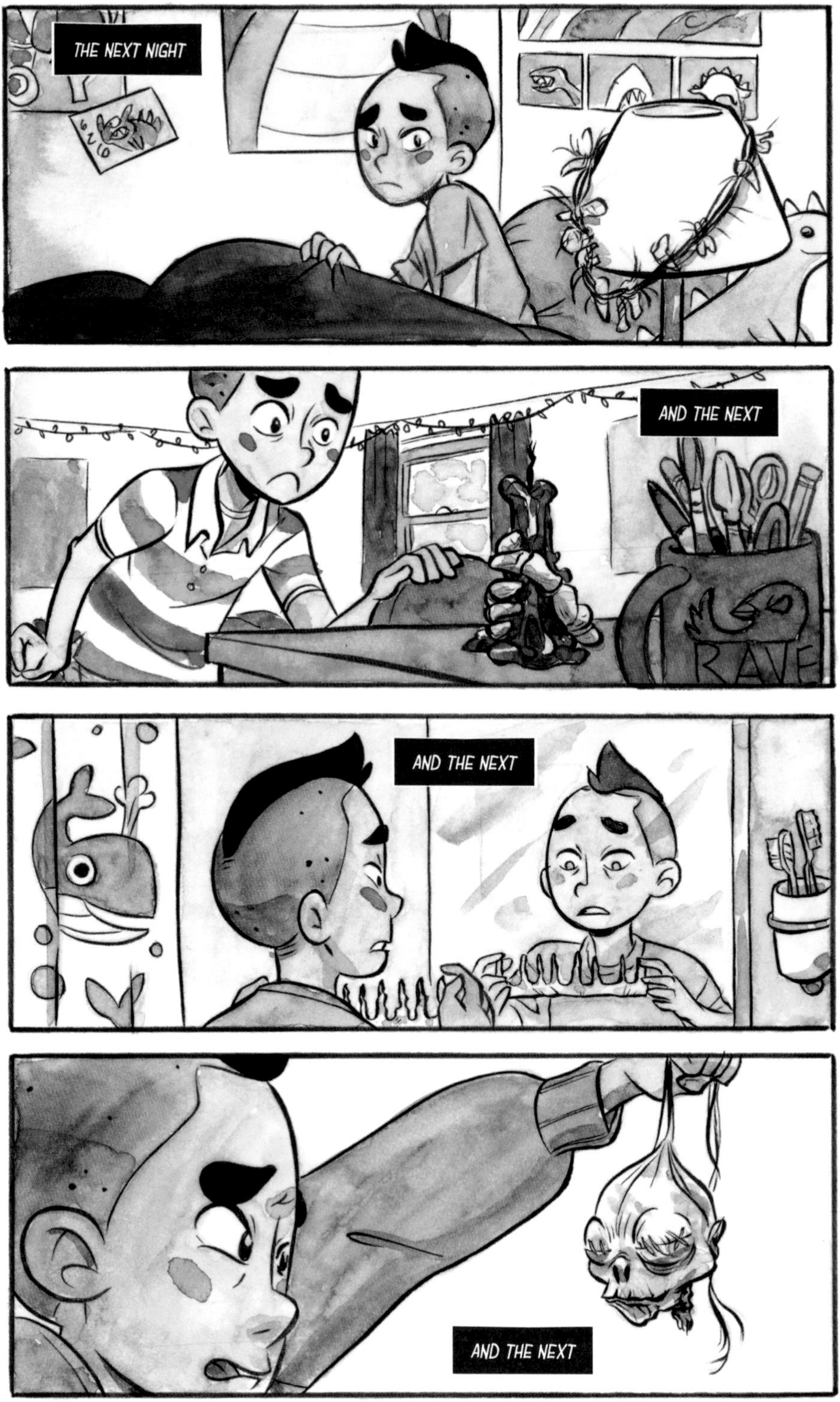
THE NEXT NIGHT
AND THE NEXT
AND THE NEXT
AND THE NEXT

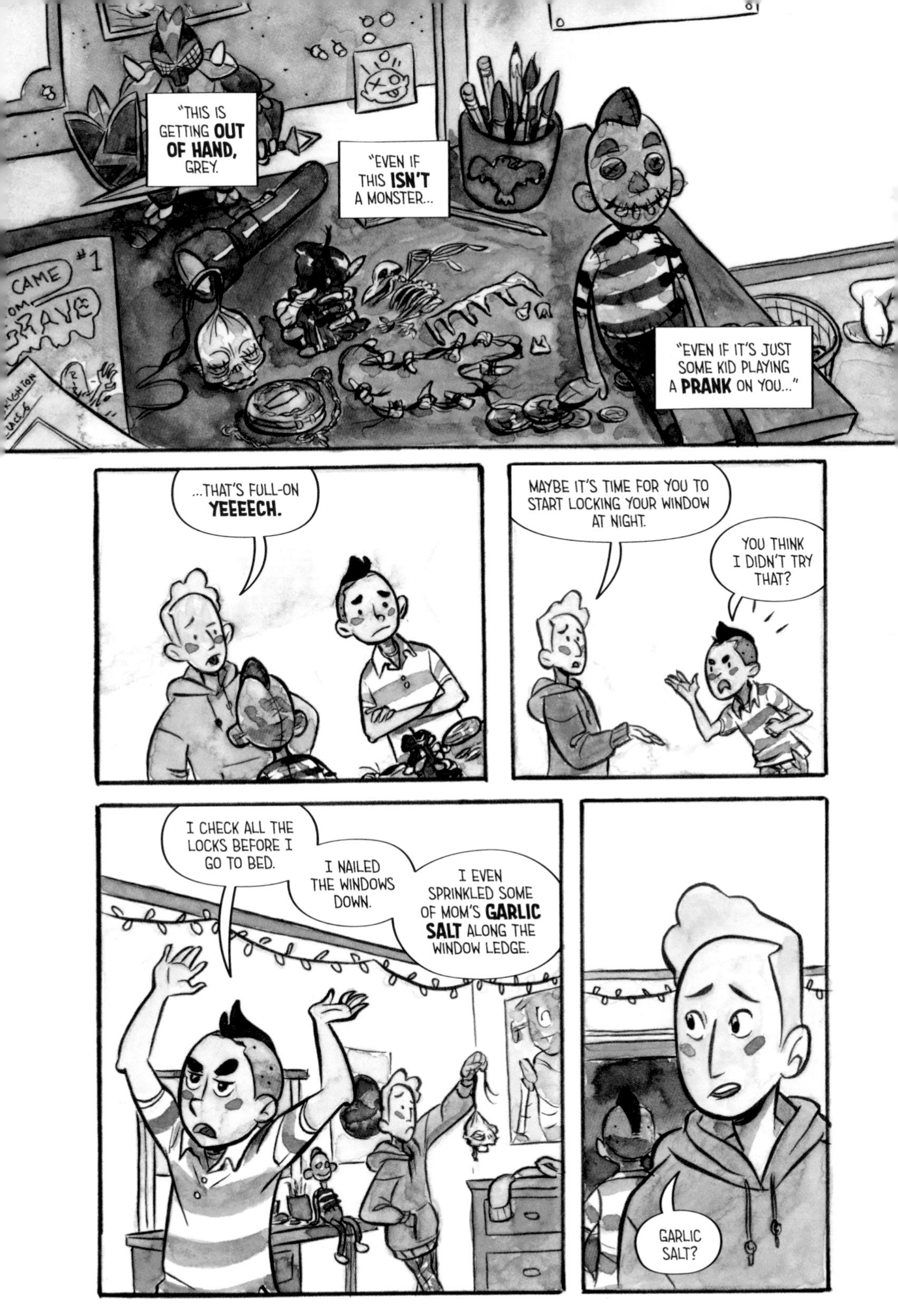
"THIS IS GETTING **OUT OF HAND,** GREY.
"EVEN IF THIS **ISN'T** A MONSTER...
"EVEN IF IT'S JUST SOME KID PLAYING A **PRANK** ON YOU..."
...THAT'S FULL-ON **YEEEECH.**
MAYBE IT'S TIME FOR YOU TO START LOCKING YOUR WINDOW AT NIGHT.
YOU THINK I DIDN'T TRY THAT?
I CHECK ALL THE LOCKS BEFORE I GO TO BED.
I NAILED THE WINDOWS DOWN.
I EVEN SPRINKLED SOME OF MOM'S **GARLIC SALT** ALONG THE WINDOW LEDGE.
GARLIC SALT?

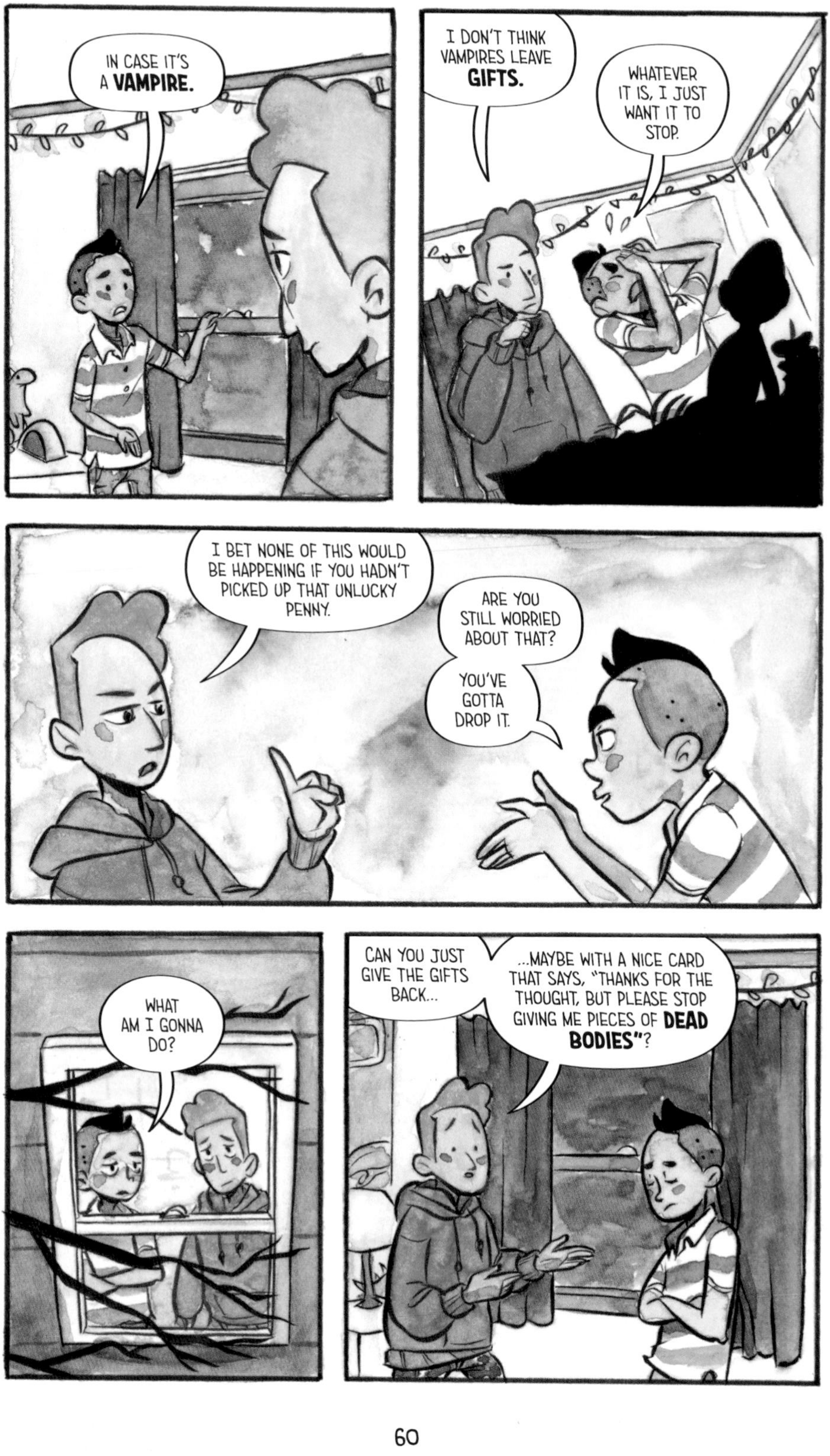
IN CASE IT'S A **VAMPIRE.**
I DON'T THINK VAMPIRES LEAVE **GIFTS.**
WHATEVER IT IS, I JUST WANT IT TO STOP.
I BET NONE OF THIS WOULD BE HAPPENING IF YOU HADN'T PICKED UP THAT UNLUCKY PENNY.
ARE YOU STILL WORRIED ABOUT THAT?
YOU'VE GOTTA DROP IT.
WHAT AM I GONNA DO?
CAN YOU JUST GIVE THE GIFTS BACK...
...MAYBE WITH A NICE CARD THAT SAYS, "THANKS FOR THE THOUGHT, BUT PLEASE STOP GIVING ME PIECES OF **DEAD BODIES**"?

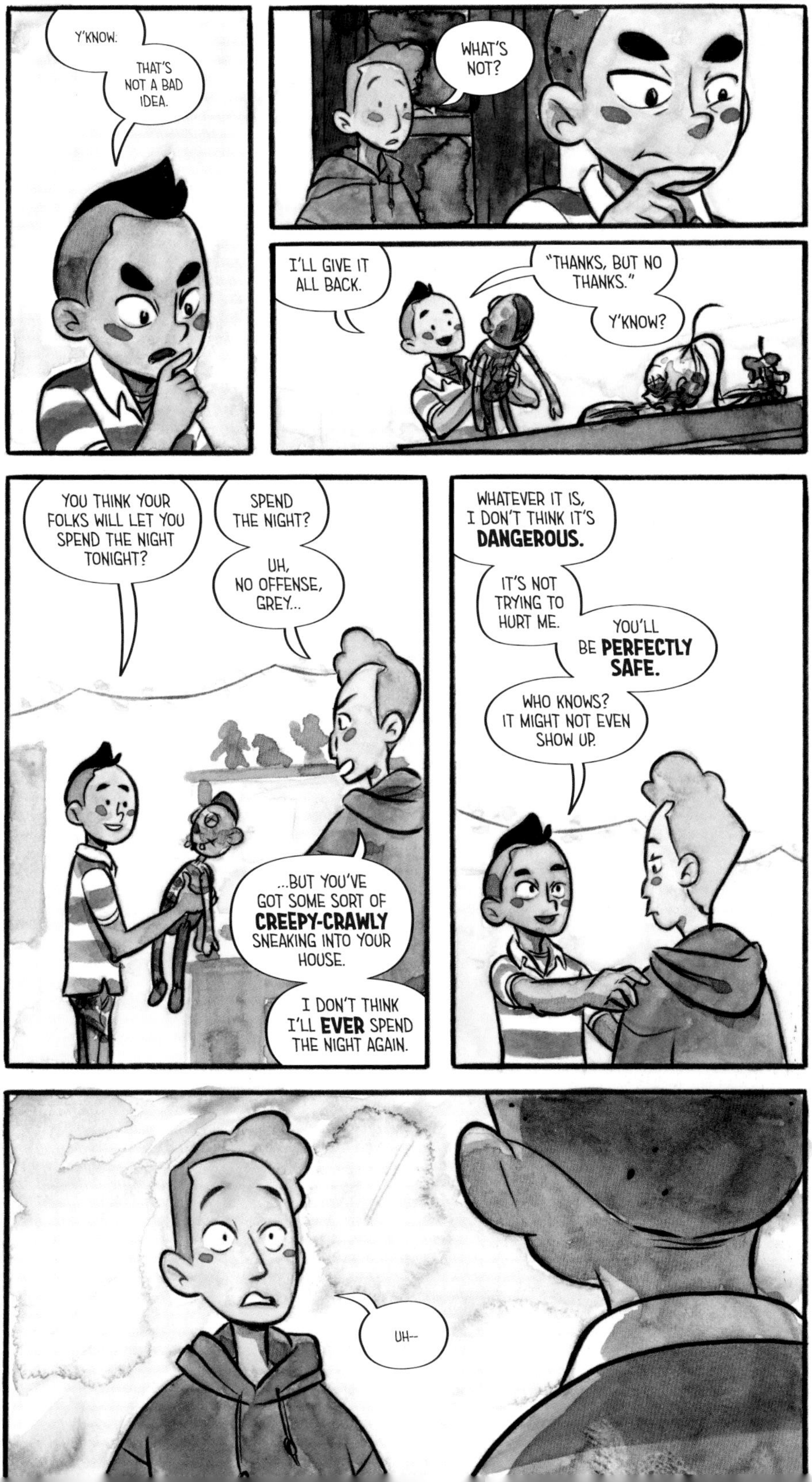
Y'KNOW:
THAT'S NOT A BAD IDEA.
WHAT'S NOT?
I'LL GIVE IT ALL BACK.
"THANKS, BUT NO THANKS."
Y'KNOW?
YOU THINK YOUR FOLKS WILL LET YOU SPEND THE NIGHT TONIGHT?
SPEND THE NIGHT?
UH, NO OFFENSE, GREY...
...BUT YOU'VE GOT SOME SORT OF CREEPY-CRAWLY SNEAKING INTO YOUR HOUSE.
I DON'T THINK I'LL EVER SPEND THE NIGHT AGAIN.
WHATEVER IT IS, I DON'T THINK IT'S DANGEROUS.
IT'S NOT TRYING TO HURT ME.
YOU'LL BE PERFECTLY SAFE.
WHO KNOWS? IT MIGHT NOT EVEN SHOW UP.
UH--

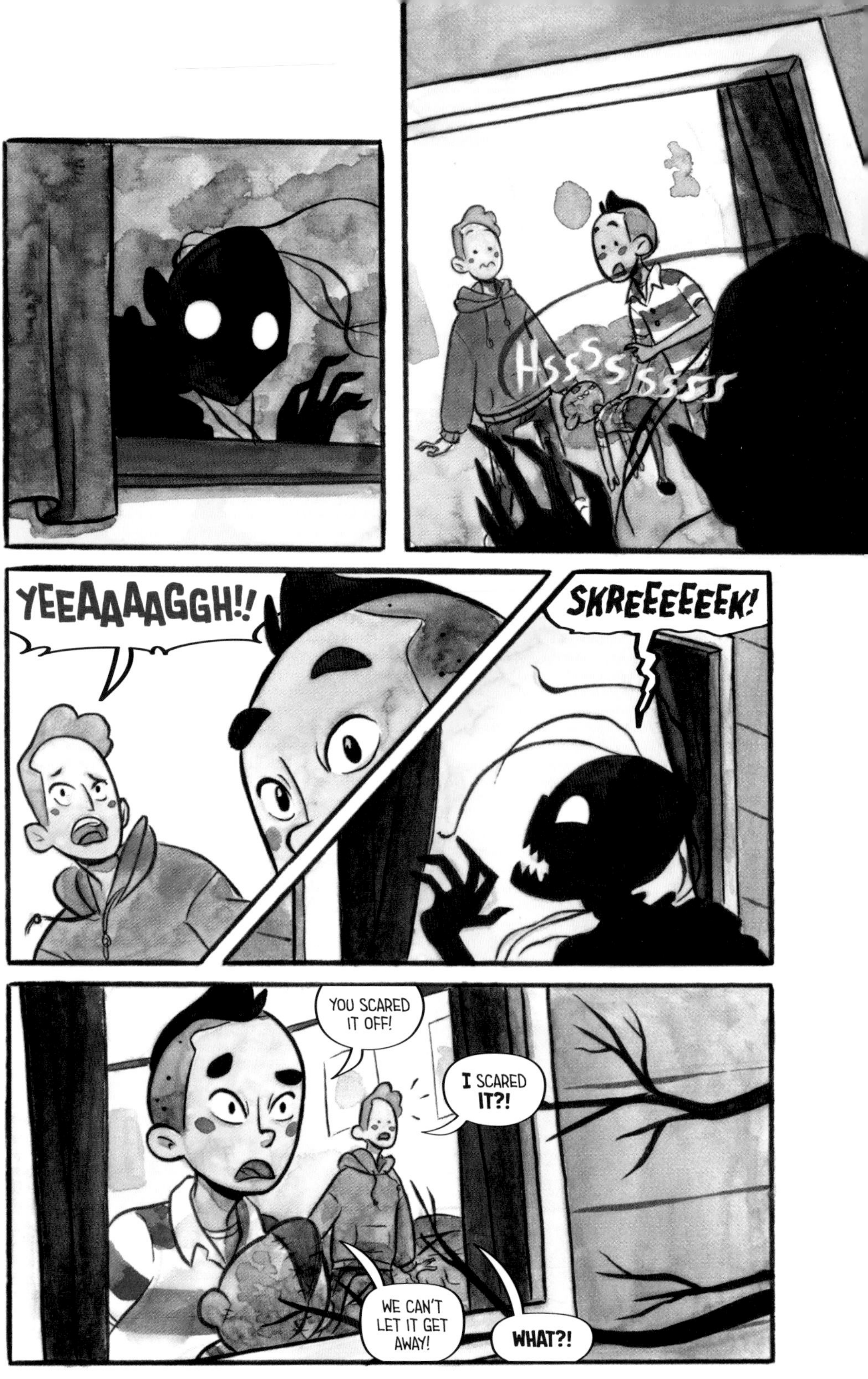
HSSSSSSSSS
YEEAAAAAGGH!!
SKREEEEEEEK!
YOU SCARED IT OFF!
I SCARED IT?!
WE CAN'T LET IT GET AWAY!
WHAT?!

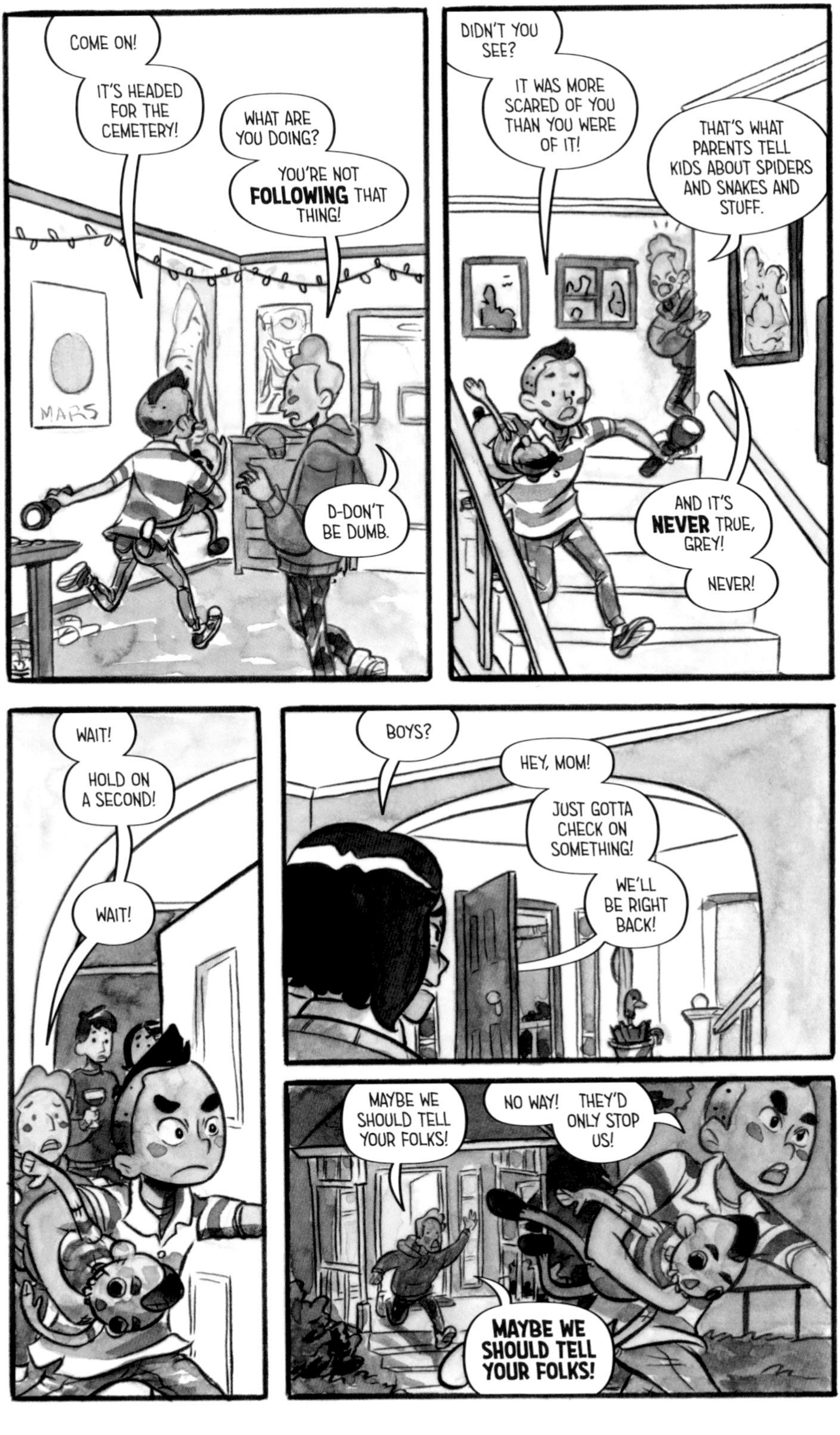
COME ON!
IT'S HEADED FOR THE CEMETERY!
WHAT ARE YOU DOING?
YOU'RE NOT **FOLLOWING** THAT THING!
MARS
D-DON'T BE DUMB.
DIDN'T YOU SEE?
IT WAS MORE SCARED OF YOU THAN YOU WERE OF IT!
THAT'S WHAT PARENTS TELL KIDS ABOUT SPIDERS AND SNAKES AND STUFF.
AND IT'S **NEVER** TRUE, GREY!
NEVER!
WAIT!
HOLD ON A SECOND!
WAIT!
BOYS?
HEY, MOM!
JUST GOTTA CHECK ON SOMETHING!
WE'LL BE RIGHT BACK!
MAYBE WE SHOULD TELL YOUR FOLKS!
NO WAY!
THEY'D ONLY STOP US!
MAYBE WE SHOULD TELL YOUR FOLKS!

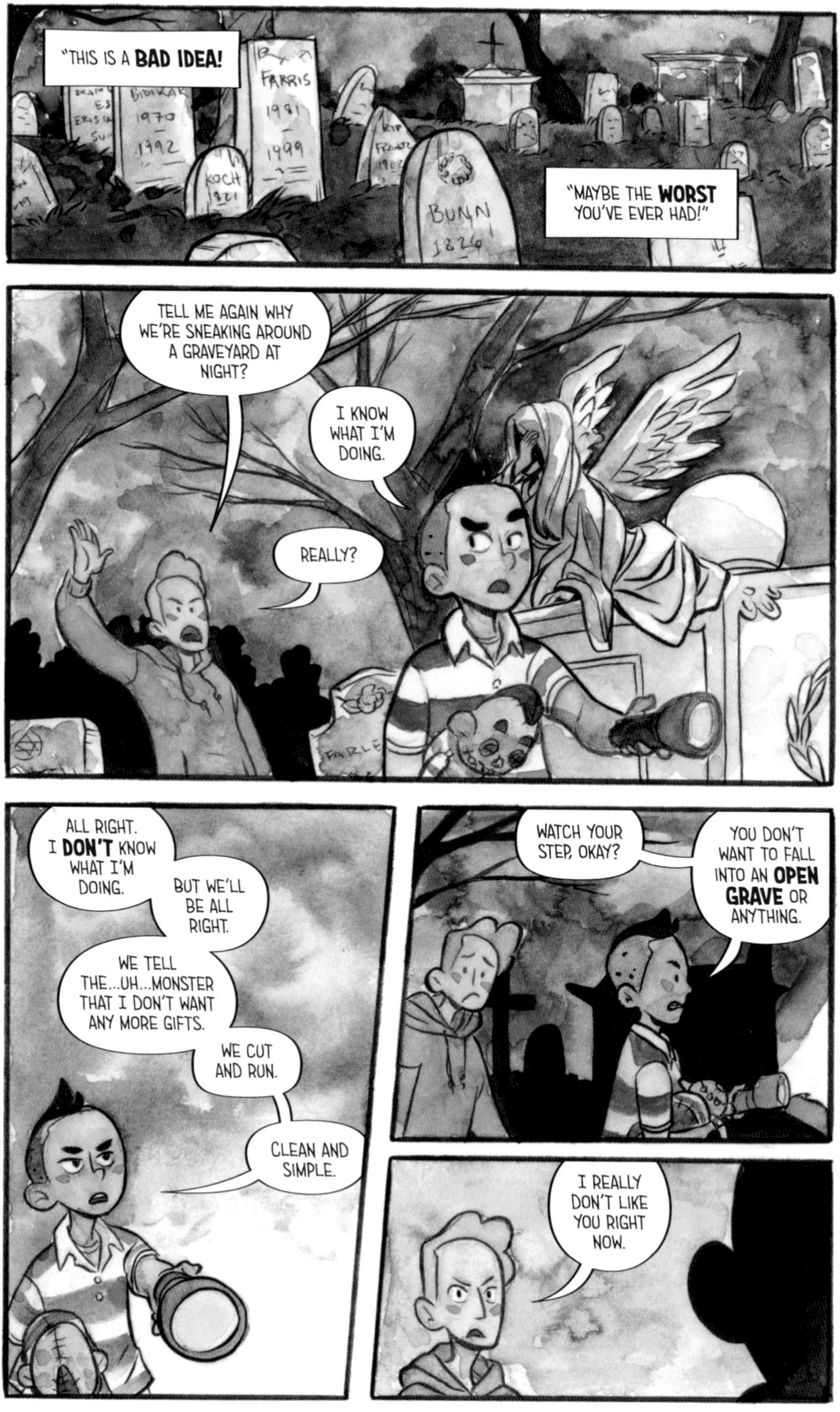
"THIS IS A **BAD IDEA!**
"MAYBE THE **WORST** YOU'VE EVER HAD!"
TELL ME AGAIN WHY WE'RE SNEAKING AROUND A GRAVEYARD AT NIGHT?
I KNOW WHAT I'M DOING.
REALLY?
ALL RIGHT. I **DON'T** KNOW WHAT I'M DOING.
BUT WE'LL BE ALL RIGHT.
WE TELL THE...UH...MONSTER THAT I DON'T WANT ANY MORE GIFTS.
WE CUT AND RUN.
CLEAN AND SIMPLE.
WATCH YOUR STEP, OKAY?
YOU DON'T WANT TO FALL INTO AN **OPEN GRAVE** OR ANYTHING.
I REALLY DON'T LIKE YOU RIGHT NOW.

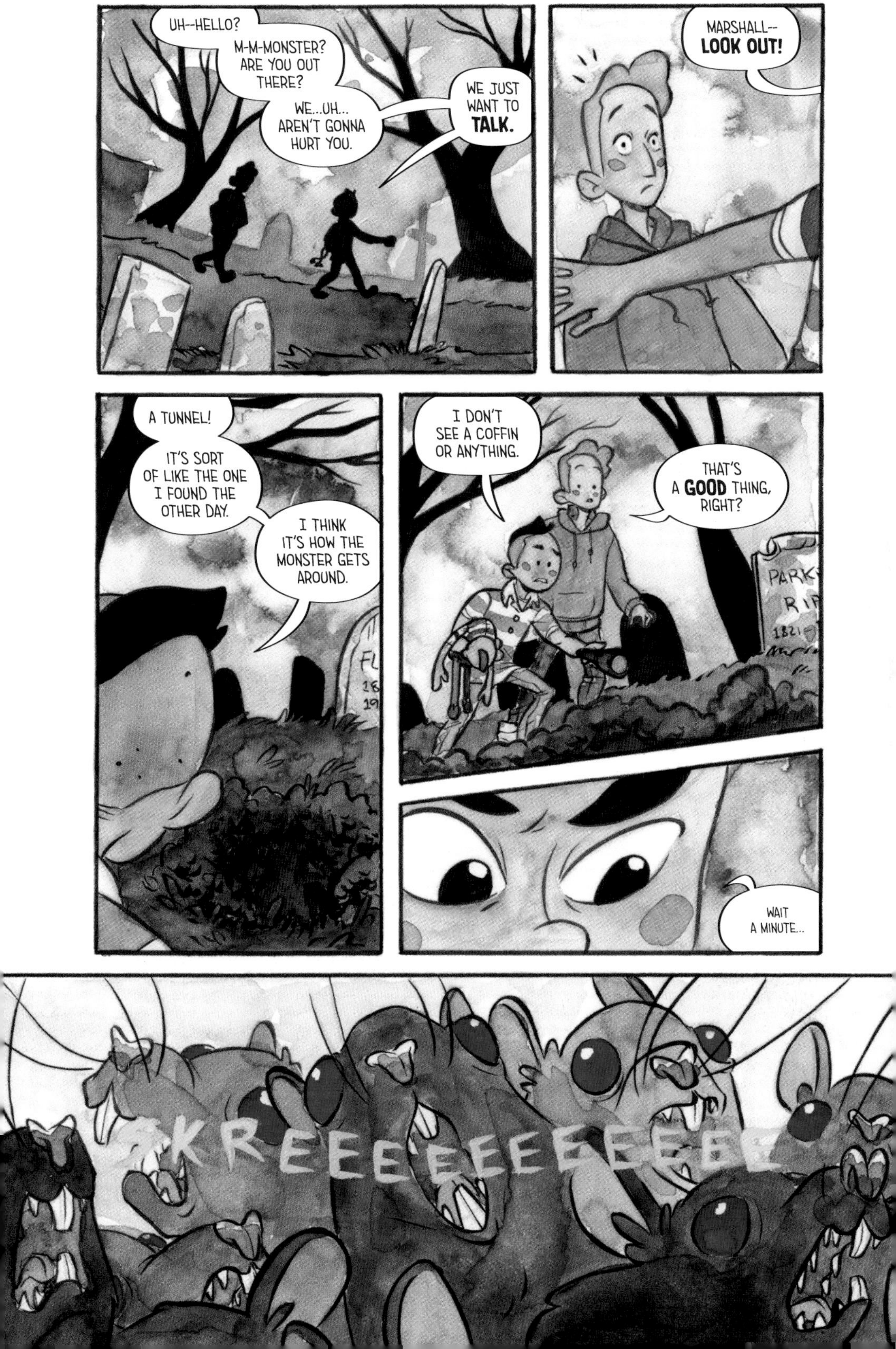
UH--HELLO?
M-M-MONSTER? ARE YOU OUT THERE?
WE...UH... AREN'T GONNA HURT YOU.
WE JUST WANT TO **TALK.**
MARSHALL-- **LOOK OUT!**
A TUNNEL!
IT'S SORT OF LIKE THE ONE I FOUND THE OTHER DAY.
I THINK IT'S HOW THE MONSTER GETS AROUND.
I DON'T SEE A COFFIN OR ANYTHING.
THAT'S A **GOOD** THING, RIGHT?
WAIT A MINUTE...
SKREEEEEEEEEEE

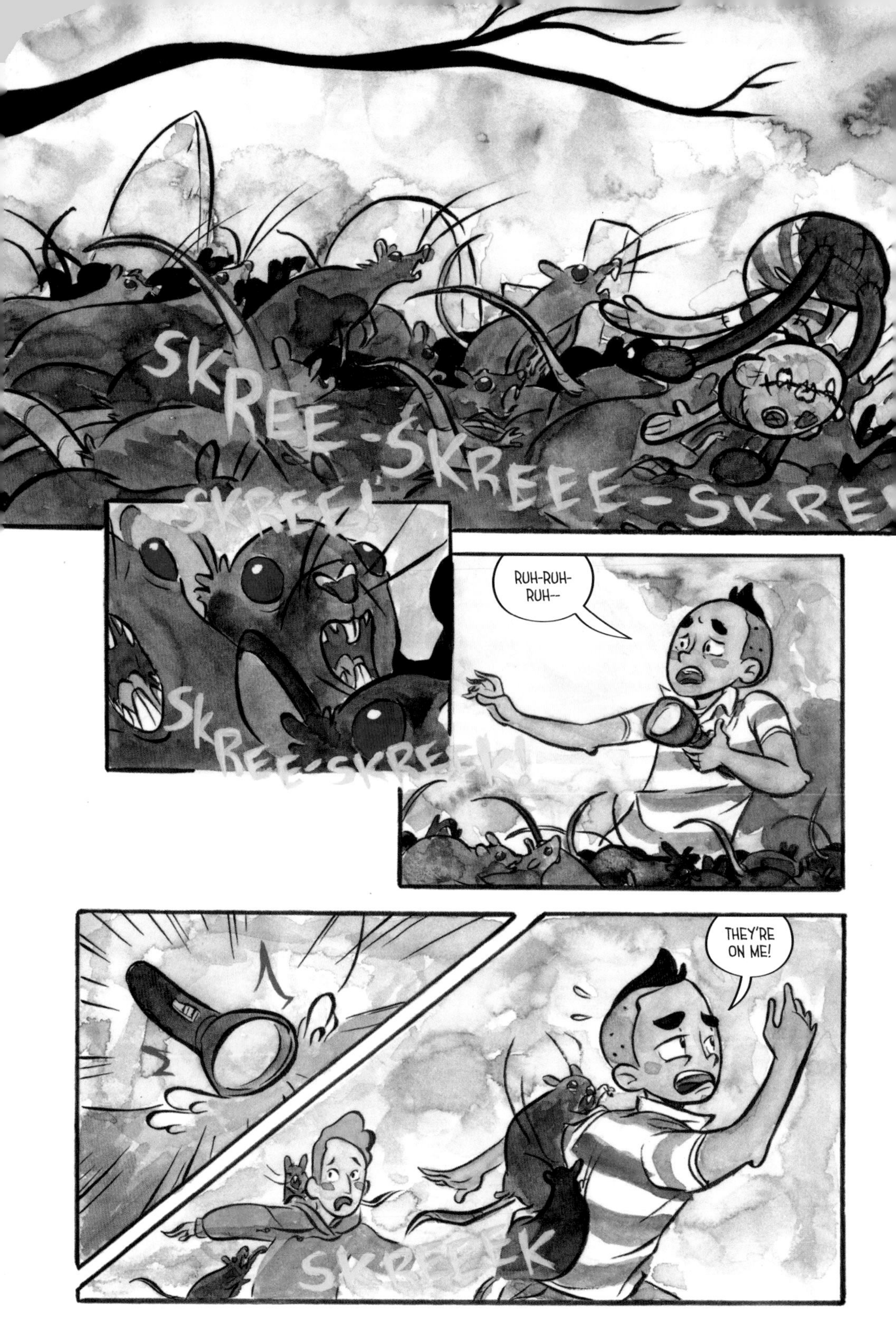
SKREE-SKREEE-SKRE
SKREE!
RUH-RUH-RUH--
SKREE-SKREEK!
THEY'RE ON ME!
SKREEEK

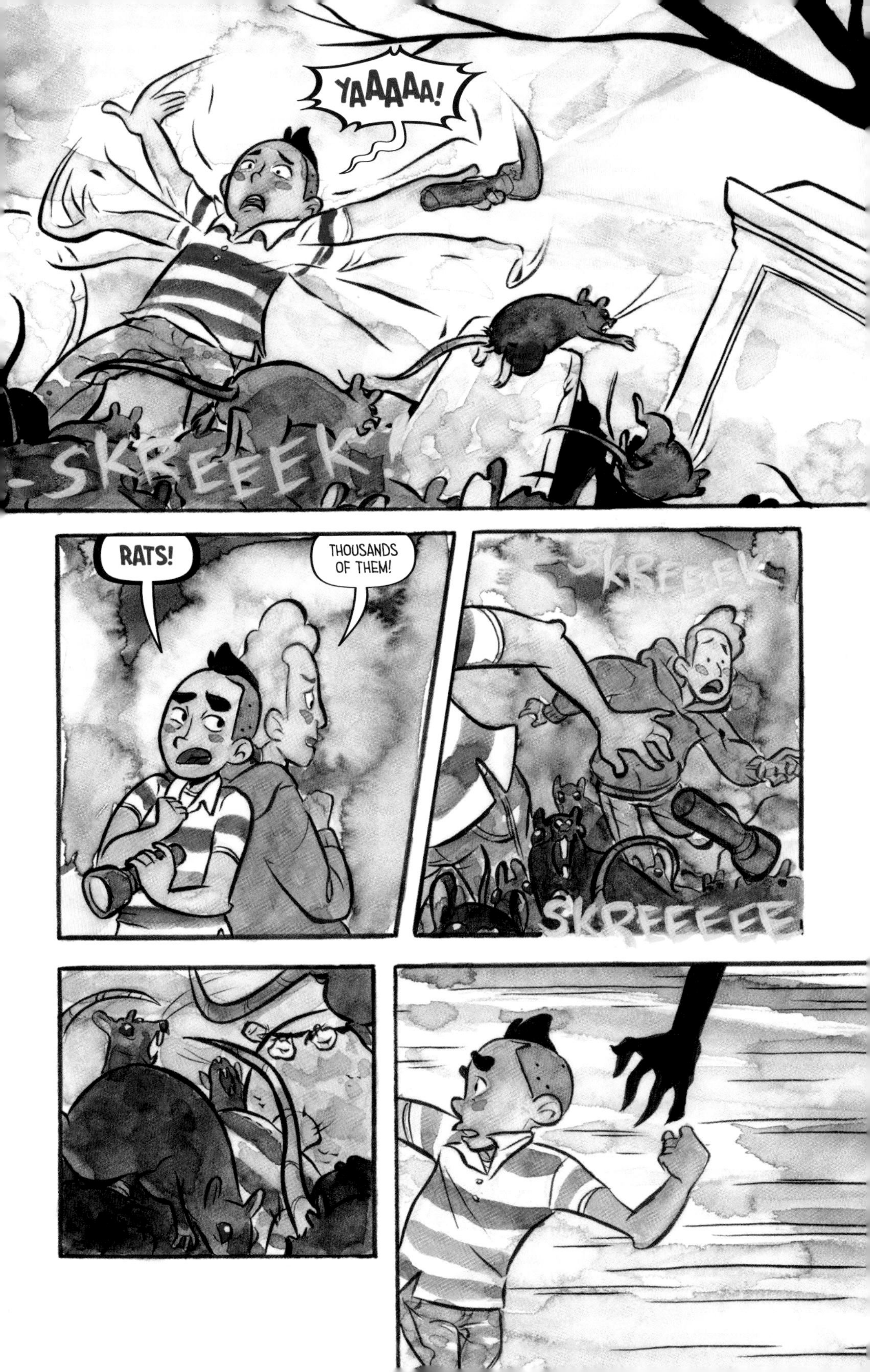
YAAAAA!
SKREEEK!
RATS!
THOUSANDS OF THEM!
SKREEEK!
SKREEEEE

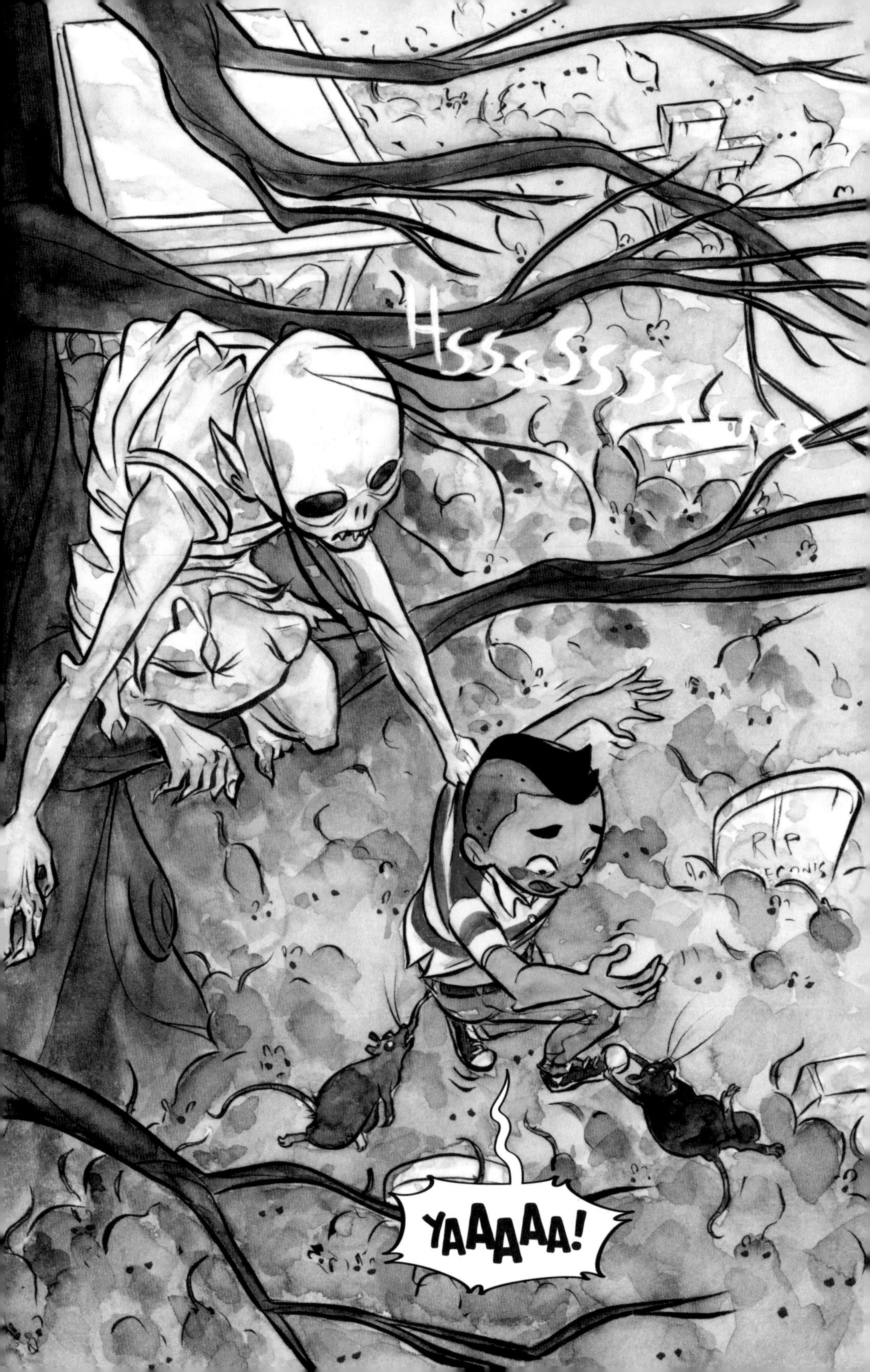
HSSSSSSSSSSS
RIP
YAAAAA!

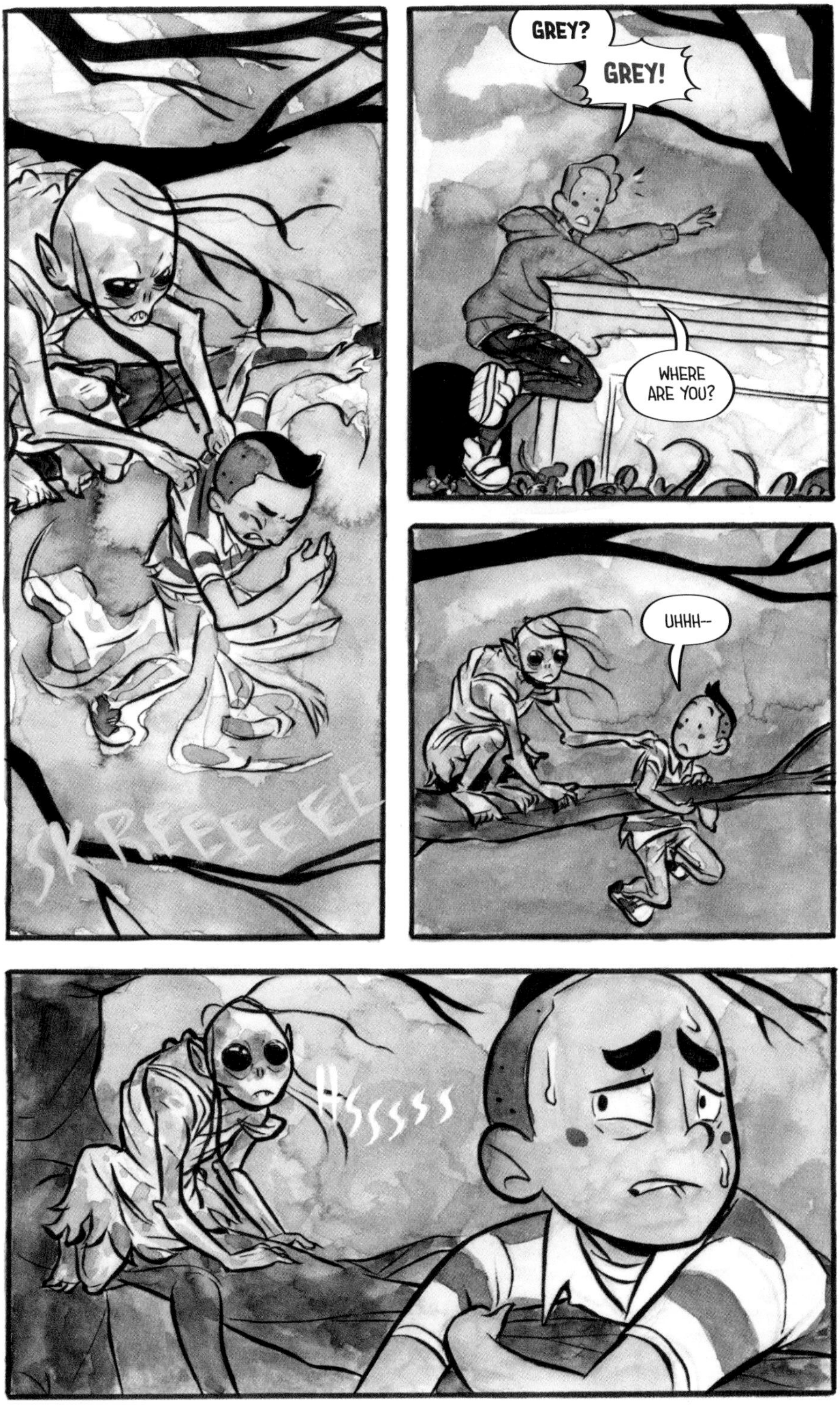
SKREEEEEE
GREY?
GREY!
WHERE ARE YOU?
UHHH--
HSSSSS

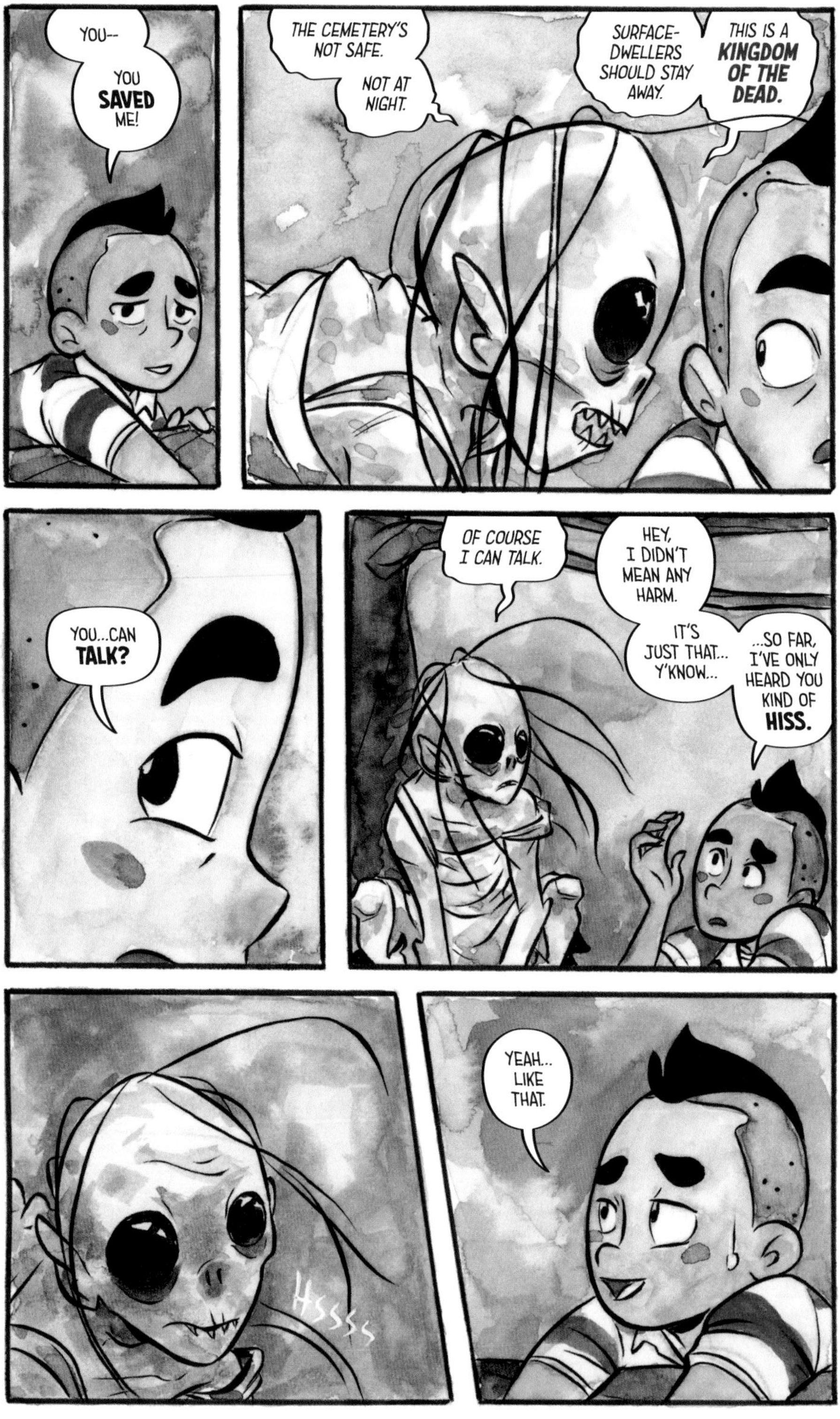
YOU--
YOU SAVED ME!
THE CEMETERY'S NOT SAFE.
NOT AT NIGHT.
SURFACE-DWELLERS SHOULD STAY AWAY.
THIS IS A KINGDOM OF THE DEAD.
YOU...CAN TALK?
OF COURSE I CAN TALK.
HEY, I DIDN'T MEAN ANY HARM.
IT'S JUST THAT... Y'KNOW...
...SO FAR, I'VE ONLY HEARD YOU KIND OF HISS.
HSSSS
YEAH... LIKE THAT.

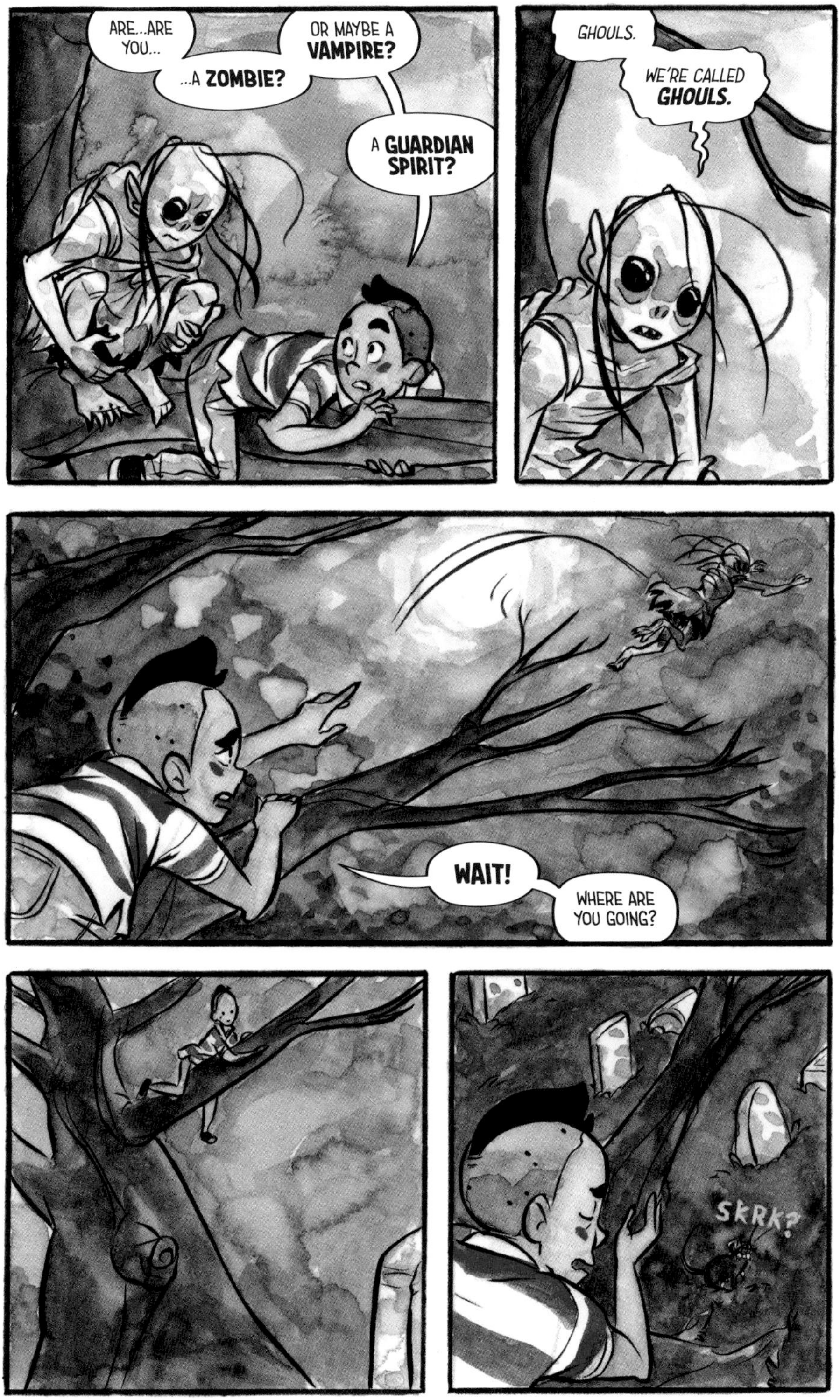
ARE...ARE YOU...
...A ZOMBIE?
OR MAYBE A VAMPIRE?
A GUARDIAN SPIRIT?
GHOULS.
WE'RE CALLED GHOULS.
WAIT!
WHERE ARE YOU GOING?
SKRK?

※HNNNN※

UNNF!

≈WUMP≈

GREY? ARE YOU ALL RIGHT?

DID YOU GET **EATEN?**

I'M OVER HERE!

DID YOU SEE HER?

THE...CREATURE!

THE **GHOUL!**

SHE WAS RIGHT HERE!

SHE WAS RIGHT HERE.

WHERE--

YOU WANNA ASK "WHERE"?

MAYBE YOU SHOULD ASK YOURSELF WHERE ALL THOSE **RATS** WENT.

I THINK MAYBE--

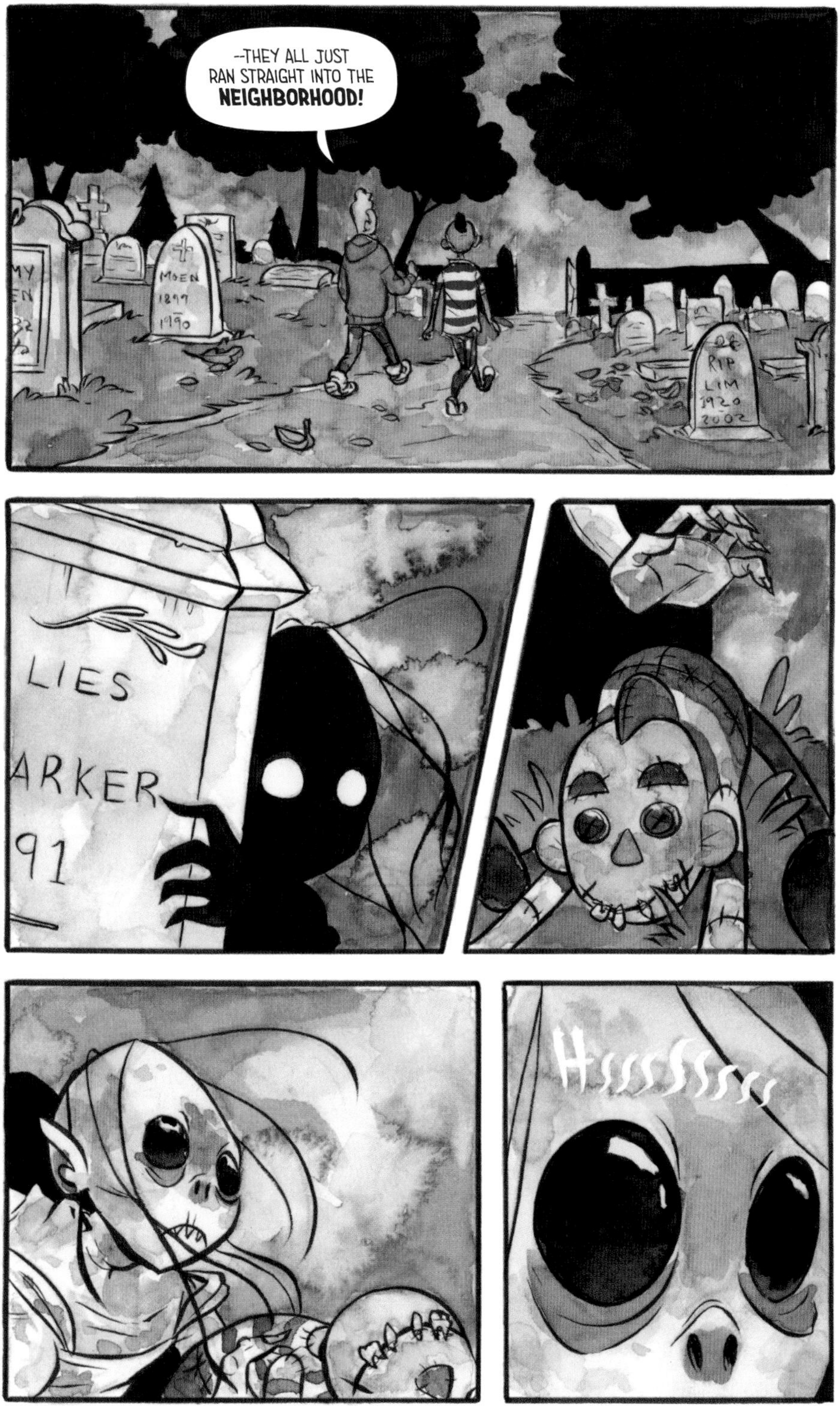
--THEY ALL JUST RAN STRAIGHT INTO THE **NEIGHBORHOOD!**
MOEN 1897 1990
RIP LIM 1920 2002
LIES
ARKER
91
Hsssssss

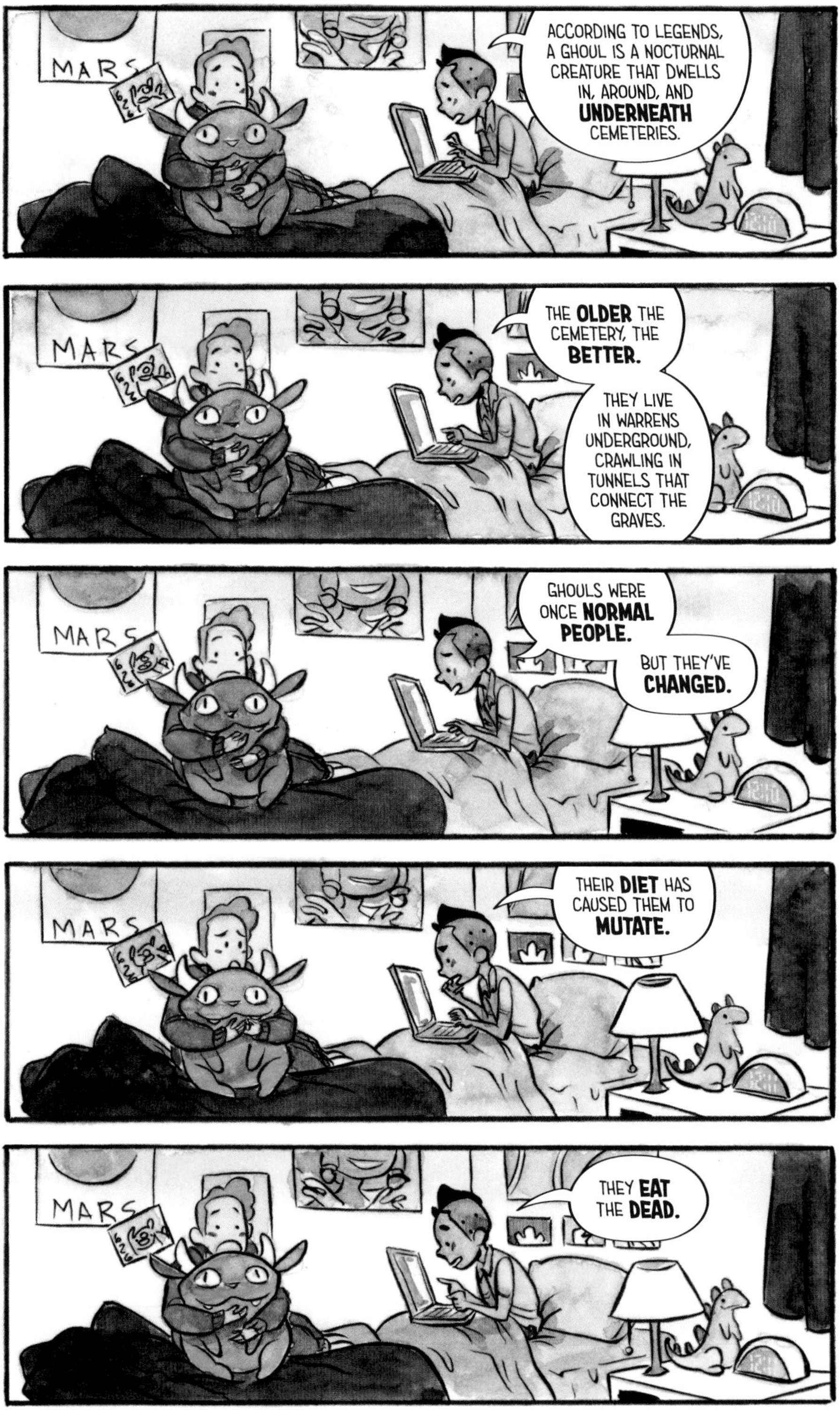
MARS
ACCORDING TO LEGENDS, A GHOUL IS A NOCTURNAL CREATURE THAT DWELLS IN, AROUND, AND **UNDERNEATH** CEMETERIES.
MARS
THE **OLDER** THE CEMETERY, THE **BETTER.**
THEY LIVE IN WARRENS UNDERGROUND, CRAWLING IN TUNNELS THAT CONNECT THE GRAVES.
MARS
GHOULS WERE ONCE **NORMAL PEOPLE.**
BUT THEY'VE **CHANGED.**
MARS
THEIR **DIET** HAS CAUSED THEM TO **MUTATE.**
MARS
THEY **EAT** THE **DEAD.**

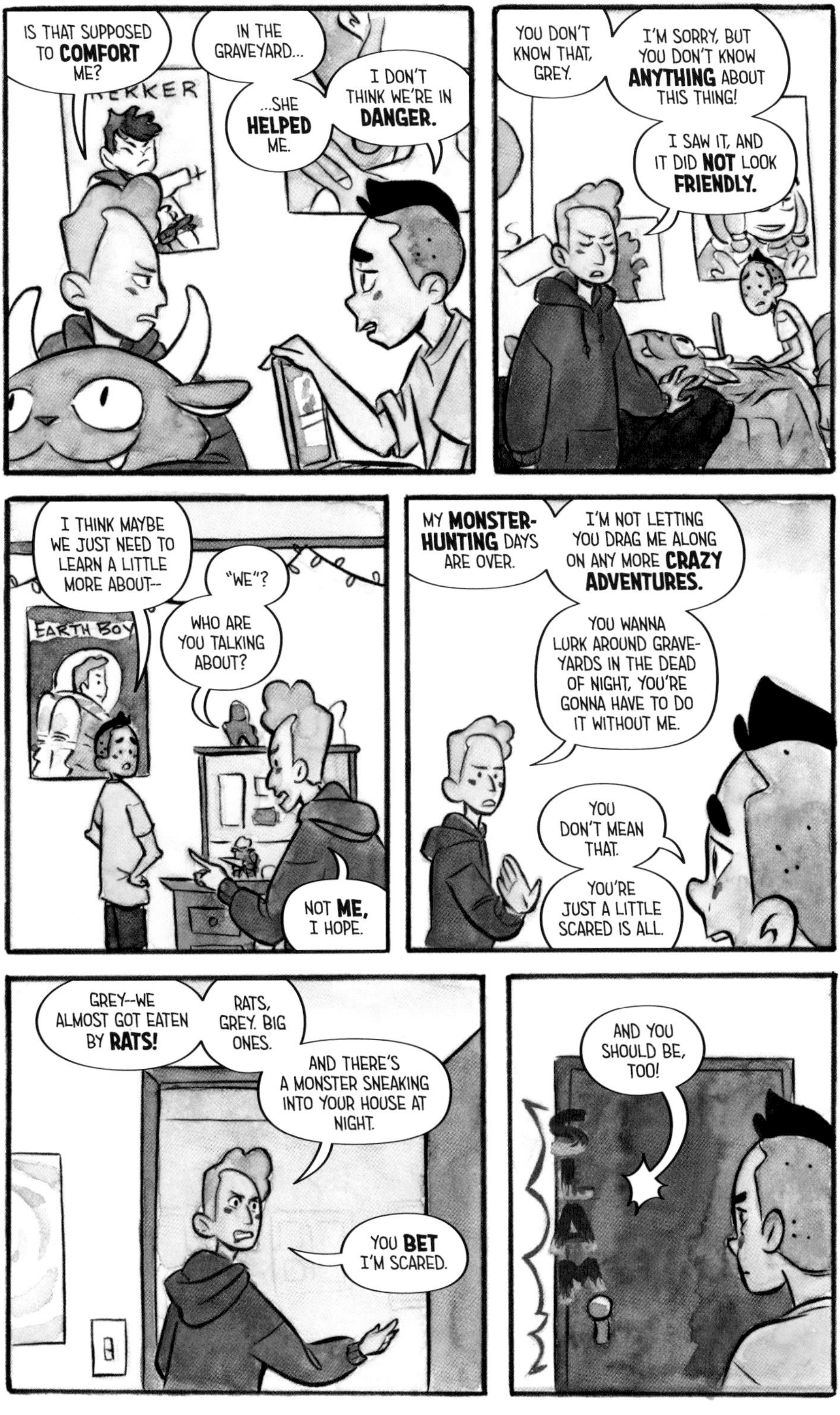
IS THAT SUPPOSED TO **COMFORT** ME?
IN THE GRAVEYARD...
...SHE **HELPED** ME.
I DON'T THINK WE'RE IN **DANGER.**
KERKER
YOU DON'T KNOW THAT, GREY.
I'M SORRY, BUT YOU DON'T KNOW **ANYTHING** ABOUT THIS THING!
I SAW IT, AND IT DID **NOT** LOOK **FRIENDLY.**
I THINK MAYBE WE JUST NEED TO LEARN A LITTLE MORE ABOUT--
"WE"?
WHO ARE YOU TALKING ABOUT?
EARTH BOY
NOT **ME,** I HOPE.
MY **MONSTER-HUNTING** DAYS ARE OVER.
I'M NOT LETTING YOU DRAG ME ALONG ON ANY MORE **CRAZY ADVENTURES.**
YOU WANNA LURK AROUND GRAVE-YARDS IN THE DEAD OF NIGHT, YOU'RE GONNA HAVE TO DO IT WITHOUT ME.
YOU DON'T MEAN THAT.
YOU'RE JUST A LITTLE SCARED IS ALL.
GREY--WE ALMOST GOT EATEN BY **RATS!**
RATS, GREY. BIG ONES.
AND THERE'S A MONSTER SNEAKING INTO YOUR HOUSE AT NIGHT.
YOU **BET** I'M SCARED.
AND YOU SHOULD BE, TOO!
SLAM

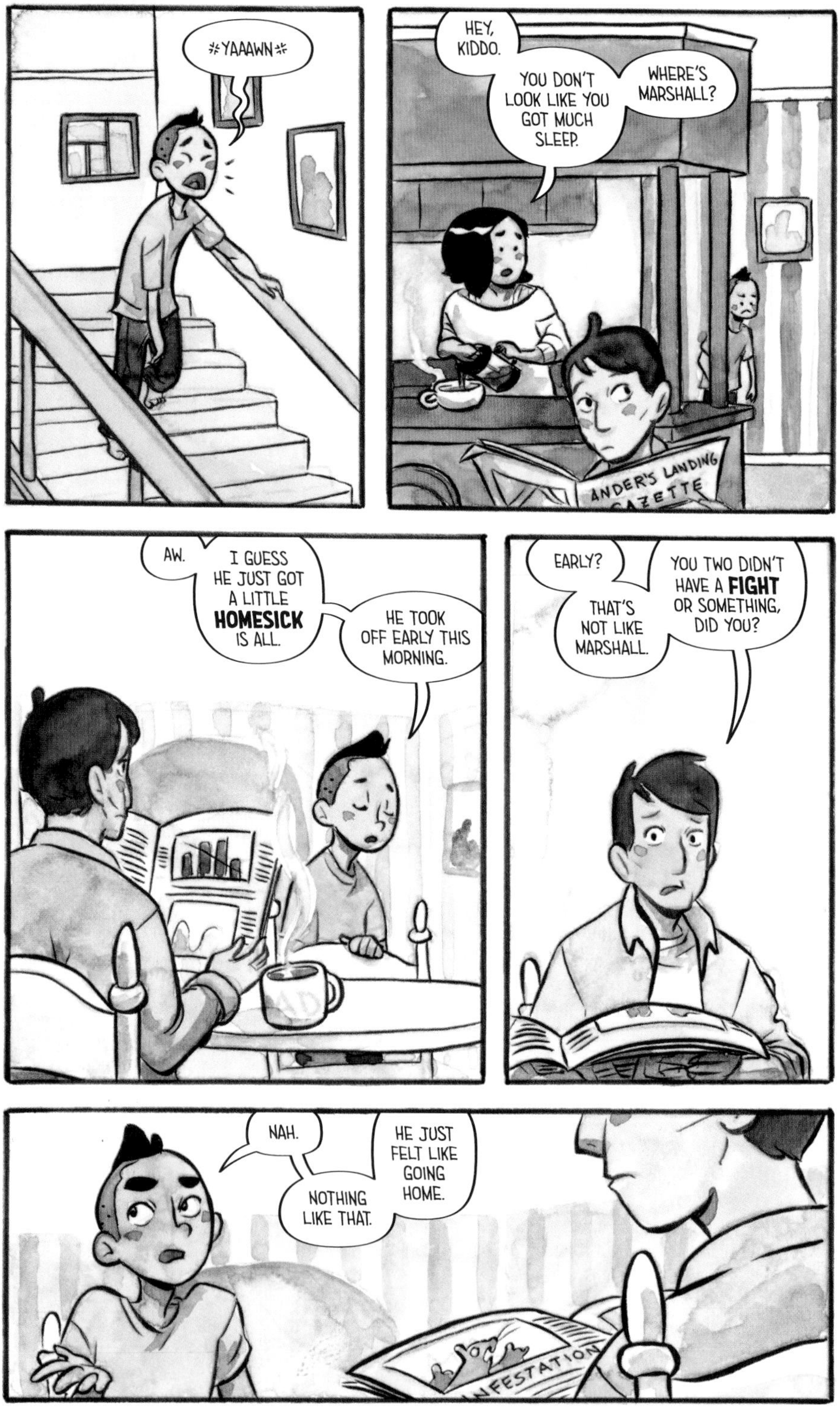

#YAAAWN#
HEY, KIDDO.
YOU DON'T LOOK LIKE YOU GOT MUCH SLEEP.
WHERE'S MARSHALL?
ANDER'S LANDING GAZETTE
AW.
I GUESS HE JUST GOT A LITTLE **HOMESICK** IS ALL.
HE TOOK OFF EARLY THIS MORNING.
EARLY?
THAT'S NOT LIKE MARSHALL.
YOU TWO DIDN'T HAVE A **FIGHT** OR SOMETHING, DID YOU?
NAH.
NOTHING LIKE THAT.
HE JUST FELT LIKE GOING HOME.
INFESTATION

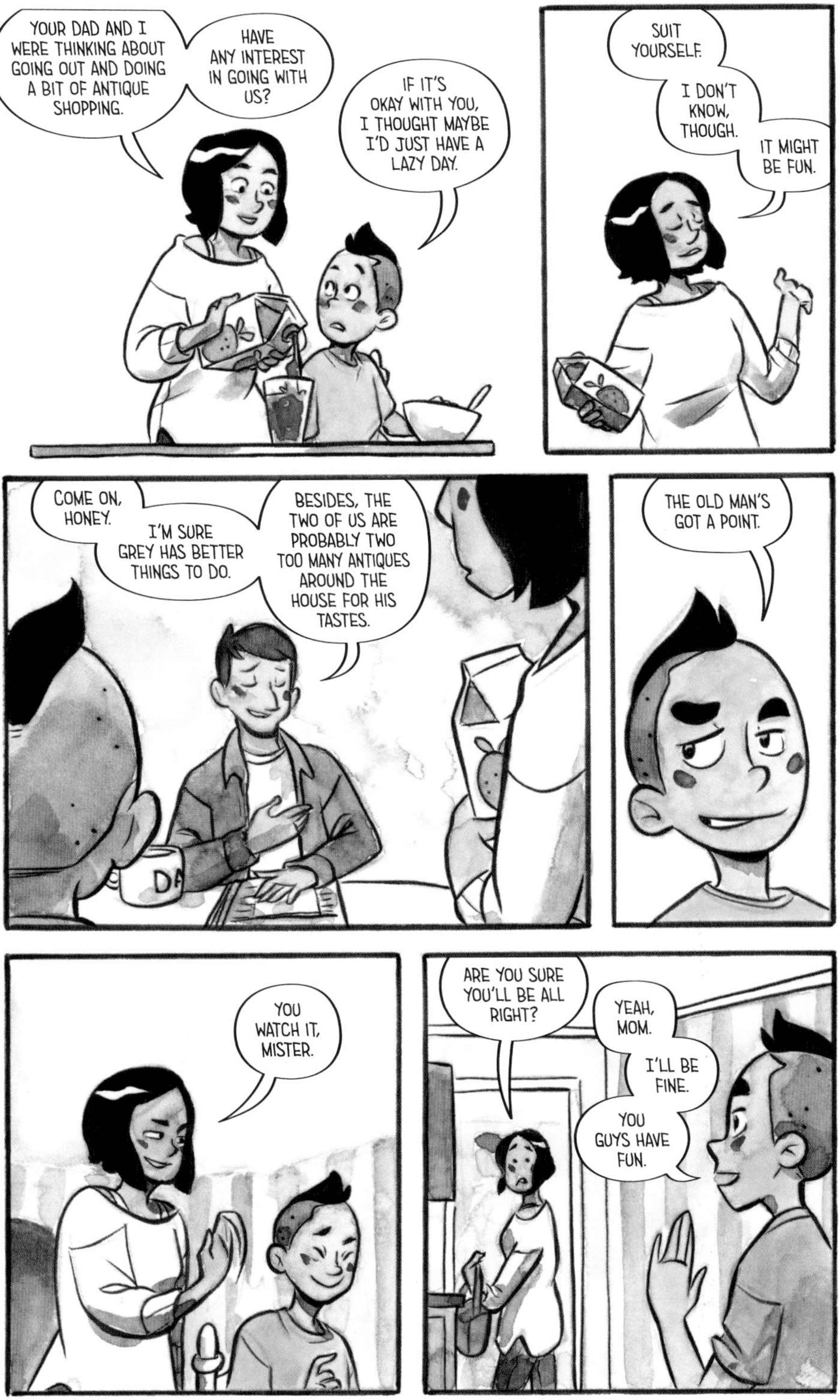
YOUR DAD AND I WERE THINKING ABOUT GOING OUT AND DOING A BIT OF ANTIQUE SHOPPING.
HAVE ANY INTEREST IN GOING WITH US?
IF IT'S OKAY WITH YOU, I THOUGHT MAYBE I'D JUST HAVE A LAZY DAY.
SUIT YOURSELF.
I DON'T KNOW, THOUGH.
IT MIGHT BE FUN.
COME ON, HONEY.
I'M SURE GREY HAS BETTER THINGS TO DO.
BESIDES, THE TWO OF US ARE PROBABLY TWO TOO MANY ANTIQUES AROUND THE HOUSE FOR HIS TASTES.
DA
THE OLD MAN'S GOT A POINT.
YOU WATCH IT, MISTER.
ARE YOU SURE YOU'LL BE ALL RIGHT?
YEAH, MOM.
I'LL BE FINE.
YOU GUYS HAVE FUN.

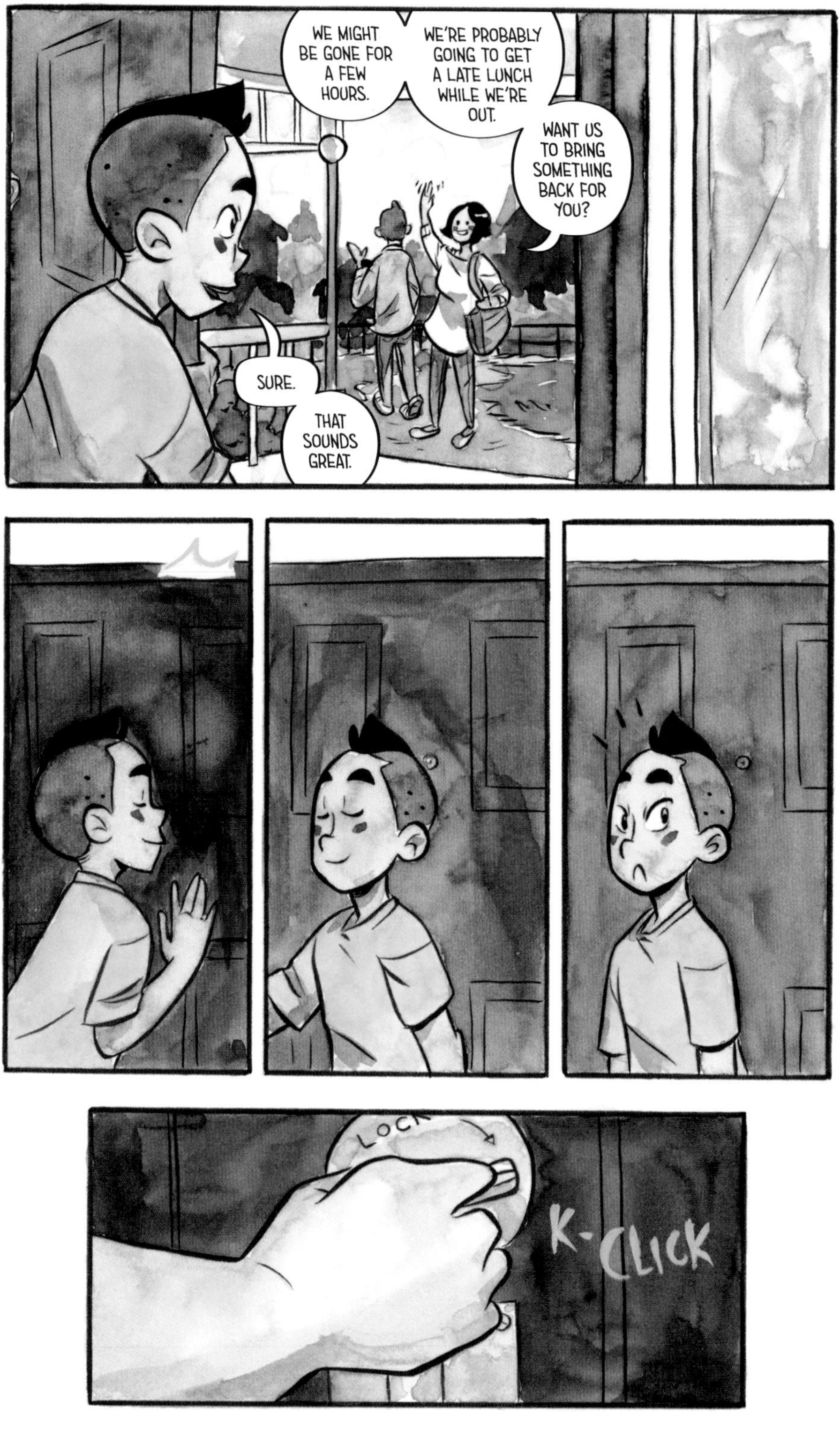
WE MIGHT BE GONE FOR A FEW HOURS.
WE'RE PROBABLY GOING TO GET A LATE LUNCH WHILE WE'RE OUT.
WANT US TO BRING SOMETHING BACK FOR YOU?
SURE.
THAT SOUNDS GREAT.
LOCK
K-CLICK

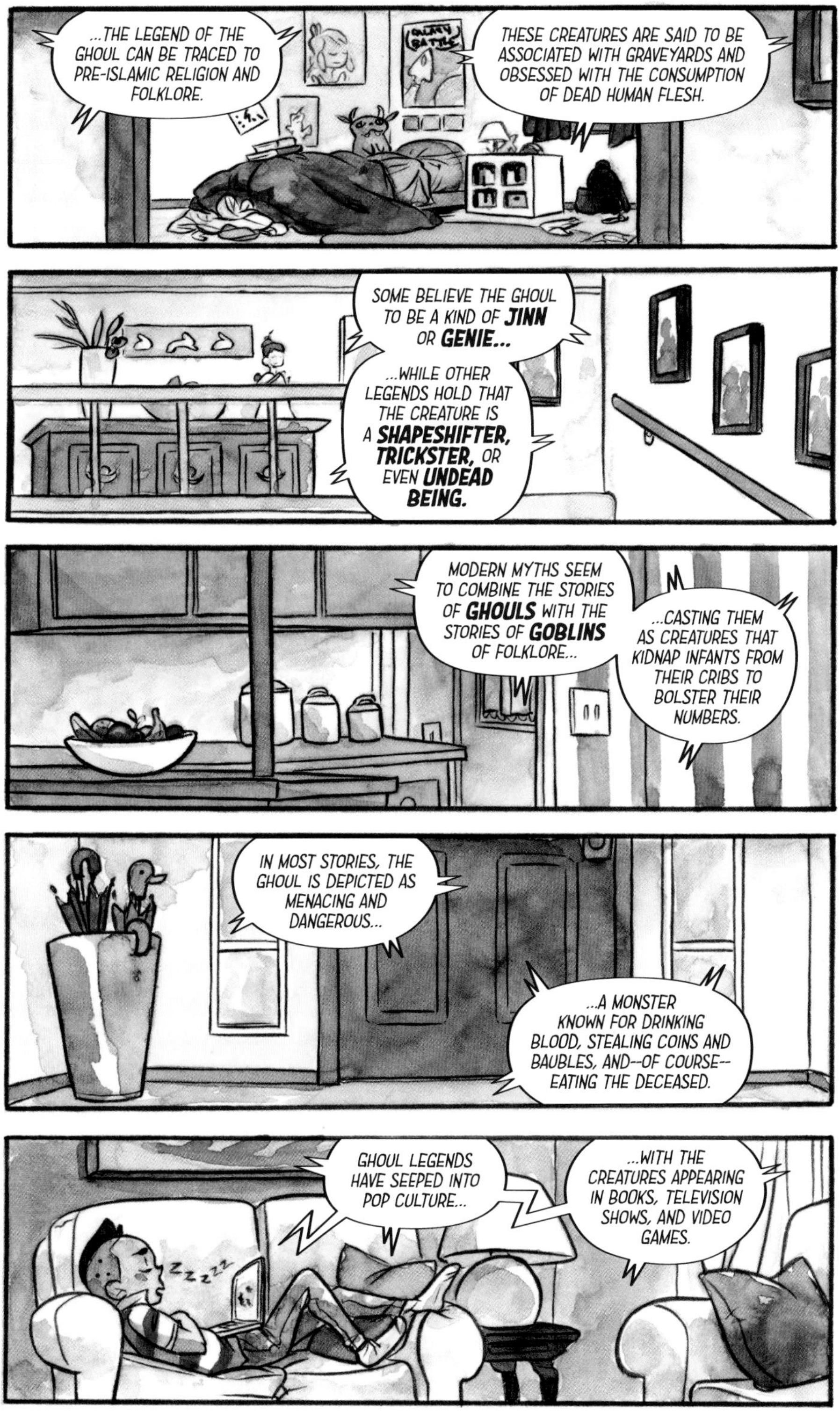
...THE LEGEND OF THE GHOUL CAN BE TRACED TO PRE-ISLAMIC RELIGION AND FOLKLORE.
THESE CREATURES ARE SAID TO BE ASSOCIATED WITH GRAVEYARDS AND OBSESSED WITH THE CONSUMPTION OF DEAD HUMAN FLESH.
SOME BELIEVE THE GHOUL TO BE A KIND OF **JINN** OR **GENIE...**
...WHILE OTHER LEGENDS HOLD THAT THE CREATURE IS A **SHAPESHIFTER, TRICKSTER,** OR EVEN **UNDEAD BEING.**
MODERN MYTHS SEEM TO COMBINE THE STORIES OF **GHOULS** WITH THE STORIES OF **GOBLINS** OF FOLKLORE...
...CASTING THEM AS CREATURES THAT KIDNAP INFANTS FROM THEIR CRIBS TO BOLSTER THEIR NUMBERS.
IN MOST STORIES, THE GHOUL IS DEPICTED AS MENACING AND DANGEROUS...
...A MONSTER KNOWN FOR DRINKING BLOOD, STEALING COINS AND BAUBLES, AND--OF COURSE--EATING THE DECEASED.
GHOUL LEGENDS HAVE SEEPED INTO POP CULTURE...
...WITH THE CREATURES APPEARING IN BOOKS, TELEVISION SHOWS, AND VIDEO GAMES.
ZZZZZ

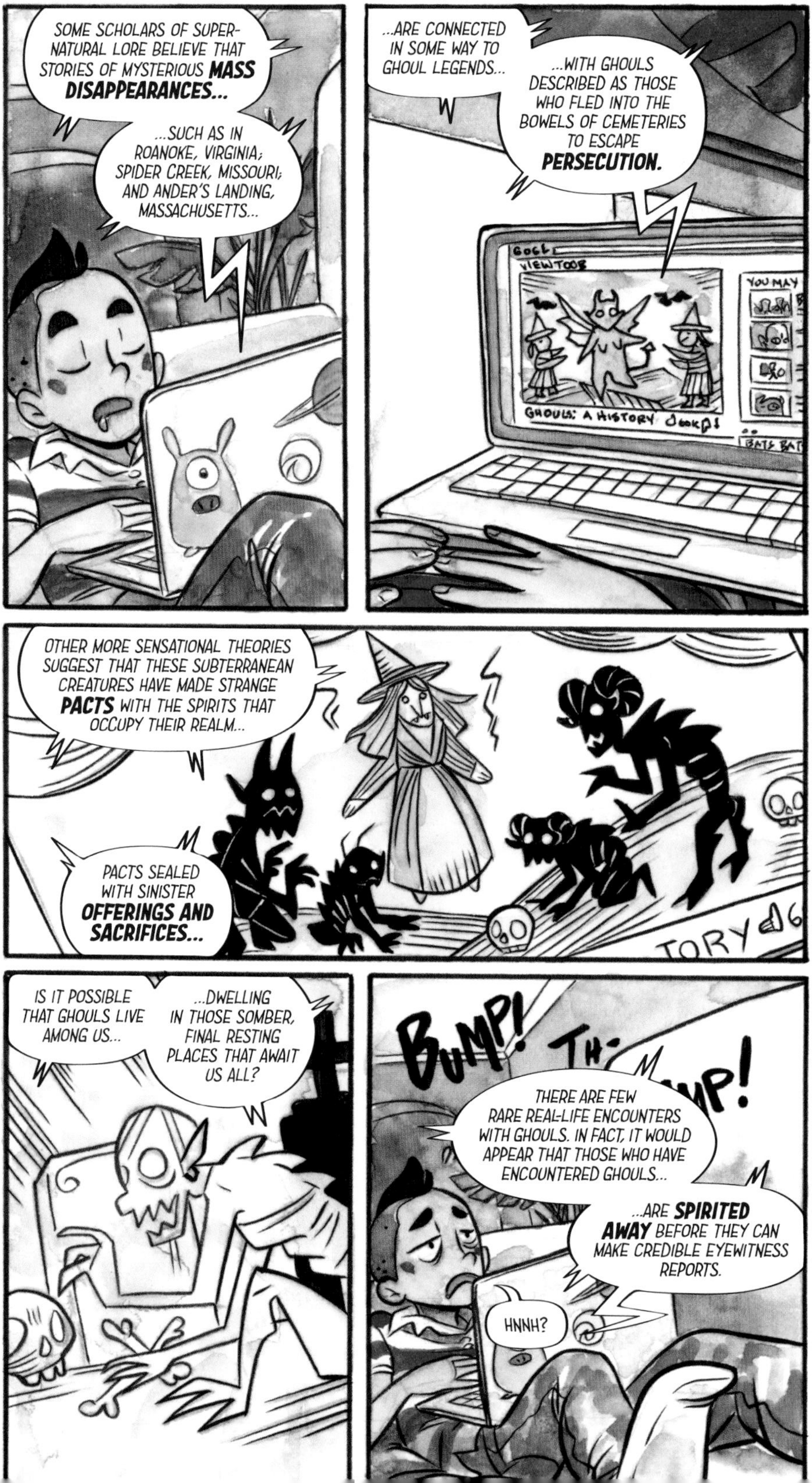
SOME SCHOLARS OF SUPER-NATURAL LORE BELIEVE THAT STORIES OF MYSTERIOUS **MASS DISAPPEARANCES...**
...SUCH AS IN ROANOKE, VIRGINIA; SPIDER CREEK, MISSOURI; AND ANDER'S LANDING, MASSACHUSETTS...
...ARE CONNECTED IN SOME WAY TO GHOUL LEGENDS...
...WITH GHOULS DESCRIBED AS THOSE WHO FLED INTO THE BOWELS OF CEMETERIES TO ESCAPE **PERSECUTION.**
GOGL
VIEWTOOB
YOU MAY
GHOULS: A HISTORY
OTHER MORE SENSATIONAL THEORIES SUGGEST THAT THESE SUBTERRANEAN CREATURES HAVE MADE STRANGE **PACTS** WITH THE SPIRITS THAT OCCUPY THEIR REALM...
PACTS SEALED WITH SINISTER **OFFERINGS AND SACRIFICES...**
IS IT POSSIBLE THAT GHOULS LIVE AMONG US...
...DWELLING IN THOSE SOMBER, FINAL RESTING PLACES THAT AWAIT US ALL?
BUMP!
TH-
THERE ARE FEW RARE REAL-LIFE ENCOUNTERS WITH GHOULS. IN FACT, IT WOULD APPEAR THAT THOSE WHO HAVE ENCOUNTERED GHOULS...
...ARE **SPIRITED AWAY** BEFORE THEY CAN MAKE CREDIBLE EYEWITNESS REPORTS.
HNNH?

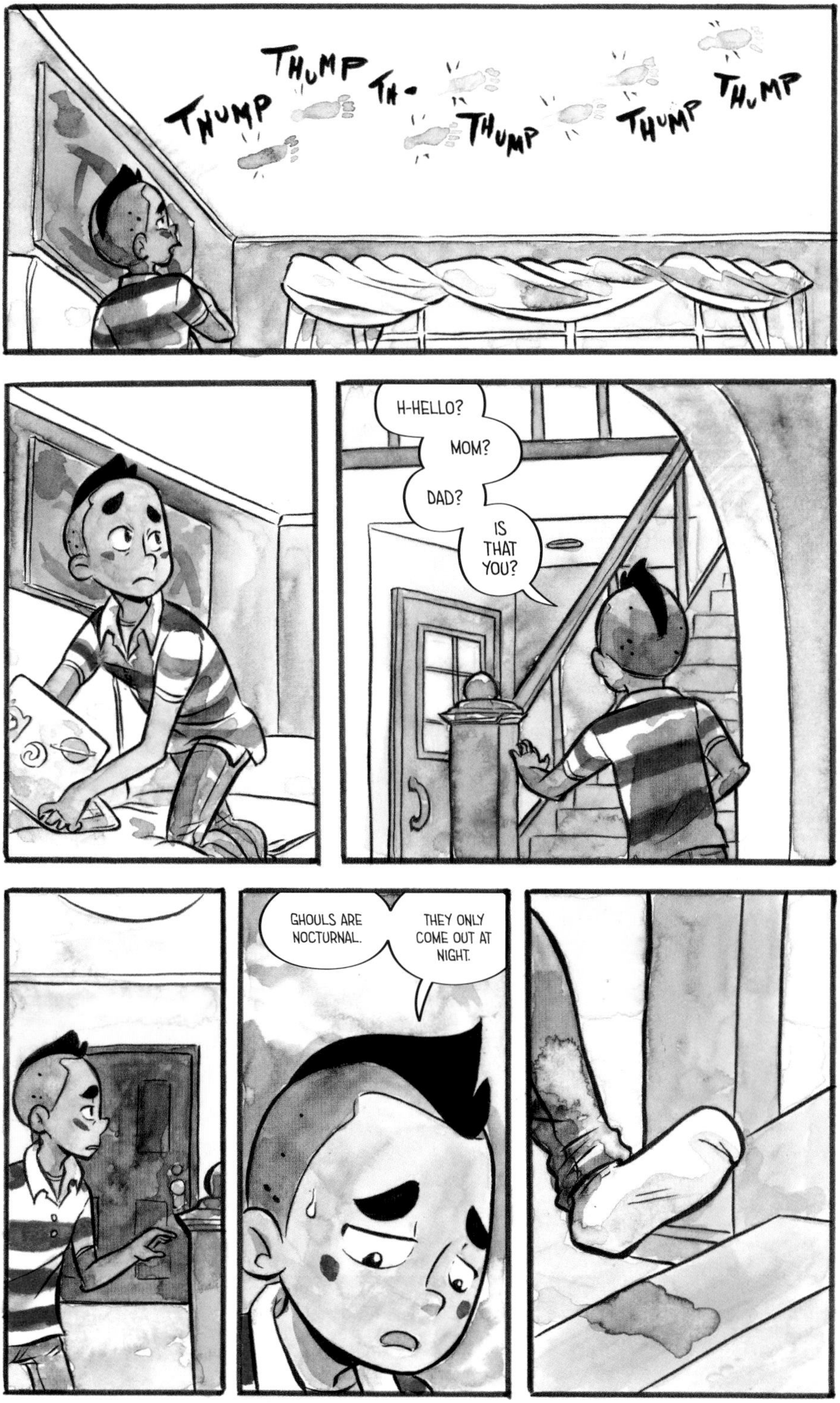
THUMP THUMP TH- THUMP THUMP THUMP
H-HELLO?
MOM?
DAD?
IS THAT YOU?
GHOULS ARE NOCTURNAL.
THEY ONLY COME OUT AT NIGHT.

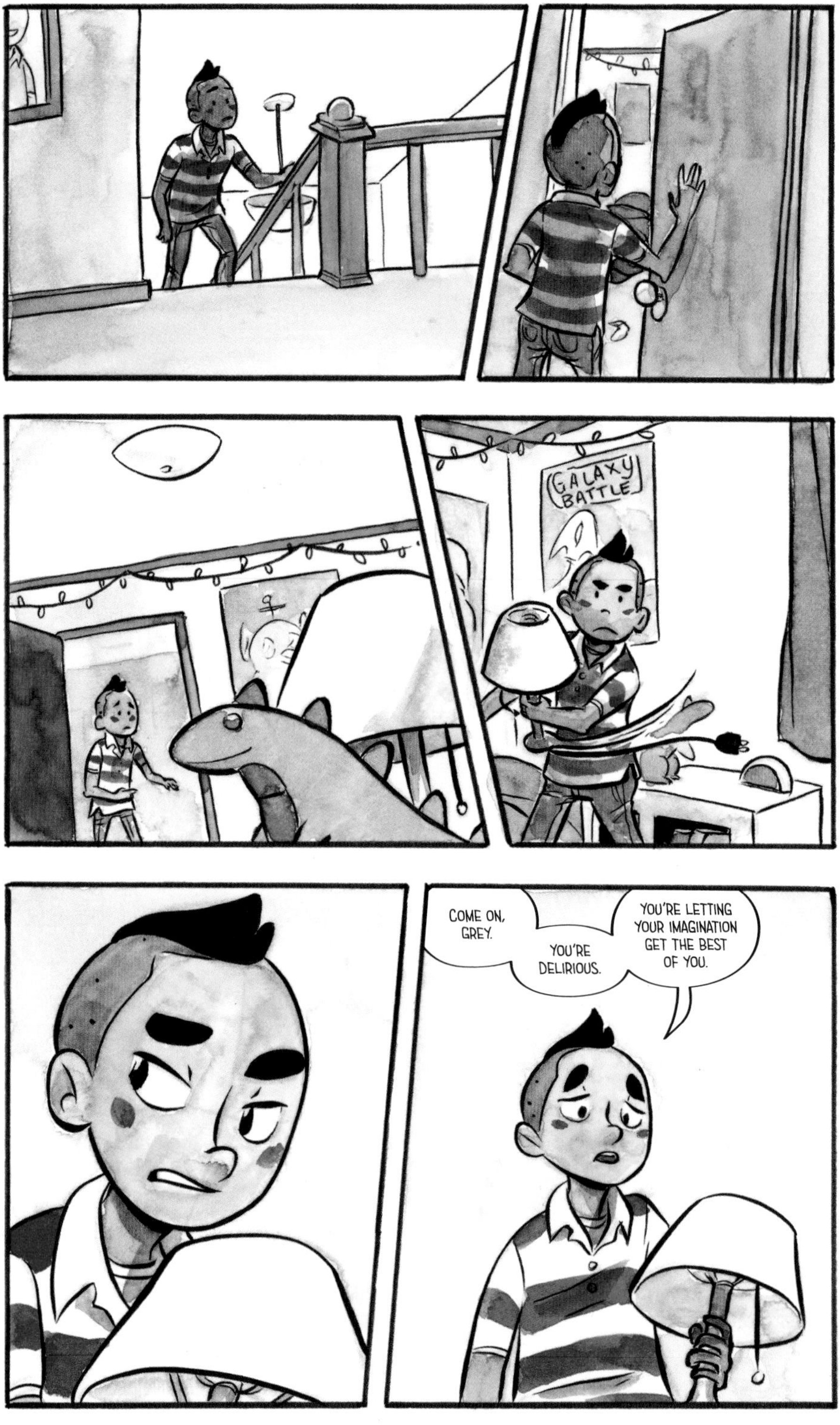
GALAXY BATTLE
COME ON, GREY.
YOU'RE DELIRIOUS.
YOU'RE LETTING YOUR IMAGINATION GET THE BEST OF YOU.

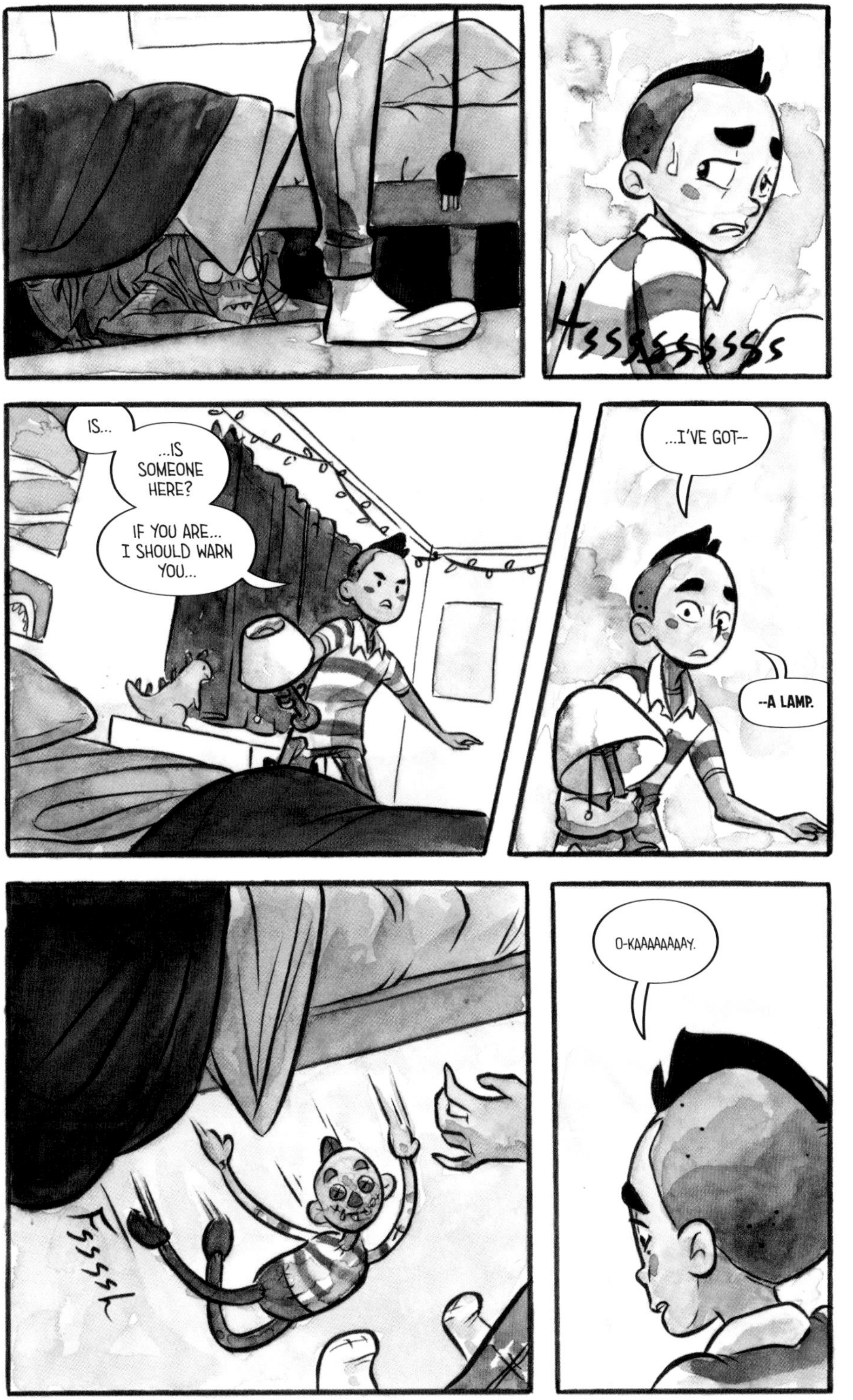
Hsssssssss
IS...
...IS SOMEONE HERE?
IF YOU ARE... I SHOULD WARN YOU...
...I'VE GOT--
--A LAMP.
Fssssh
O-KAAAAAAAAY.

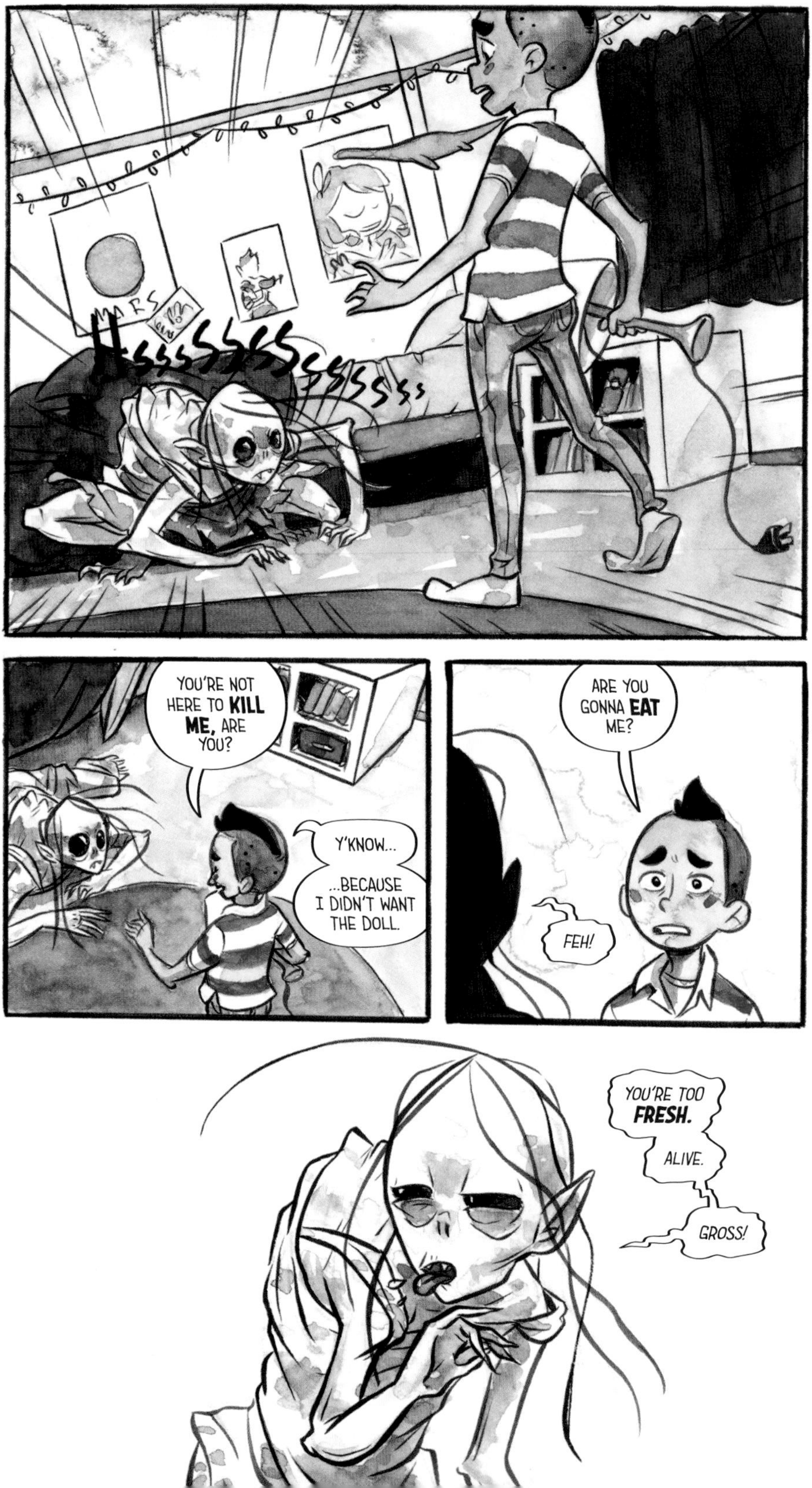
MARS
HSSSSSSSSSSSSSSSSS
YOU'RE NOT HERE TO KILL ME, ARE YOU?
Y'KNOW...
...BECAUSE I DIDN'T WANT THE DOLL.
ARE YOU GONNA EAT ME?
FEH!
YOU'RE TOO FRESH.
ALIVE.
GROSS!

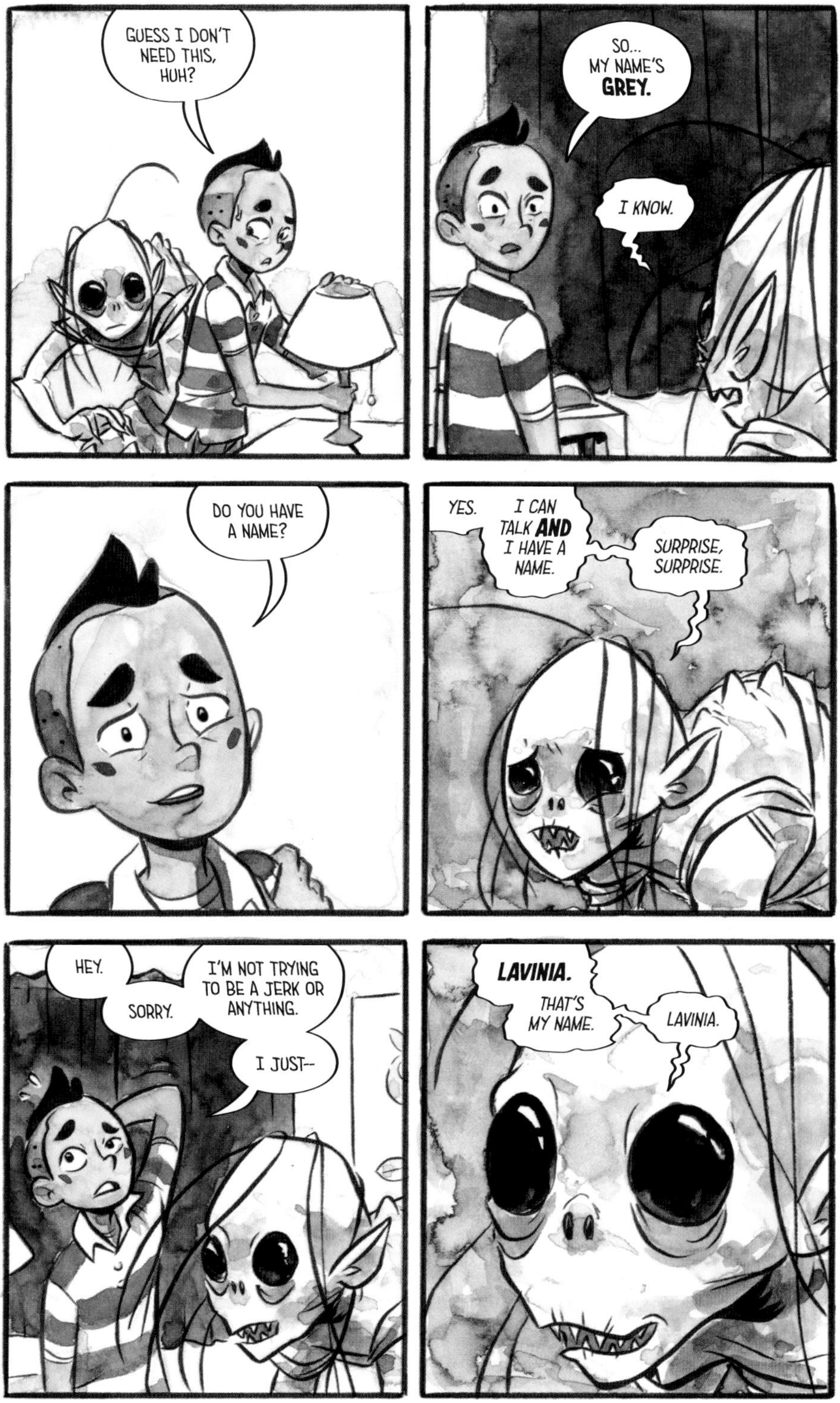
GUESS I DON'T NEED THIS, HUH?
SO... MY NAME'S **GREY.**
I KNOW.
DO YOU HAVE A NAME?
YES.
I CAN TALK **AND** I HAVE A NAME.
SURPRISE, SURPRISE.
HEY.
SORRY.
I'M NOT TRYING TO BE A JERK OR ANYTHING.
I JUST--
LAVINIA.
THAT'S MY NAME.
LAVINIA.

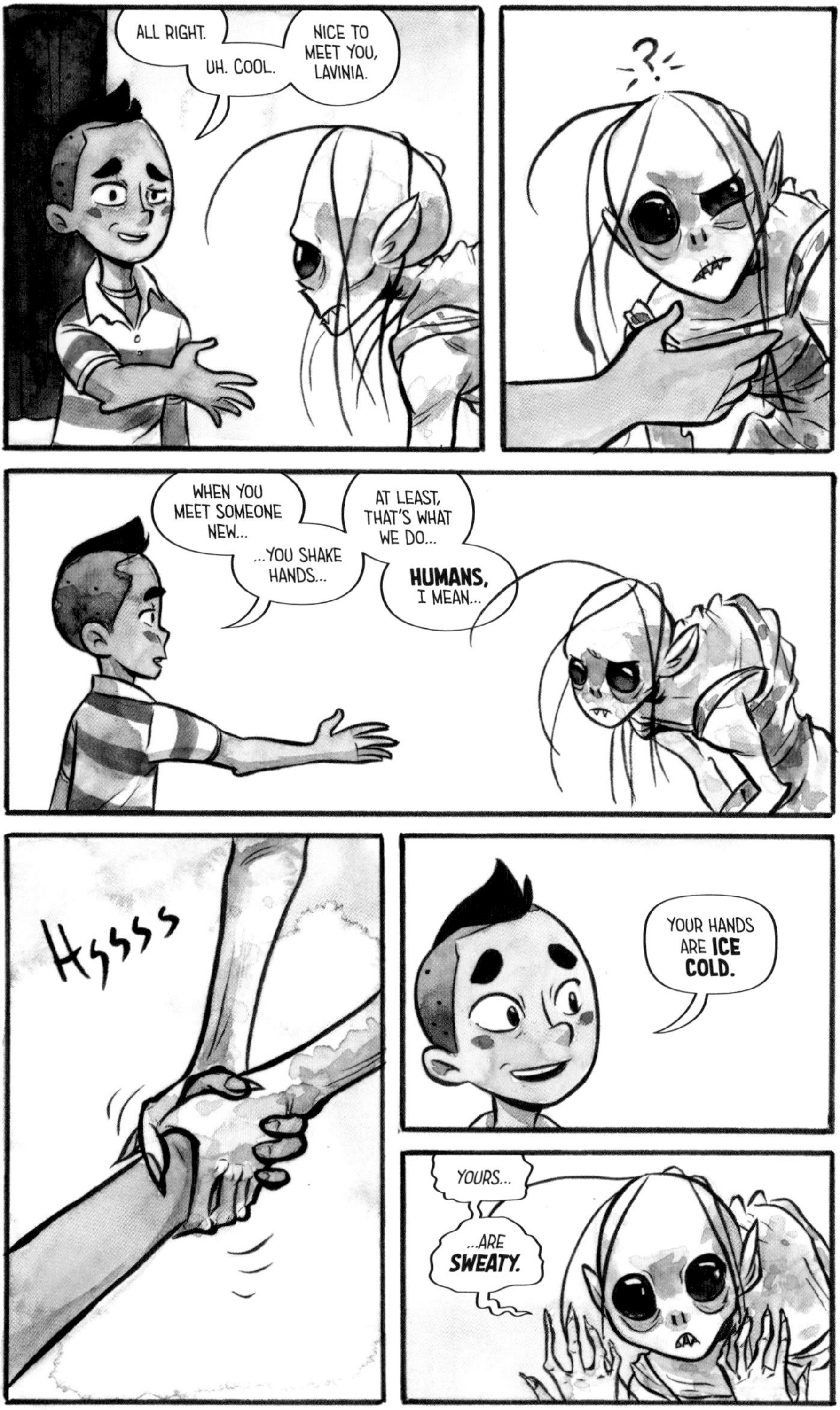
ALL RIGHT.
UH. COOL.
NICE TO MEET YOU, LAVINIA.
?
WHEN YOU MEET SOMEONE NEW...
...YOU SHAKE HANDS...
AT LEAST, THAT'S WHAT WE DO...
HUMANS, I MEAN...
Hssss
YOUR HANDS ARE ICE COLD.
YOURS...
...ARE SWEATY.

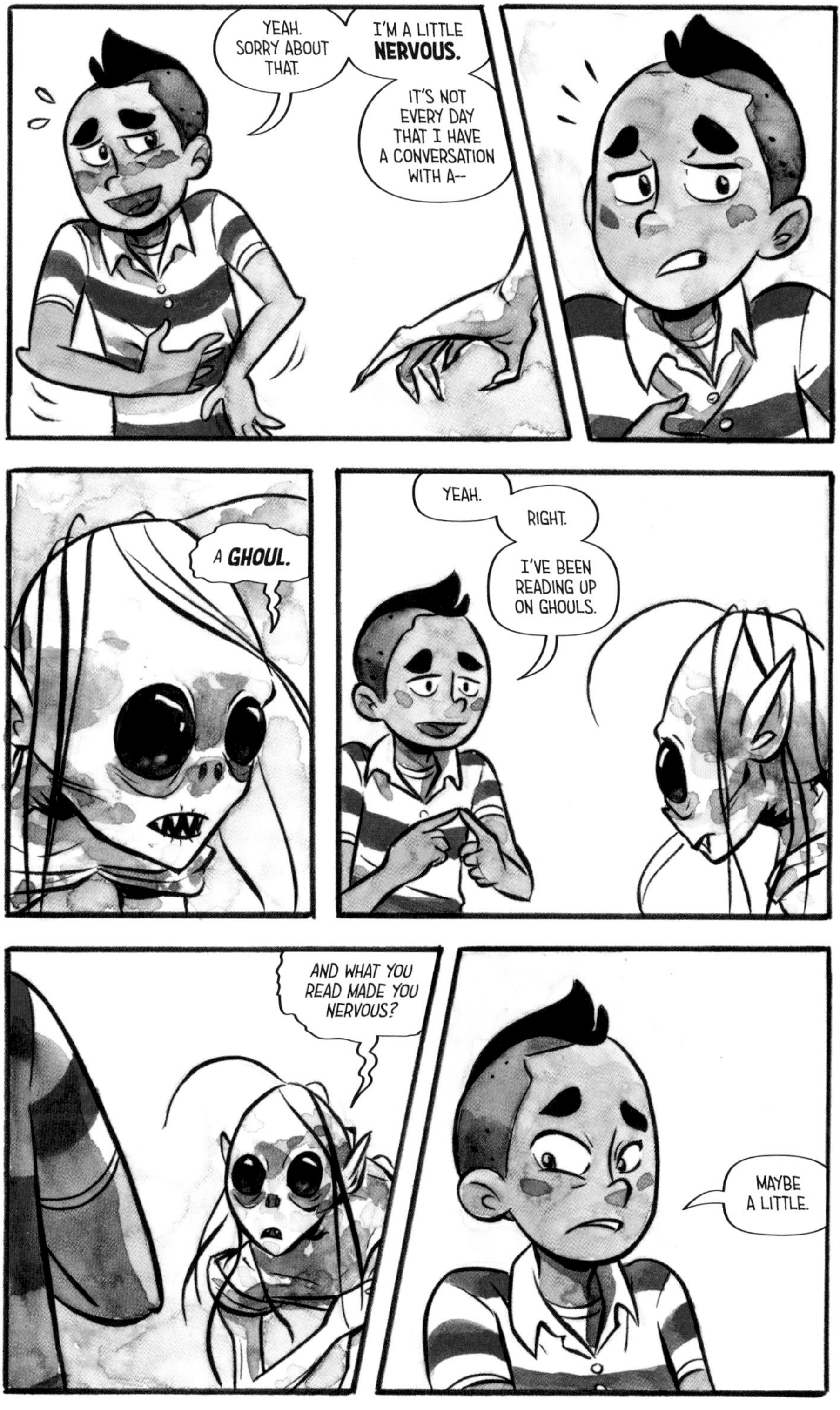
YEAH. SORRY ABOUT THAT.
I'M A LITTLE **NERVOUS.**
IT'S NOT EVERY DAY THAT I HAVE A CONVERSATION WITH A--
A **GHOUL.**
YEAH.
RIGHT.
I'VE BEEN READING UP ON GHOULS.
AND WHAT YOU READ MADE YOU NERVOUS?
MAYBE A LITTLE.

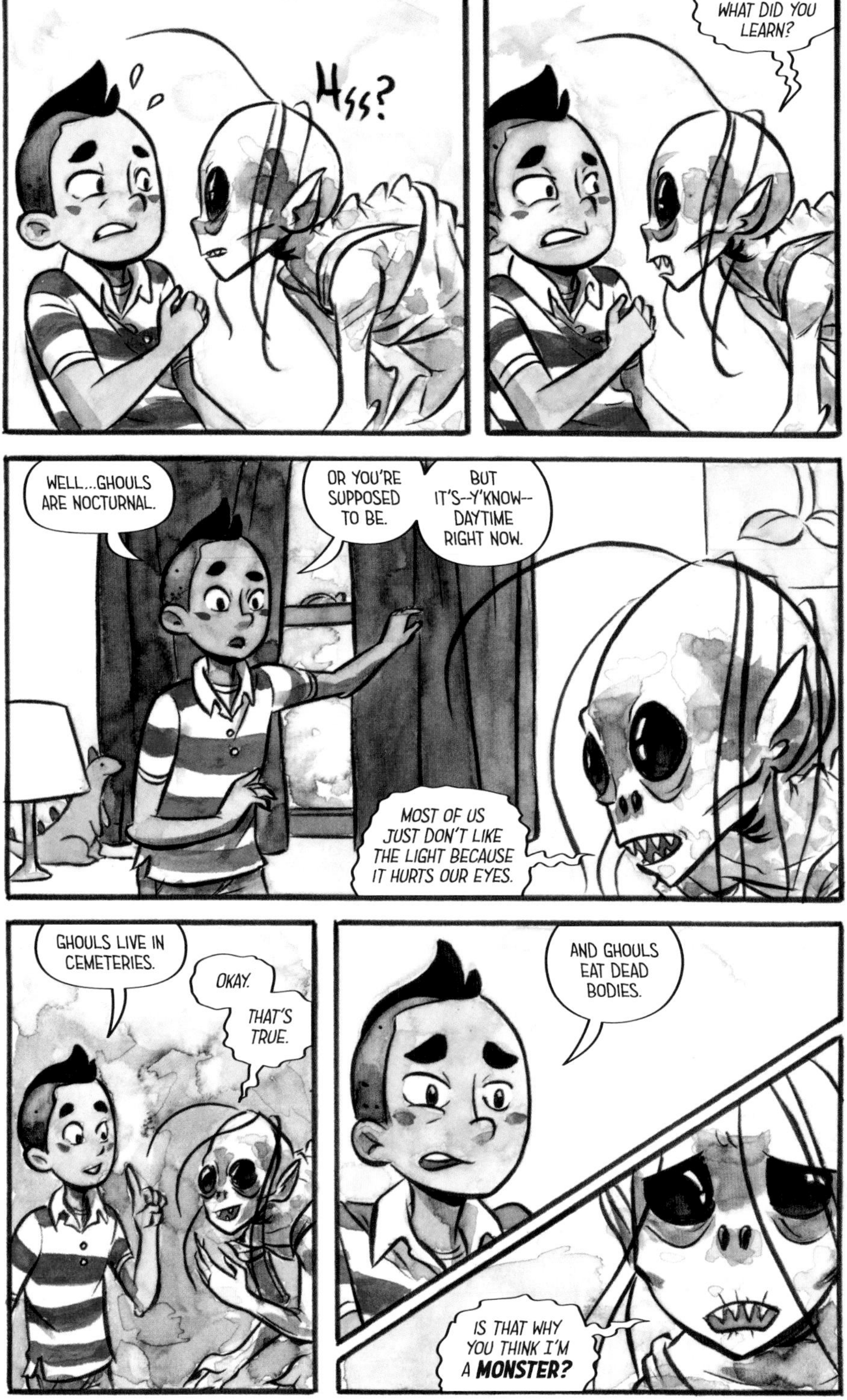
Hss?
WHAT DID YOU LEARN?
WELL...GHOULS ARE NOCTURNAL.
OR YOU'RE SUPPOSED TO BE.
BUT IT'S--Y'KNOW--DAYTIME RIGHT NOW.
MOST OF US JUST DON'T LIKE THE LIGHT BECAUSE IT HURTS OUR EYES.
GHOULS LIVE IN CEMETERIES.
OKAY.
THAT'S TRUE.
AND GHOULS EAT DEAD BODIES.
IS THAT WHY YOU THINK I'M A MONSTER?

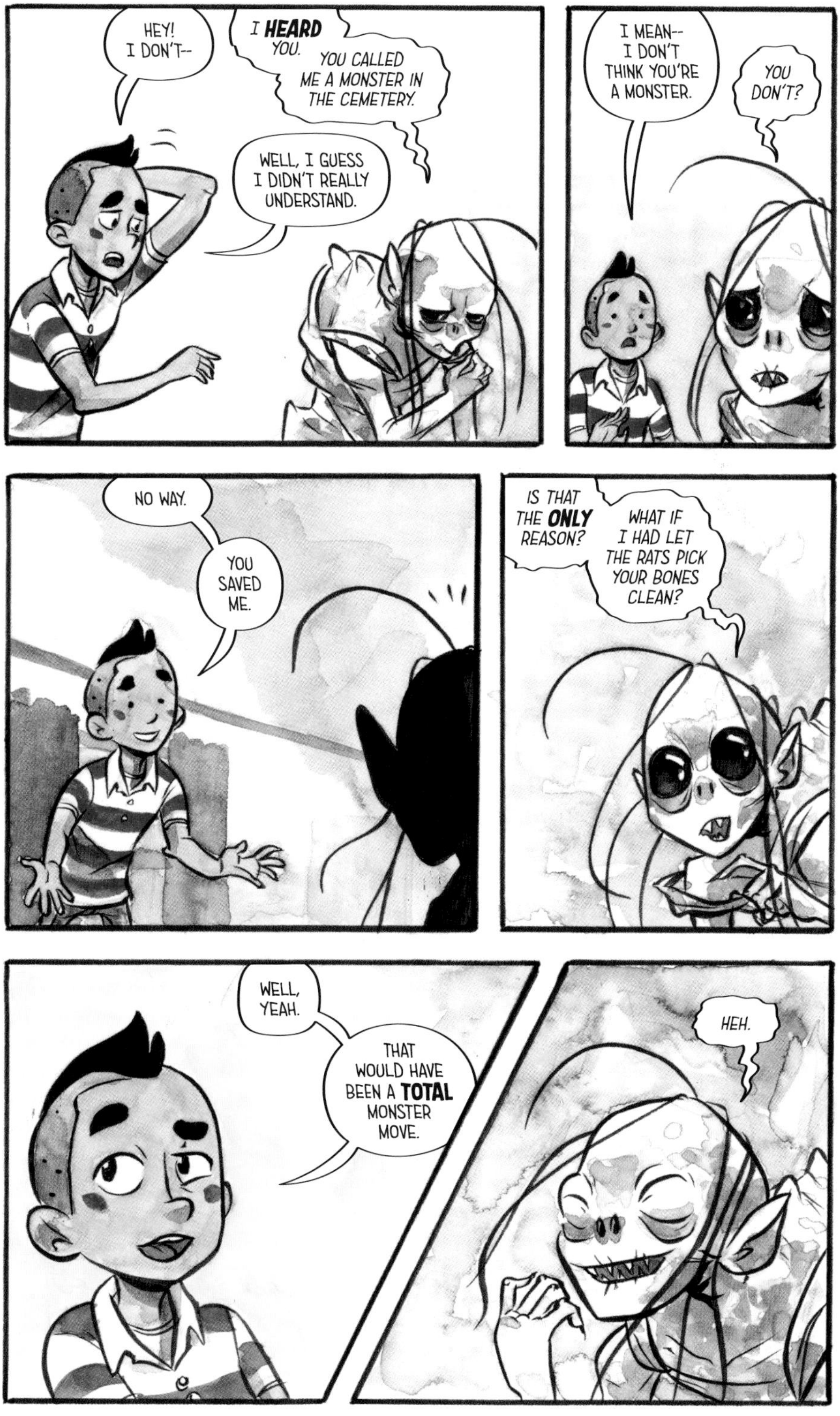
HEY! I DON'T--
I **HEARD** YOU.
YOU CALLED ME A MONSTER IN THE CEMETERY.
WELL, I GUESS I DIDN'T REALLY UNDERSTAND.
I MEAN-- I DON'T THINK YOU'RE A MONSTER.
YOU DON'T?
NO WAY.
YOU SAVED ME.
IS THAT THE **ONLY** REASON?
WHAT IF I HAD LET THE RATS PICK YOUR BONES CLEAN?
WELL, YEAH.
THAT WOULD HAVE BEEN A **TOTAL** MONSTER MOVE.
HEH.

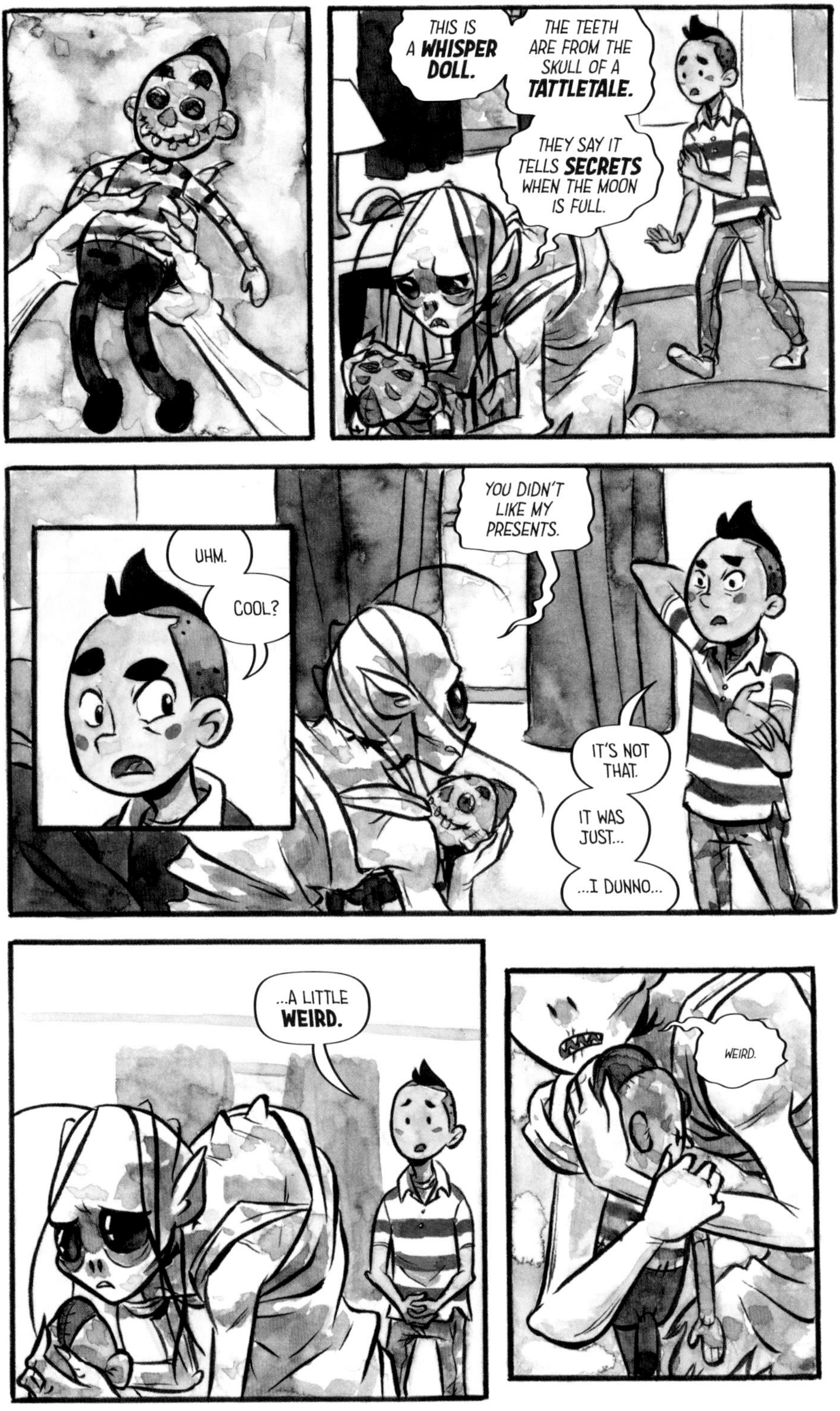
THIS IS A **WHISPER DOLL.**
THE TEETH ARE FROM THE SKULL OF A **TATTLETALE.**
THEY SAY IT TELLS **SECRETS** WHEN THE MOON IS FULL.
YOU DIDN'T LIKE MY PRESENTS.
UHM.
COOL?
IT'S NOT THAT.
IT WAS JUST...
...I DUNNO...
...A LITTLE **WEIRD.**
WEIRD.

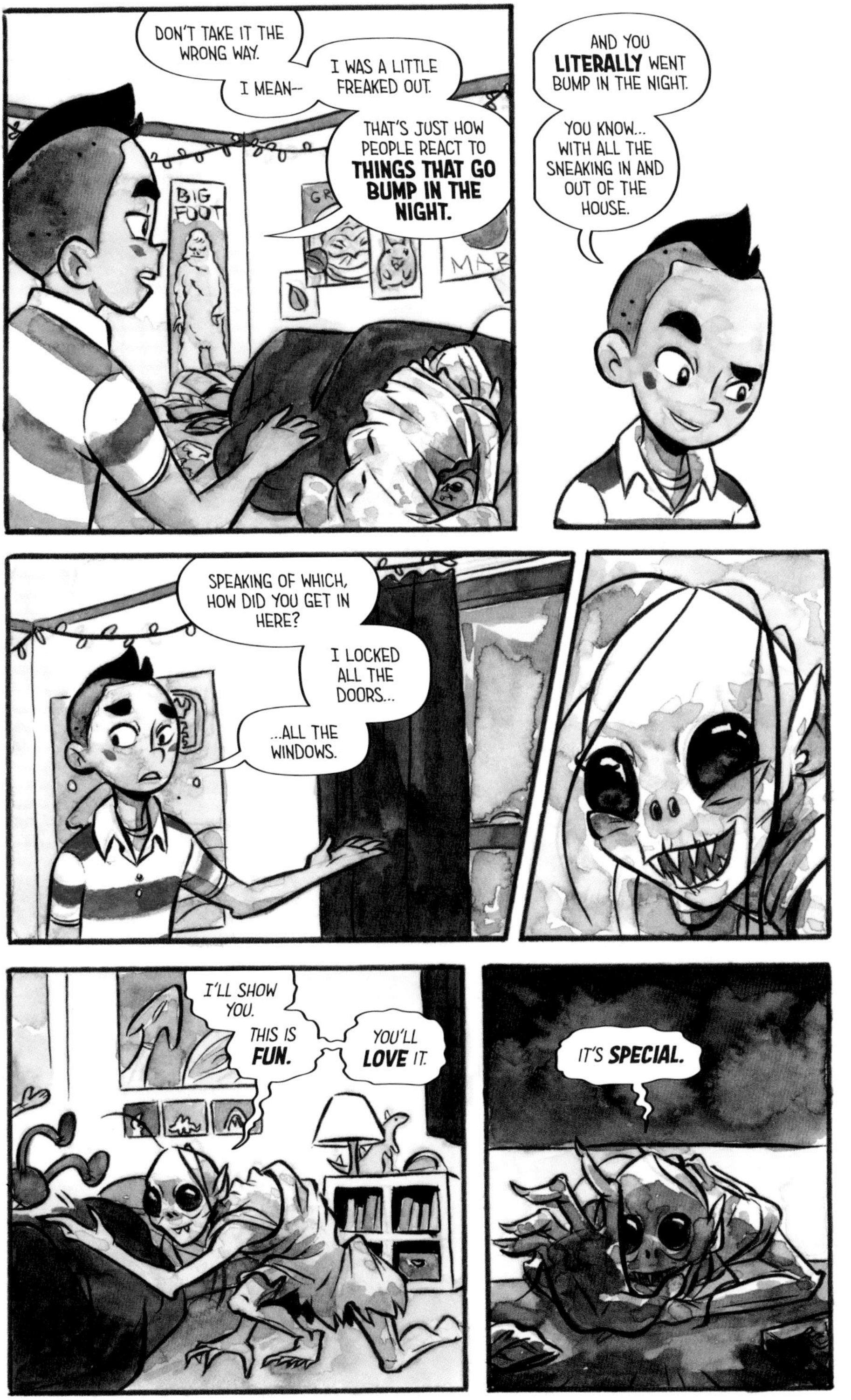
DON'T TAKE IT THE WRONG WAY.
I MEAN--
I WAS A LITTLE FREAKED OUT.
THAT'S JUST HOW PEOPLE REACT TO **THINGS THAT GO BUMP IN THE NIGHT.**
BIG FOOT
AND YOU **LITERALLY** WENT BUMP IN THE NIGHT.
YOU KNOW... WITH ALL THE SNEAKING IN AND OUT OF THE HOUSE.
SPEAKING OF WHICH, HOW DID YOU GET IN HERE?
I LOCKED ALL THE DOORS...
...ALL THE WINDOWS.
I'LL SHOW YOU.
THIS IS ***FUN.***
YOU'LL ***LOVE*** *IT.*
IT'S ***SPECIAL.***

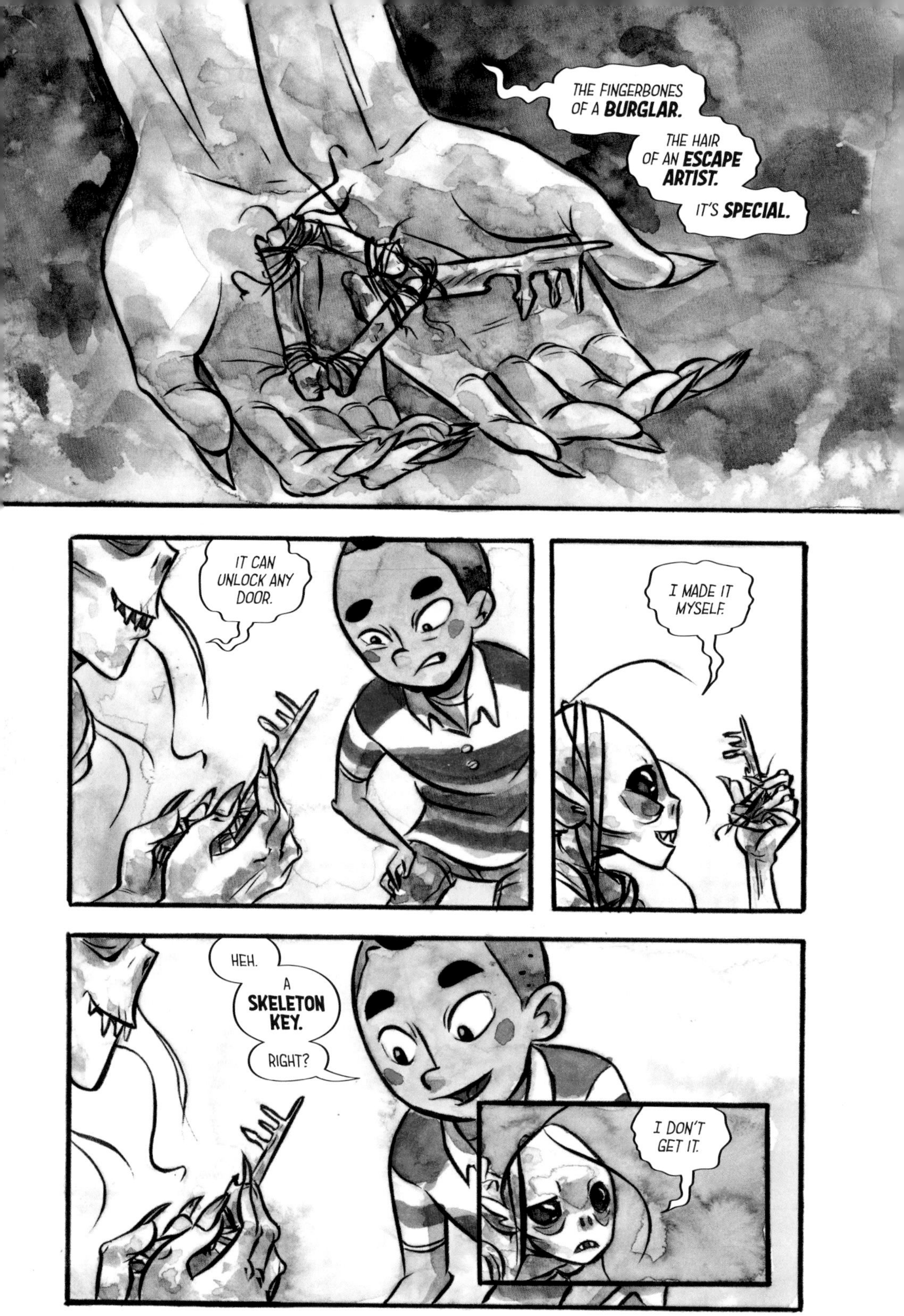
THE FINGERBONES OF A BURGLAR.
THE HAIR OF AN ESCAPE ARTIST.
IT'S SPECIAL.
IT CAN UNLOCK ANY DOOR.
I MADE IT MYSELF.
HEH.
A SKELETON KEY.
RIGHT?
I DON'T GET IT.

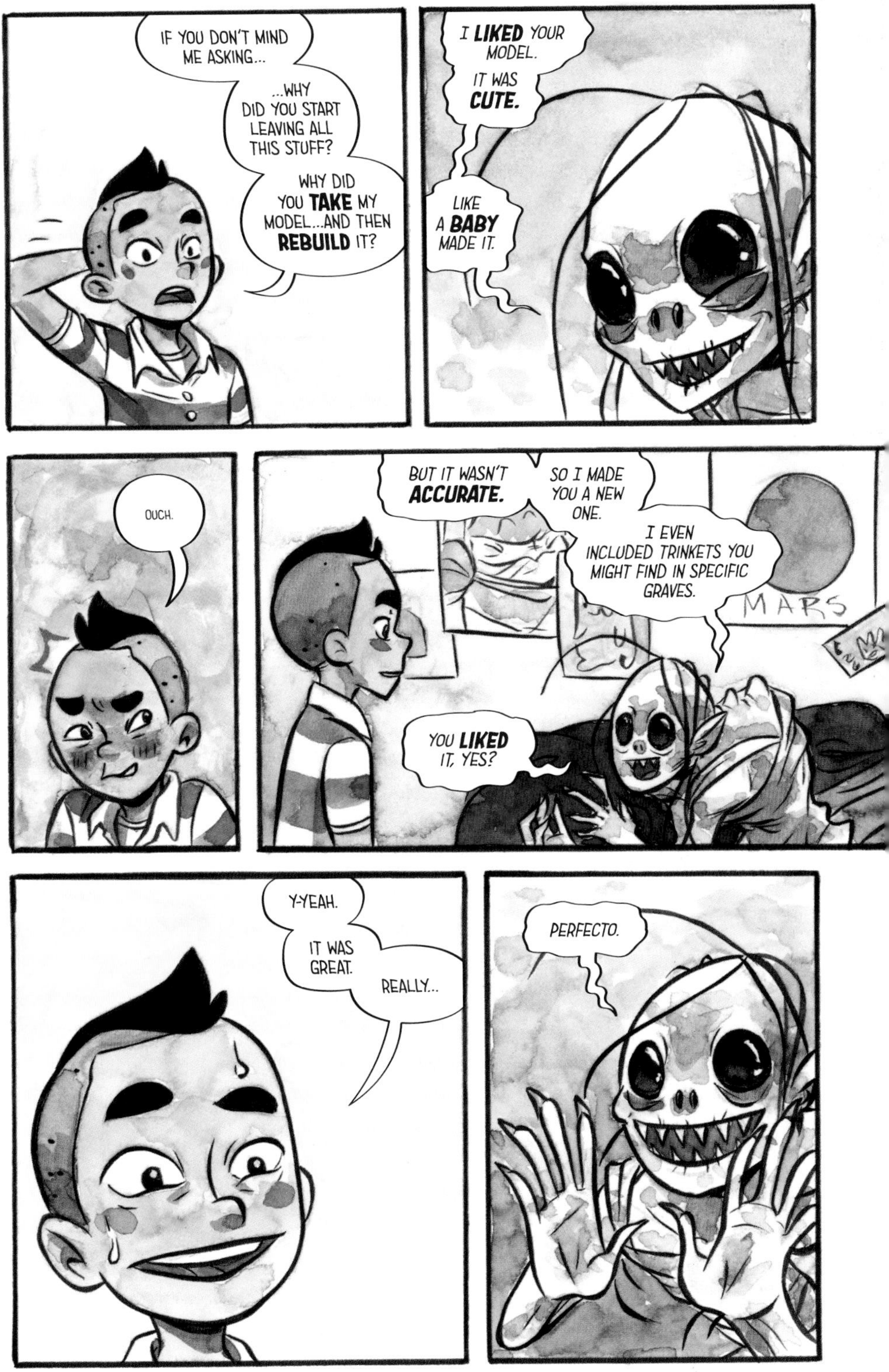
IF YOU DON'T MIND ME ASKING...
...WHY DID YOU START LEAVING ALL THIS STUFF?
WHY DID YOU TAKE MY MODEL...AND THEN REBUILD IT?
I LIKED YOUR MODEL.
IT WAS CUTE.
LIKE A BABY MADE IT.
OUCH.
BUT IT WASN'T ACCURATE.
SO I MADE YOU A NEW ONE.
I EVEN INCLUDED TRINKETS YOU MIGHT FIND IN SPECIFIC GRAVES.
MARS
YOU LIKED IT, YES?
Y-YEAH.
IT WAS GREAT.
REALLY...
PERFECTO.

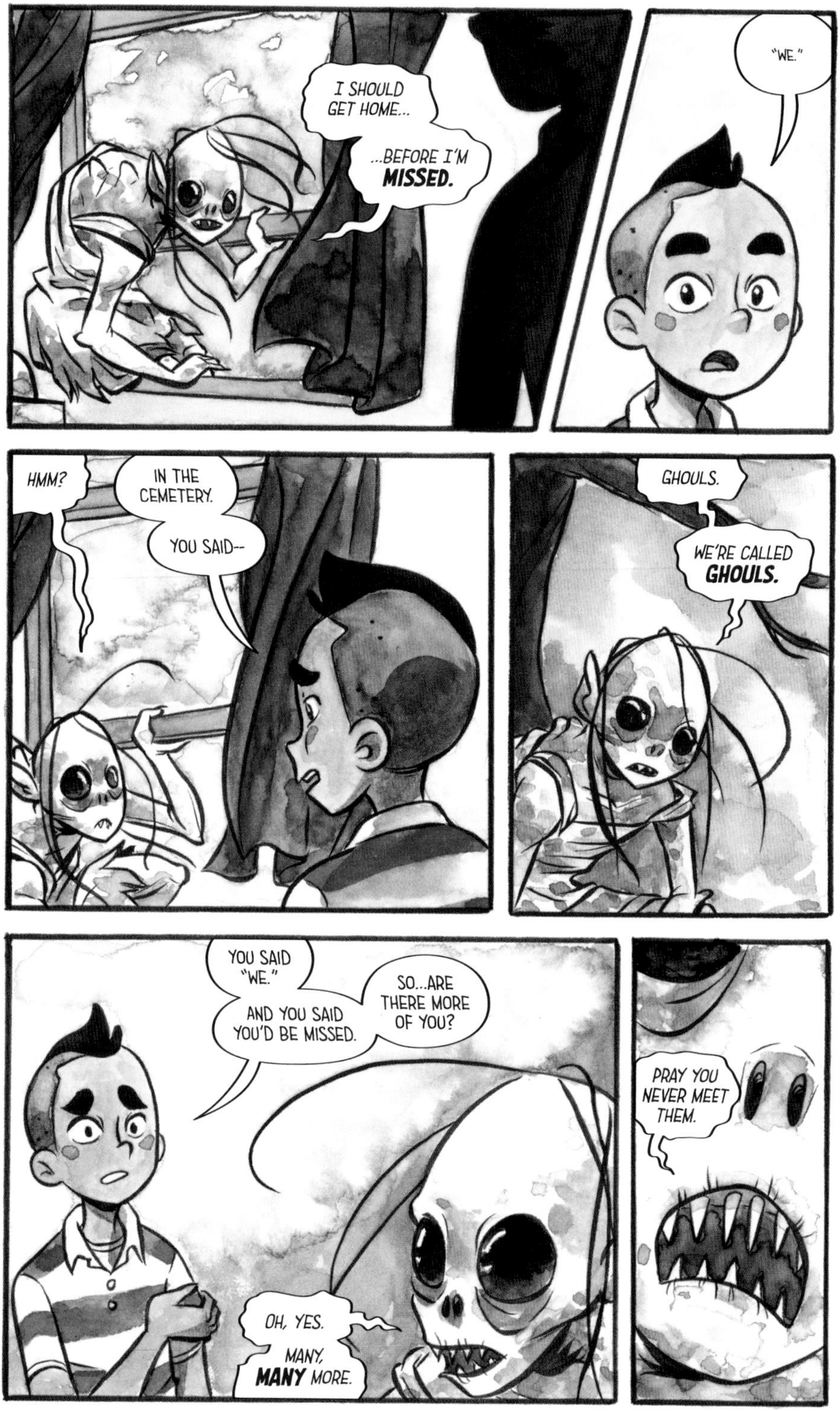
I SHOULD GET HOME...
...BEFORE I'M **MISSED.**
"WE."
HMM?
IN THE CEMETERY.
YOU SAID--
GHOULS.
WE'RE CALLED **GHOULS.**
YOU SAID "WE."
AND YOU SAID YOU'D BE MISSED.
SO...ARE THERE MORE OF YOU?
OH, YES.
MANY, **MANY** MORE.
PRAY YOU NEVER MEET THEM.

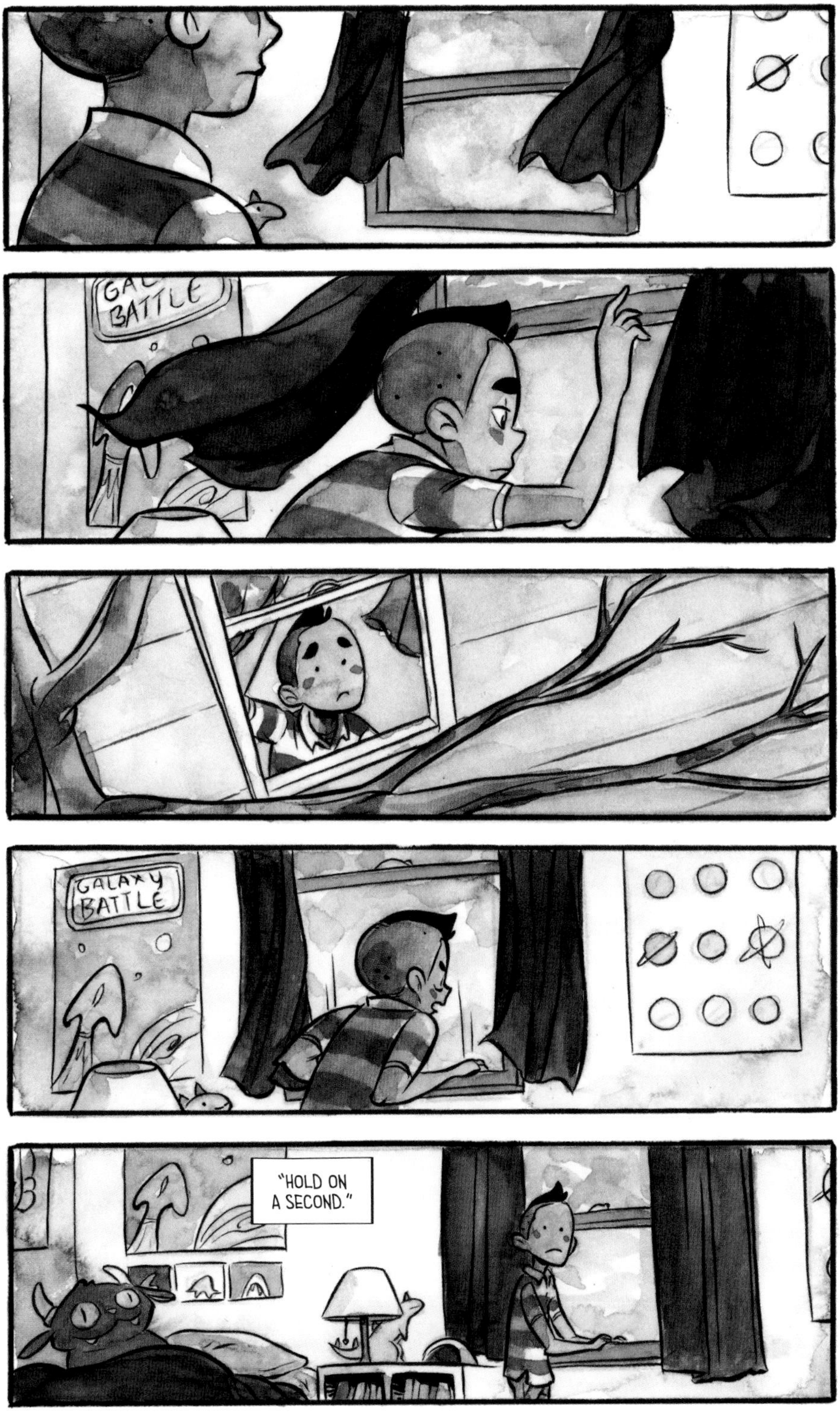
GALAXY BATTLE
"HOLD ON A SECOND."

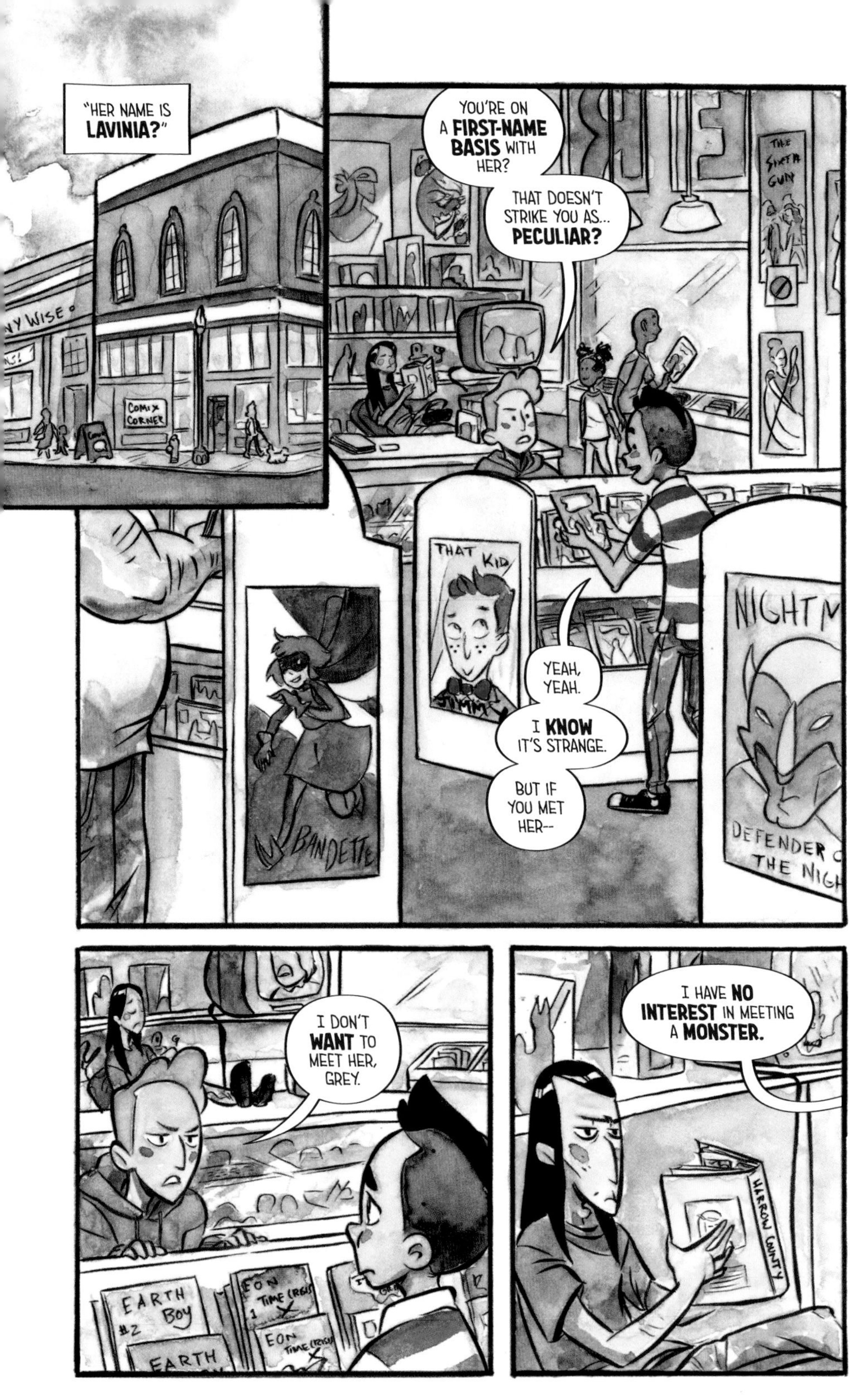
"HER NAME IS **LAVINIA?**"
COMIX CORNER
YOU'RE ON A **FIRST-NAME BASIS** WITH HER?
THAT DOESN'T STRIKE YOU AS... **PECULIAR?**
THAT KID
BANDETTE
YEAH, YEAH.
I **KNOW** IT'S STRANGE.
BUT IF YOU MET HER--
DEFENDER O THE NIGH
I DON'T **WANT** TO MEET HER, GREY.
EARTH BOY #2
I HAVE **NO INTEREST** IN MEETING A **MONSTER.**
HARROW COUNTY

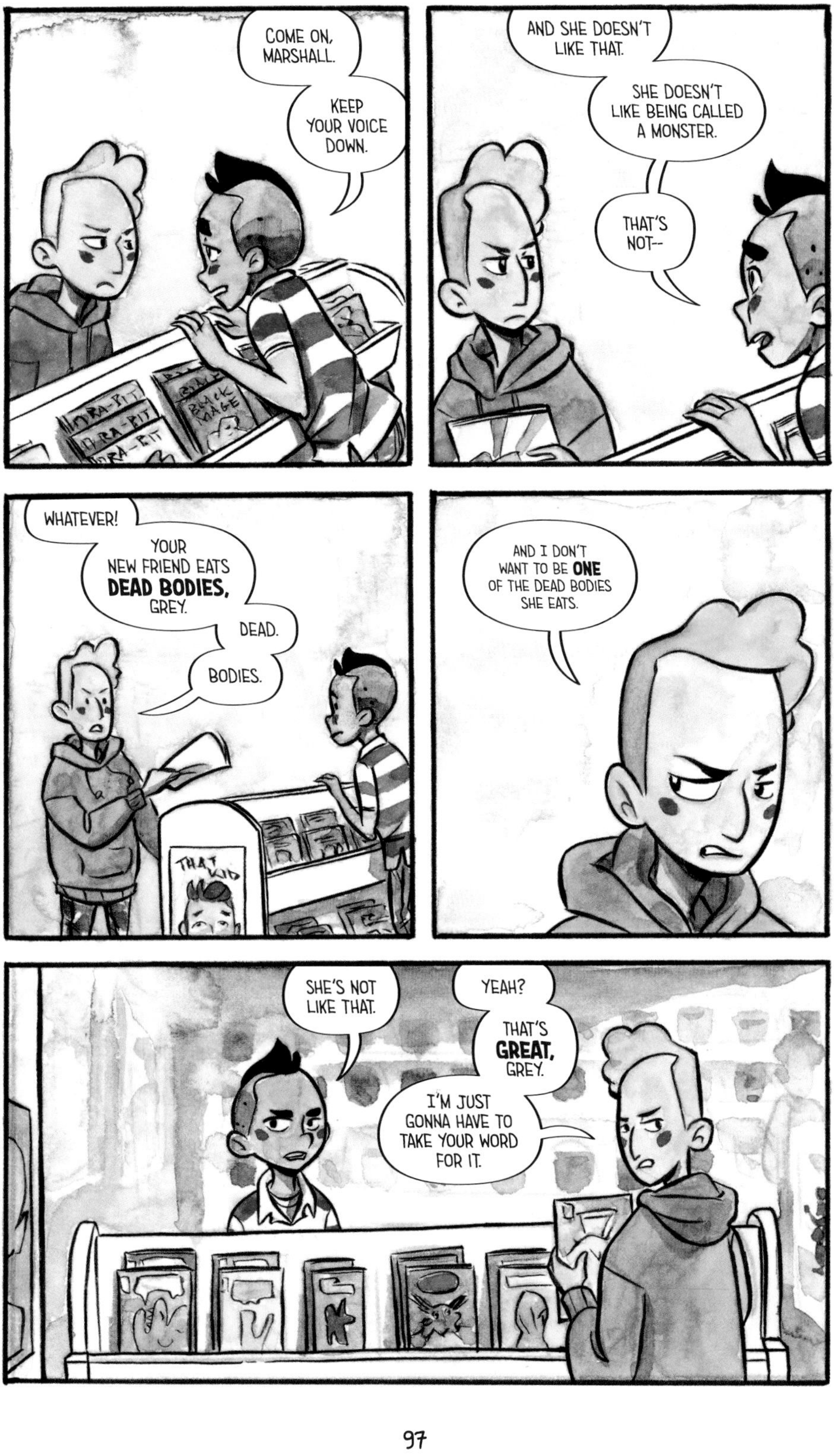
COME ON, MARSHALL.
KEEP YOUR VOICE DOWN.
AND SHE DOESN'T LIKE THAT.
SHE DOESN'T LIKE BEING CALLED A MONSTER.
THAT'S NOT--
WHATEVER!
YOUR NEW FRIEND EATS **DEAD BODIES,** GREY.
DEAD.
BODIES.
AND I DON'T WANT TO BE **ONE** OF THE DEAD BODIES SHE EATS.
SHE'S NOT LIKE THAT.
YEAH?
THAT'S **GREAT,** GREY.
I'M JUST GONNA HAVE TO TAKE YOUR WORD FOR IT.

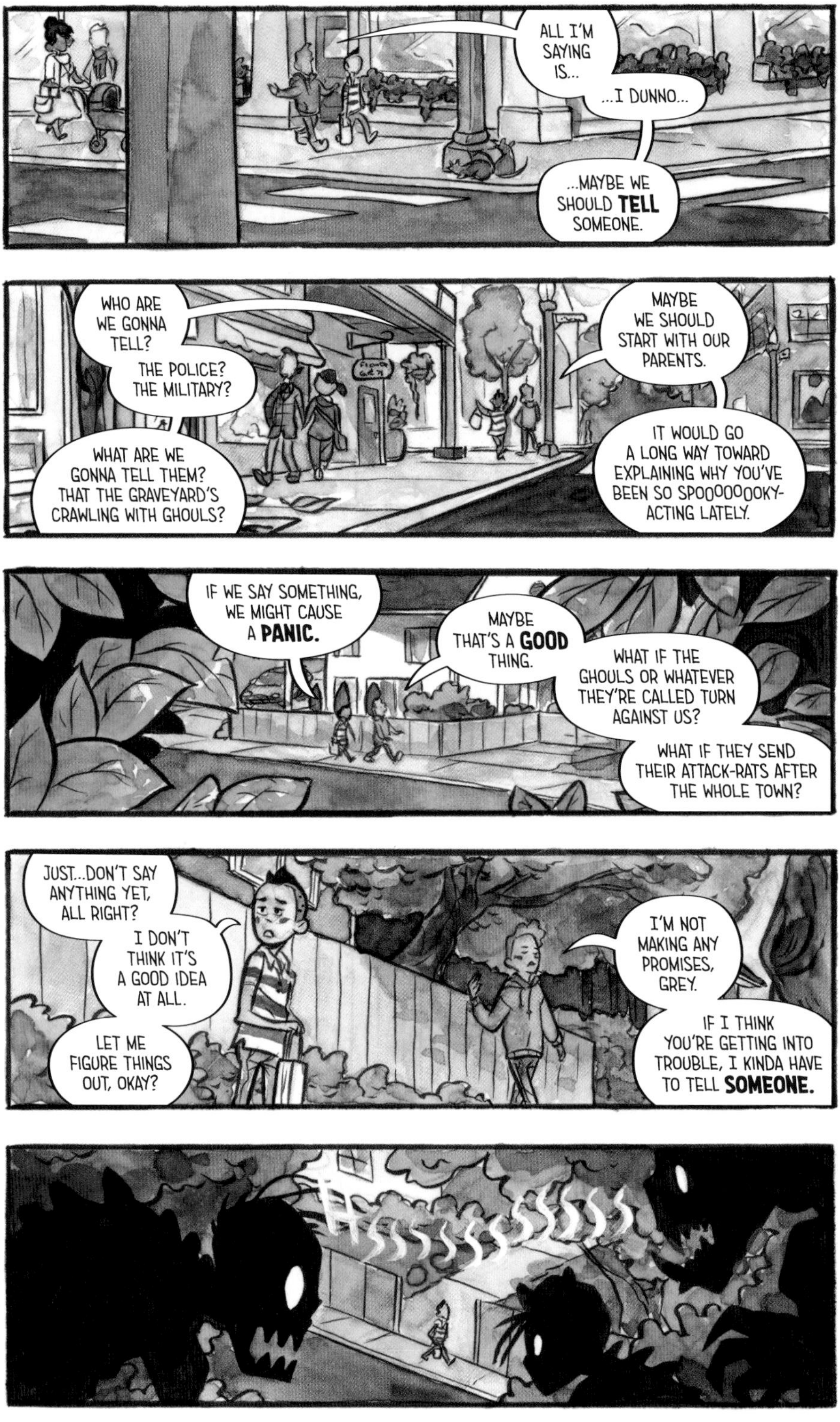
ALL I'M SAYING IS...
...I DUNNO...
...MAYBE WE SHOULD **TELL** SOMEONE.
WHO ARE WE GONNA TELL?
THE POLICE? THE MILITARY?
WHAT ARE WE GONNA TELL THEM? THAT THE GRAVEYARD'S CRAWLING WITH GHOULS?
MAYBE WE SHOULD START WITH OUR PARENTS.
IT WOULD GO A LONG WAY TOWARD EXPLAINING WHY YOU'VE BEEN SO SPOOOOOOOKY-ACTING LATELY.
IF WE SAY SOMETHING, WE MIGHT CAUSE A **PANIC.**
MAYBE THAT'S A **GOOD** THING.
WHAT IF THE GHOULS OR WHATEVER THEY'RE CALLED TURN AGAINST US?
WHAT IF THEY SEND THEIR ATTACK-RATS AFTER THE WHOLE TOWN?
JUST...DON'T SAY ANYTHING YET, ALL RIGHT?
I DON'T THINK IT'S A GOOD IDEA AT ALL.
LET ME FIGURE THINGS OUT, OKAY?
I'M NOT MAKING ANY PROMISES, GREY.
IF I THINK YOU'RE GETTING INTO TROUBLE, I KINDA HAVE TO TELL **SOMEONE.**
HSSSSSSSSSSS

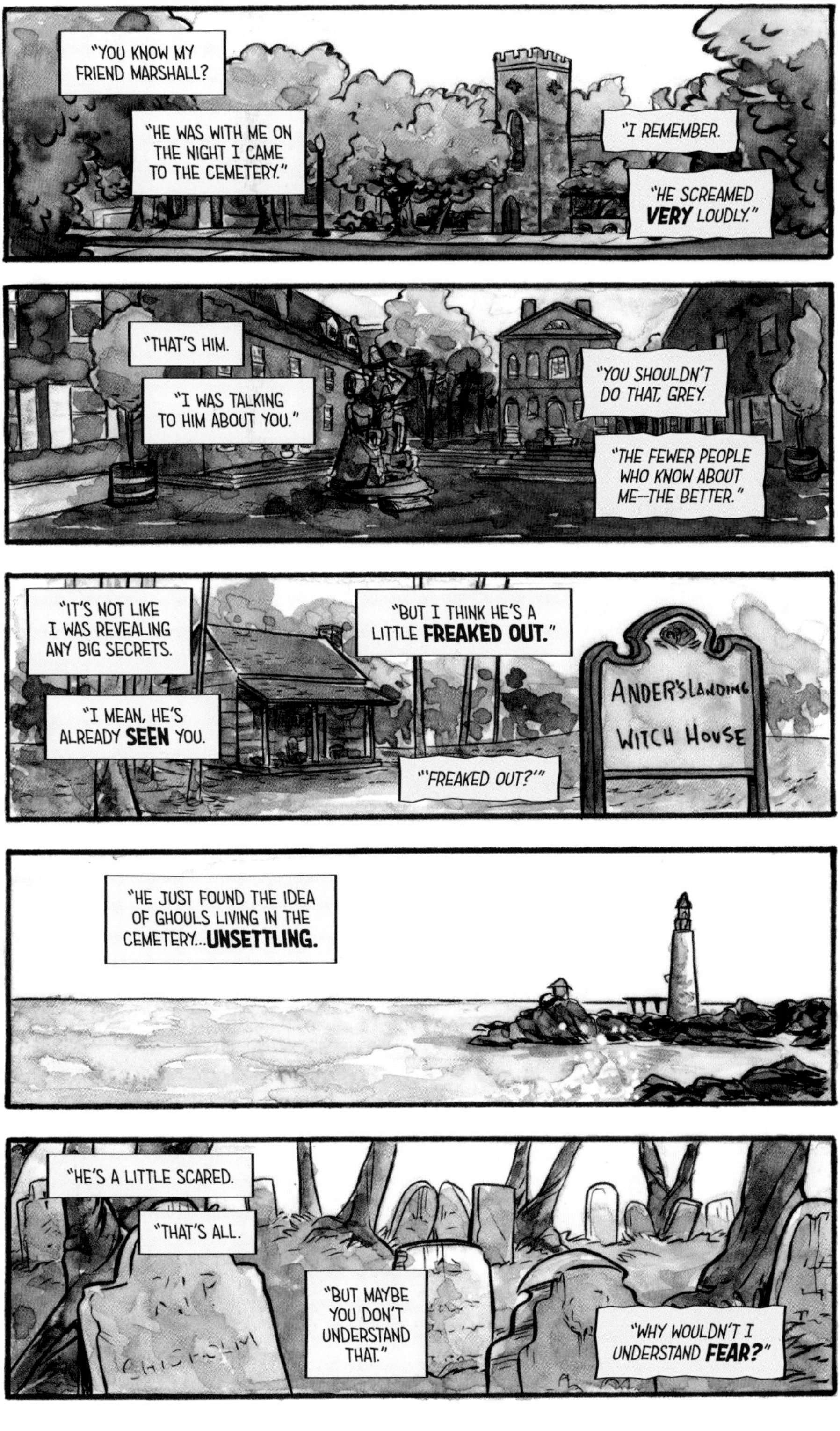
"YOU KNOW MY FRIEND MARSHALL?
"HE WAS WITH ME ON THE NIGHT I CAME TO THE CEMETERY."
"I REMEMBER.
"HE SCREAMED VERY LOUDLY."
"THAT'S HIM.
"I WAS TALKING TO HIM ABOUT YOU."
"YOU SHOULDN'T DO THAT, GREY.
"THE FEWER PEOPLE WHO KNOW ABOUT ME--THE BETTER."
"IT'S NOT LIKE I WAS REVEALING ANY BIG SECRETS.
"I MEAN, HE'S ALREADY SEEN YOU.
"BUT I THINK HE'S A LITTLE FREAKED OUT."
"'FREAKED OUT?'"
ANDER'S LANDING
WITCH HOUSE
"HE JUST FOUND THE IDEA OF GHOULS LIVING IN THE CEMETERY...UNSETTLING.
"HE'S A LITTLE SCARED.
"THAT'S ALL.
"BUT MAYBE YOU DON'T UNDERSTAND THAT."
"WHY WOULDN'T I UNDERSTAND FEAR?"

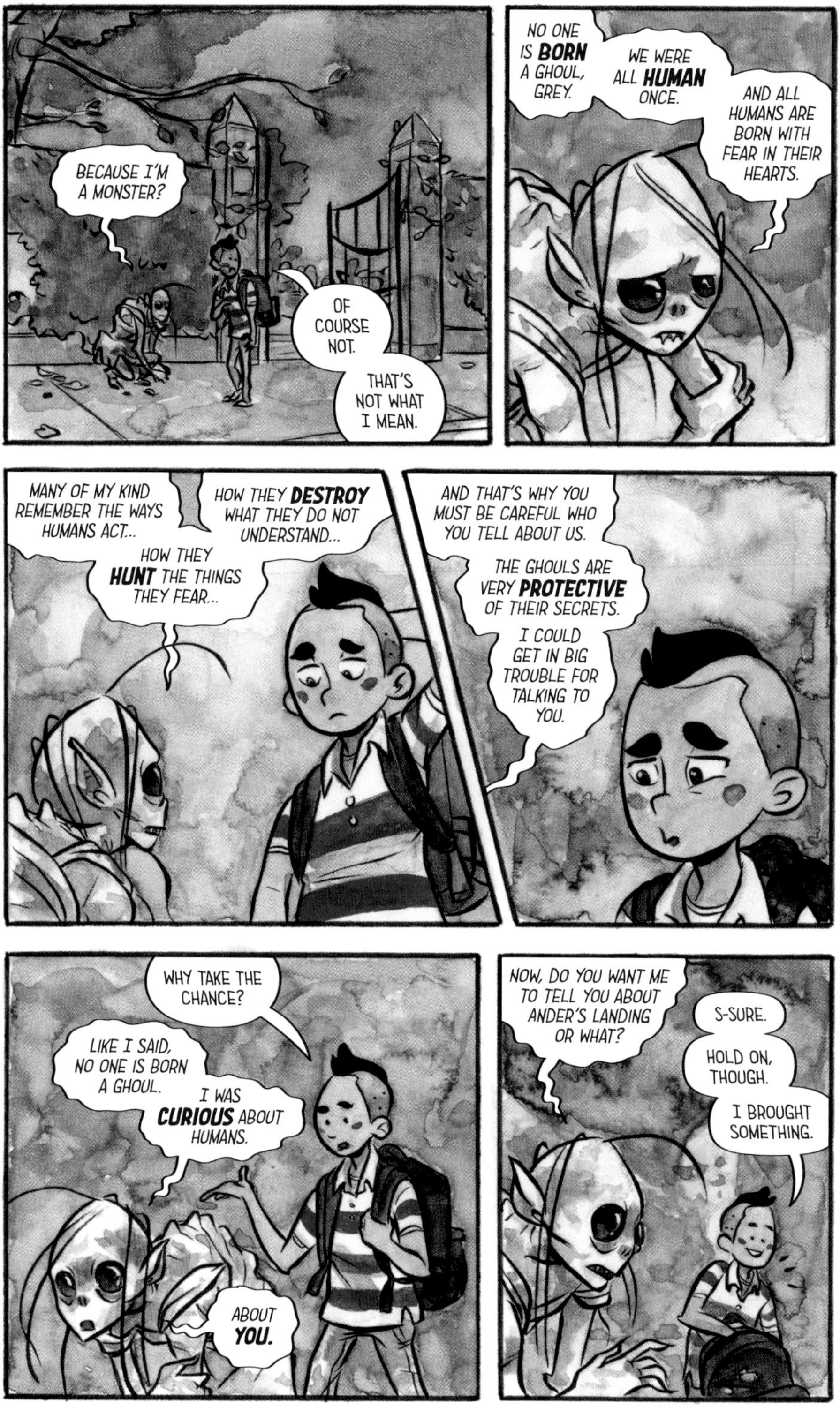
BECAUSE I'M A MONSTER?
OF COURSE NOT.
THAT'S NOT WHAT I MEAN.
NO ONE IS **BORN** A GHOUL, GREY.
WE WERE ALL **HUMAN** ONCE.
AND ALL HUMANS ARE BORN WITH FEAR IN THEIR HEARTS.
MANY OF MY KIND REMEMBER THE WAYS HUMANS ACT...
HOW THEY **DESTROY** WHAT THEY DO NOT UNDERSTAND...
HOW THEY **HUNT** THE THINGS THEY FEAR...
AND THAT'S WHY YOU MUST BE CAREFUL WHO YOU TELL ABOUT US.
THE GHOULS ARE VERY **PROTECTIVE** OF THEIR SECRETS.
I COULD GET IN BIG TROUBLE FOR TALKING TO YOU.
WHY TAKE THE CHANCE?
LIKE I SAID, NO ONE IS BORN A GHOUL.
I WAS **CURIOUS** ABOUT HUMANS.
ABOUT **YOU.**
NOW, DO YOU WANT ME TO TELL YOU ABOUT ANDER'S LANDING OR WHAT?
S-SURE.
HOLD ON, THOUGH.
I BROUGHT SOMETHING.

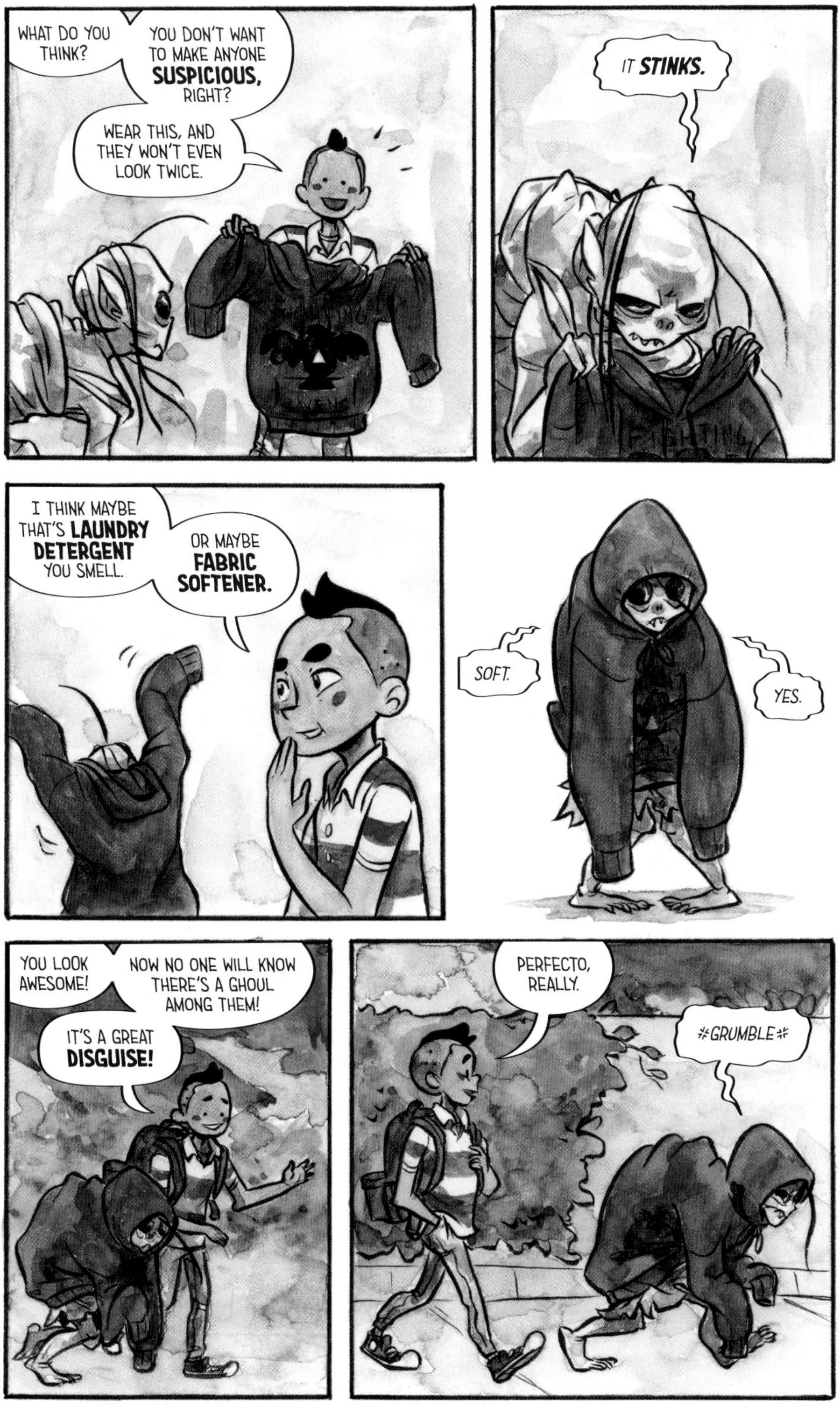

WHAT DO YOU THINK?
YOU DON'T WANT TO MAKE ANYONE **SUSPICIOUS,** RIGHT?
WEAR THIS, AND THEY WON'T EVEN LOOK TWICE.
IT **STINKS.**
I THINK MAYBE THAT'S **LAUNDRY DETERGENT** YOU SMELL.
OR MAYBE **FABRIC SOFTENER.**
SOFT.
YES.
YOU LOOK AWESOME!
NOW NO ONE WILL KNOW THERE'S A GHOUL AMONG THEM!
IT'S A GREAT **DISGUISE!**
PERFECTO, REALLY.
GRUMBLE

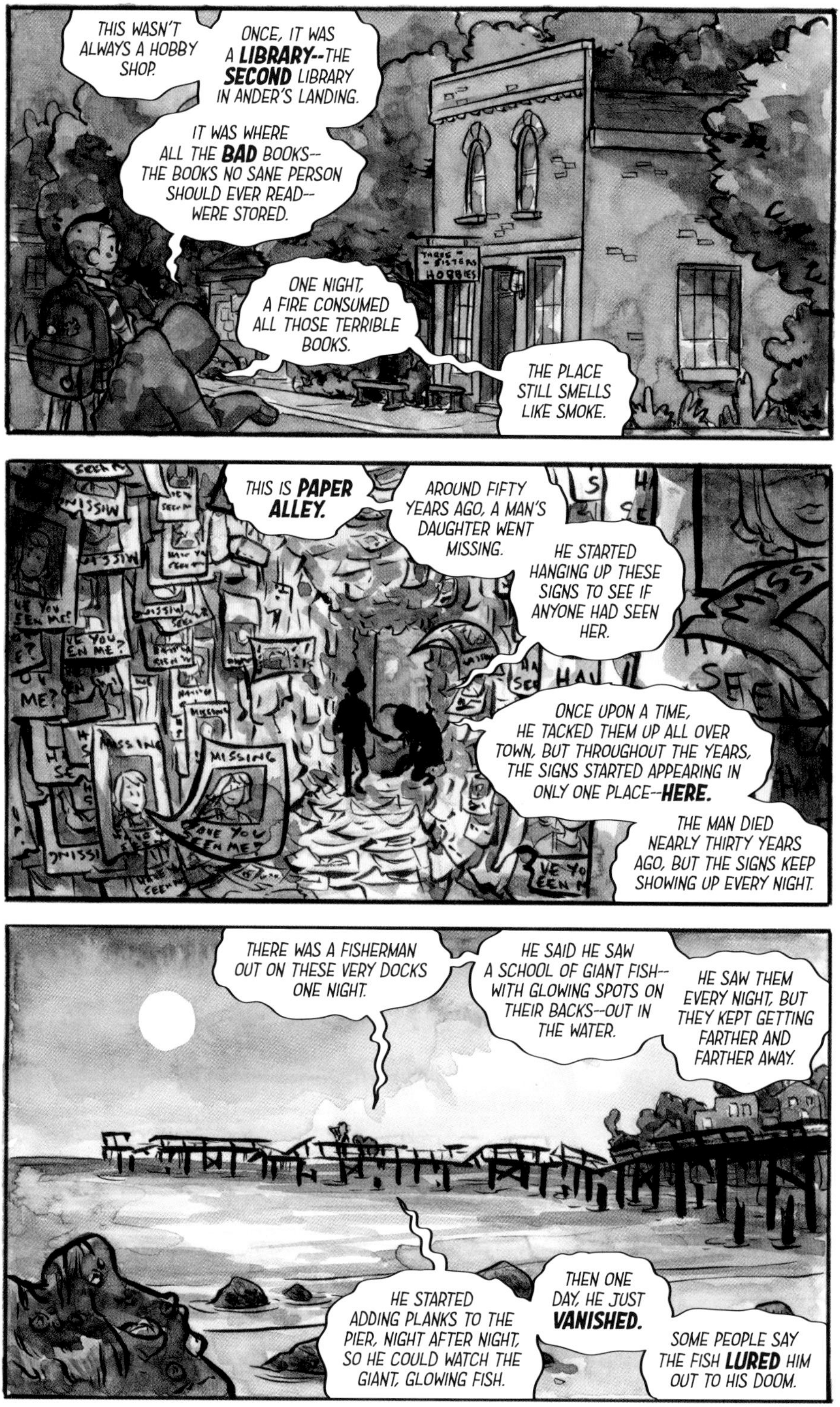
THIS WASN'T ALWAYS A HOBBY SHOP.
ONCE, IT WAS A **LIBRARY**--THE **SECOND** LIBRARY IN ANDER'S LANDING.
IT WAS WHERE ALL THE **BAD** BOOKS-- THE BOOKS NO SANE PERSON SHOULD EVER READ-- WERE STORED.
ONE NIGHT, A FIRE CONSUMED ALL THOSE TERRIBLE BOOKS.
THE PLACE STILL SMELLS LIKE SMOKE.
THIS IS **PAPER ALLEY.**
AROUND FIFTY YEARS AGO, A MAN'S DAUGHTER WENT MISSING.
HE STARTED HANGING UP THESE SIGNS TO SEE IF ANYONE HAD SEEN HER.
ONCE UPON A TIME, HE TACKED THEM UP ALL OVER TOWN, BUT THROUGHOUT THE YEARS, THE SIGNS STARTED APPEARING IN ONLY ONE PLACE--**HERE.**
THE MAN DIED NEARLY THIRTY YEARS AGO, BUT THE SIGNS KEEP SHOWING UP EVERY NIGHT.
THERE WAS A FISHERMAN OUT ON THESE VERY DOCKS ONE NIGHT.
HE SAID HE SAW A SCHOOL OF GIANT FISH-- WITH GLOWING SPOTS ON THEIR BACKS--OUT IN THE WATER.
HE SAW THEM EVERY NIGHT, BUT THEY KEPT GETTING FARTHER AND FARTHER AWAY.
HE STARTED ADDING PLANKS TO THE PIER, NIGHT AFTER NIGHT, SO HE COULD WATCH THE GIANT, GLOWING FISH.
THEN ONE DAY, HE JUST **VANISHED.**
SOME PEOPLE SAY THE FISH **LURED** HIM OUT TO HIS DOOM.

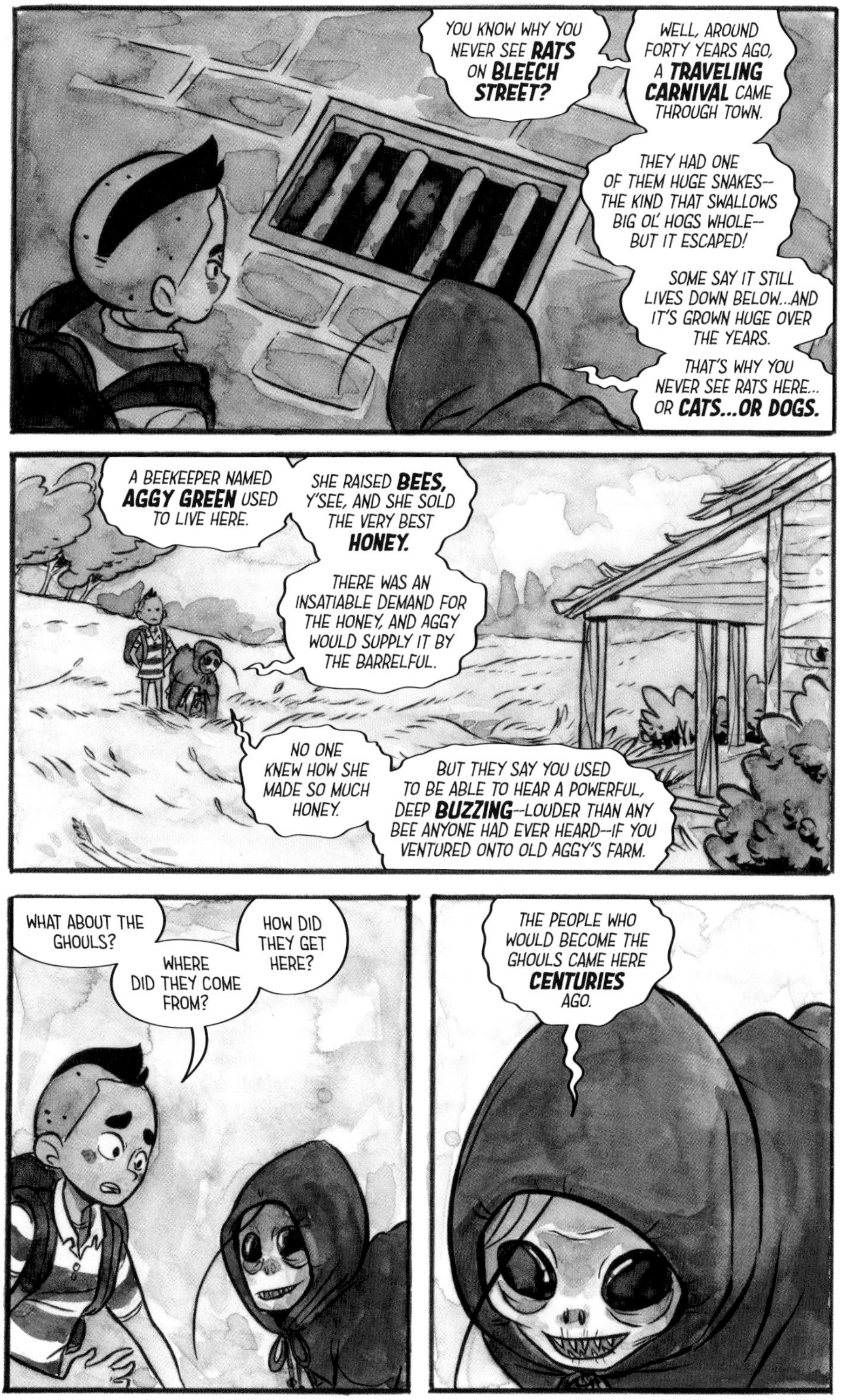
YOU KNOW WHY YOU NEVER SEE RATS ON BLEECH STREET?
WELL, AROUND FORTY YEARS AGO, A TRAVELING CARNIVAL CAME THROUGH TOWN.
THEY HAD ONE OF THEM HUGE SNAKES-- THE KIND THAT SWALLOWS BIG OL' HOGS WHOLE-- BUT IT ESCAPED!
SOME SAY IT STILL LIVES DOWN BELOW...AND IT'S GROWN HUGE OVER THE YEARS.
THAT'S WHY YOU NEVER SEE RATS HERE... OR CATS...OR DOGS.
A BEEKEEPER NAMED AGGY GREEN USED TO LIVE HERE.
SHE RAISED BEES, Y'SEE, AND SHE SOLD THE VERY BEST HONEY.
THERE WAS AN INSATIABLE DEMAND FOR THE HONEY, AND AGGY WOULD SUPPLY IT BY THE BARRELFUL.
NO ONE KNEW HOW SHE MADE SO MUCH HONEY.
BUT THEY SAY YOU USED TO BE ABLE TO HEAR A POWERFUL, DEEP BUZZING--LOUDER THAN ANY BEE ANYONE HAD EVER HEARD--IF YOU VENTURED ONTO OLD AGGY'S FARM.
WHAT ABOUT THE GHOULS?
WHERE DID THEY COME FROM?
HOW DID THEY GET HERE?
THE PEOPLE WHO WOULD BECOME THE GHOULS CAME HERE CENTURIES AGO.

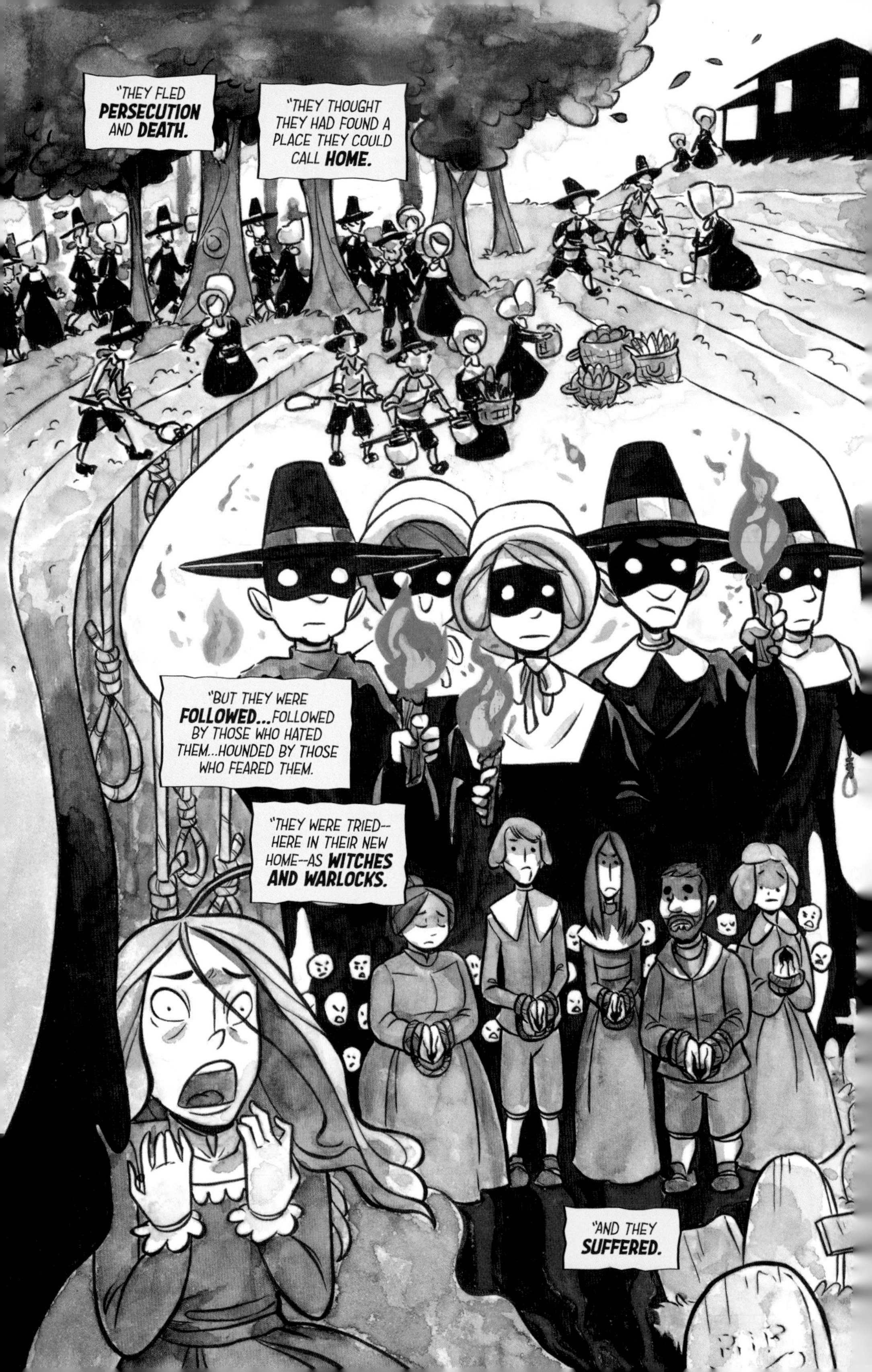
"THEY FLED **PERSECUTION** AND **DEATH.**
"THEY THOUGHT THEY HAD FOUND A PLACE THEY COULD CALL **HOME.**
"BUT THEY WERE **FOLLOWED...** FOLLOWED BY THOSE WHO HATED THEM...HOUNDED BY THOSE WHO FEARED THEM.
"THEY WERE TRIED-- HERE IN THEIR NEW HOME--AS **WITCHES AND WARLOCKS.**
"AND THEY **SUFFERED.**

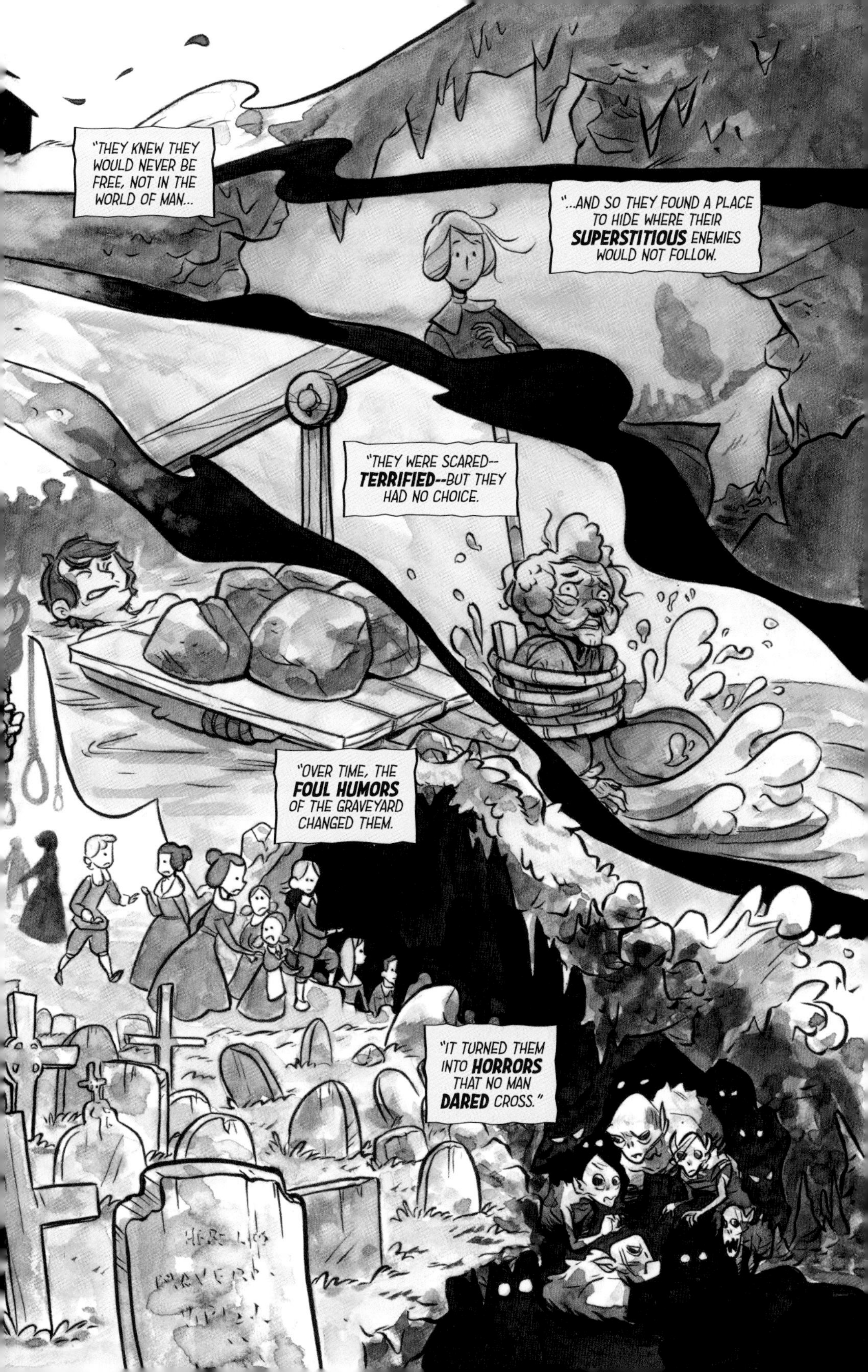
"THEY KNEW THEY WOULD NEVER BE FREE, NOT IN THE WORLD OF MAN...
"...AND SO THEY FOUND A PLACE TO HIDE WHERE THEIR SUPERSTITIOUS ENEMIES WOULD NOT FOLLOW.
"THEY WERE SCARED-- TERRIFIED--BUT THEY HAD NO CHOICE.
"OVER TIME, THE FOUL HUMORS OF THE GRAVEYARD CHANGED THEM.
"IT TURNED THEM INTO HORRORS THAT NO MAN DARED CROSS."

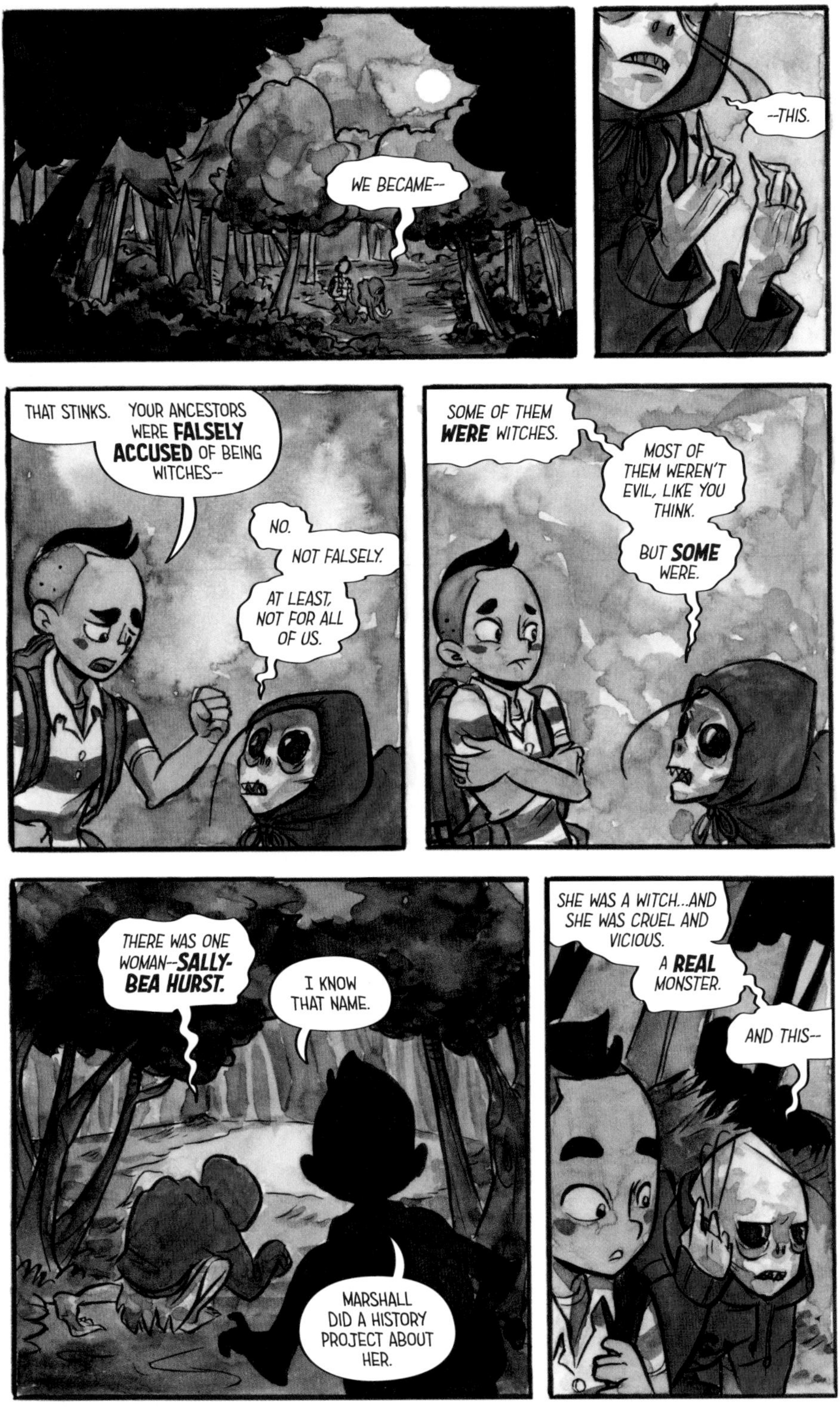
WE BECAME--
--THIS.
THAT STINKS.
YOUR ANCESTORS WERE FALSELY ACCUSED OF BEING WITCHES--
NO.
NOT FALSELY.
AT LEAST, NOT FOR ALL OF US.
SOME OF THEM WERE WITCHES.
MOST OF THEM WEREN'T EVIL, LIKE YOU THINK.
BUT SOME WERE.
THERE WAS ONE WOMAN--SALLY-BEA HURST.
I KNOW THAT NAME.
MARSHALL DID A HISTORY PROJECT ABOUT HER.
SHE WAS A WITCH...AND SHE WAS CRUEL AND VICIOUS.
A REAL MONSTER.
AND THIS--

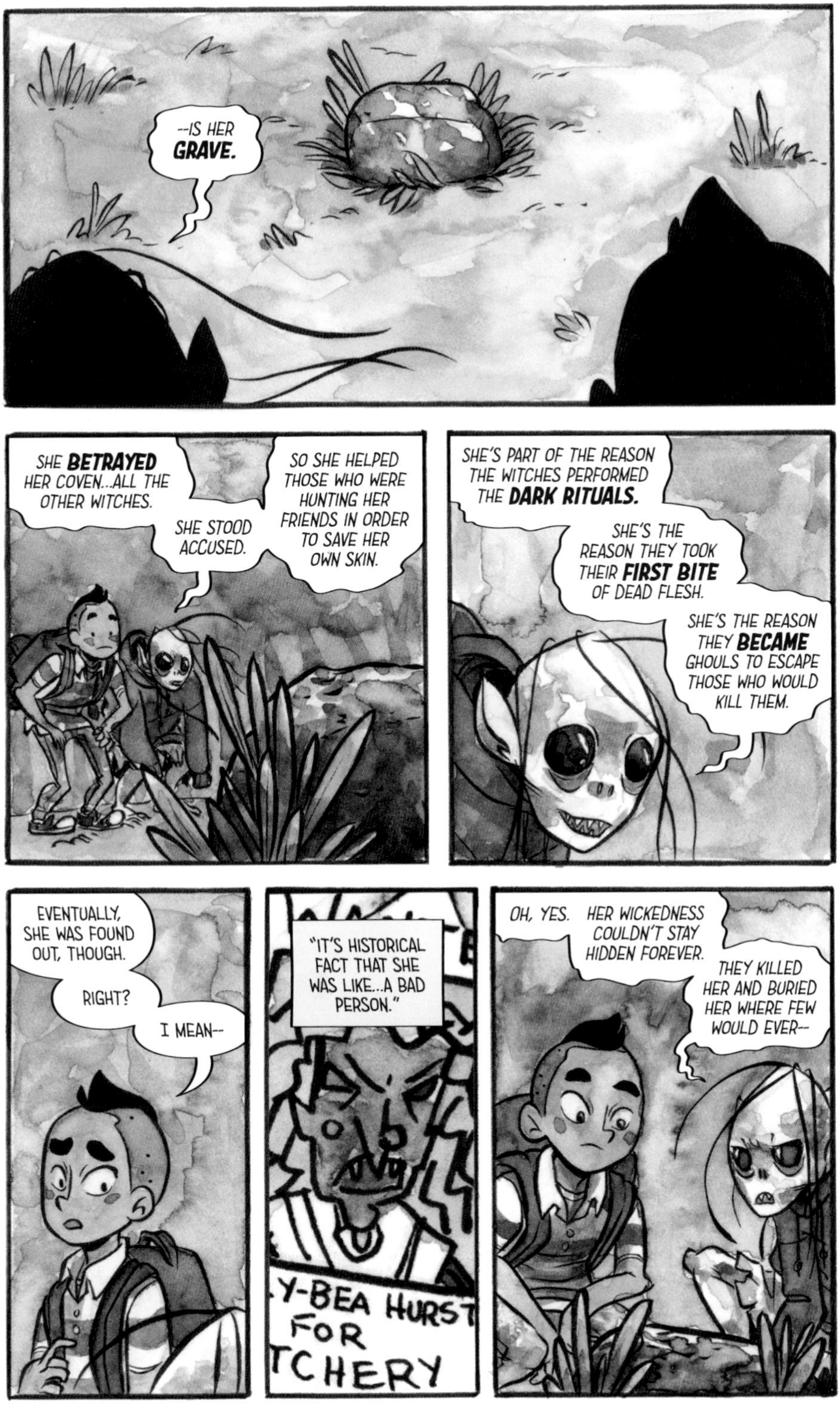
--IS HER GRAVE.
SHE BETRAYED HER COVEN...ALL THE OTHER WITCHES.
SHE STOOD ACCUSED.
SO SHE HELPED THOSE WHO WERE HUNTING HER FRIENDS IN ORDER TO SAVE HER OWN SKIN.
SHE'S PART OF THE REASON THE WITCHES PERFORMED THE DARK RITUALS.
SHE'S THE REASON THEY TOOK THEIR FIRST BITE OF DEAD FLESH.
SHE'S THE REASON THEY BECAME GHOULS TO ESCAPE THOSE WHO WOULD KILL THEM.
EVENTUALLY, SHE WAS FOUND OUT, THOUGH.
RIGHT?
I MEAN--
"IT'S HISTORICAL FACT THAT SHE WAS LIKE...A BAD PERSON."
Y-BEA HURST
FOR
TCHERY
OH, YES.
HER WICKEDNESS COULDN'T STAY HIDDEN FOREVER.
THEY KILLED HER AND BURIED HER WHERE FEW WOULD EVER--

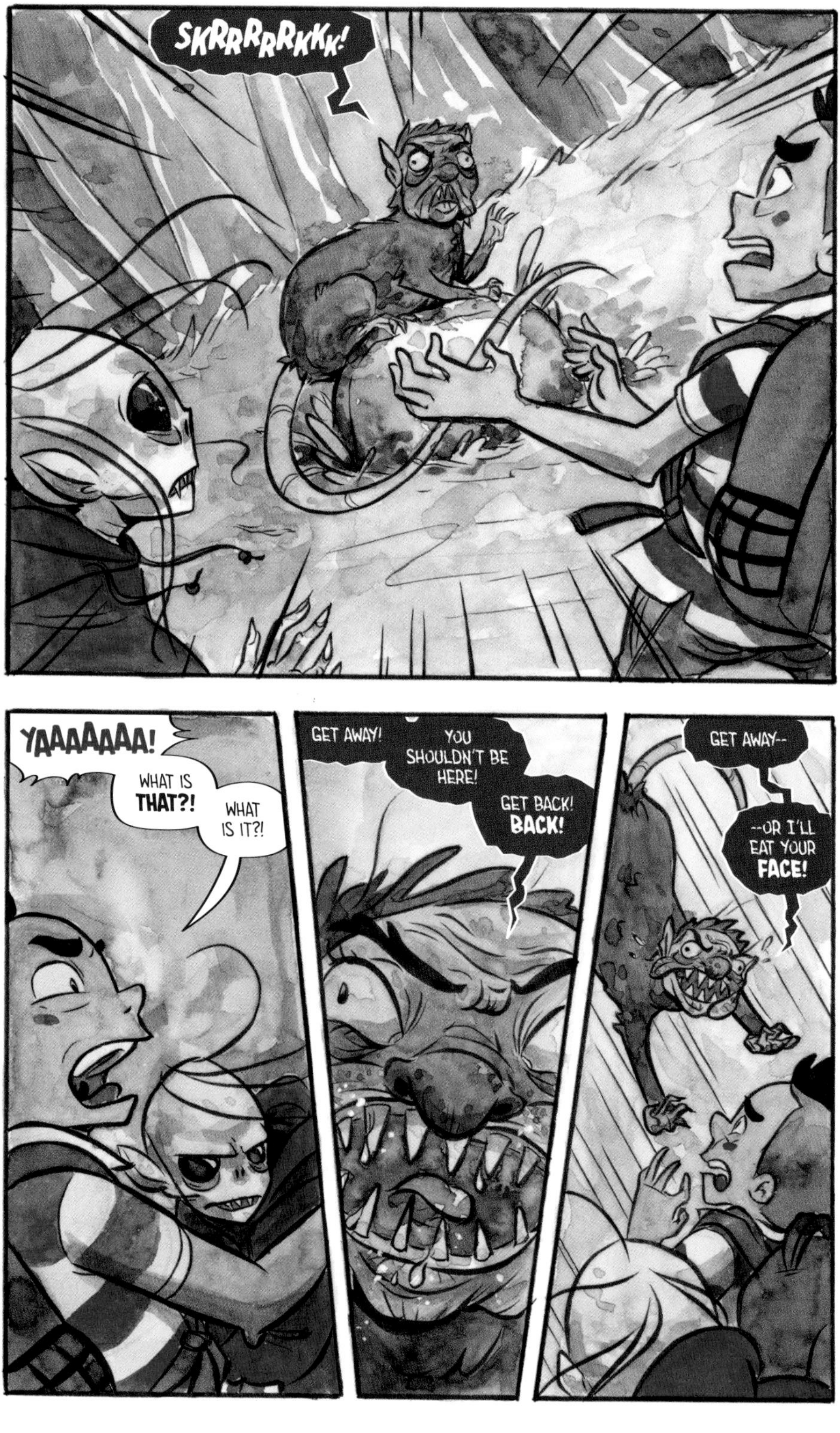
SKRRRRRKKK!
YAAAAAAA!
WHAT IS THAT?!
WHAT IS IT?!
GET AWAY!
YOU SHOULDN'T BE HERE!
GET BACK! BACK!
GET AWAY--
--OR I'LL EAT YOUR FACE!

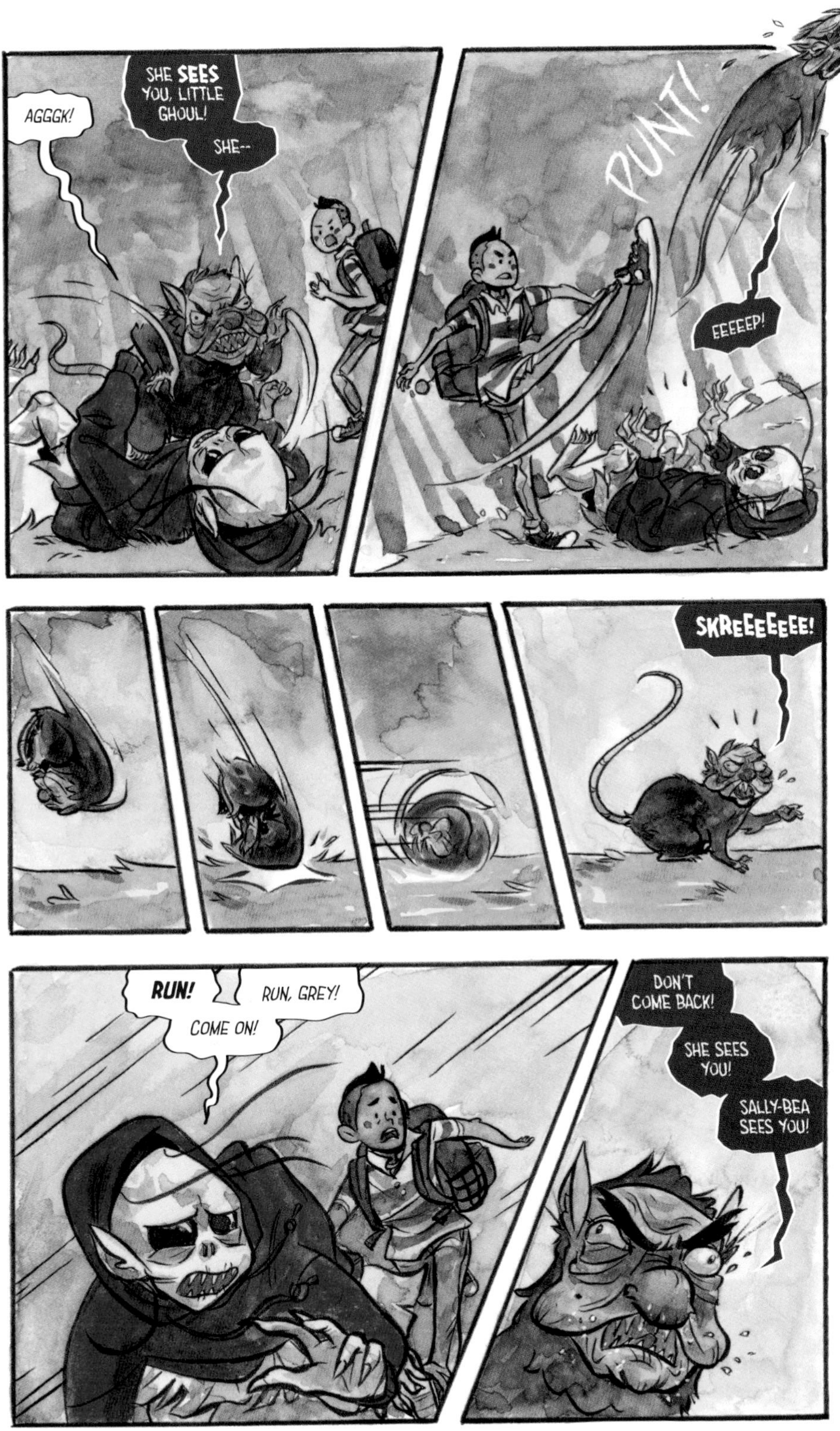

AGGGK!
SHE SEES YOU, LITTLE GHOUL!
SHE--
PUNT!
EEEEEP!
SKREEEEEEE!
RUN!
RUN, GREY!
COME ON!
DON'T COME BACK!
SHE SEES YOU!
SALLY-BEA SEES YOU!

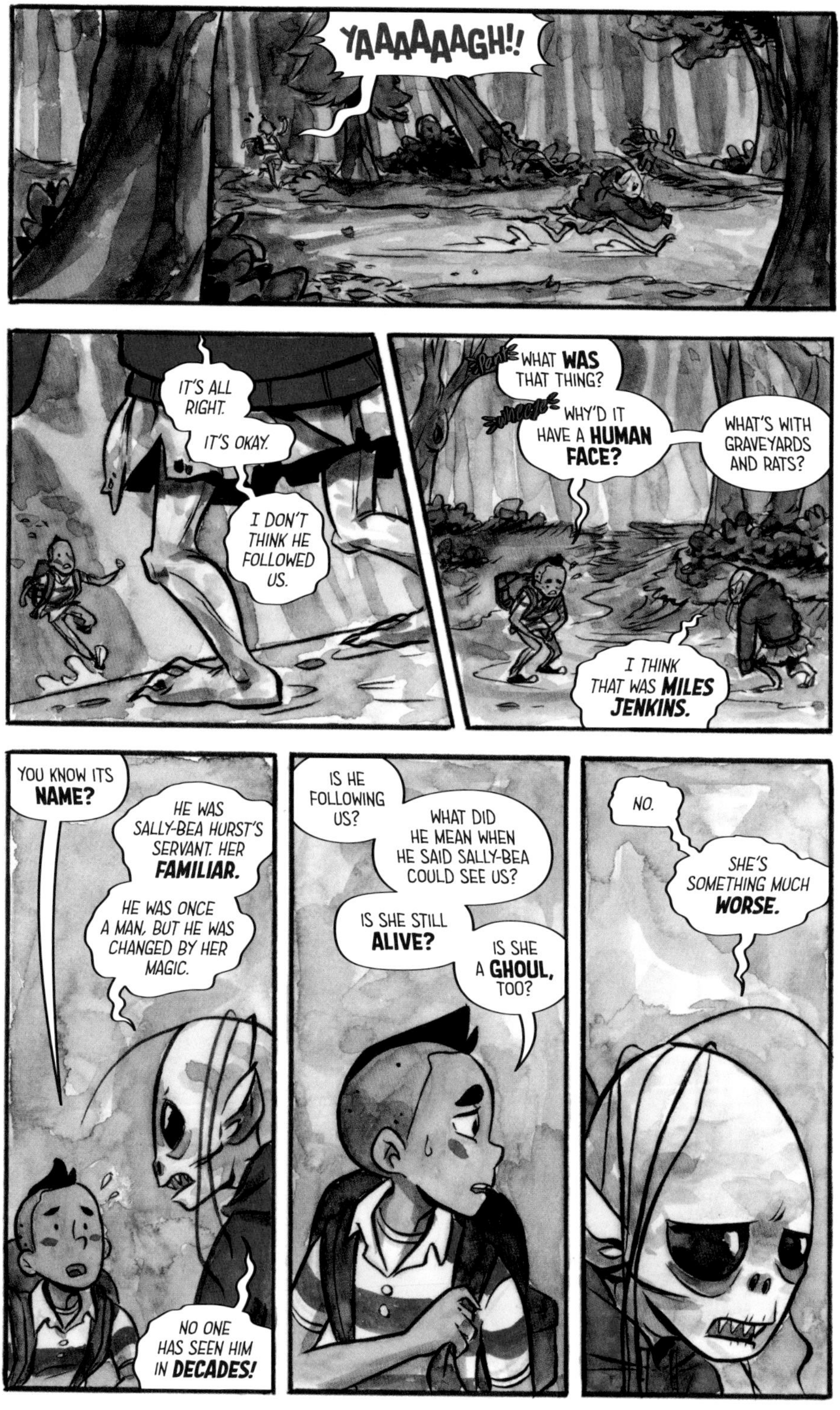
YAAAAAAGH!!
IT'S ALL RIGHT.
IT'S OKAY.
I DON'T THINK HE FOLLOWED US.
WHAT WAS THAT THING?
WHY'D IT HAVE A HUMAN FACE?
WHAT'S WITH GRAVEYARDS AND RATS?
I THINK THAT WAS MILES JENKINS.
YOU KNOW ITS NAME?
HE WAS SALLY-BEA HURST'S SERVANT. HER FAMILIAR.
HE WAS ONCE A MAN, BUT HE WAS CHANGED BY HER MAGIC.
NO ONE HAS SEEN HIM IN DECADES!
IS HE FOLLOWING US?
WHAT DID HE MEAN WHEN HE SAID SALLY-BEA COULD SEE US?
IS SHE STILL ALIVE?
IS SHE A GHOUL, TOO?
NO.
SHE'S SOMETHING MUCH WORSE.

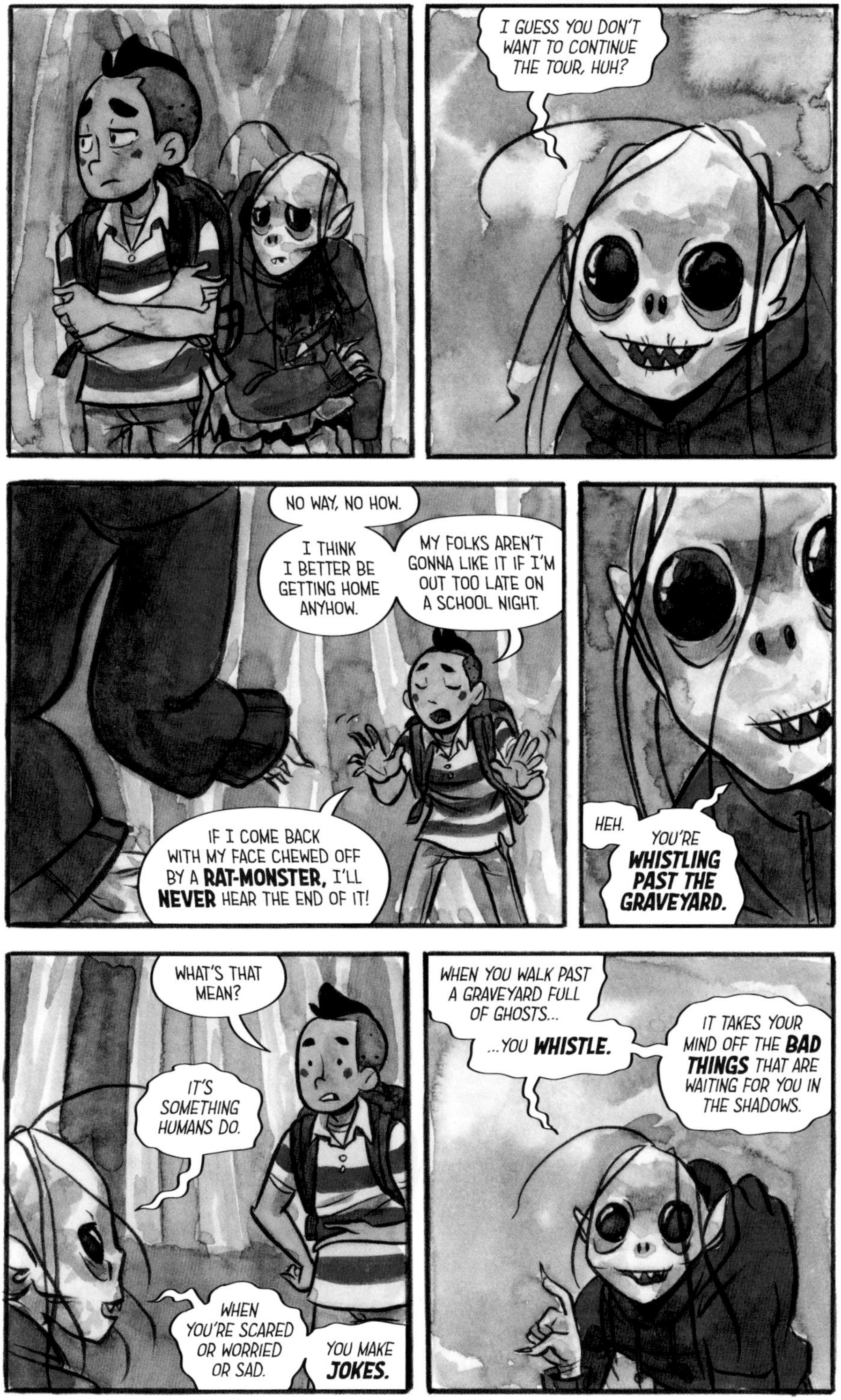
I GUESS YOU DON'T WANT TO CONTINUE THE TOUR, HUH?
NO WAY, NO HOW.
I THINK I BETTER BE GETTING HOME ANYHOW.
MY FOLKS AREN'T GONNA LIKE IT IF I'M OUT TOO LATE ON A SCHOOL NIGHT.
IF I COME BACK WITH MY FACE CHEWED OFF BY A RAT-MONSTER, I'LL NEVER HEAR THE END OF IT!
HEH.
YOU'RE WHISTLING PAST THE GRAVEYARD.
WHAT'S THAT MEAN?
IT'S SOMETHING HUMANS DO.
WHEN YOU'RE SCARED OR WORRIED OR SAD.
YOU MAKE JOKES.
WHEN YOU WALK PAST A GRAVEYARD FULL OF GHOSTS...
...YOU WHISTLE.
IT TAKES YOUR MIND OFF THE BAD THINGS THAT ARE WAITING FOR YOU IN THE SHADOWS.

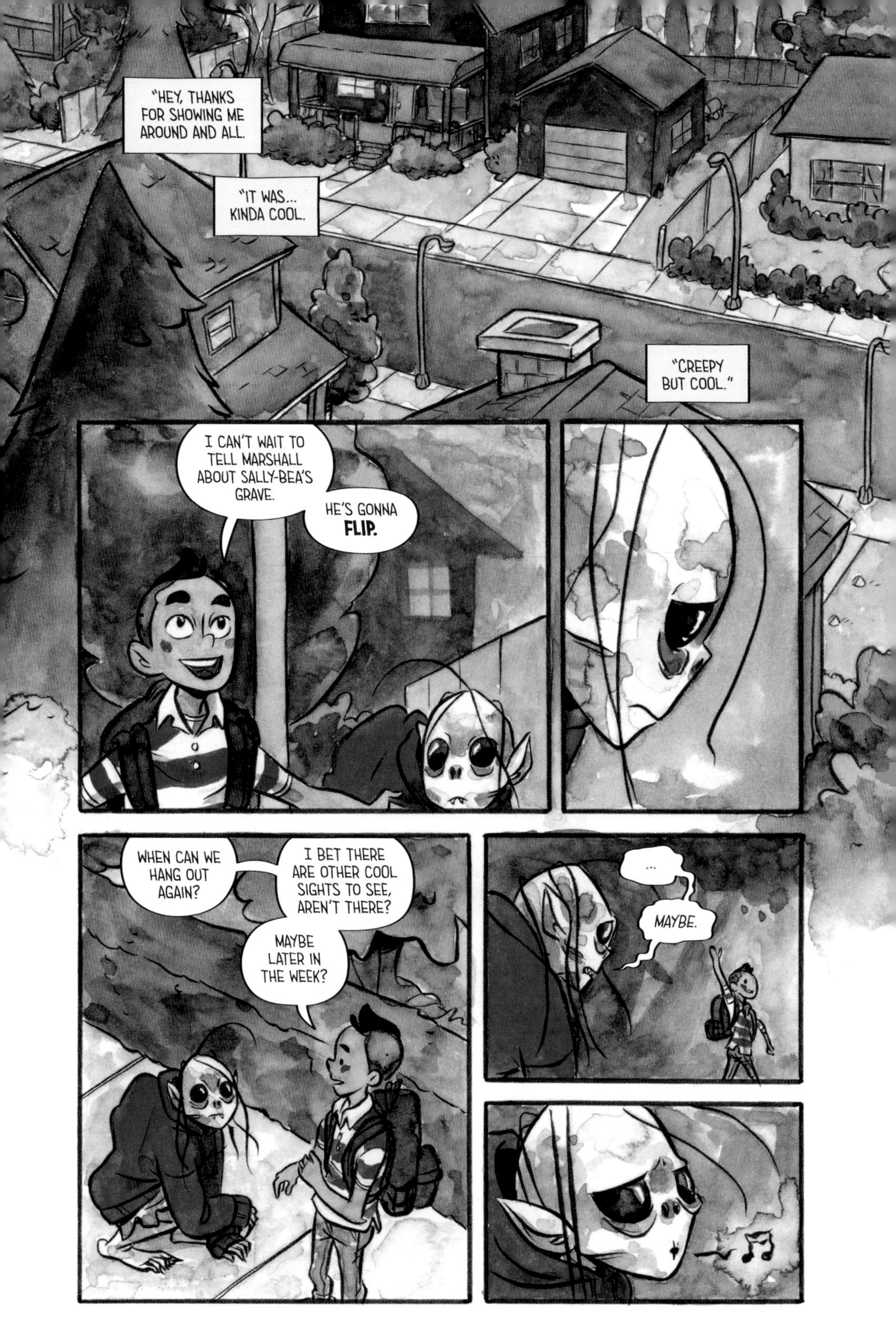
"HEY, THANKS FOR SHOWING ME AROUND AND ALL.
"IT WAS... KINDA COOL.
"CREEPY BUT COOL."
I CAN'T WAIT TO TELL MARSHALL ABOUT SALLY-BEA'S GRAVE.
HE'S GONNA **FLIP.**
WHEN CAN WE HANG OUT AGAIN?
I BET THERE ARE OTHER COOL SIGHTS TO SEE, AREN'T THERE?
MAYBE LATER IN THE WEEK?
...
MAYBE.

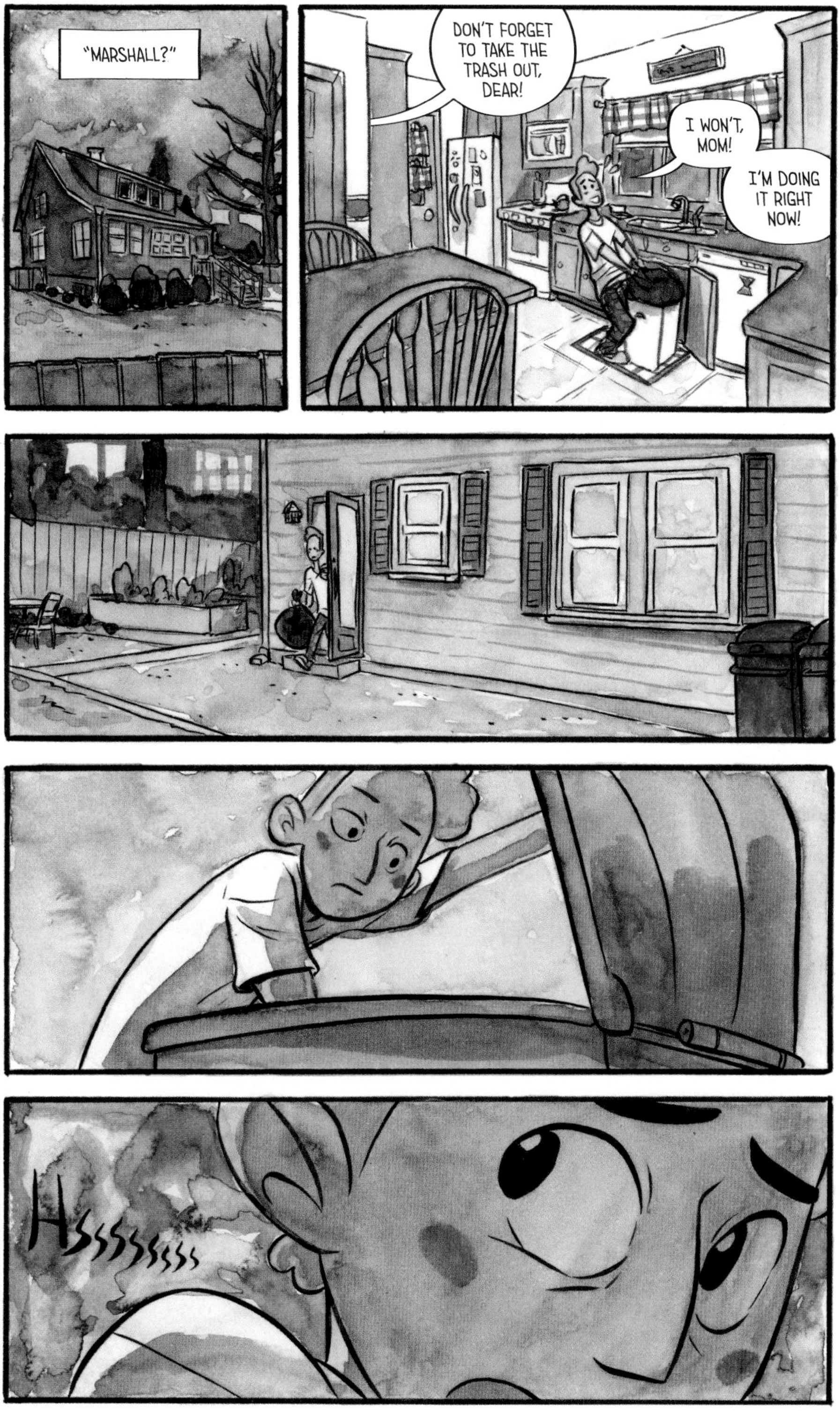

"MARSHALL?"
DON'T FORGET TO TAKE THE TRASH OUT, DEAR!
I WON'T, MOM!
I'M DOING IT RIGHT NOW!
Hsssssss

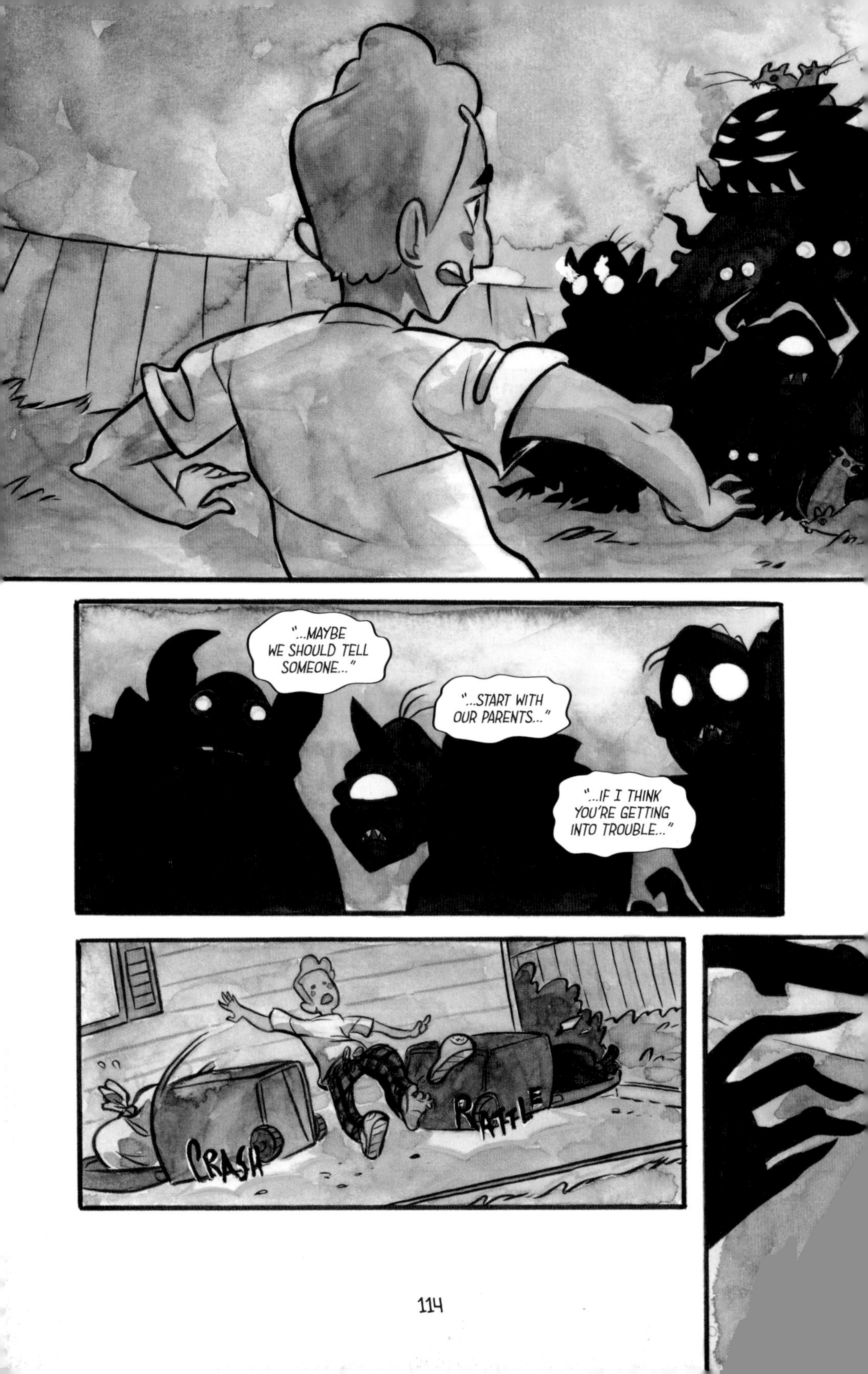
"...MAYBE WE SHOULD TELL SOMEONE..."
"...START WITH OUR PARENTS..."
"...IF I THINK YOU'RE GETTING INTO TROUBLE..."
CRASH
RATTLE

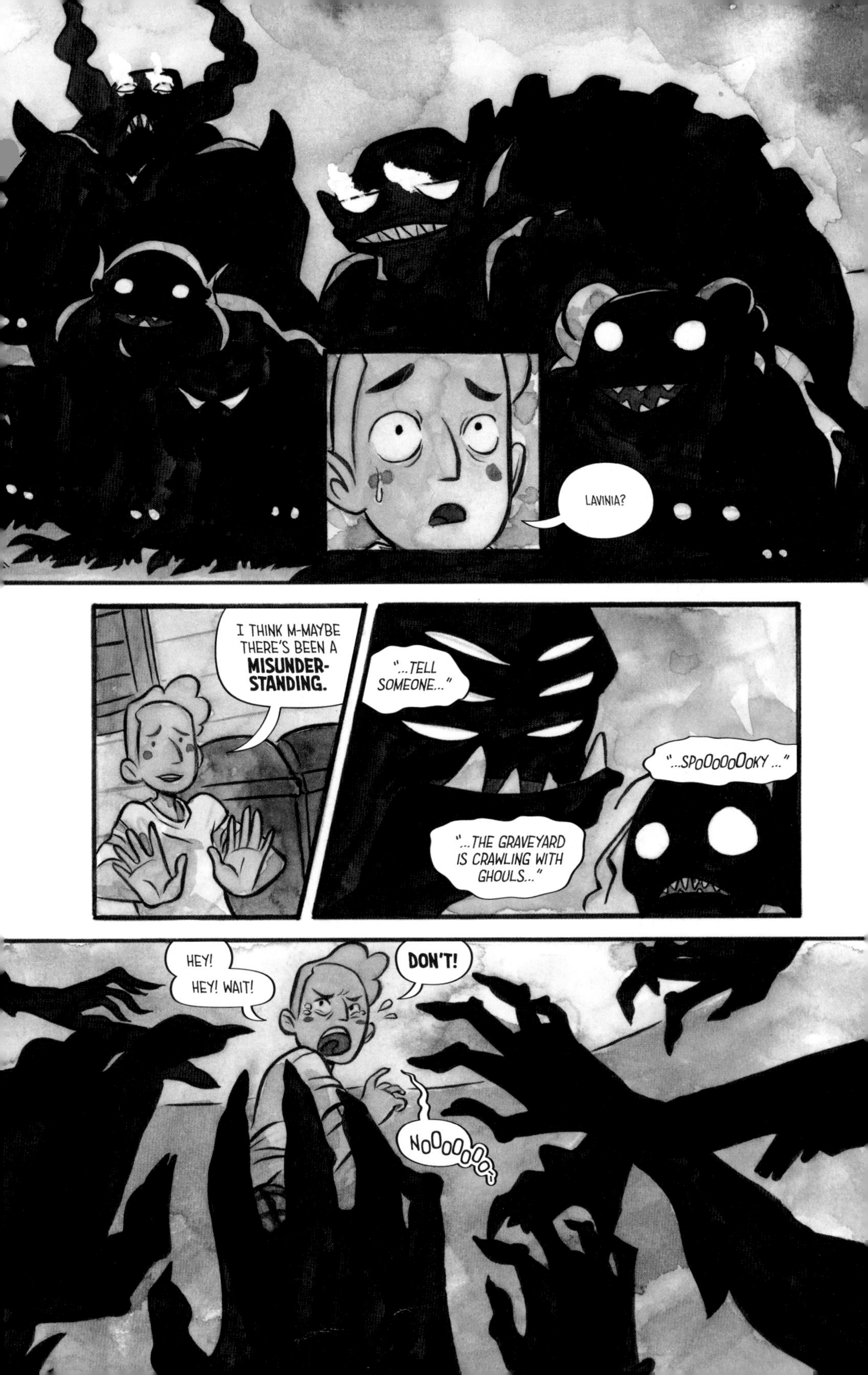
LAVINIA?
I THINK M-MAYBE THERE'S BEEN A MISUNDERSTANDING.
"...TELL SOMEONE..."
"...SPOOOOOOOKY ..."
"...THE GRAVEYARD IS CRAWLING WITH GHOULS..."
HEY!
HEY! WAIT!
DON'T!
NOOOOOOO-

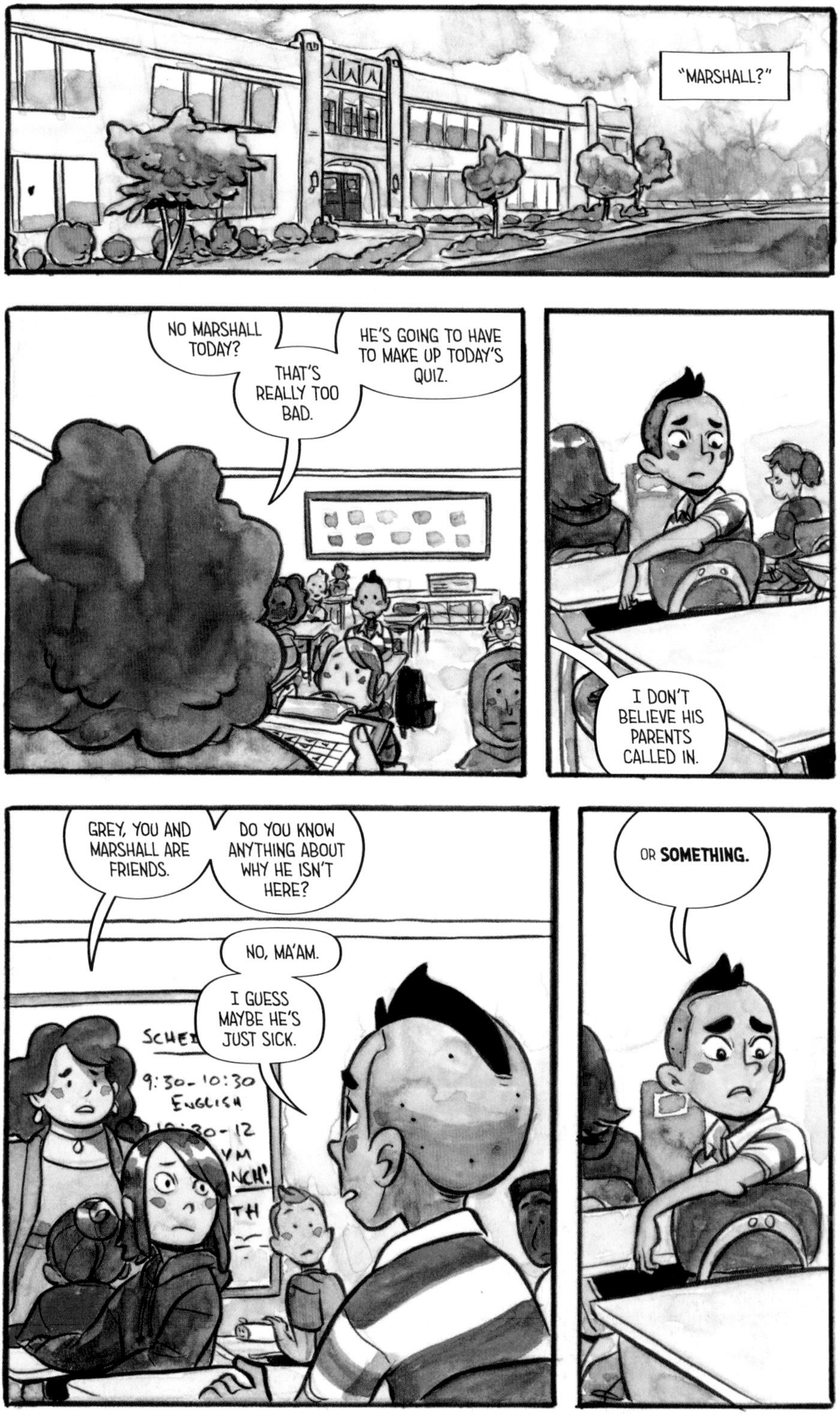
"MARSHALL?"
NO MARSHALL TODAY?
THAT'S REALLY TOO BAD.
HE'S GOING TO HAVE TO MAKE UP TODAY'S QUIZ.
I DON'T BELIEVE HIS PARENTS CALLED IN.
GREY, YOU AND MARSHALL ARE FRIENDS.
DO YOU KNOW ANYTHING ABOUT WHY HE ISN'T HERE?
NO, MA'AM.
I GUESS MAYBE HE'S JUST SICK.
OR **SOMETHING.**

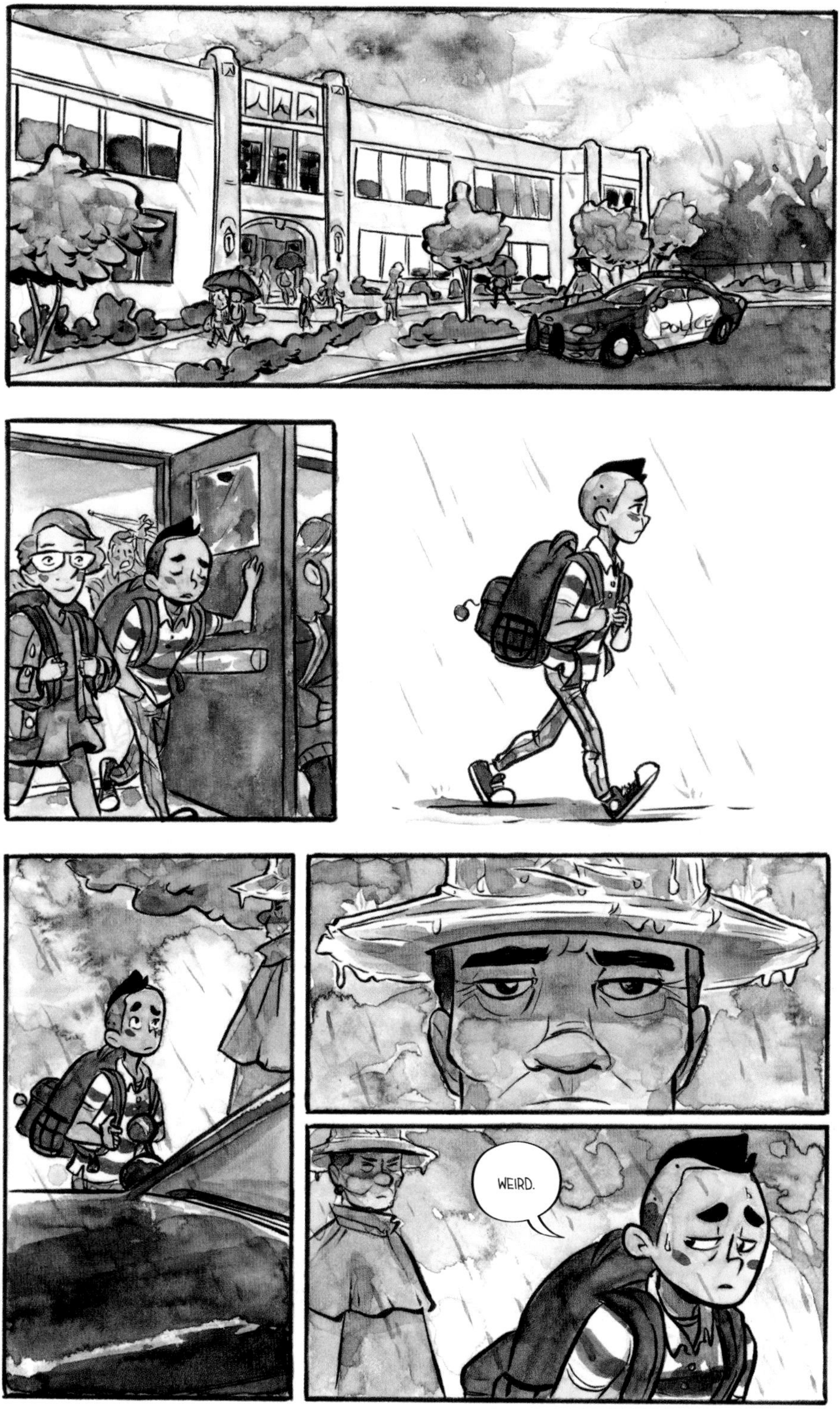
POLICE
WEIRD.

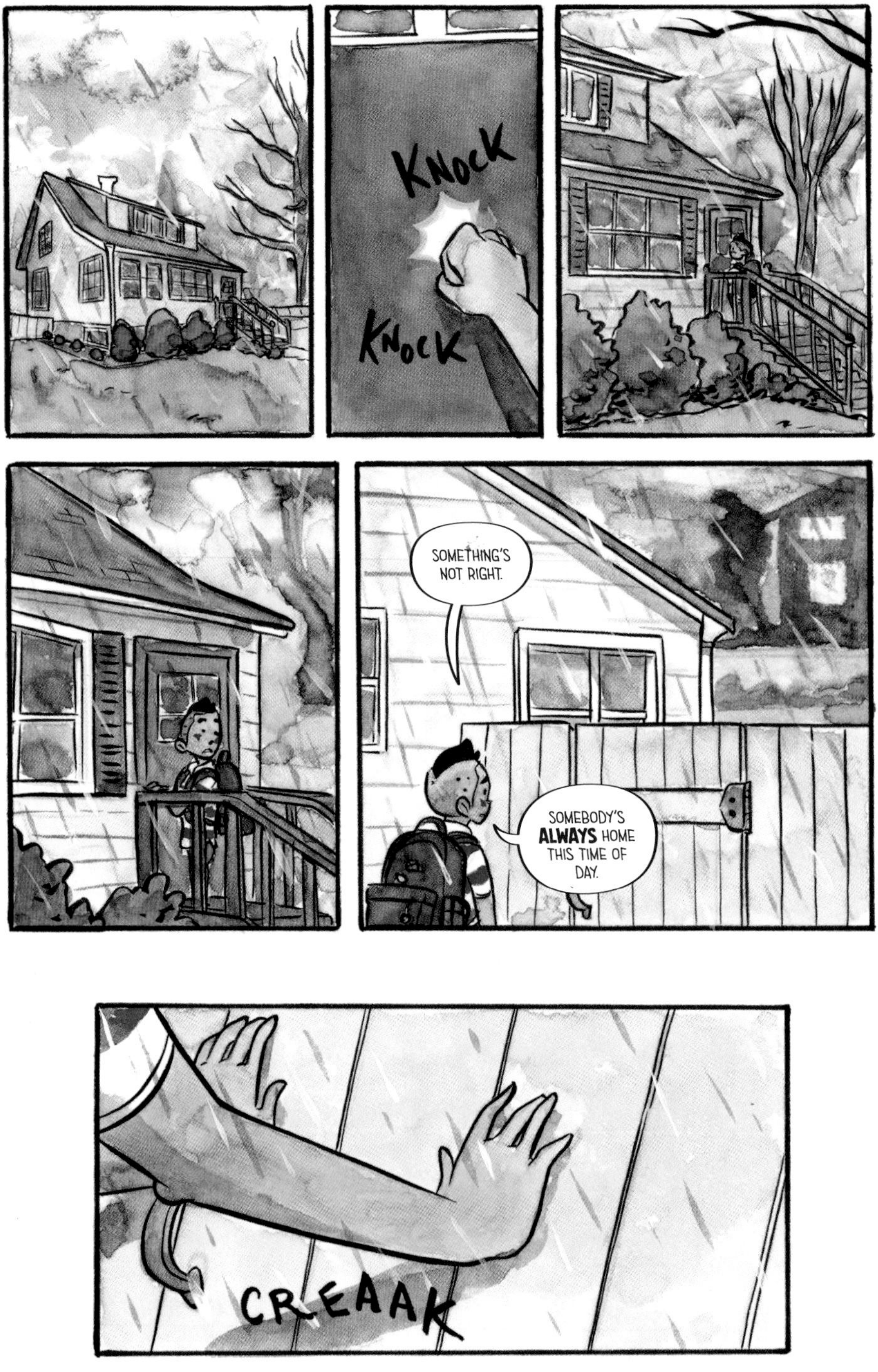
KNOCK
KNOCK
SOMETHING'S NOT RIGHT.
SOMEBODY'S **ALWAYS** HOME THIS TIME OF DAY.
CREAAK

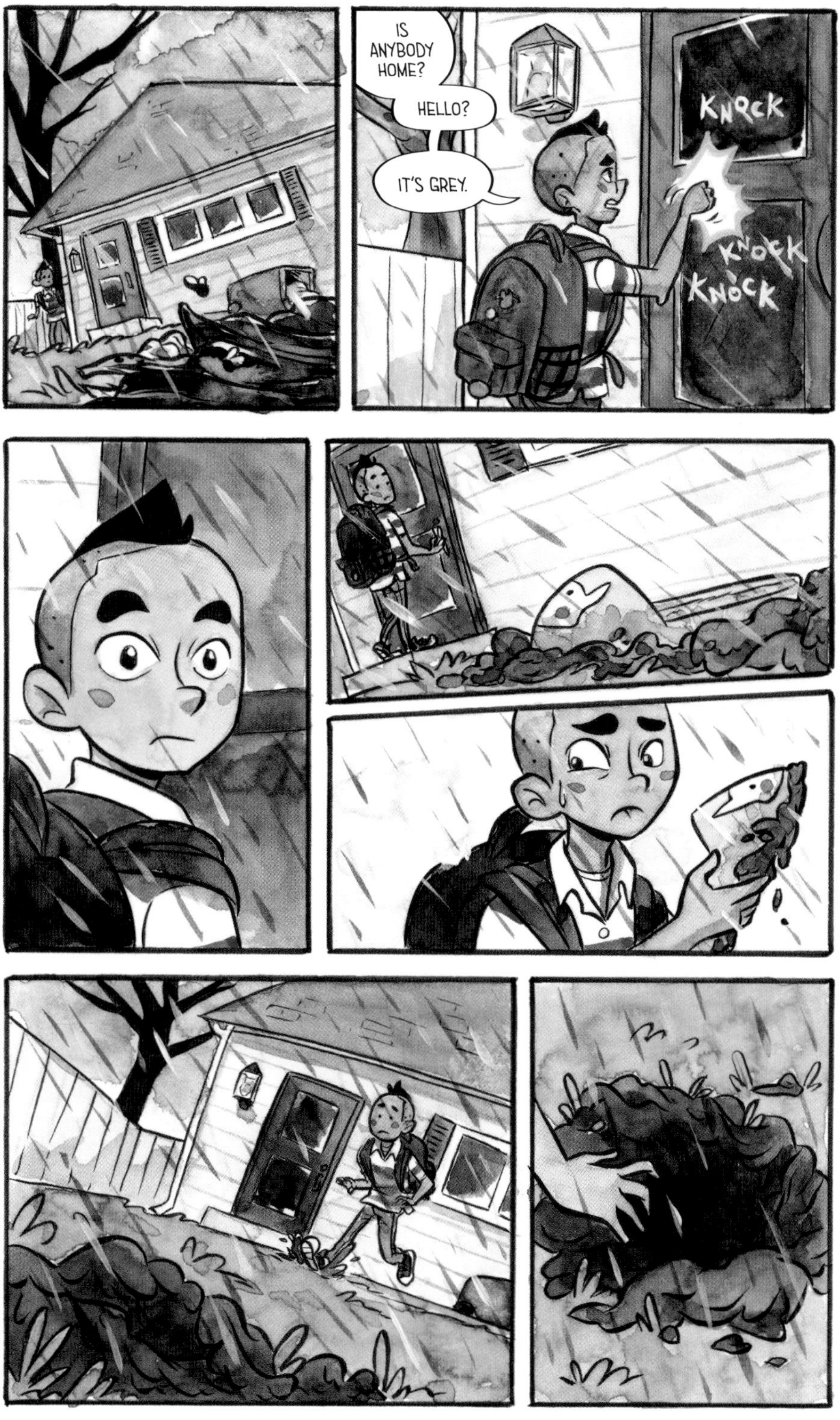
IS ANYBODY HOME?
HELLO?
IT'S GREY.
KNOCK
KNOCK
KNOCK

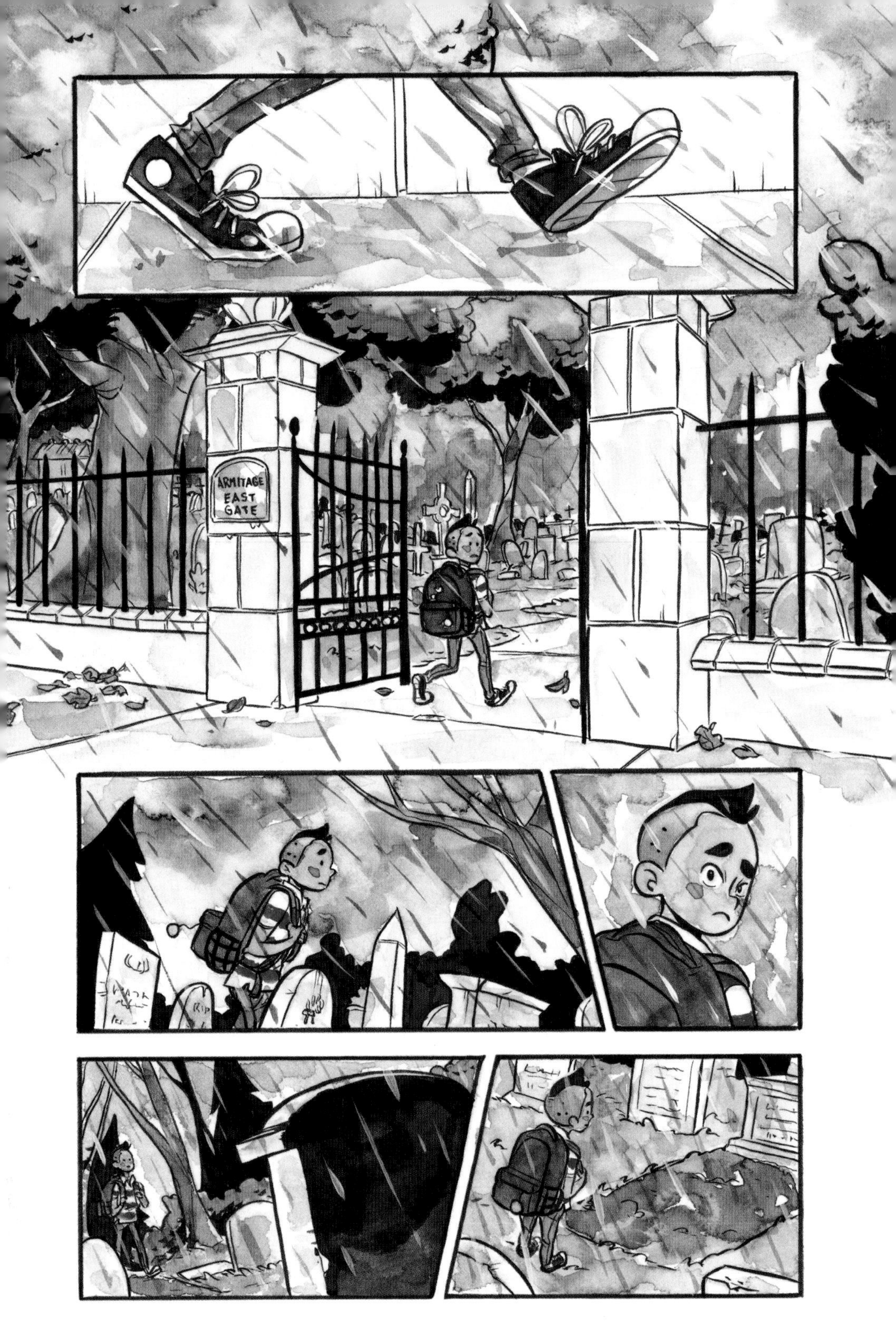
ARMITAGE
EAST
GATE

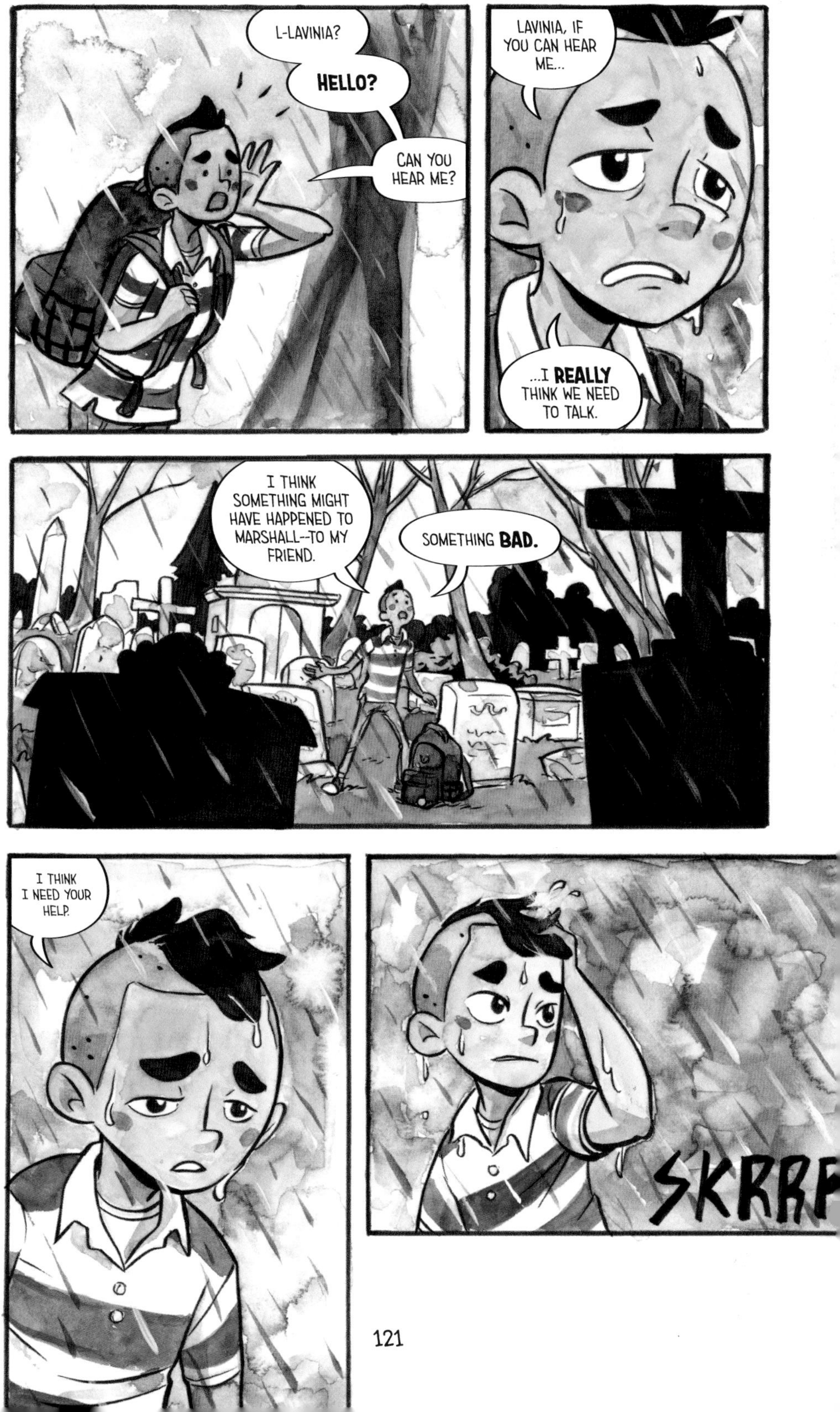
L-LAVINIA?
HELLO?
CAN YOU HEAR ME?
LAVINIA, IF YOU CAN HEAR ME...
...I **REALLY** THINK WE NEED TO TALK.
I THINK SOMETHING MIGHT HAVE HAPPENED TO MARSHALL--TO MY FRIEND.
SOMETHING **BAD.**
I THINK I NEED YOUR HELP.
SKRRF

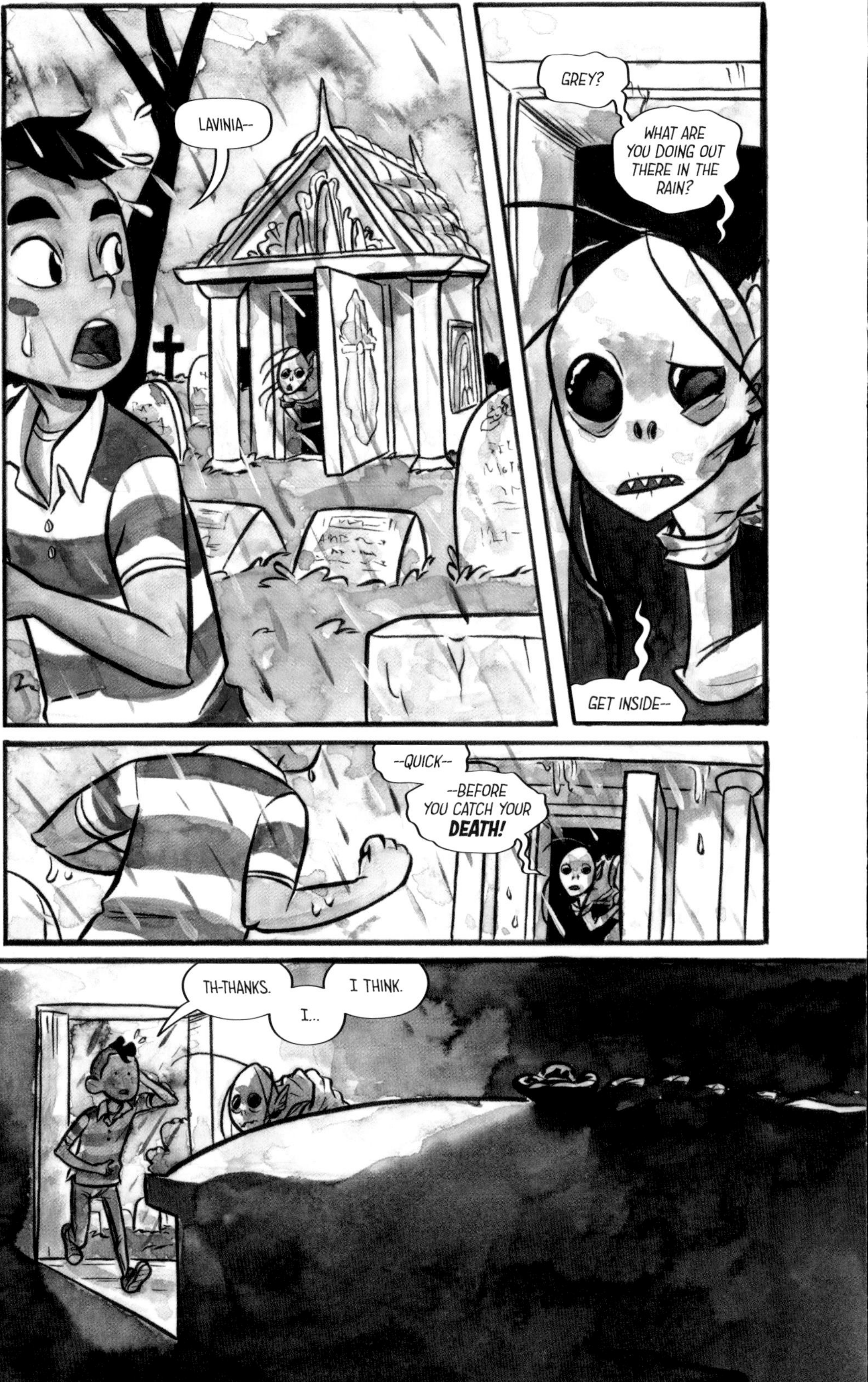
LAVINIA--
GREY?
WHAT ARE YOU DOING OUT THERE IN THE RAIN?
GET INSIDE--
--QUICK--
--BEFORE YOU CATCH YOUR **DEATH!**
TH-THANKS.
I...
I THINK.

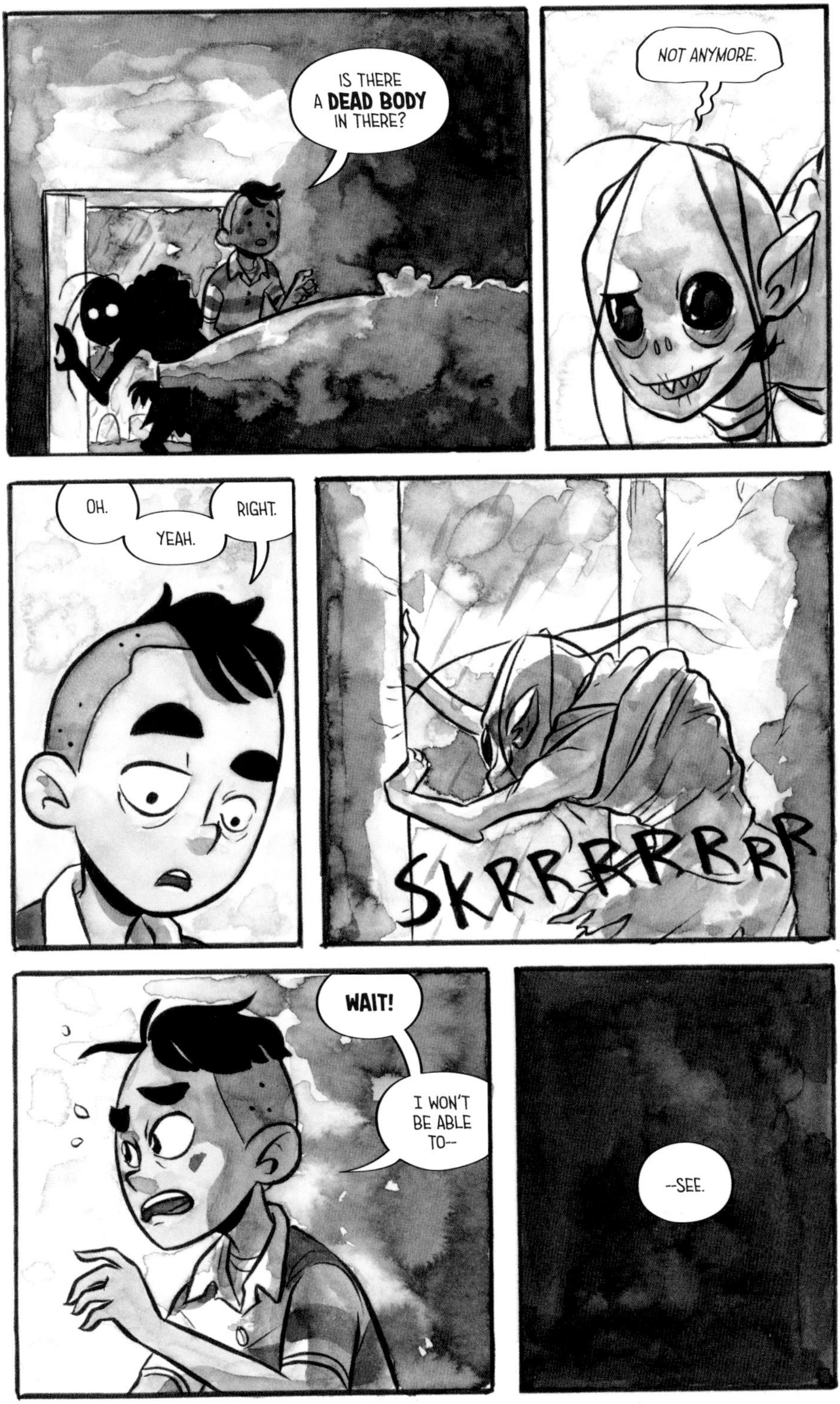
IS THERE A **DEAD BODY** IN THERE?
NOT ANYMORE.
OH.
YEAH.
RIGHT.
SKRRRRRRRR
WAIT!
I WON'T BE ABLE TO--
--SEE.

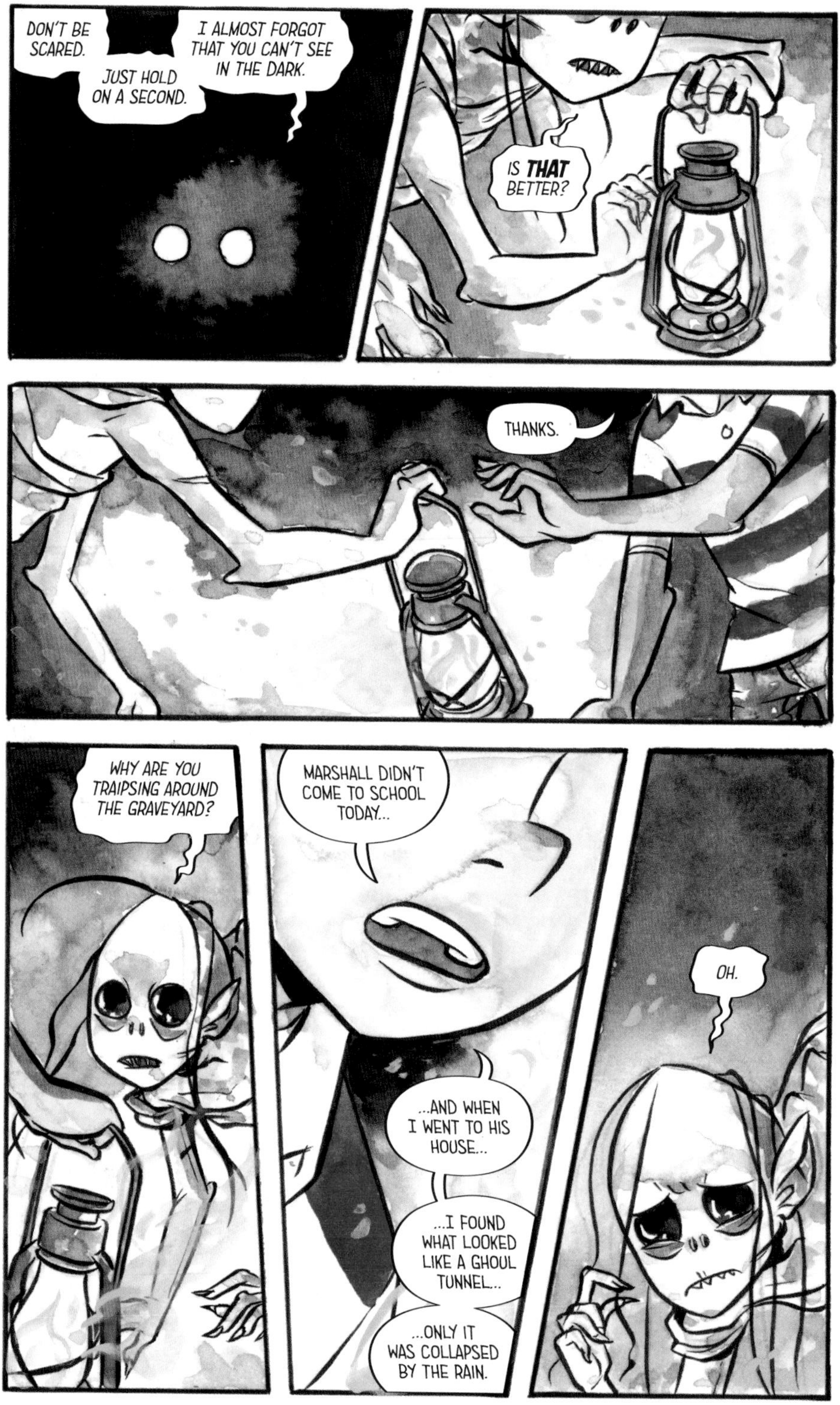
DON'T BE SCARED.
JUST HOLD ON A SECOND.
I ALMOST FORGOT THAT YOU CAN'T SEE IN THE DARK.
IS **THAT** BETTER?
THANKS.
WHY ARE YOU TRAIPSING AROUND THE GRAVEYARD?
MARSHALL DIDN'T COME TO SCHOOL TODAY...
...AND WHEN I WENT TO HIS HOUSE...
...I FOUND WHAT LOOKED LIKE A GHOUL TUNNEL...
...ONLY IT WAS COLLAPSED BY THE RAIN.
OH.

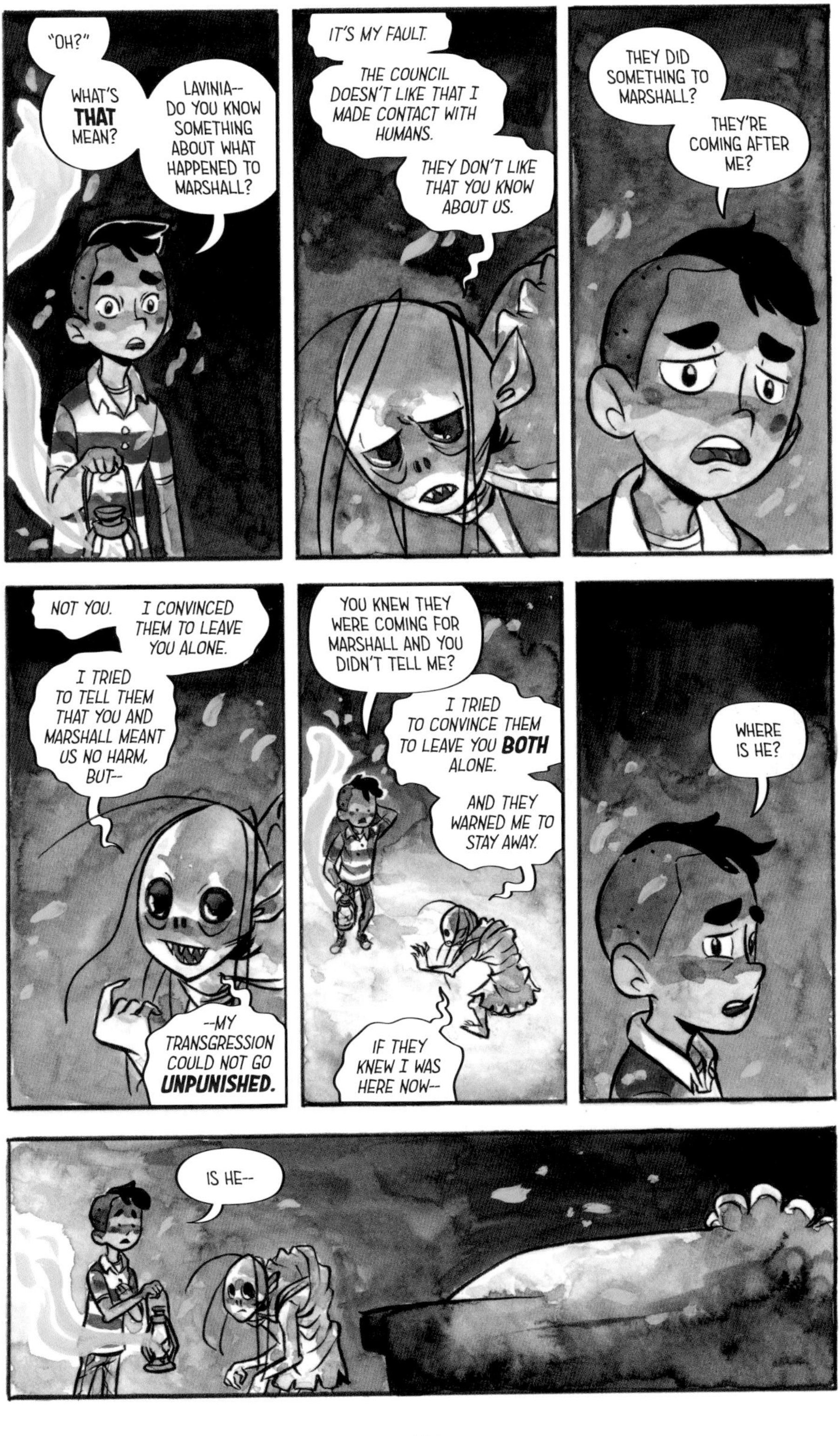
"OH?"
WHAT'S **THAT** MEAN?
LAVINIA-- DO YOU KNOW SOMETHING ABOUT WHAT HAPPENED TO MARSHALL?
IT'S MY FAULT.
THE COUNCIL DOESN'T LIKE THAT I MADE CONTACT WITH HUMANS.
THEY DON'T LIKE THAT YOU KNOW ABOUT US.
THEY DID SOMETHING TO MARSHALL?
THEY'RE COMING AFTER ME?
NOT YOU.
I CONVINCED THEM TO LEAVE YOU ALONE.
I TRIED TO TELL THEM THAT YOU AND MARSHALL MEANT US NO HARM, BUT--
--MY TRANSGRESSION COULD NOT GO **UNPUNISHED.**
YOU KNEW THEY WERE COMING FOR MARSHALL AND YOU DIDN'T TELL ME?
I TRIED TO CONVINCE THEM TO LEAVE YOU **BOTH** ALONE.
AND THEY WARNED ME TO STAY AWAY.
IF THEY KNEW I WAS HERE NOW--
WHERE IS HE?
IS HE--

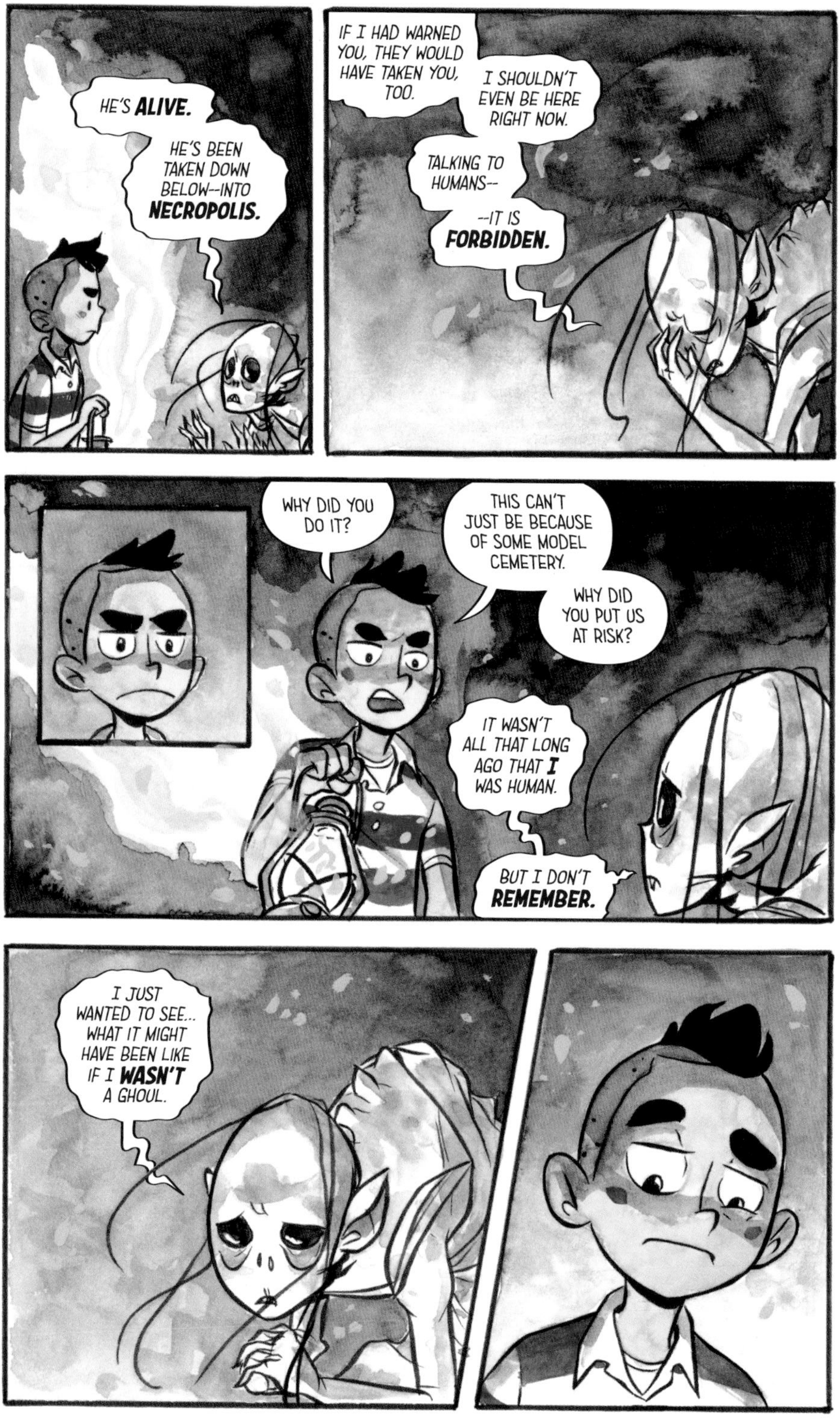
HE'S **ALIVE.**
HE'S BEEN TAKEN DOWN BELOW--INTO **NECROPOLIS.**
IF I HAD WARNED YOU, THEY WOULD HAVE TAKEN YOU, TOO.
I SHOULDN'T EVEN BE HERE RIGHT NOW.
TALKING TO HUMANS--
--IT IS **FORBIDDEN.**
WHY DID YOU DO IT?
THIS CAN'T JUST BE BECAUSE OF SOME MODEL CEMETERY.
WHY DID YOU PUT US AT RISK?
IT WASN'T ALL THAT LONG AGO THAT **I** WAS HUMAN.
BUT I DON'T **REMEMBER.**
I JUST WANTED TO SEE... WHAT IT MIGHT HAVE BEEN LIKE IF I **WASN'T** A GHOUL.

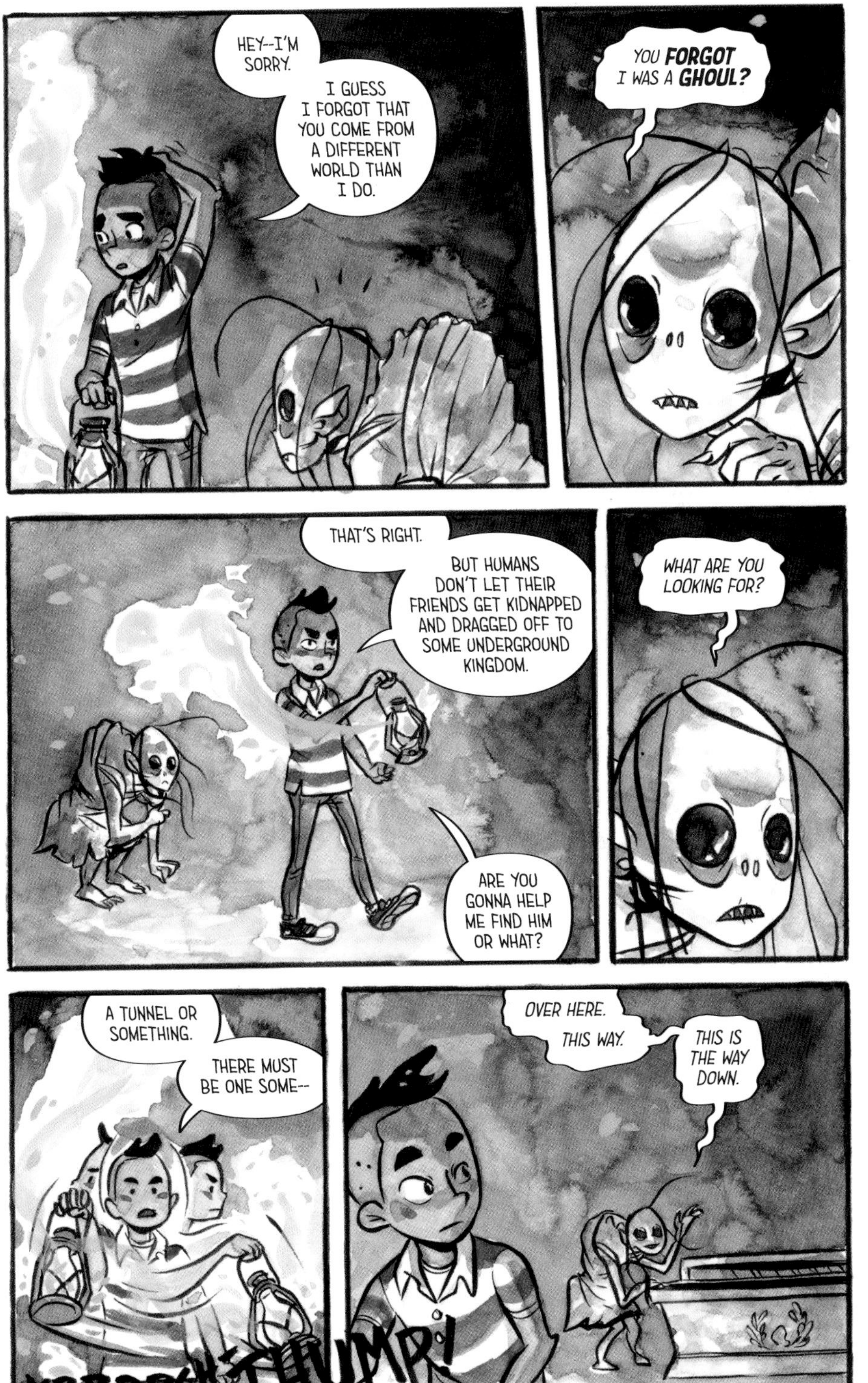
HEY--I'M SORRY.
I GUESS I FORGOT THAT YOU COME FROM A DIFFERENT WORLD THAN I DO.
YOU **FORGOT** I WAS A **GHOUL?**
THAT'S RIGHT.
BUT HUMANS DON'T LET THEIR FRIENDS GET KIDNAPPED AND DRAGGED OFF TO SOME UNDERGROUND KINGDOM.
ARE YOU GONNA HELP ME FIND HIM OR WHAT?
WHAT ARE YOU LOOKING FOR?
A TUNNEL OR SOMETHING.
THERE MUST BE ONE SOME--
KRRRRSH THUMP!
OVER HERE.
THIS WAY.
THIS IS THE WAY DOWN.

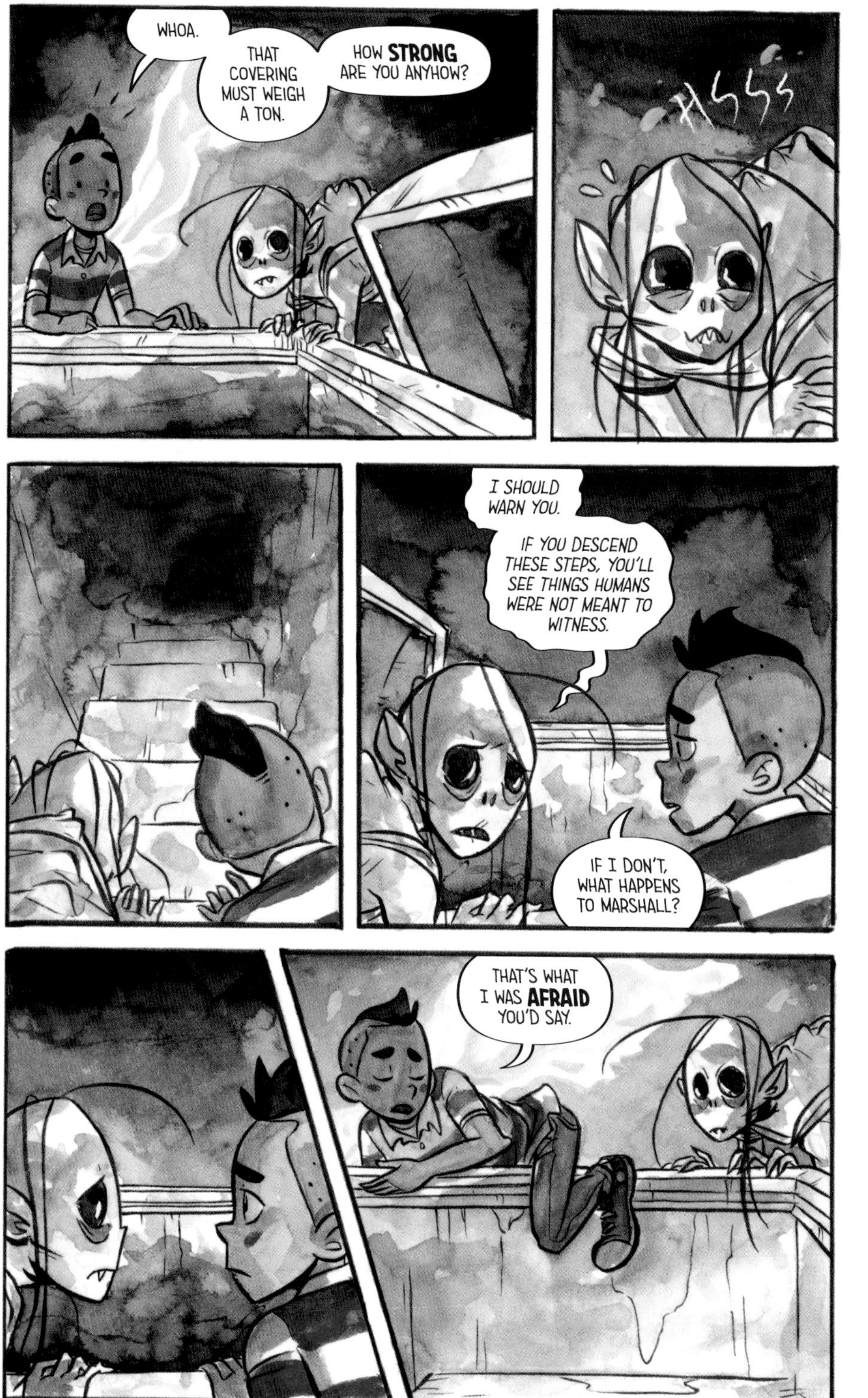
WHOA.
THAT COVERING MUST WEIGH A TON.
HOW **STRONG** ARE YOU ANYHOW?
HSSS
I SHOULD WARN YOU.
IF YOU DESCEND THESE STEPS, YOU'LL SEE THINGS HUMANS WERE NOT MEANT TO WITNESS.
IF I DON'T, WHAT HAPPENS TO MARSHALL?
THAT'S WHAT I WAS **AFRAID** YOU'D SAY.

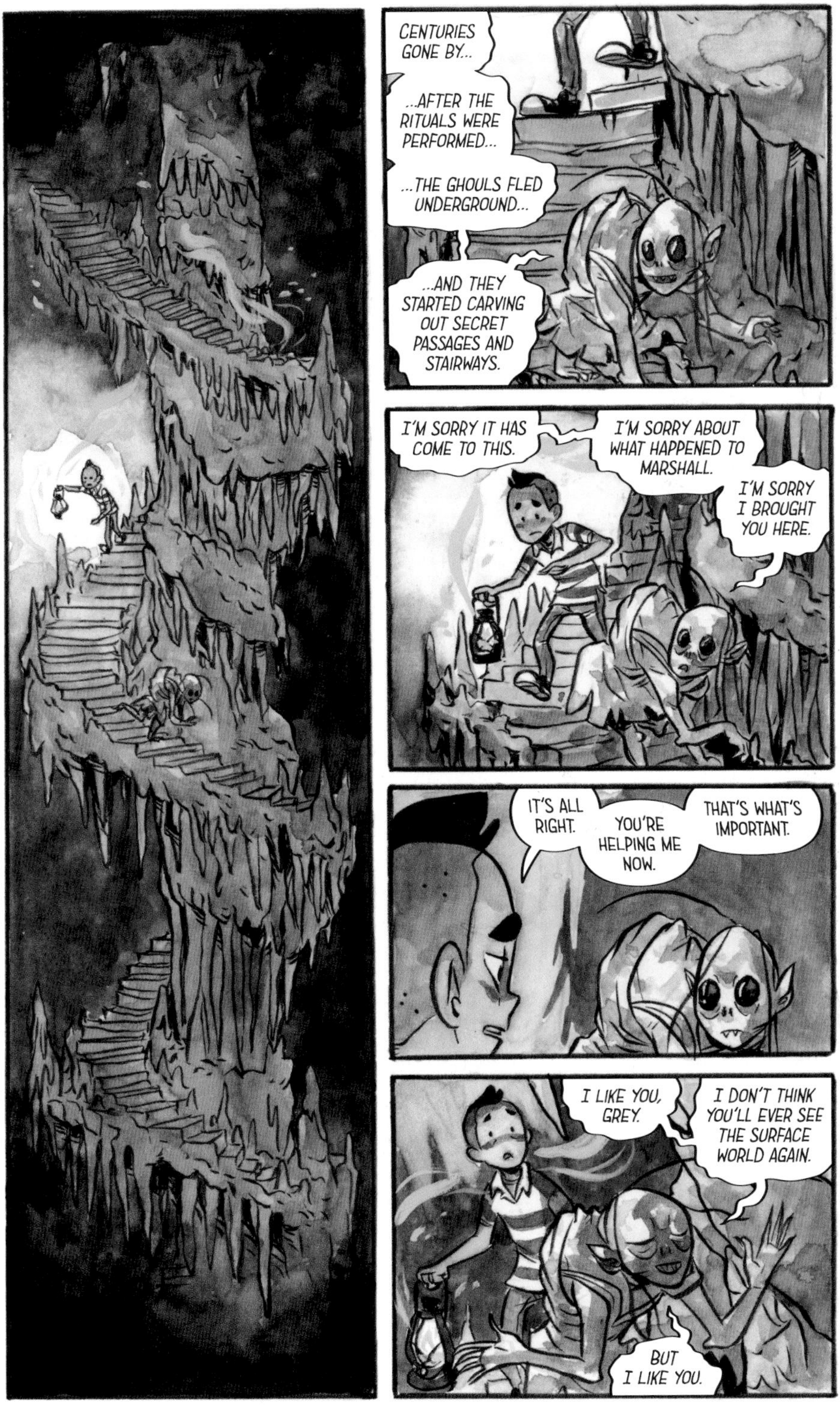
CENTURIES GONE BY...
...AFTER THE RITUALS WERE PERFORMED...
...THE GHOULS FLED UNDERGROUND...
...AND THEY STARTED CARVING OUT SECRET PASSAGES AND STAIRWAYS.
I'M SORRY IT HAS COME TO THIS.
I'M SORRY ABOUT WHAT HAPPENED TO MARSHALL.
I'M SORRY I BROUGHT YOU HERE.
IT'S ALL RIGHT.
YOU'RE HELPING ME NOW.
THAT'S WHAT'S IMPORTANT.
I LIKE YOU, GREY.
I DON'T THINK YOU'LL EVER SEE THE SURFACE WORLD AGAIN.
BUT I LIKE YOU.

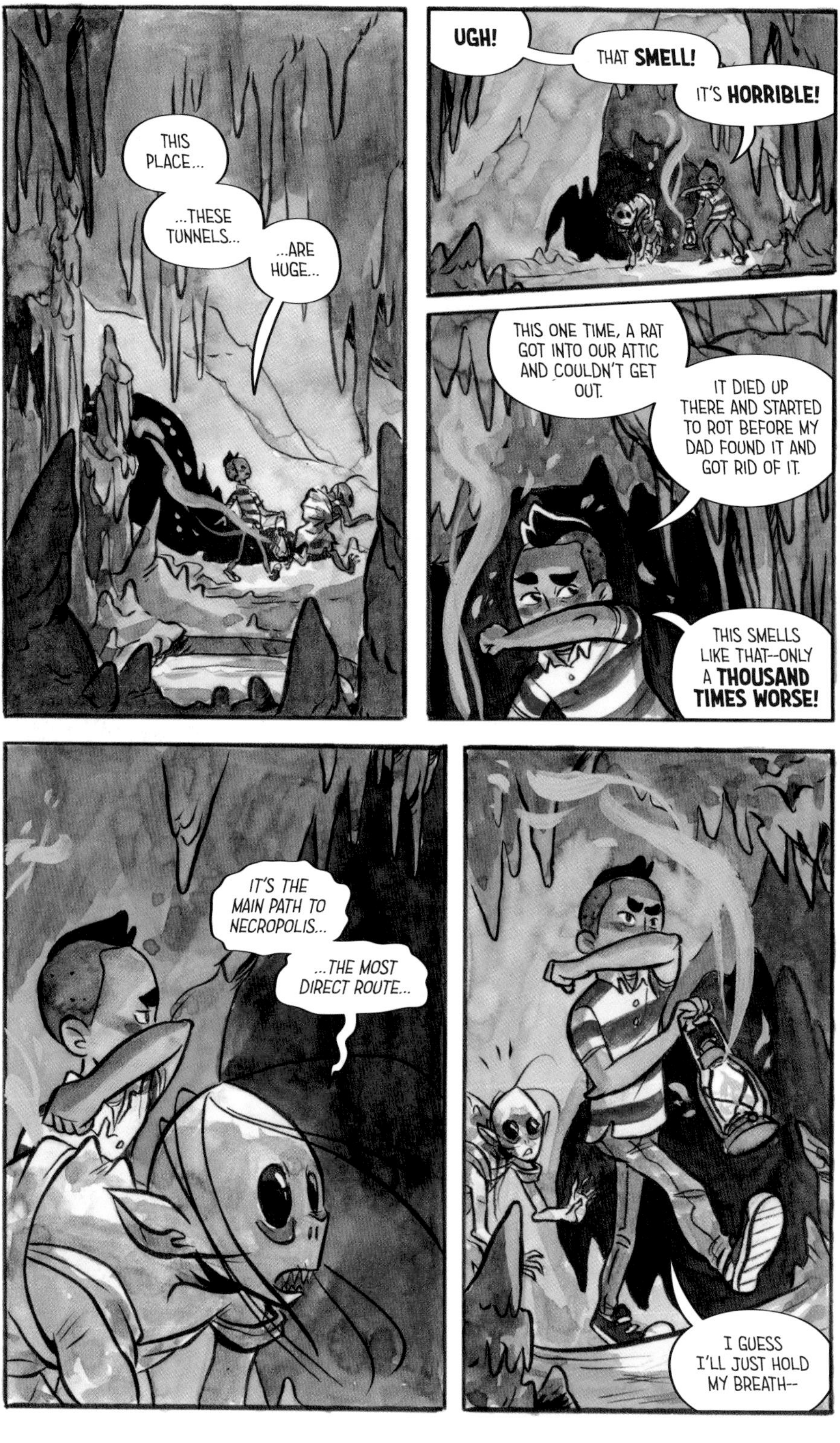
THIS PLACE...
...THESE TUNNELS...
...ARE HUGE...
UGH!
THAT SMELL!
IT'S HORRIBLE!
THIS ONE TIME, A RAT GOT INTO OUR ATTIC AND COULDN'T GET OUT.
IT DIED UP THERE AND STARTED TO ROT BEFORE MY DAD FOUND IT AND GOT RID OF IT.
THIS SMELLS LIKE THAT--ONLY A THOUSAND TIMES WORSE!
IT'S THE MAIN PATH TO NECROPOLIS...
...THE MOST DIRECT ROUTE...
I GUESS I'LL JUST HOLD MY BREATH--

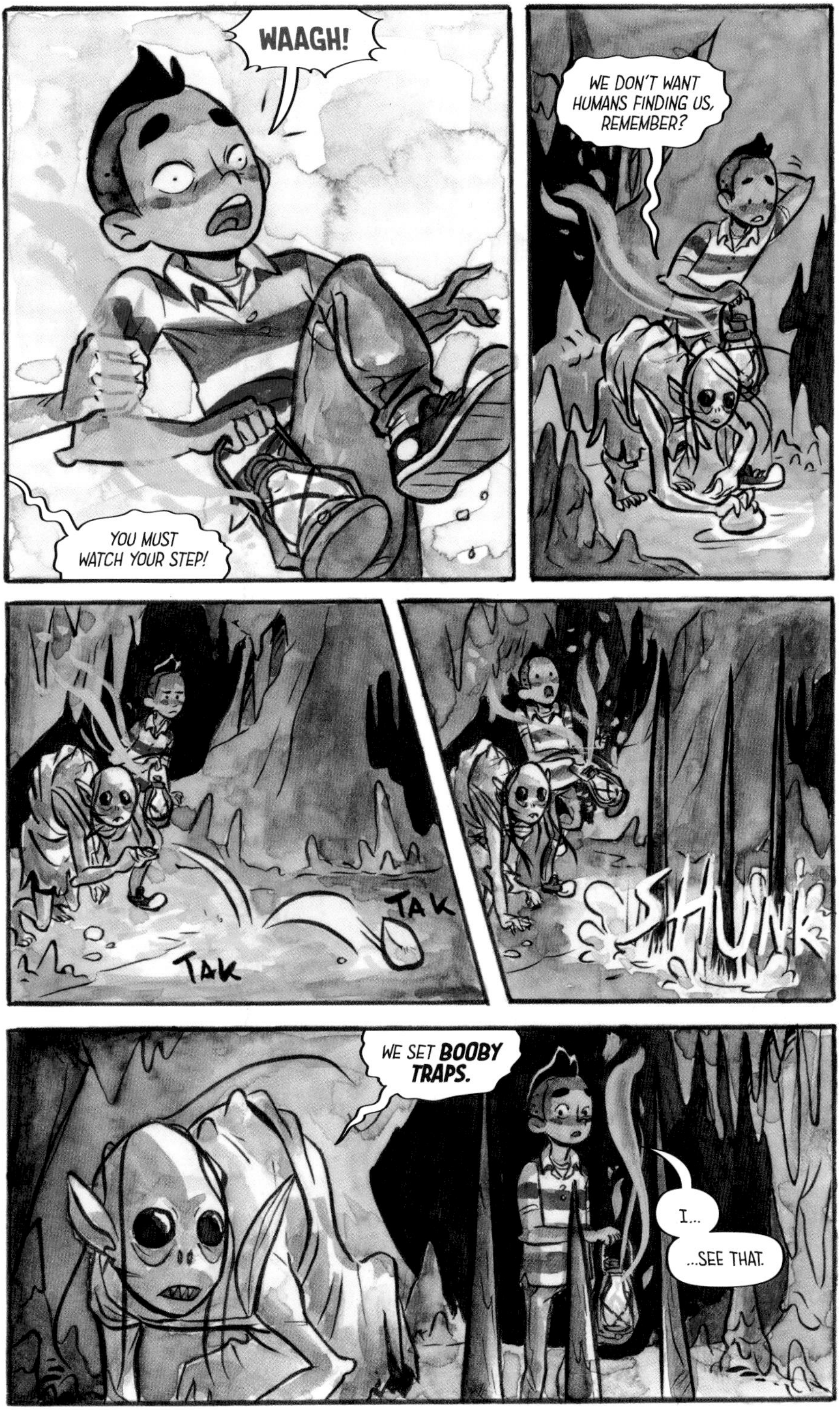
WAAGH!
YOU MUST WATCH YOUR STEP!
WE DON'T WANT HUMANS FINDING US, REMEMBER?
TAK
TAK
SHUNK
WE SET **BOOBY TRAPS.**
I...
...SEE THAT.

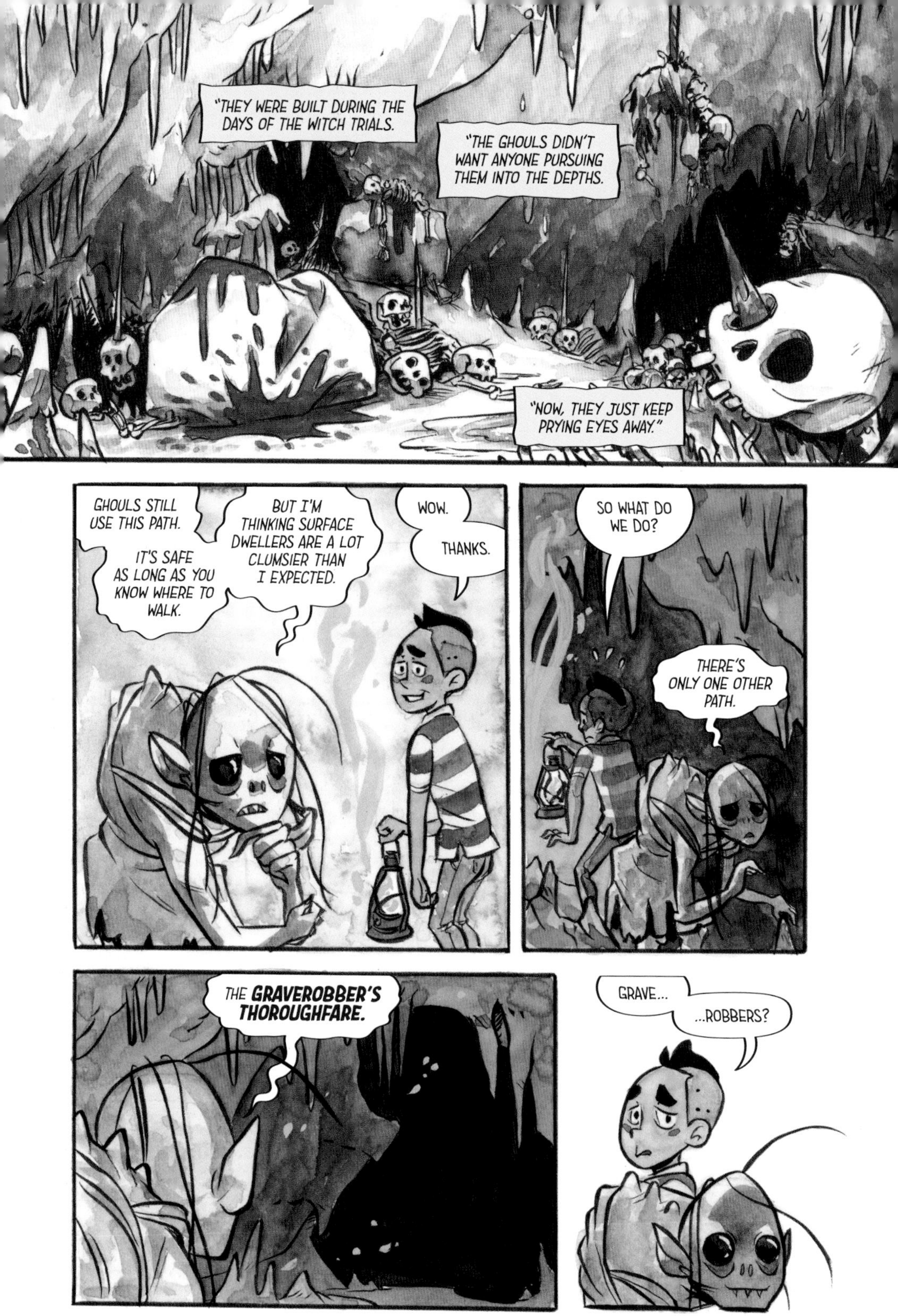
"THEY WERE BUILT DURING THE DAYS OF THE WITCH TRIALS.
"THE GHOULS DIDN'T WANT ANYONE PURSUING THEM INTO THE DEPTHS.
"NOW, THEY JUST KEEP PRYING EYES AWAY."
GHOULS STILL USE THIS PATH.
IT'S SAFE AS LONG AS YOU KNOW WHERE TO WALK.
BUT I'M THINKING SURFACE DWELLERS ARE A LOT CLUMSIER THAN I EXPECTED.
WOW.
THANKS.
SO WHAT DO WE DO?
THERE'S ONLY ONE OTHER PATH.
THE **GRAVEROBBER'S THOROUGHFARE.**
GRAVE...
...ROBBERS?

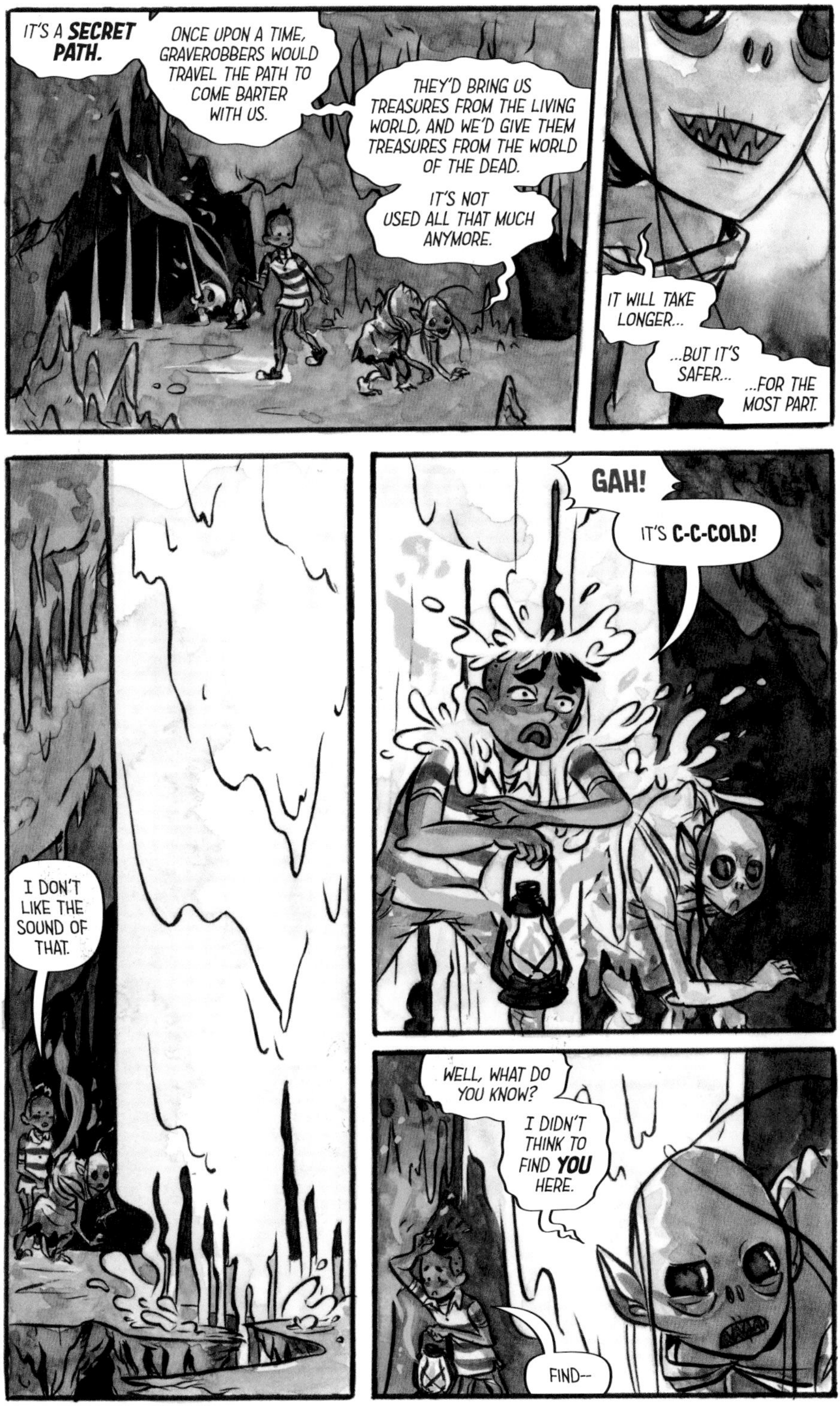

IT'S A **SECRET PATH.**
ONCE UPON A TIME, GRAVEROBBERS WOULD TRAVEL THE PATH TO COME BARTER WITH US.
THEY'D BRING US TREASURES FROM THE LIVING WORLD, AND WE'D GIVE THEM TREASURES FROM THE WORLD OF THE DEAD.
IT'S NOT USED ALL THAT MUCH ANYMORE.
IT WILL TAKE LONGER...
...BUT IT'S SAFER...
...FOR THE MOST PART.
I DON'T LIKE THE SOUND OF THAT.
GAH!
IT'S **C-C-COLD!**
WELL, WHAT DO YOU KNOW?
I DIDN'T THINK TO FIND **YOU** HERE.
FIND--

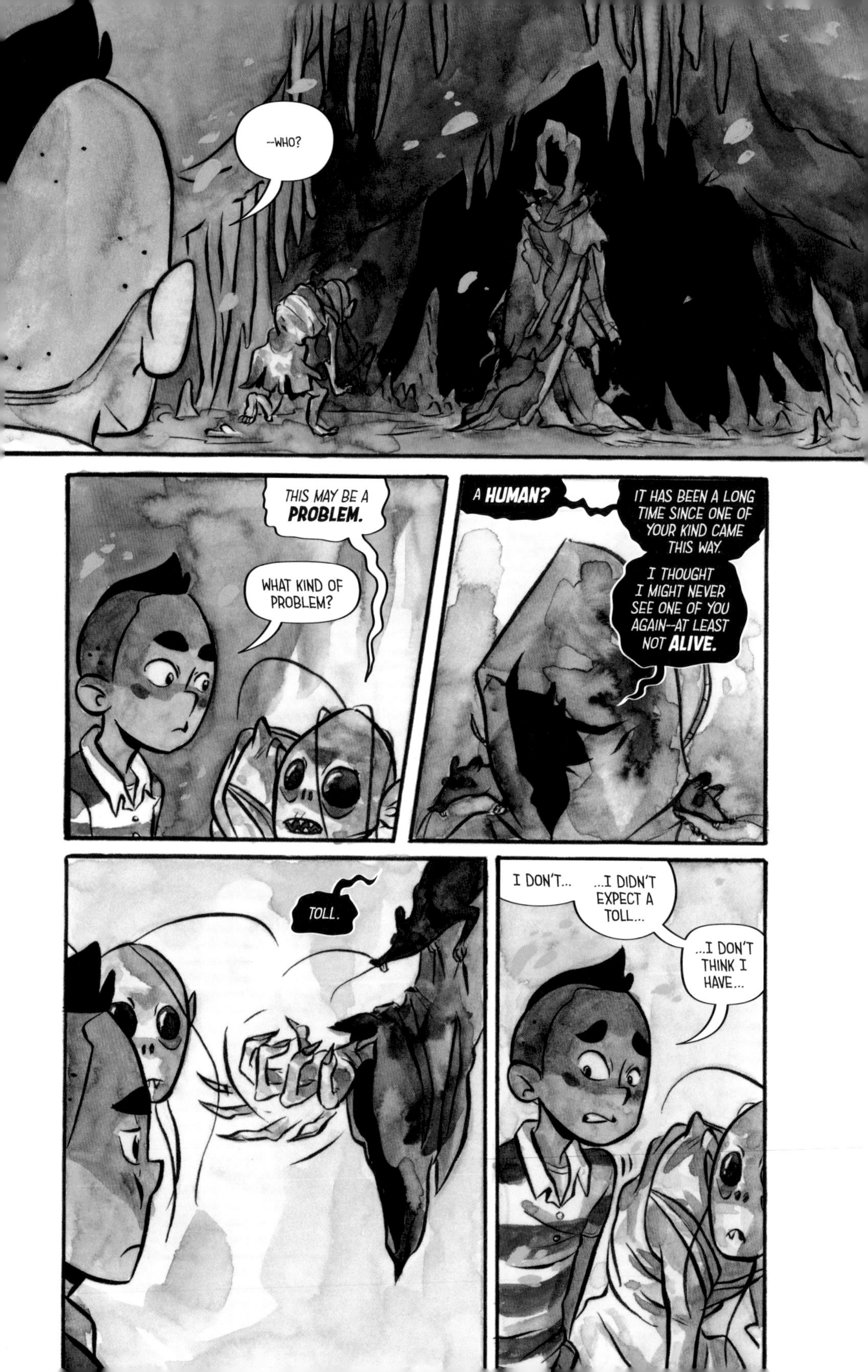
--WHO?
THIS MAY BE A PROBLEM.
WHAT KIND OF PROBLEM?
A HUMAN?
IT HAS BEEN A LONG TIME SINCE ONE OF YOUR KIND CAME THIS WAY.
I THOUGHT I MIGHT NEVER SEE ONE OF YOU AGAIN--AT LEAST NOT ALIVE.
TOLL.
I DON'T...
...I DIDN'T EXPECT A TOLL...
...I DON'T THINK I HAVE...

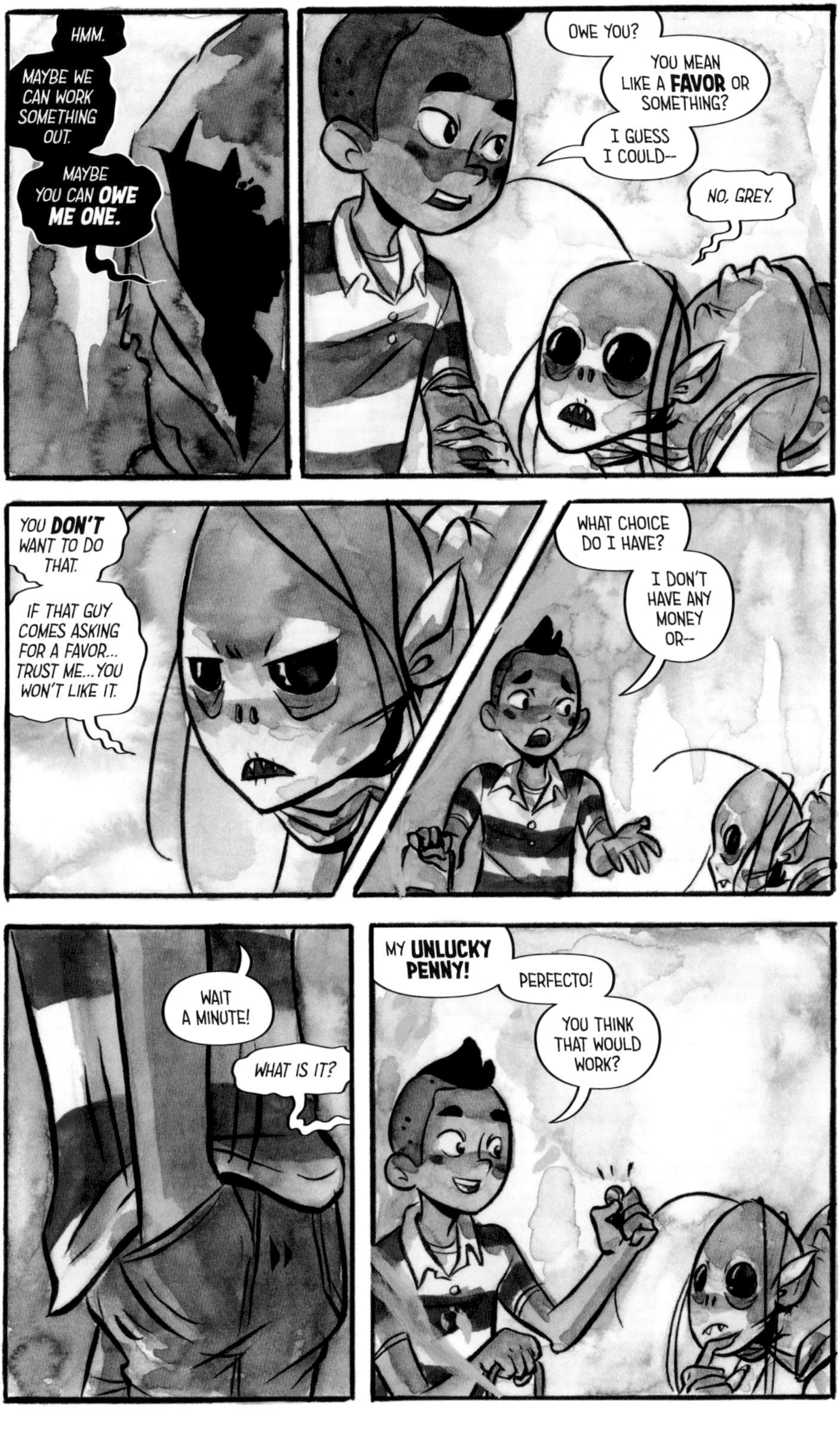
HMM.
MAYBE WE CAN WORK SOMETHING OUT.
MAYBE YOU CAN **OWE ME ONE.**
OWE YOU?
YOU MEAN LIKE A **FAVOR** OR SOMETHING?
I GUESS I COULD--
NO, GREY.
YOU **DON'T** WANT TO DO THAT.
IF THAT GUY COMES ASKING FOR A FAVOR... TRUST ME...YOU WON'T LIKE IT.
WHAT CHOICE DO I HAVE?
I DON'T HAVE ANY MONEY OR--
WAIT A MINUTE!
WHAT IS IT?
MY **UNLUCKY PENNY!**
PERFECTO!
YOU THINK THAT WOULD WORK?

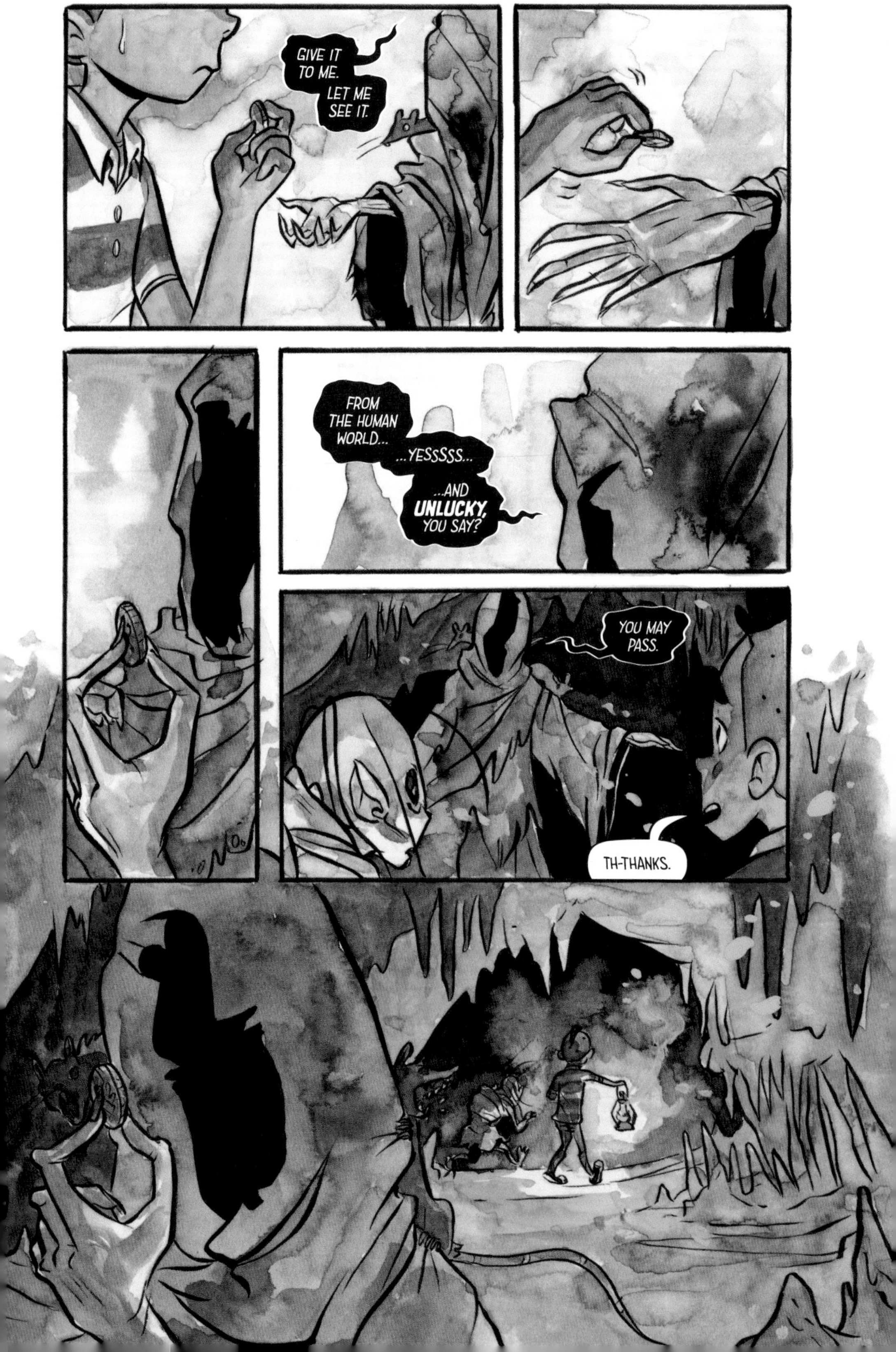
GIVE IT TO ME.
LET ME SEE IT.
FROM THE HUMAN WORLD...
...YESSSSS...
...AND **UNLUCKY,** YOU SAY?
YOU MAY PASS.
TH-THANKS.

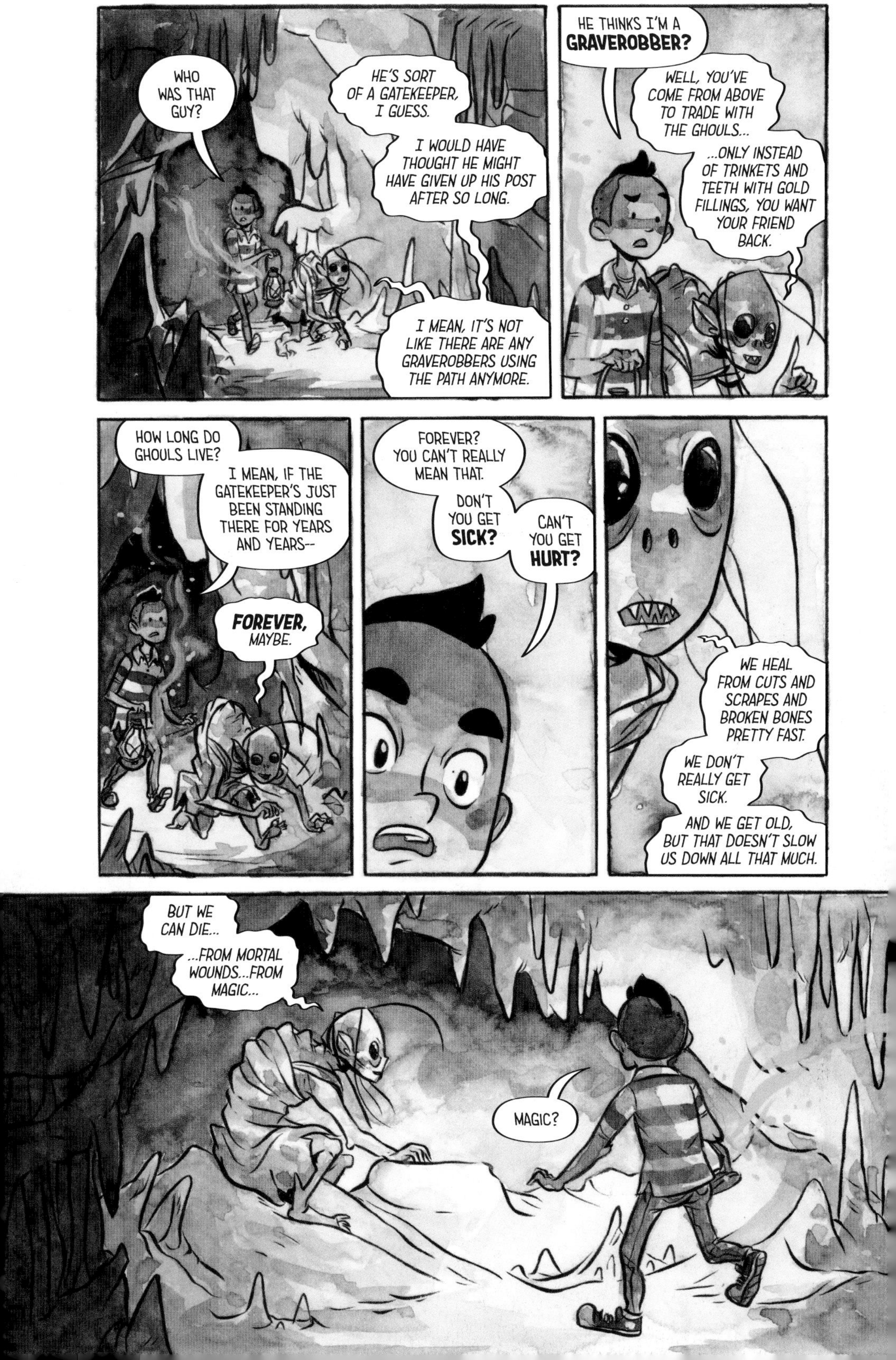
WHO WAS THAT GUY?
HE'S SORT OF A GATEKEEPER, I GUESS.
I WOULD HAVE THOUGHT HE MIGHT HAVE GIVEN UP HIS POST AFTER SO LONG.
I MEAN, IT'S NOT LIKE THERE ARE ANY GRAVEROBBERS USING THE PATH ANYMORE.
HE THINKS I'M A **GRAVEROBBER?**
WELL, YOU'VE COME FROM ABOVE TO TRADE WITH THE GHOULS...
...ONLY INSTEAD OF TRINKETS AND TEETH WITH GOLD FILLINGS, YOU WANT YOUR FRIEND BACK.
HOW LONG DO GHOULS LIVE?
I MEAN, IF THE GATEKEEPER'S JUST BEEN STANDING THERE FOR YEARS AND YEARS--
FOREVER, MAYBE.
FOREVER? YOU CAN'T REALLY MEAN THAT.
DON'T YOU GET **SICK?**
CAN'T YOU GET **HURT?**
WE HEAL FROM CUTS AND SCRAPES AND BROKEN BONES PRETTY FAST.
WE DON'T REALLY GET SICK.
AND WE GET OLD, BUT THAT DOESN'T SLOW US DOWN ALL THAT MUCH.
BUT WE CAN DIE...
...FROM MORTAL WOUNDS...FROM MAGIC...
MAGIC?

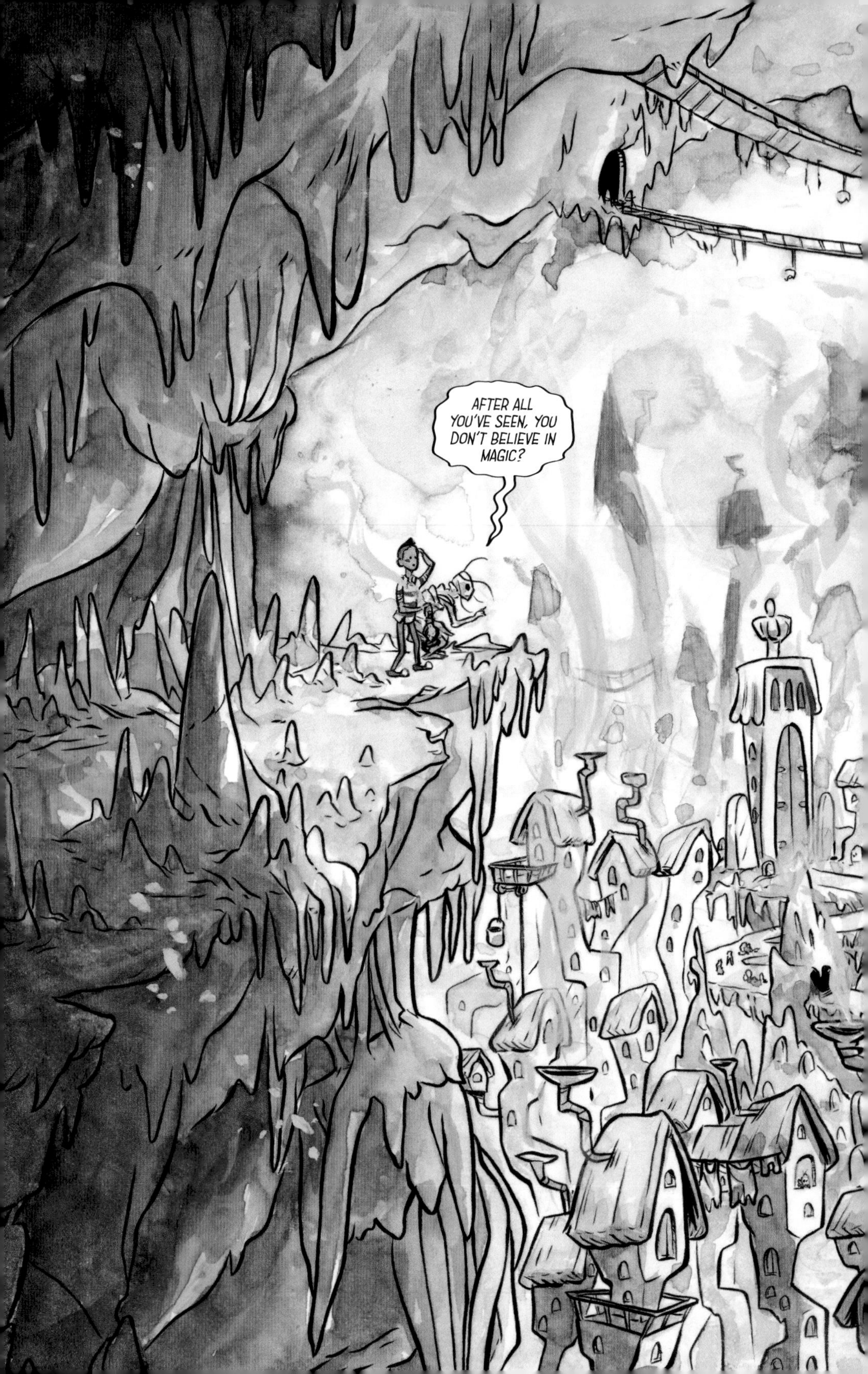
AFTER ALL YOU'VE SEEN, YOU DON'T BELIEVE IN MAGIC?

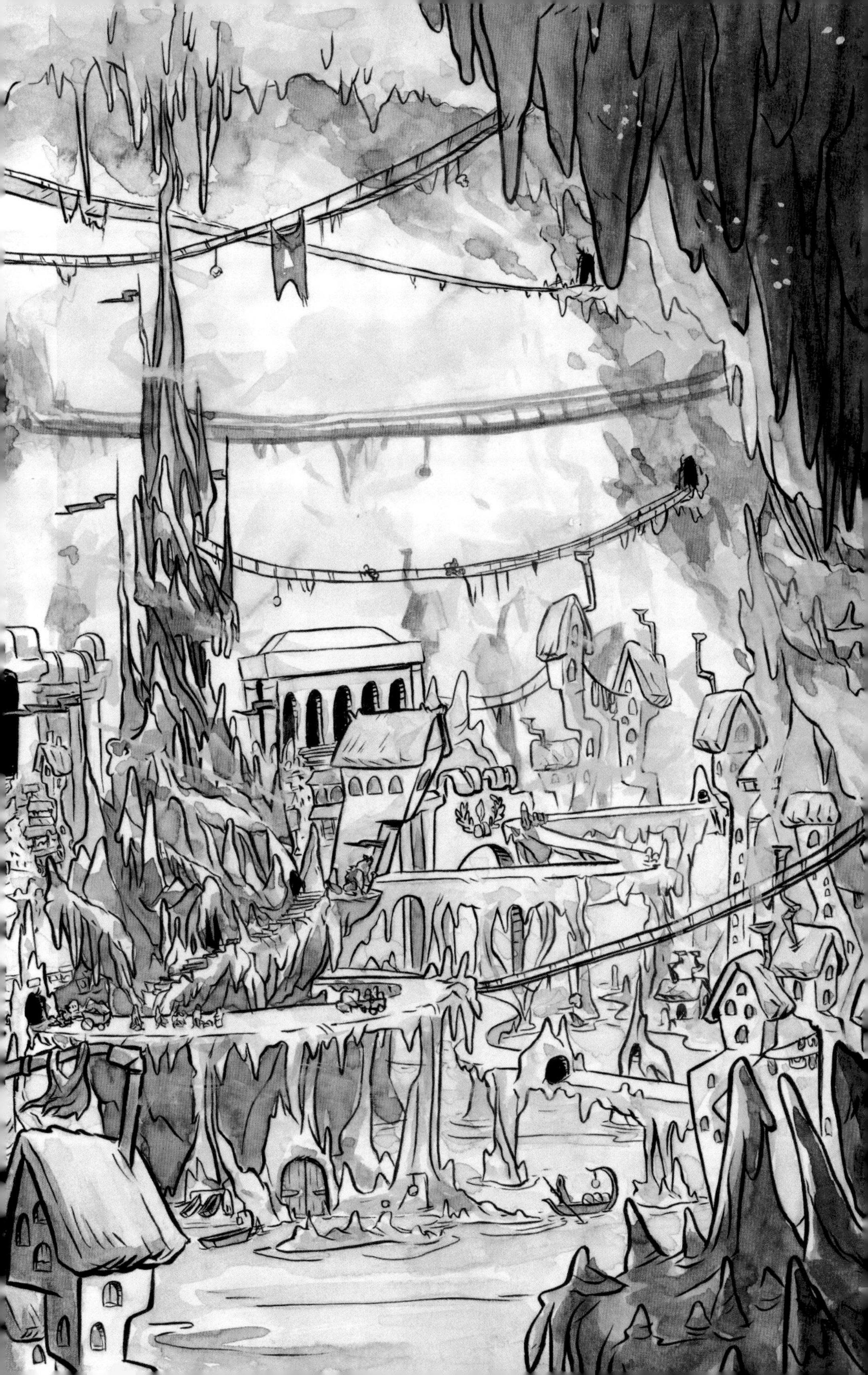

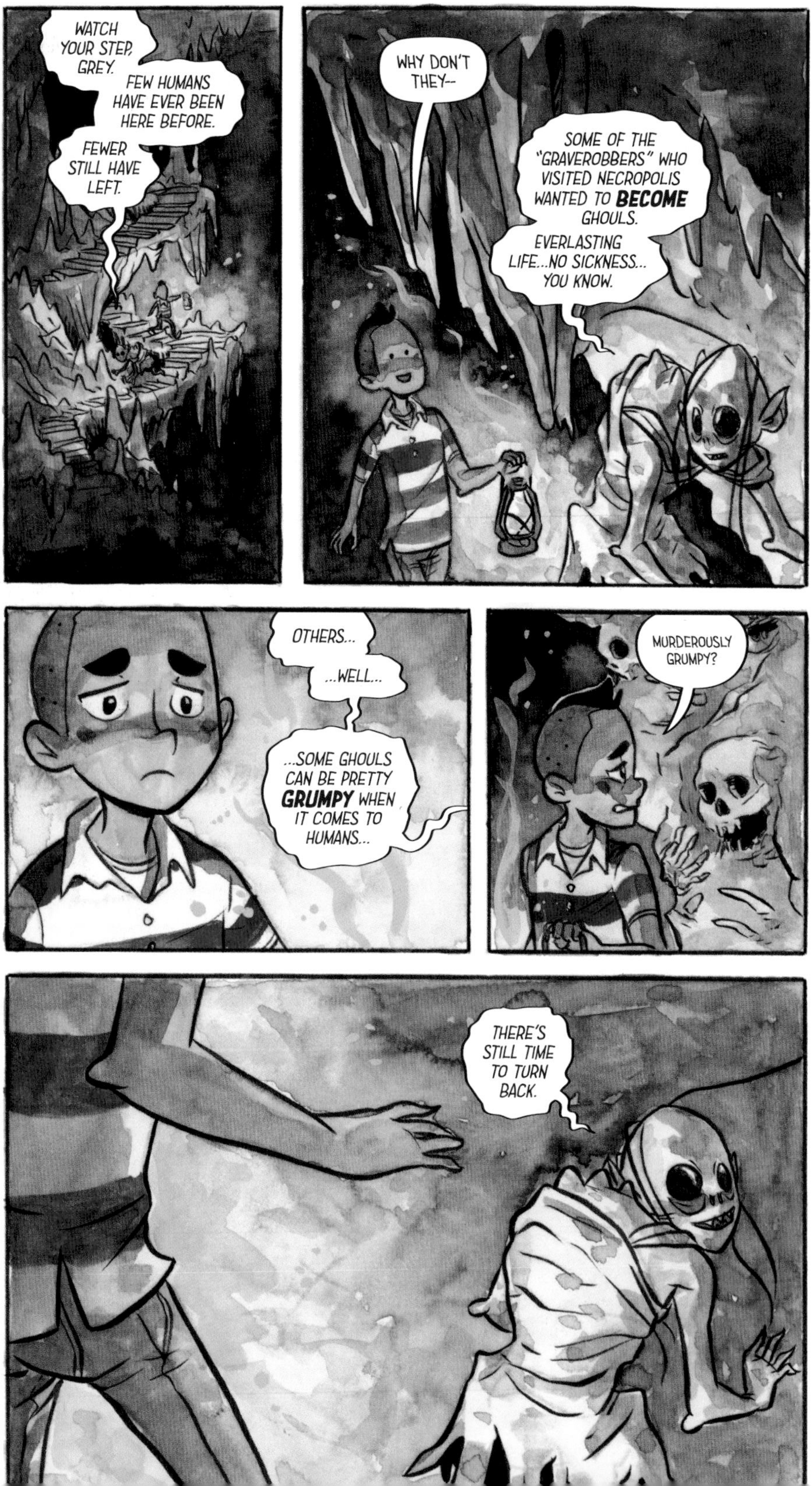
WATCH YOUR STEP, GREY.
FEW HUMANS HAVE EVER BEEN HERE BEFORE.
FEWER STILL HAVE LEFT.
WHY DON'T THEY--
SOME OF THE "GRAVEROBBERS" WHO VISITED NECROPOLIS WANTED TO **BECOME** GHOULS.
EVERLASTING LIFE...NO SICKNESS... YOU KNOW.
OTHERS...
...WELL...
...SOME GHOULS CAN BE PRETTY **GRUMPY** WHEN IT COMES TO HUMANS...
MURDEROUSLY GRUMPY?
THERE'S STILL TIME TO TURN BACK.

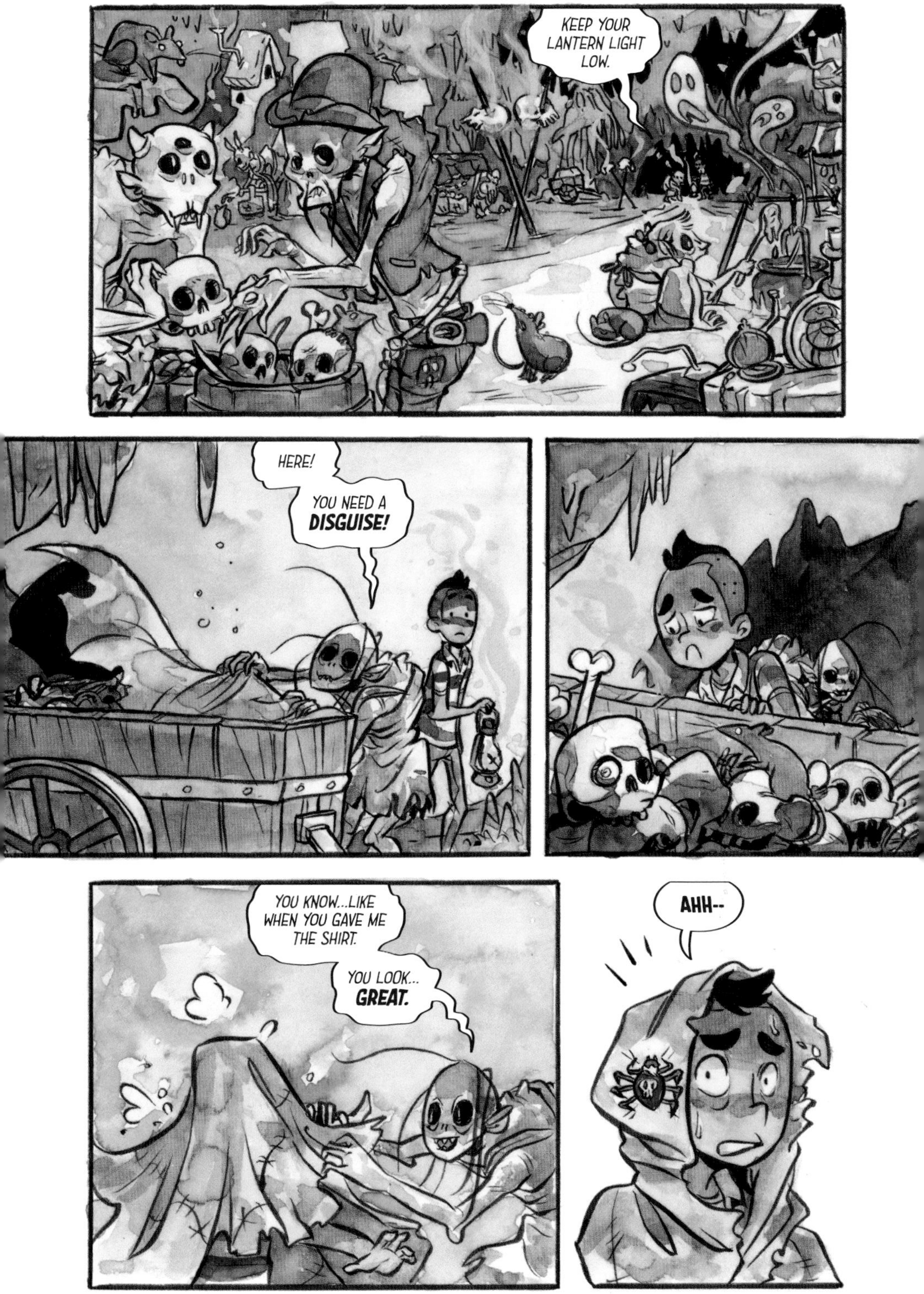
KEEP YOUR LANTERN LIGHT LOW.
HERE!
YOU NEED A DISGUISE!
YOU KNOW...LIKE WHEN YOU GAVE ME THE SHIRT.
YOU LOOK... GREAT.
AHH--

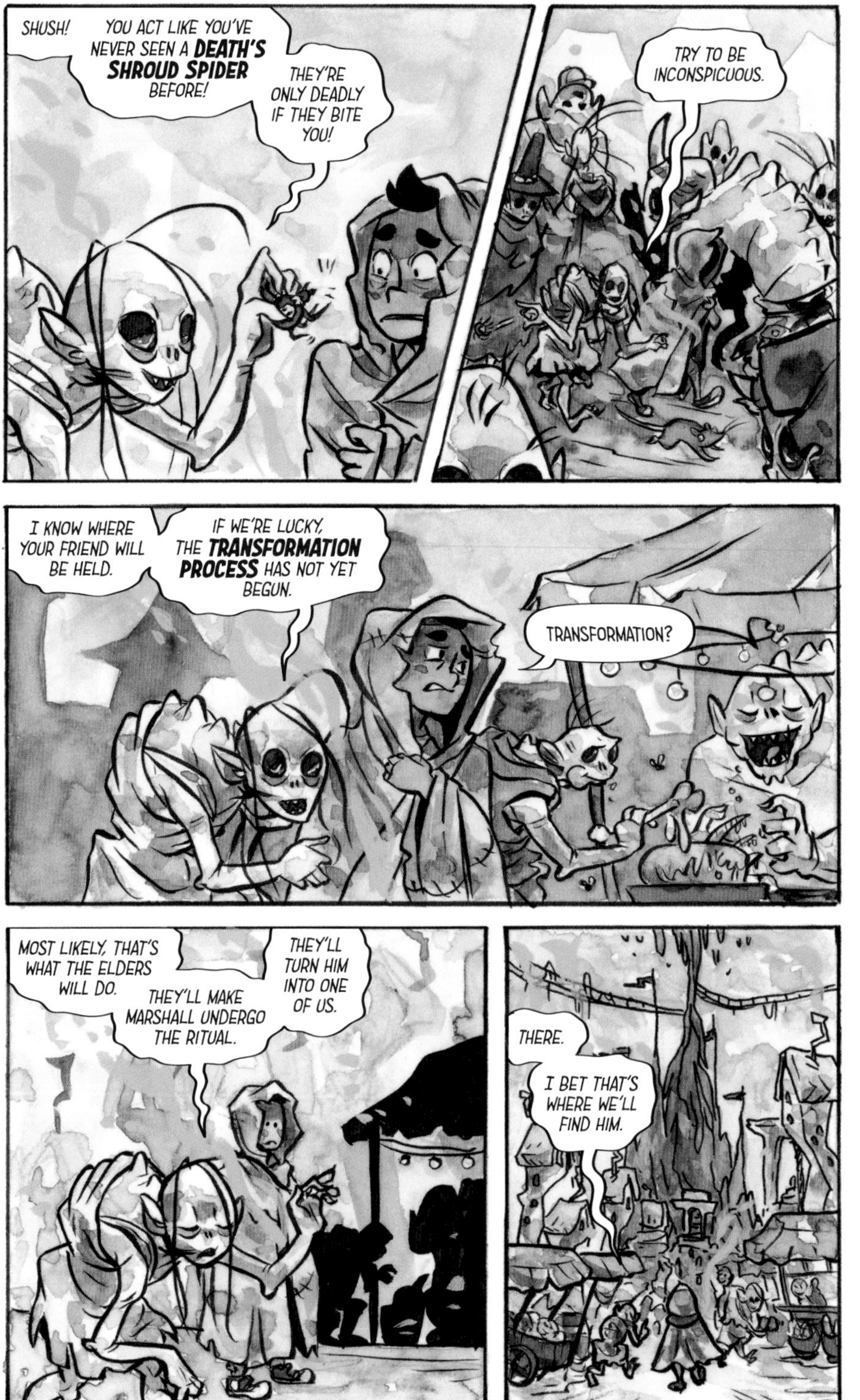
SHUSH!
YOU ACT LIKE YOU'VE NEVER SEEN A DEATH'S SHROUD SPIDER BEFORE!
THEY'RE ONLY DEADLY IF THEY BITE YOU!
TRY TO BE INCONSPICUOUS.
I KNOW WHERE YOUR FRIEND WILL BE HELD.
IF WE'RE LUCKY, THE TRANSFORMATION PROCESS HAS NOT YET BEGUN.
TRANSFORMATION?
MOST LIKELY, THAT'S WHAT THE ELDERS WILL DO.
THEY'LL MAKE MARSHALL UNDERGO THE RITUAL.
THEY'LL TURN HIM INTO ONE OF US.
THERE.
I BET THAT'S WHERE WE'LL FIND HIM.

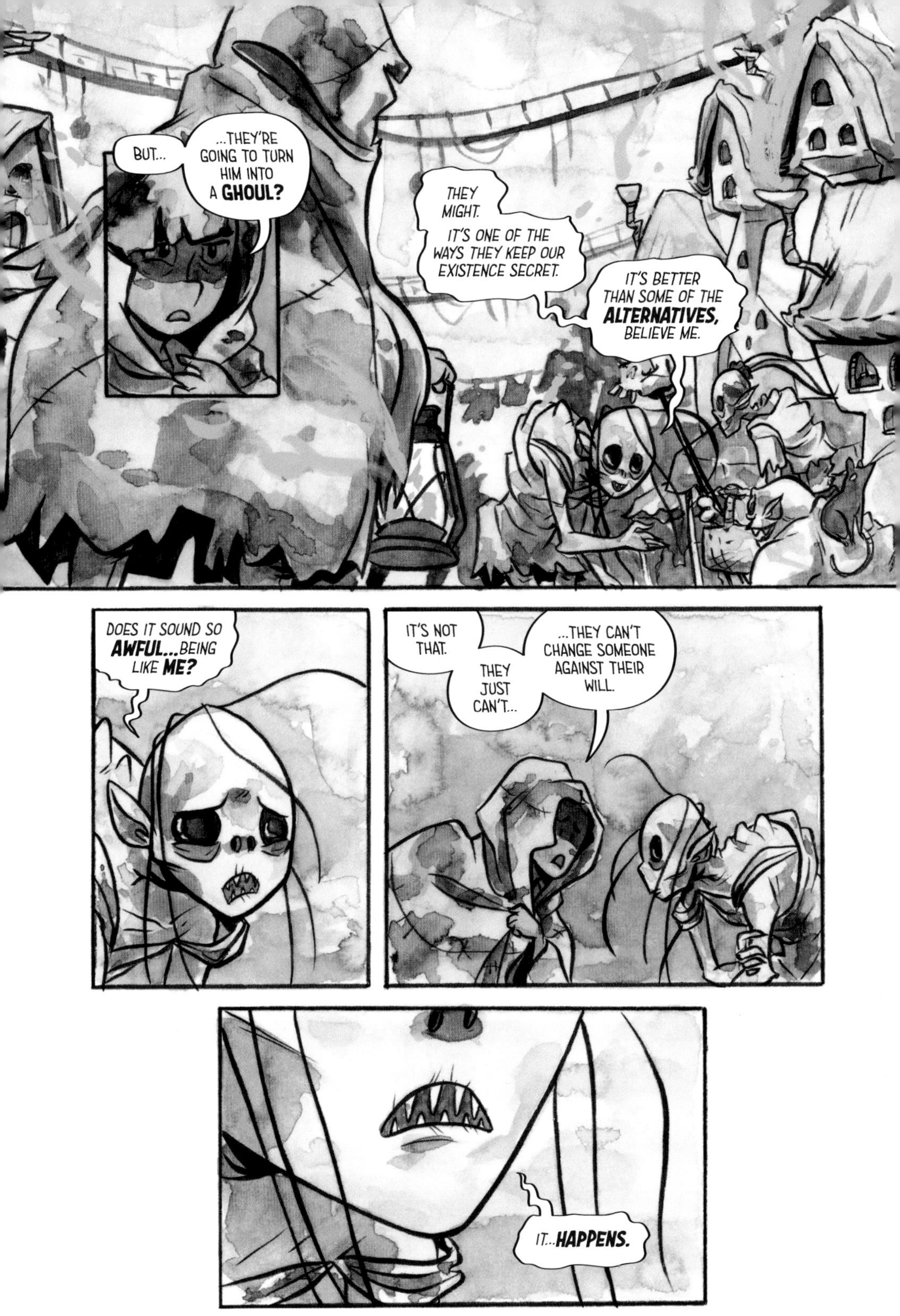

BUT...
...THEY'RE GOING TO TURN HIM INTO A GHOUL?
THEY MIGHT.
IT'S ONE OF THE WAYS THEY KEEP OUR EXISTENCE SECRET.
IT'S BETTER THAN SOME OF THE ALTERNATIVES, BELIEVE ME.
DOES IT SOUND SO AWFUL...BEING LIKE ME?
IT'S NOT THAT.
THEY JUST CAN'T...
...THEY CAN'T CHANGE SOMEONE AGAINST THEIR WILL.
IT...HAPPENS.

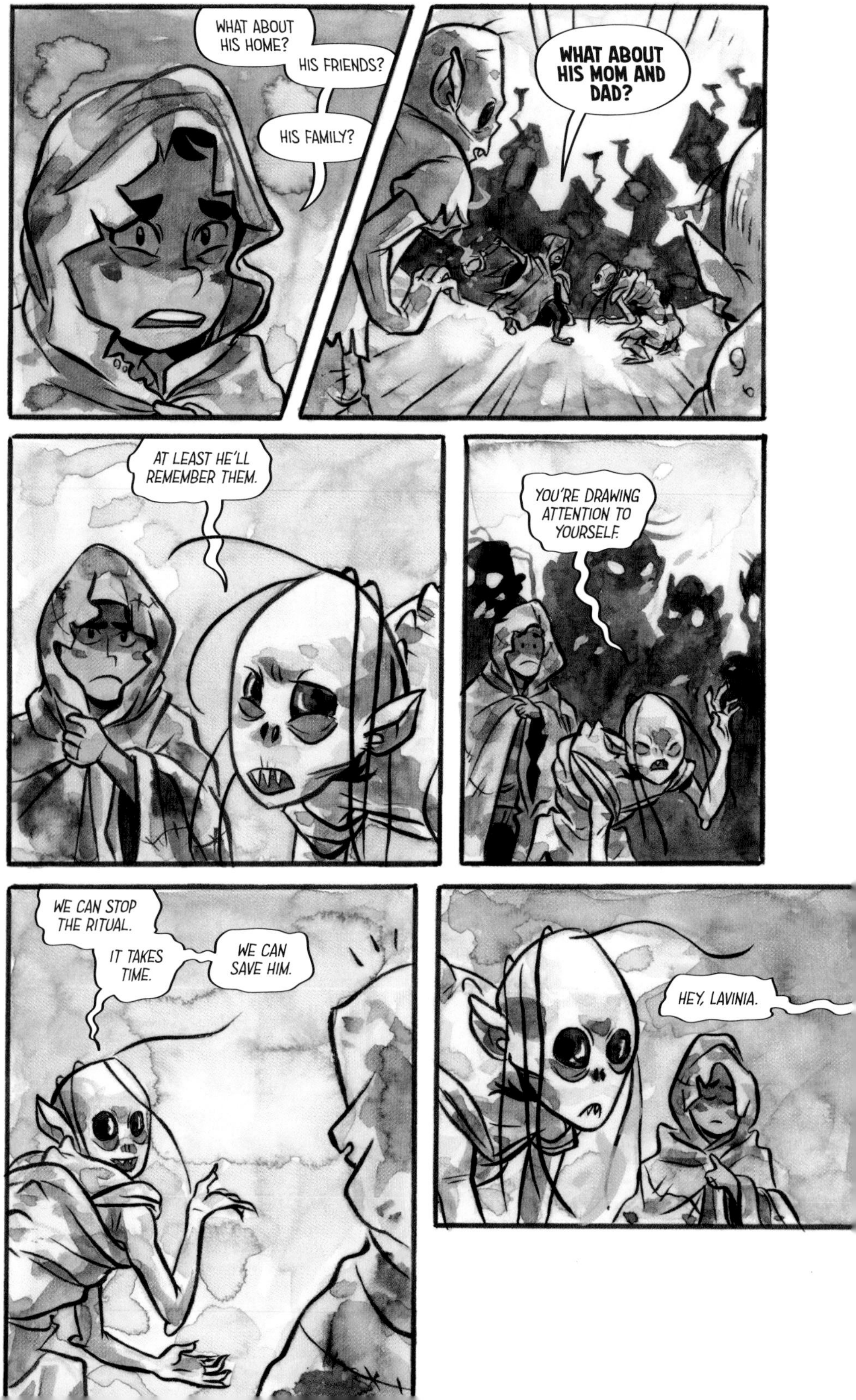
WHAT ABOUT HIS HOME?
HIS FRIENDS?
HIS FAMILY?
WHAT ABOUT HIS MOM AND DAD?
AT LEAST HE'LL REMEMBER THEM.
YOU'RE DRAWING ATTENTION TO YOURSELF.
WE CAN STOP THE RITUAL.
IT TAKES TIME.
WE CAN SAVE HIM.
HEY, LAVINIA.

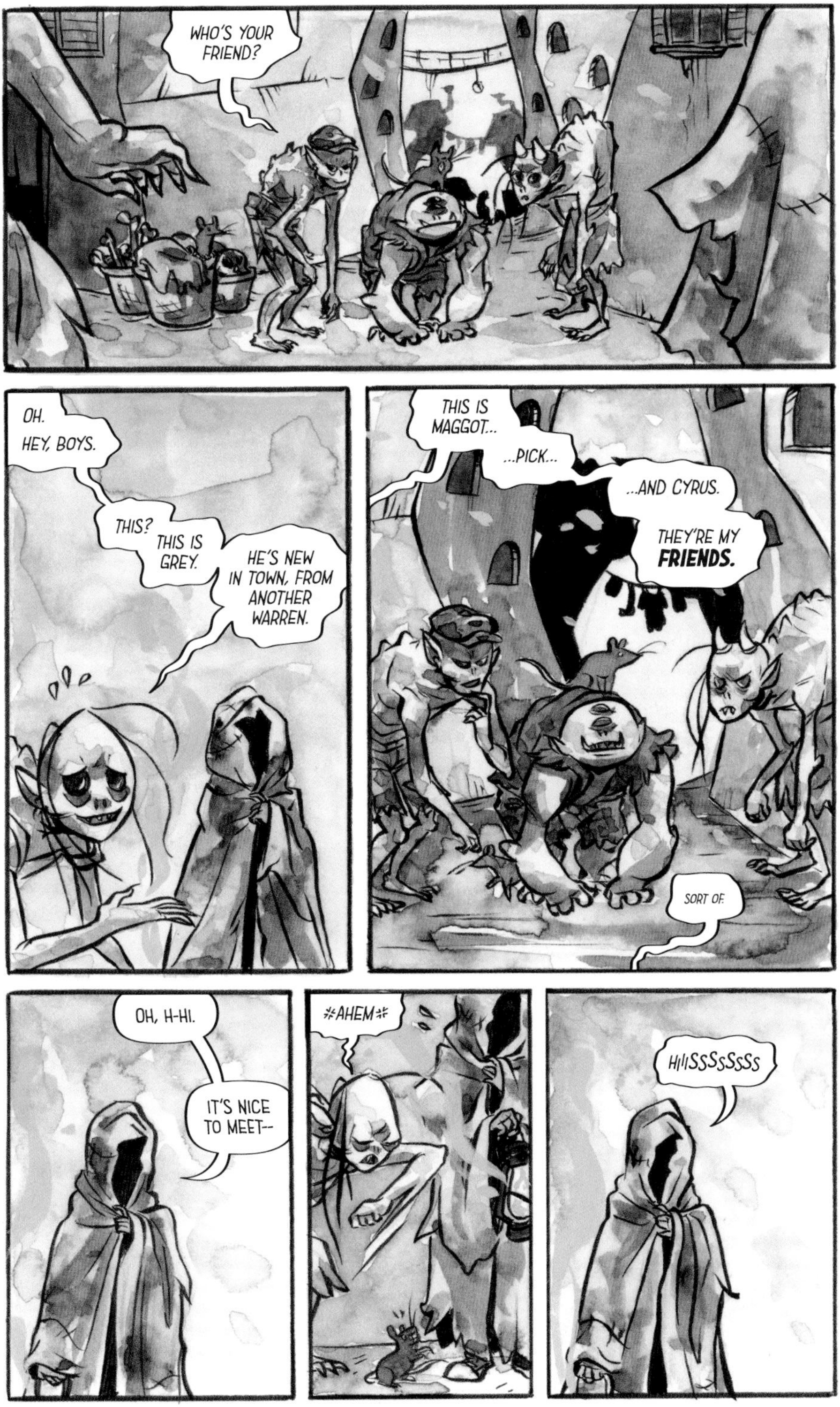
WHO'S YOUR FRIEND?
OH.
HEY, BOYS.
THIS?
THIS IS GREY.
HE'S NEW IN TOWN, FROM ANOTHER WARREN.
THIS IS MAGGOT...
...PICK...
...AND CYRUS.
THEY'RE MY **FRIENDS.**
SORT OF.
OH, H-HI.
IT'S NICE TO MEET--
#AHEM#
HIIISSSSSSSS

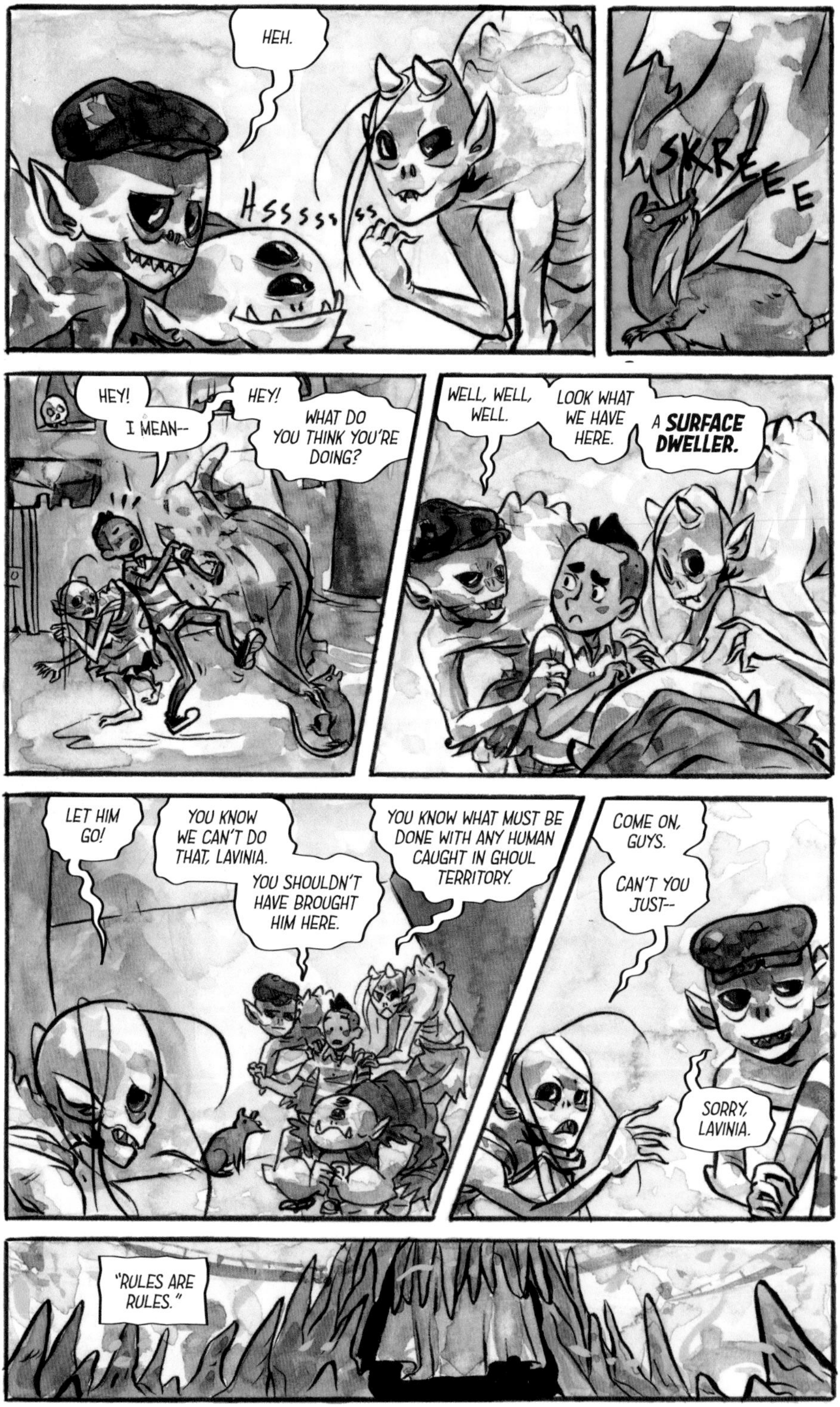
HEH.
HSSSSSSSS
SKREEEE
HEY!
I MEAN--
HEY!
WHAT DO YOU THINK YOU'RE DOING?
WELL, WELL, WELL.
LOOK WHAT WE HAVE HERE.
A SURFACE DWELLER.
LET HIM GO!
YOU KNOW WE CAN'T DO THAT, LAVINIA.
YOU SHOULDN'T HAVE BROUGHT HIM HERE.
YOU KNOW WHAT MUST BE DONE WITH ANY HUMAN CAUGHT IN GHOUL TERRITORY.
COME ON, GUYS.
CAN'T YOU JUST--
SORRY, LAVINIA.
"RULES ARE RULES."

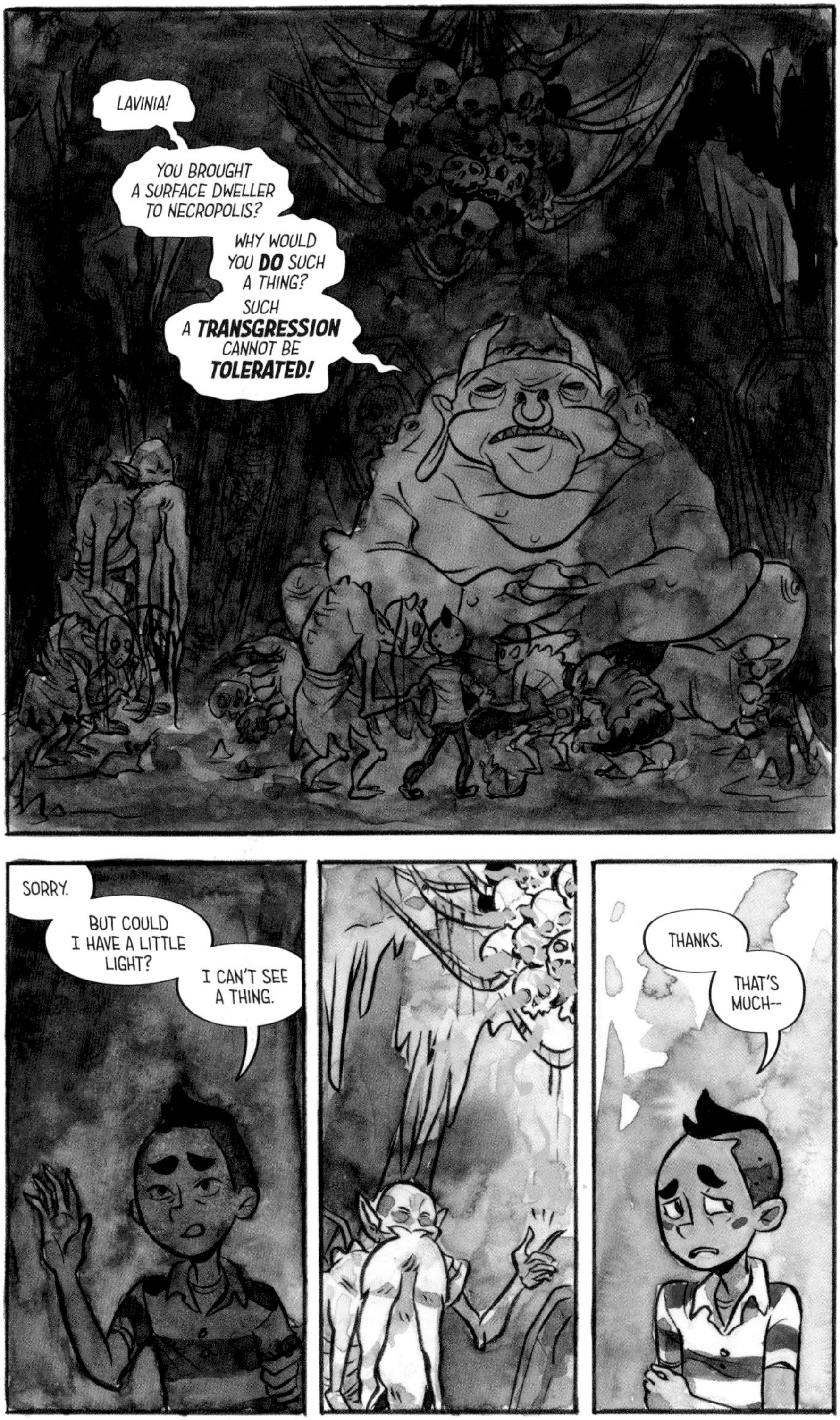
LAVINIA!
YOU BROUGHT A SURFACE DWELLER TO NECROPOLIS?
WHY WOULD YOU **DO** SUCH A THING?
SUCH A **TRANSGRESSION** CANNOT BE **TOLERATED!**
SORRY.
BUT COULD I HAVE A LITTLE LIGHT?
I CAN'T SEE A THING.
THANKS.
THAT'S MUCH--

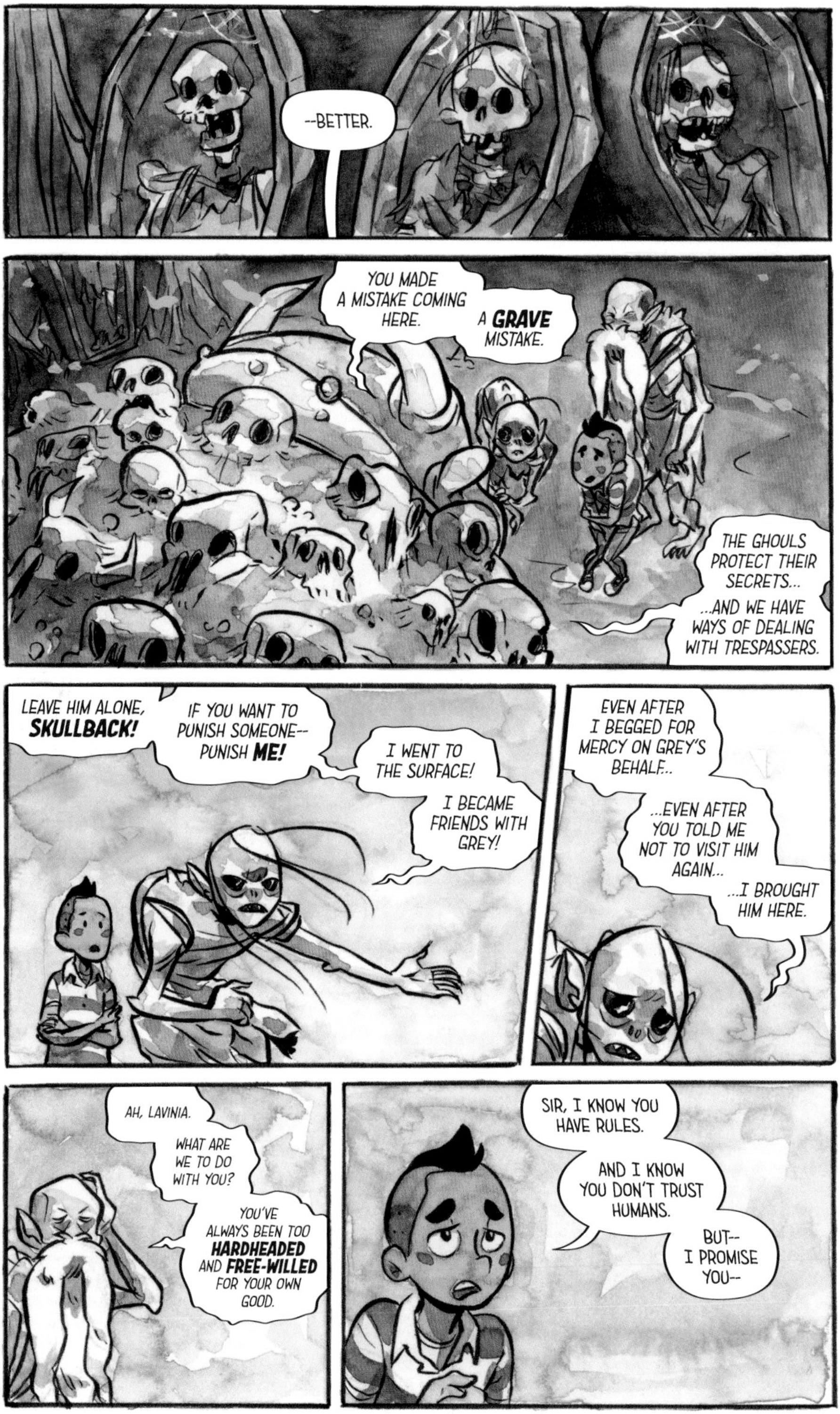
--BETTER.
YOU MADE A MISTAKE COMING HERE.
A **GRAVE** MISTAKE.
THE GHOULS PROTECT THEIR SECRETS...
...AND WE HAVE WAYS OF DEALING WITH TRESPASSERS.
LEAVE HIM ALONE, **SKULLBACK!**
IF YOU WANT TO PUNISH SOMEONE-- PUNISH **ME!**
I WENT TO THE SURFACE!
I BECAME FRIENDS WITH GREY!
EVEN AFTER I BEGGED FOR MERCY ON GREY'S BEHALF...
...EVEN AFTER YOU TOLD ME NOT TO VISIT HIM AGAIN...
...I BROUGHT HIM HERE.
AH, LAVINIA.
WHAT ARE WE TO DO WITH YOU?
YOU'VE ALWAYS BEEN TOO **HARDHEADED** AND **FREE-WILLED** FOR YOUR OWN GOOD.
SIR, I KNOW YOU HAVE RULES.
AND I KNOW YOU DON'T TRUST HUMANS.
BUT-- I PROMISE YOU--

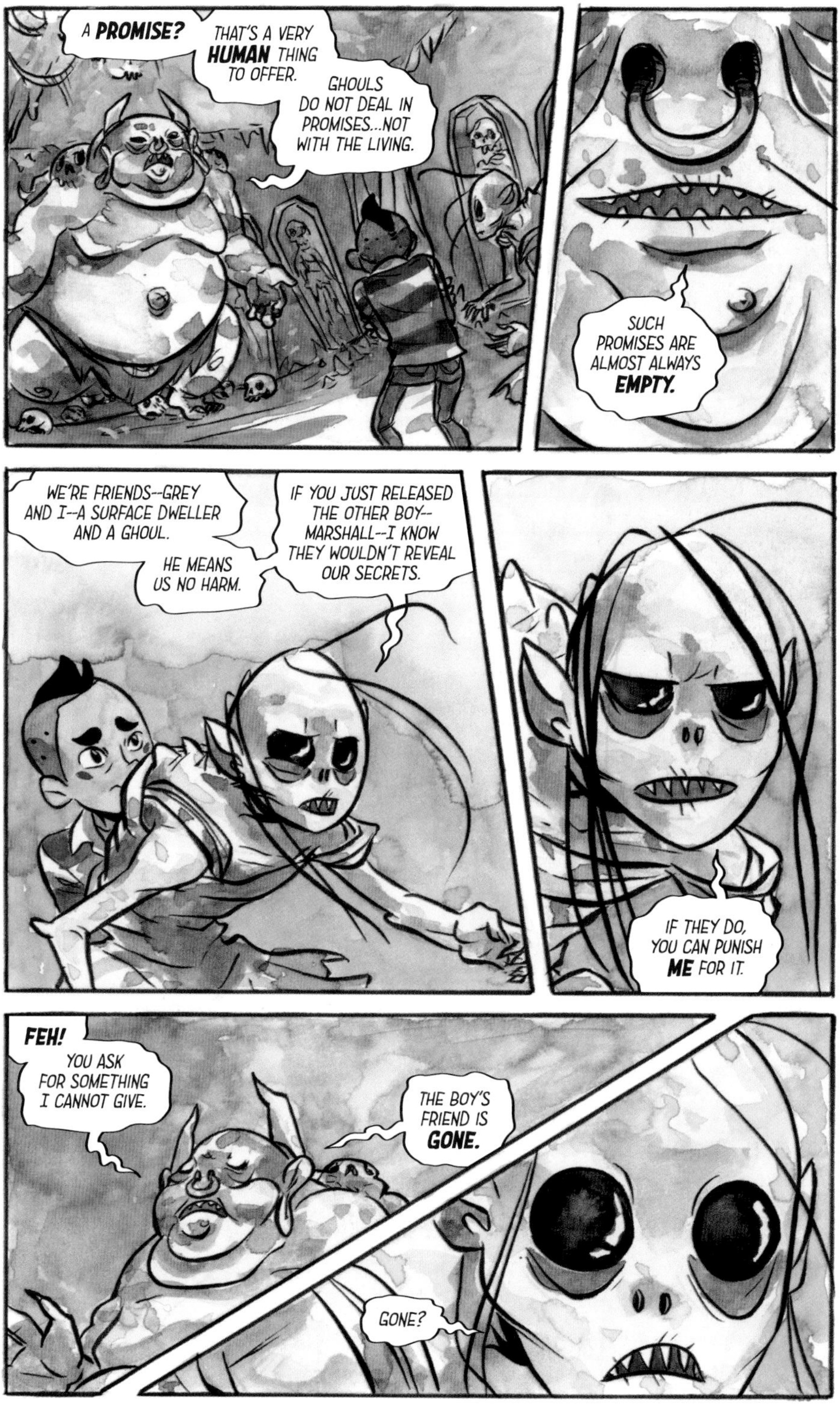
A **PROMISE?**
THAT'S A VERY **HUMAN** THING TO OFFER.
GHOULS DO NOT DEAL IN PROMISES...NOT WITH THE LIVING.
SUCH PROMISES ARE ALMOST ALWAYS **EMPTY.**
WE'RE FRIENDS--GREY AND I--A SURFACE DWELLER AND A GHOUL.
HE MEANS US NO HARM.
IF YOU JUST RELEASED THE OTHER BOY--MARSHALL--I KNOW THEY WOULDN'T REVEAL OUR SECRETS.
IF THEY DO, YOU CAN PUNISH **ME** FOR IT.
FEH!
YOU ASK FOR SOMETHING I CANNOT GIVE.
THE BOY'S FRIEND IS **GONE.**
GONE?

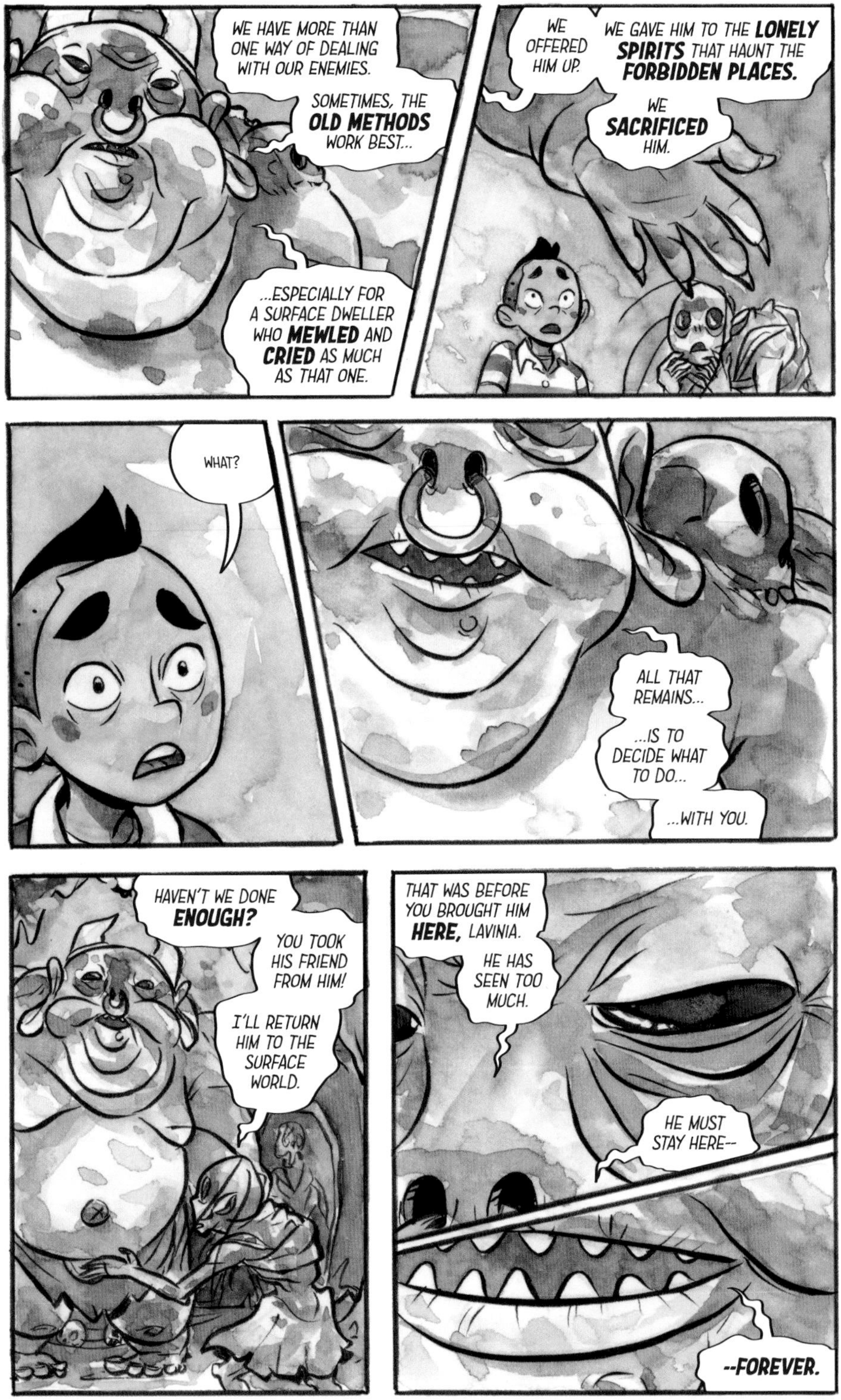
WE HAVE MORE THAN ONE WAY OF DEALING WITH OUR ENEMIES.
SOMETIMES, THE **OLD METHODS** WORK BEST...
...ESPECIALLY FOR A SURFACE DWELLER WHO **MEWLED** AND **CRIED** AS MUCH AS THAT ONE.
WE OFFERED HIM UP.
WE GAVE HIM TO THE **LONELY SPIRITS** THAT HAUNT THE **FORBIDDEN PLACES.**
WE **SACRIFICED** HIM.
WHAT?
ALL THAT REMAINS...
...IS TO DECIDE WHAT TO DO...
...WITH YOU.
HAVEN'T WE DONE **ENOUGH?**
YOU TOOK HIS FRIEND FROM HIM!
I'LL RETURN HIM TO THE SURFACE WORLD.
THAT WAS BEFORE YOU BROUGHT HIM **HERE,** LAVINIA.
HE HAS SEEN TOO MUCH.
HE MUST STAY HERE--
--FOREVER.

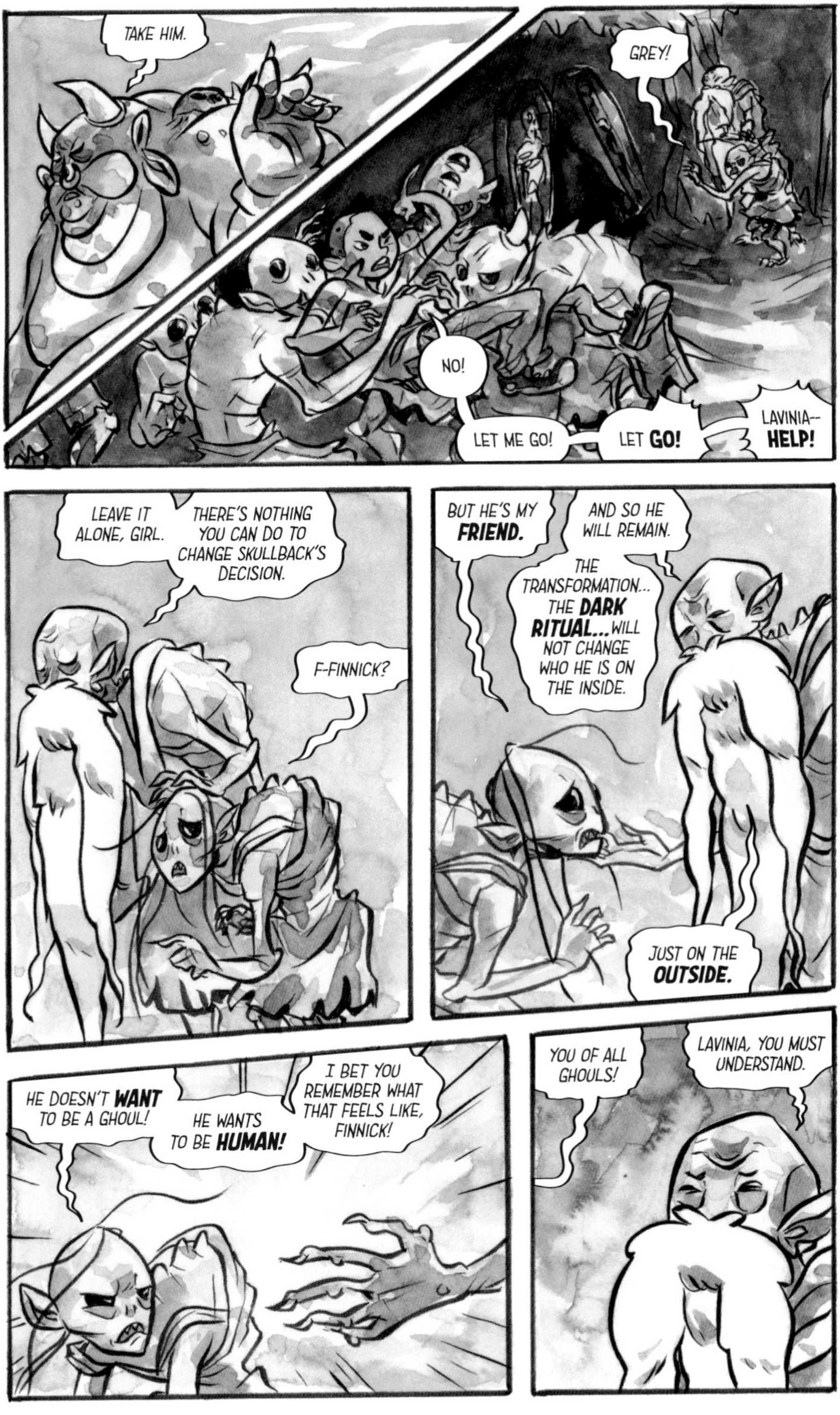
TAKE HIM.
GREY!
NO!
LET ME GO!
LET **GO!**
LAVINIA-- **HELP!**
LEAVE IT ALONE, GIRL.
THERE'S NOTHING YOU CAN DO TO CHANGE SKULLBACK'S DECISION.
F-FINNICK?
BUT HE'S MY **FRIEND.**
AND SO HE WILL REMAIN.
THE TRANSFORMATION... THE **DARK RITUAL...** WILL NOT CHANGE WHO HE IS ON THE INSIDE.
JUST ON THE **OUTSIDE.**
HE DOESN'T **WANT** TO BE A GHOUL!
HE WANTS TO BE **HUMAN!**
I BET YOU REMEMBER WHAT THAT FEELS LIKE, FINNICK!
YOU OF ALL GHOULS!
LAVINIA, YOU MUST UNDERSTAND.

"THERE IS
NOTHING
WE CAN DO."

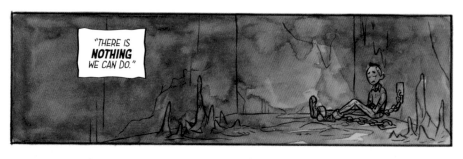

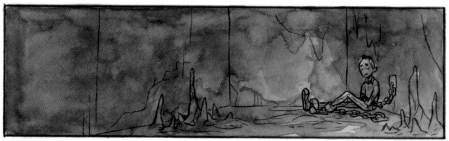

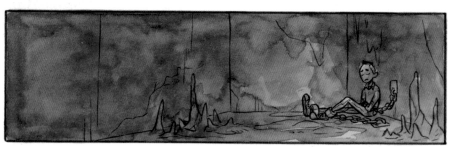

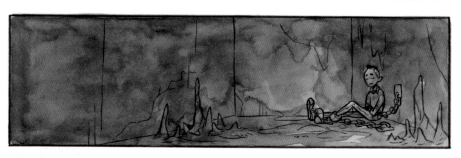

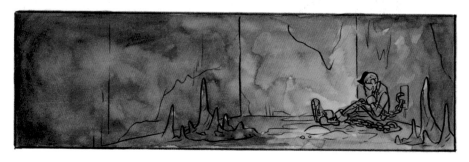

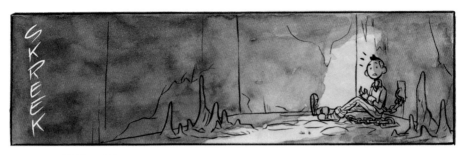

LAVINIA?

ARE YOU... **RESCUING** ME?

WE NEED TO GET YOU OUT OF HERE.

THEY'LL **STARVE** YOU FOR A FEW DAYS...THEN DRAG IN A CORPSE...ONE THAT'S BEEN SPECIALLY SEASONED WITH ALL SORTS OF WEIRD ALCHEMICAL SOLUTIONS AND HERBS...

BUT YOU DON'T WANT THAT.

YOU DON'T WANT TO BE LIKE **ME.**

DON'T WORRY.

I WOULDN'T HAVE LET THAT HAPPEN.

I MIGHT NOT HAVE HAD A CHOICE, BUT **YOU** DO.

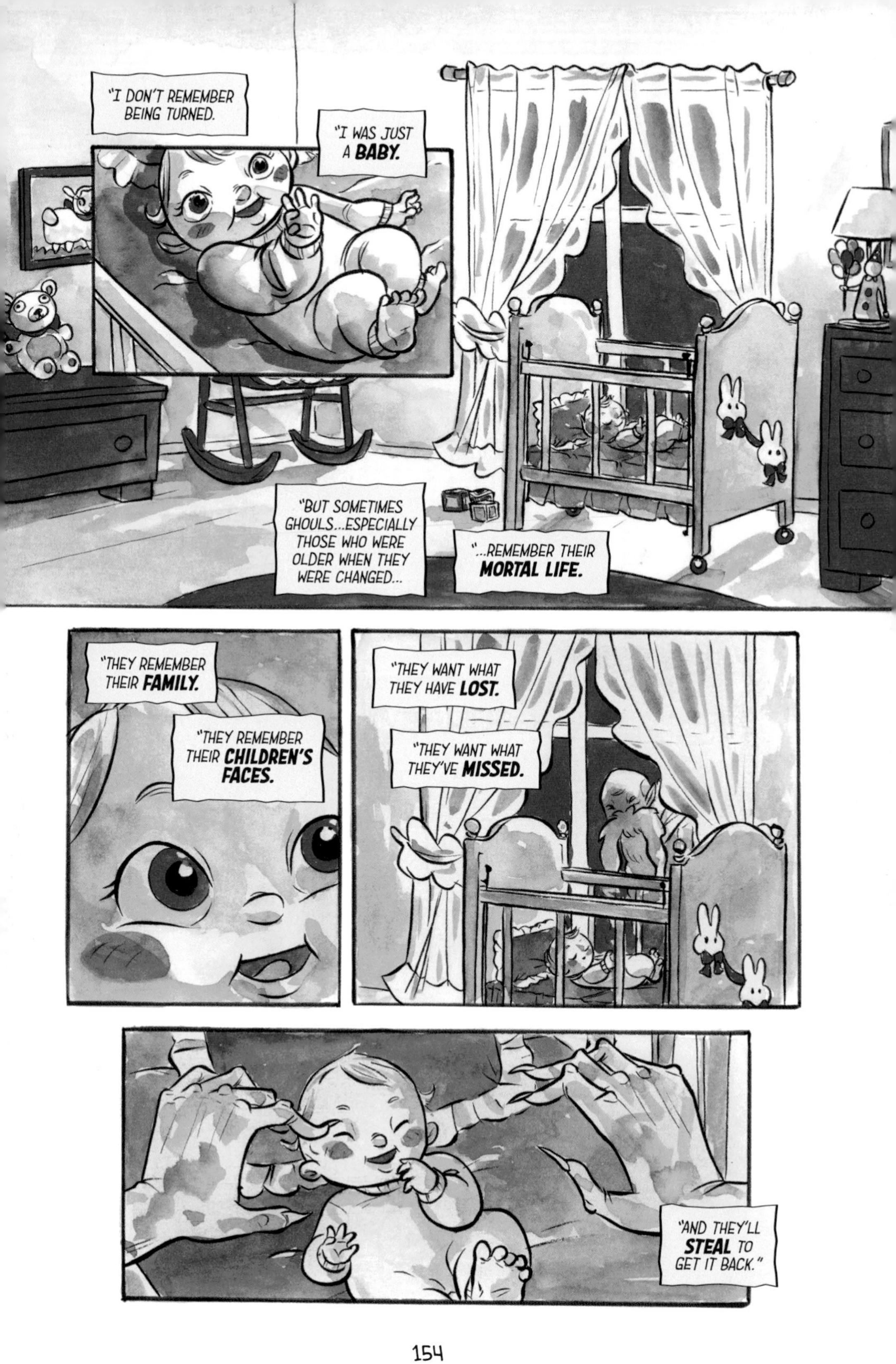
"I DON'T REMEMBER BEING TURNED.
"I WAS JUST A **BABY.**
"BUT SOMETIMES GHOULS...ESPECIALLY THOSE WHO WERE OLDER WHEN THEY WERE CHANGED...
"...REMEMBER THEIR **MORTAL LIFE.**
"THEY REMEMBER THEIR **FAMILY.**
"THEY REMEMBER THEIR **CHILDREN'S FACES.**
"THEY WANT WHAT THEY HAVE **LOST.**
"THEY WANT WHAT THEY'VE **MISSED.**
"AND THEY'LL **STEAL** TO GET IT BACK."

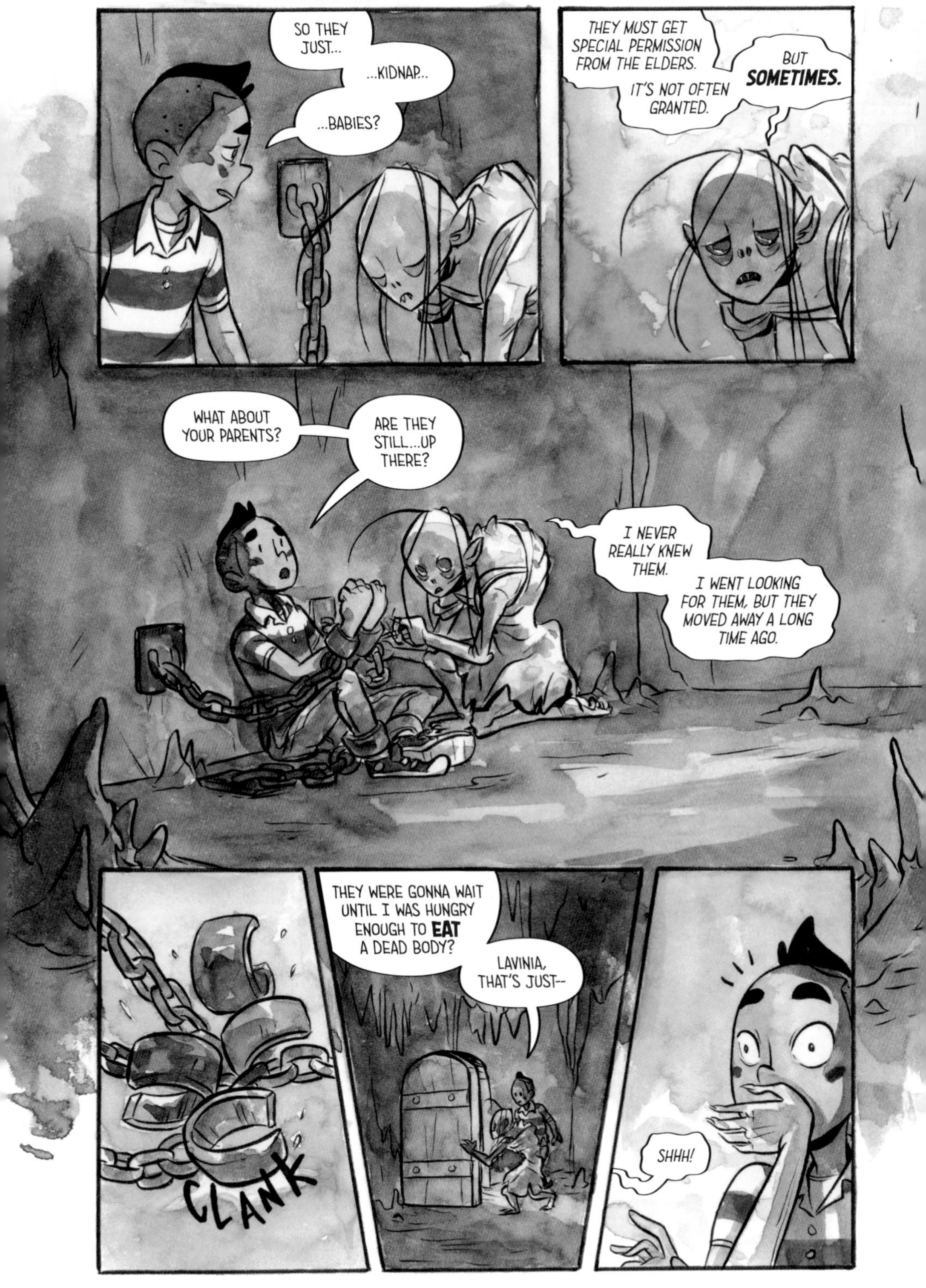
SO THEY JUST...
...KIDNAP...
...BABIES?
THEY MUST GET SPECIAL PERMISSION FROM THE ELDERS.
IT'S NOT OFTEN GRANTED.
BUT **SOMETIMES.**
WHAT ABOUT YOUR PARENTS?
ARE THEY STILL...UP THERE?
I NEVER REALLY KNEW THEM.
I WENT LOOKING FOR THEM, BUT THEY MOVED AWAY A LONG TIME AGO.
CLANK
THEY WERE GONNA WAIT UNTIL I WAS HUNGRY ENOUGH TO **EAT** A DEAD BODY?
LAVINIA, THAT'S JUST--
SHHH!

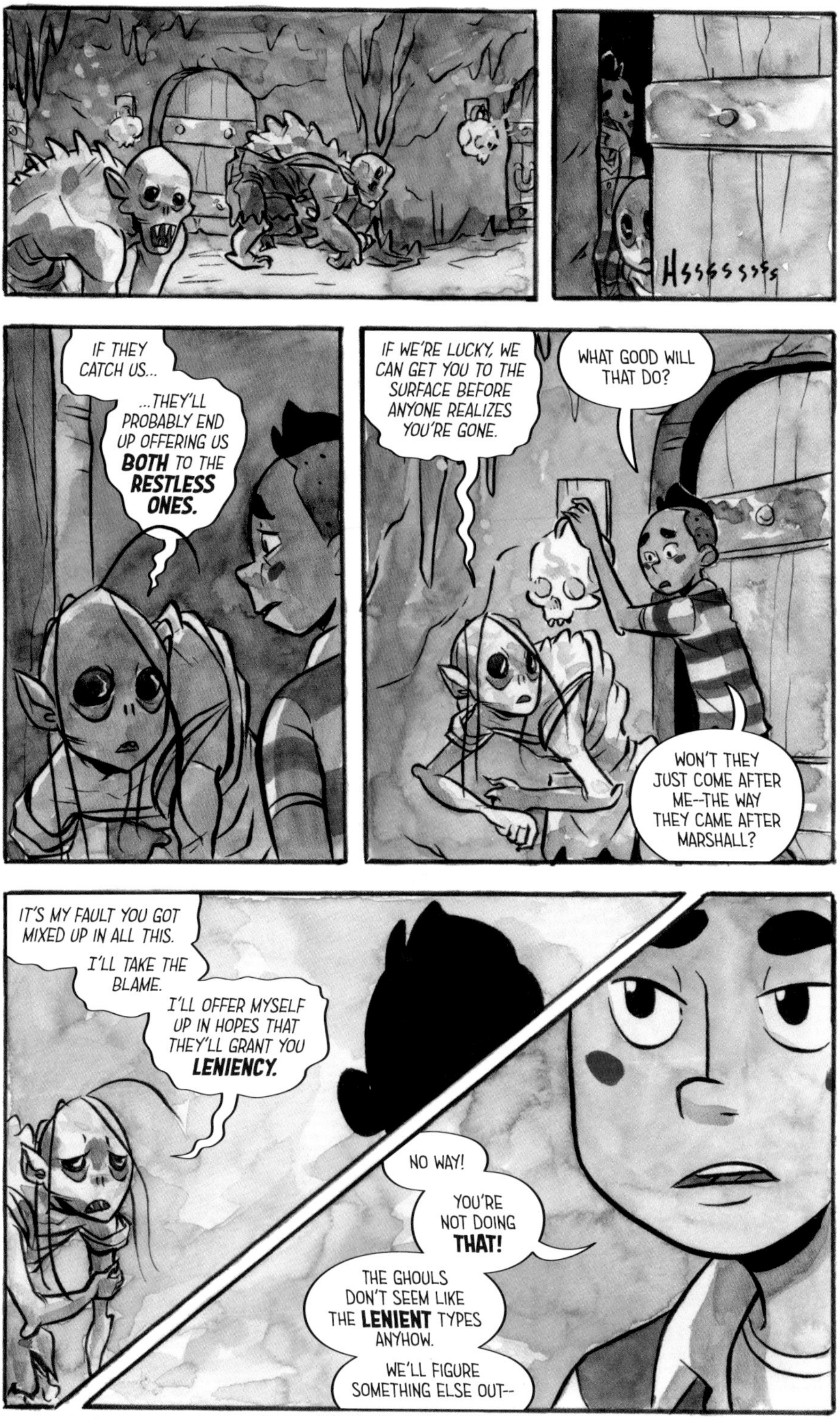
Hsssssss
IF THEY CATCH US...
...THEY'LL PROBABLY END UP OFFERING US **BOTH** TO THE **RESTLESS ONES.**
IF WE'RE LUCKY, WE CAN GET YOU TO THE SURFACE BEFORE ANYONE REALIZES YOU'RE GONE.
WHAT GOOD WILL THAT DO?
WON'T THEY JUST COME AFTER ME--THE WAY THEY CAME AFTER MARSHALL?
IT'S MY FAULT YOU GOT MIXED UP IN ALL THIS.
I'LL TAKE THE BLAME.
I'LL OFFER MYSELF UP IN HOPES THAT THEY'LL GRANT YOU **LENIENCY.**
NO WAY!
YOU'RE NOT DOING **THAT!**
THE GHOULS DON'T SEEM LIKE THE **LENIENT** TYPES ANYHOW.
WE'LL FIGURE SOMETHING ELSE OUT--

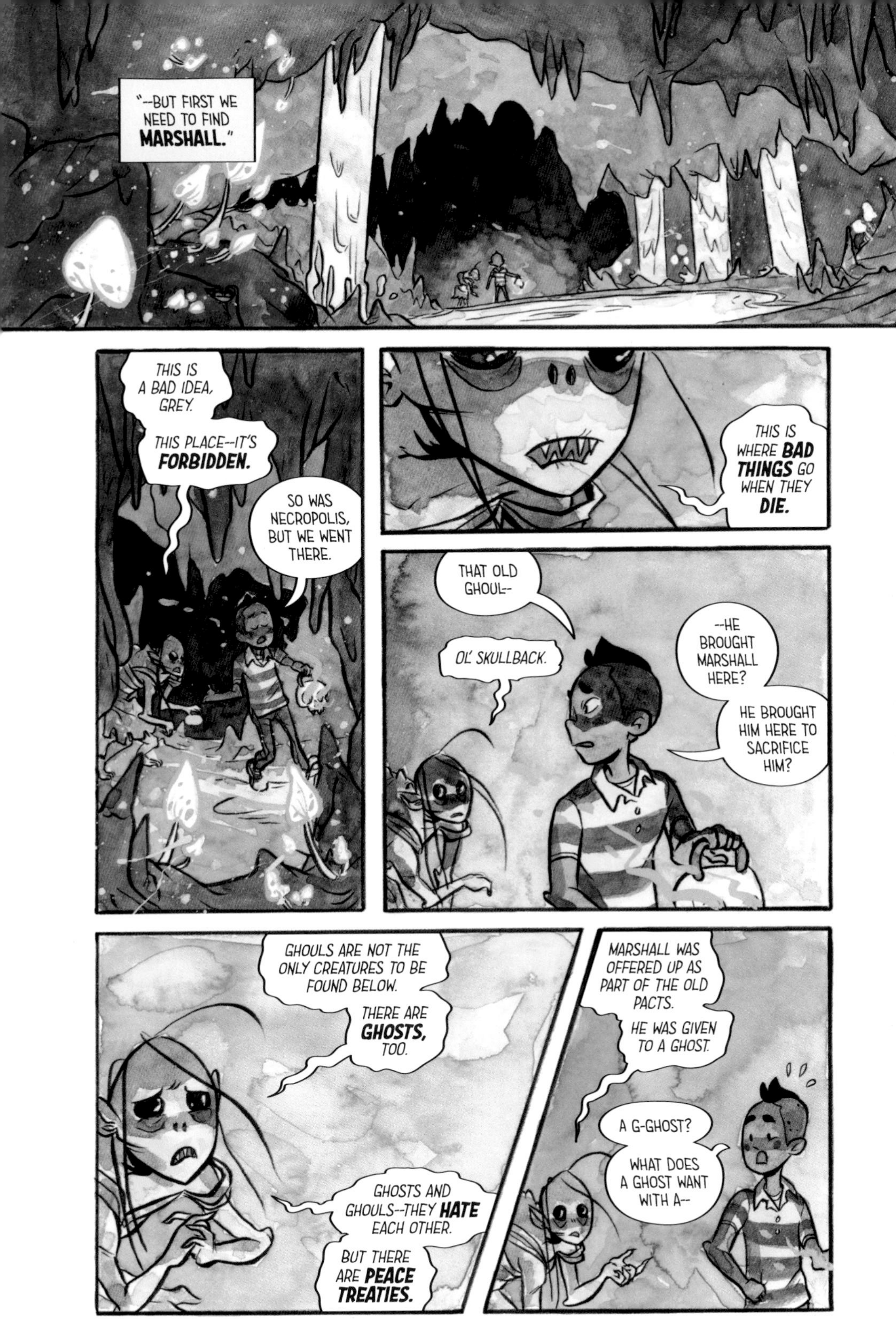
"--BUT FIRST WE NEED TO FIND MARSHALL."
THIS IS A BAD IDEA, GREY.
THIS PLACE--IT'S FORBIDDEN.
SO WAS NECROPOLIS, BUT WE WENT THERE.
THIS IS WHERE BAD THINGS GO WHEN THEY DIE.
THAT OLD GHOUL--
OL' SKULLBACK.
--HE BROUGHT MARSHALL HERE?
HE BROUGHT HIM HERE TO SACRIFICE HIM?
GHOULS ARE NOT THE ONLY CREATURES TO BE FOUND BELOW.
THERE ARE GHOSTS, TOO.
GHOSTS AND GHOULS--THEY HATE EACH OTHER.
BUT THERE ARE PEACE TREATIES.
MARSHALL WAS OFFERED UP AS PART OF THE OLD PACTS.
HE WAS GIVEN TO A GHOST.
A G-GHOST?
WHAT DOES A GHOST WANT WITH A--

TH-THAT SOUND!

IT'S HORRIBLE!

AAAUUUUUUVVVGGGGG

IT'S A **HOWLING GARDEN.**

DON'T WORRY. WE'LL BE SAFE.

IF WE MOVE FAST.

OOOUL

WHOEVER'S IN THE CASKETS...

...THEY'RE **SCREAMING.**

REAAAUUUUGH

YEAH.

GHOSTS CAN BE SUCH BABIES.

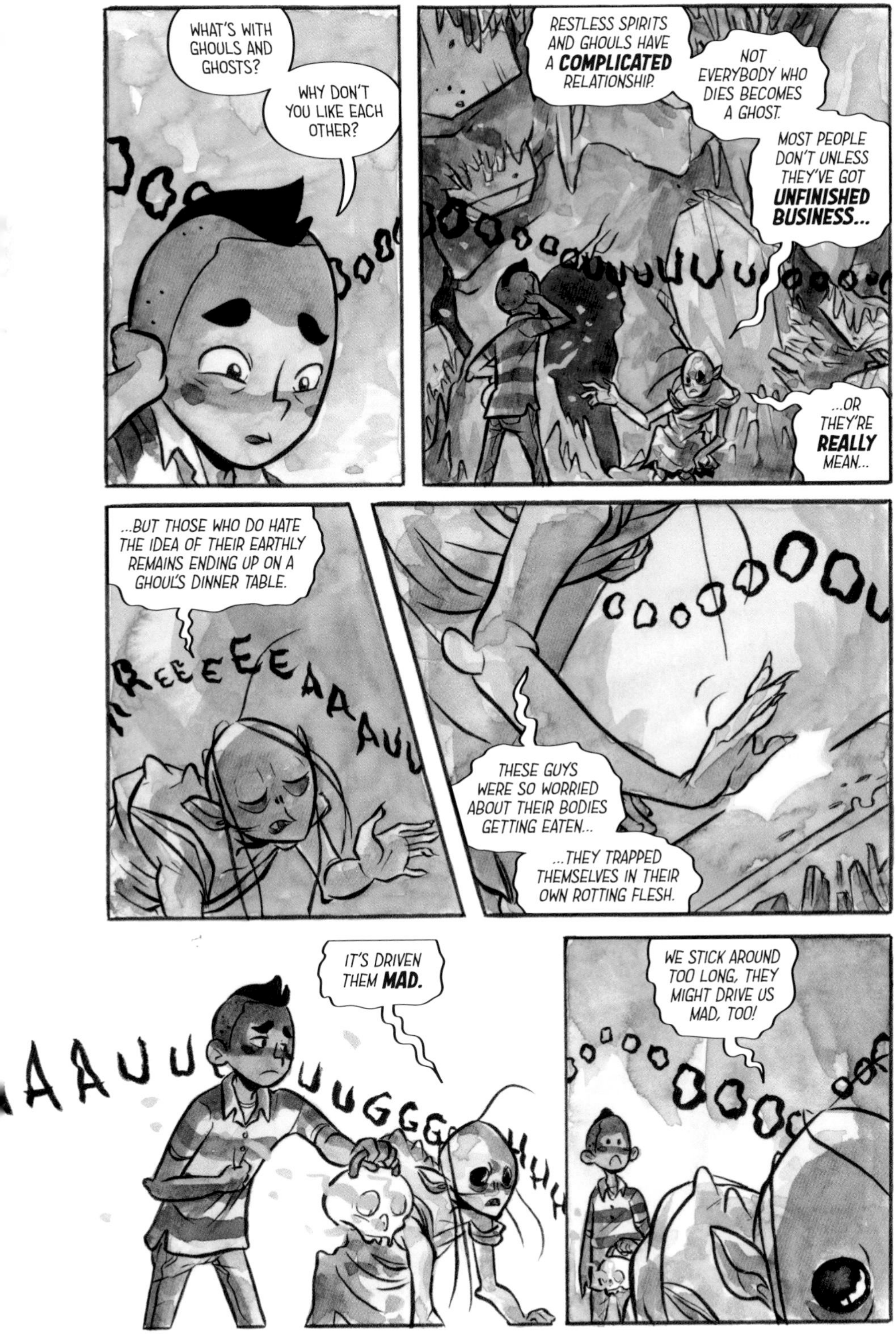
WHAT'S WITH GHOULS AND GHOSTS?
WHY DON'T YOU LIKE EACH OTHER?
RESTLESS SPIRITS AND GHOULS HAVE A **COMPLICATED** RELATIONSHIP.
NOT EVERYBODY WHO DIES BECOMES A GHOST.
MOST PEOPLE DON'T UNLESS THEY'VE GOT **UNFINISHED BUSINESS...**
...OR THEY'RE **REALLY** MEAN...
...BUT THOSE WHO DO HATE THE IDEA OF THEIR EARTHLY REMAINS ENDING UP ON A GHOUL'S DINNER TABLE.
REEEEEAAAAUU
THESE GUYS WERE SO WORRIED ABOUT THEIR BODIES GETTING EATEN...
...THEY TRAPPED THEMSELVES IN THEIR OWN ROTTING FLESH.
IT'S DRIVEN THEM **MAD.**
AAAUUUUUGGGHHHH
WE STICK AROUND TOO LONG, THEY MIGHT DRIVE US MAD, TOO!

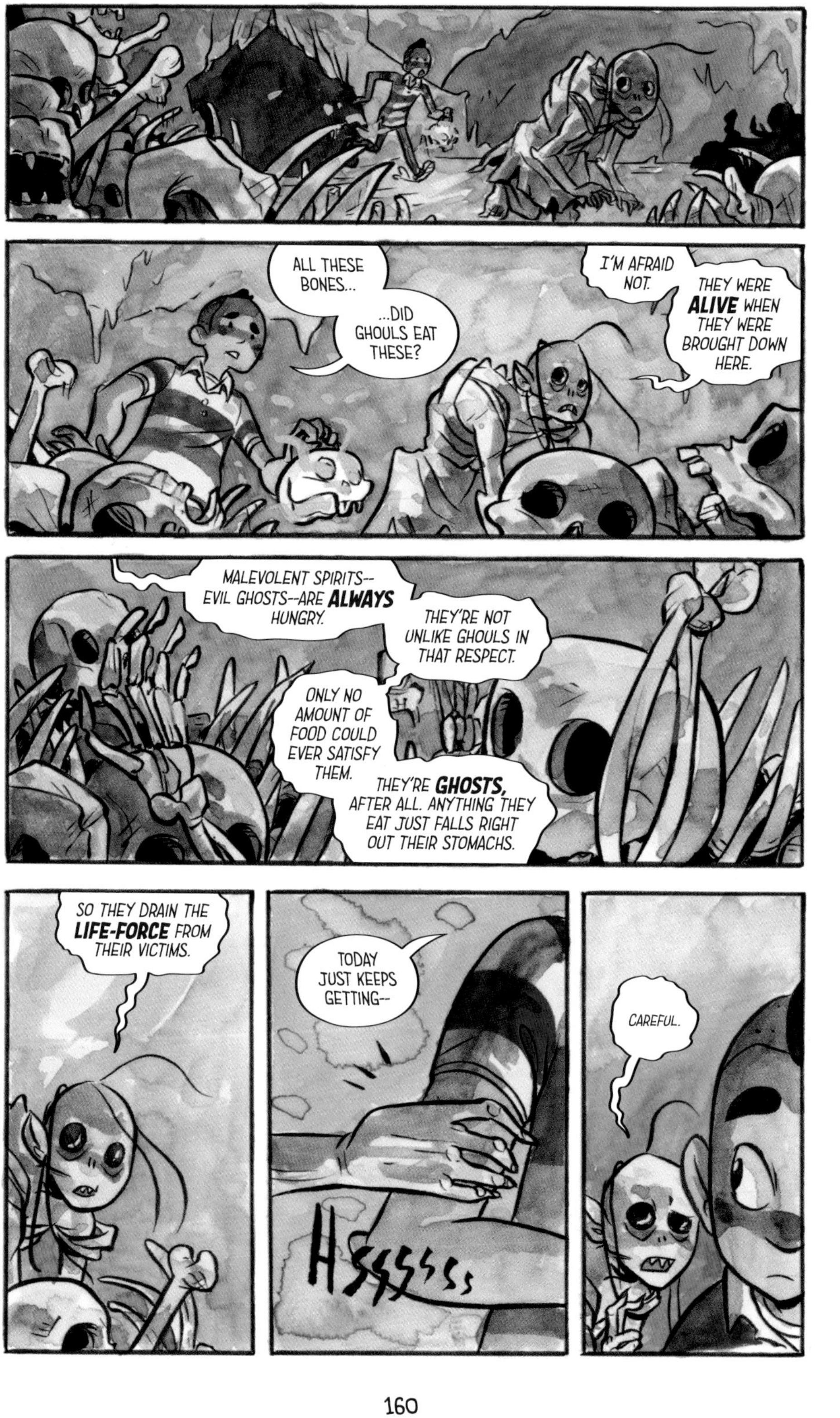
ALL THESE BONES...
...DID GHOULS EAT THESE?
I'M AFRAID NOT.
THEY WERE **ALIVE** WHEN THEY WERE BROUGHT DOWN HERE.
MALEVOLENT SPIRITS--EVIL GHOSTS--ARE **ALWAYS** HUNGRY.
THEY'RE NOT UNLIKE GHOULS IN THAT RESPECT.
ONLY NO AMOUNT OF FOOD COULD EVER SATISFY THEM.
THEY'RE **GHOSTS,** AFTER ALL. ANYTHING THEY EAT JUST FALLS RIGHT OUT THEIR STOMACHS.
SO THEY DRAIN THE **LIFE-FORCE** FROM THEIR VICTIMS.
TODAY JUST KEEPS GETTING--
HSSSSSss
CAREFUL.

ULP!

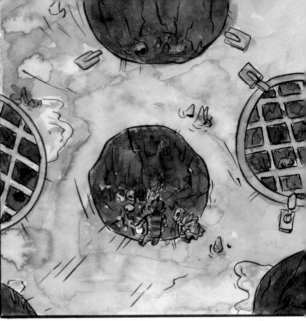

IF GHOSTS D-D-DRAIN THE LIFE FROM THEIR VICTIMS...

...I GUESS THIS IS LIKE THEIR **PANTRY.**

IT'S **COLD** HERE.

DO YOU FEEL IT?

SOMETHING **POWERFUL...**SOMETHING **EVIL...**LURKS NEARBY.

C-C-COLD?

I B-B-BARELY NOTICED.

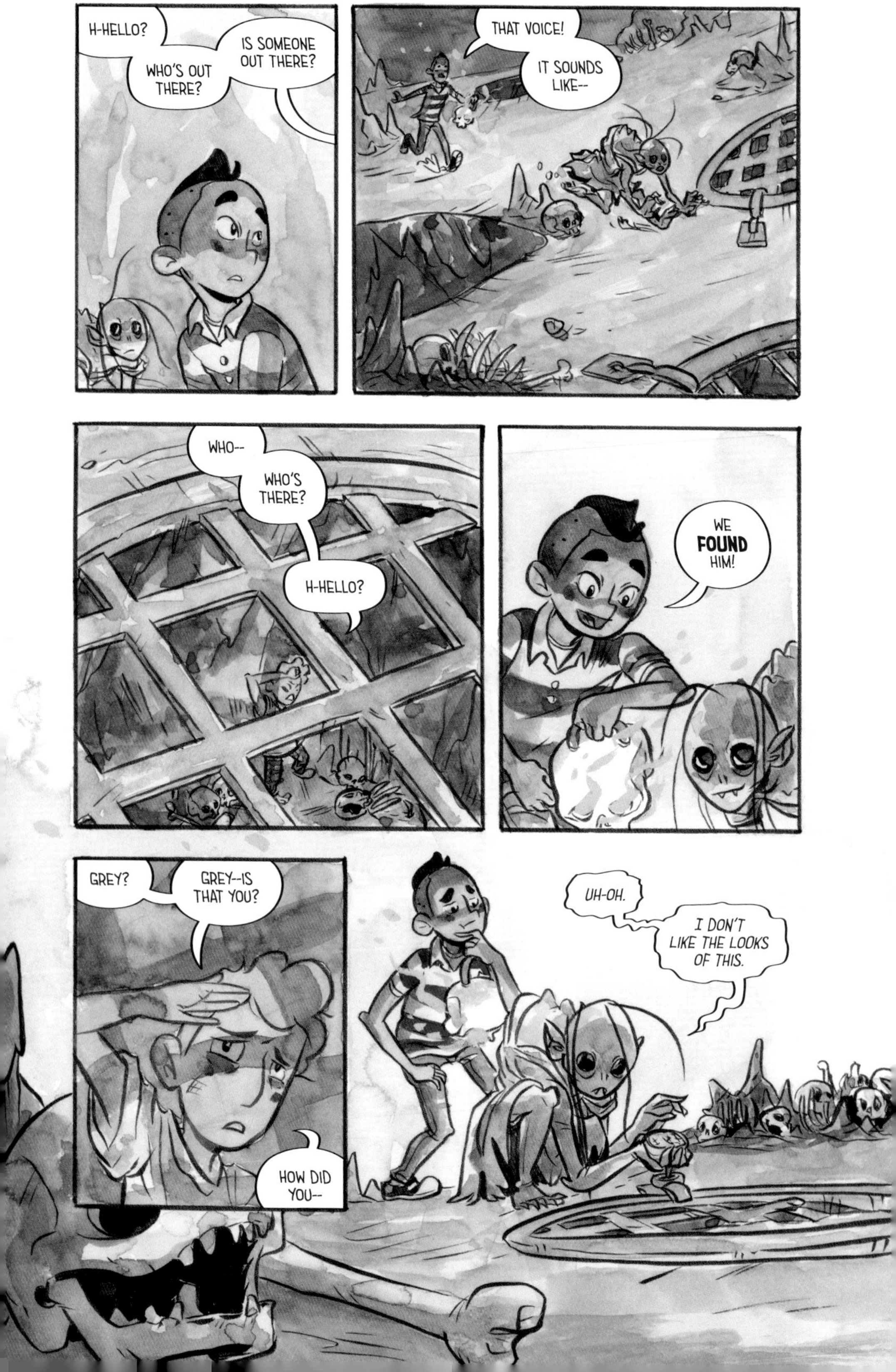
H-HELLO?
WHO'S OUT THERE?
IS SOMEONE OUT THERE?
THAT VOICE!
IT SOUNDS LIKE--
WHO--
WHO'S THERE?
H-HELLO?
WE **FOUND** HIM!
GREY?
GREY--IS THAT YOU?
HOW DID YOU--
UH-OH.
I DON'T LIKE THE LOOKS OF THIS.

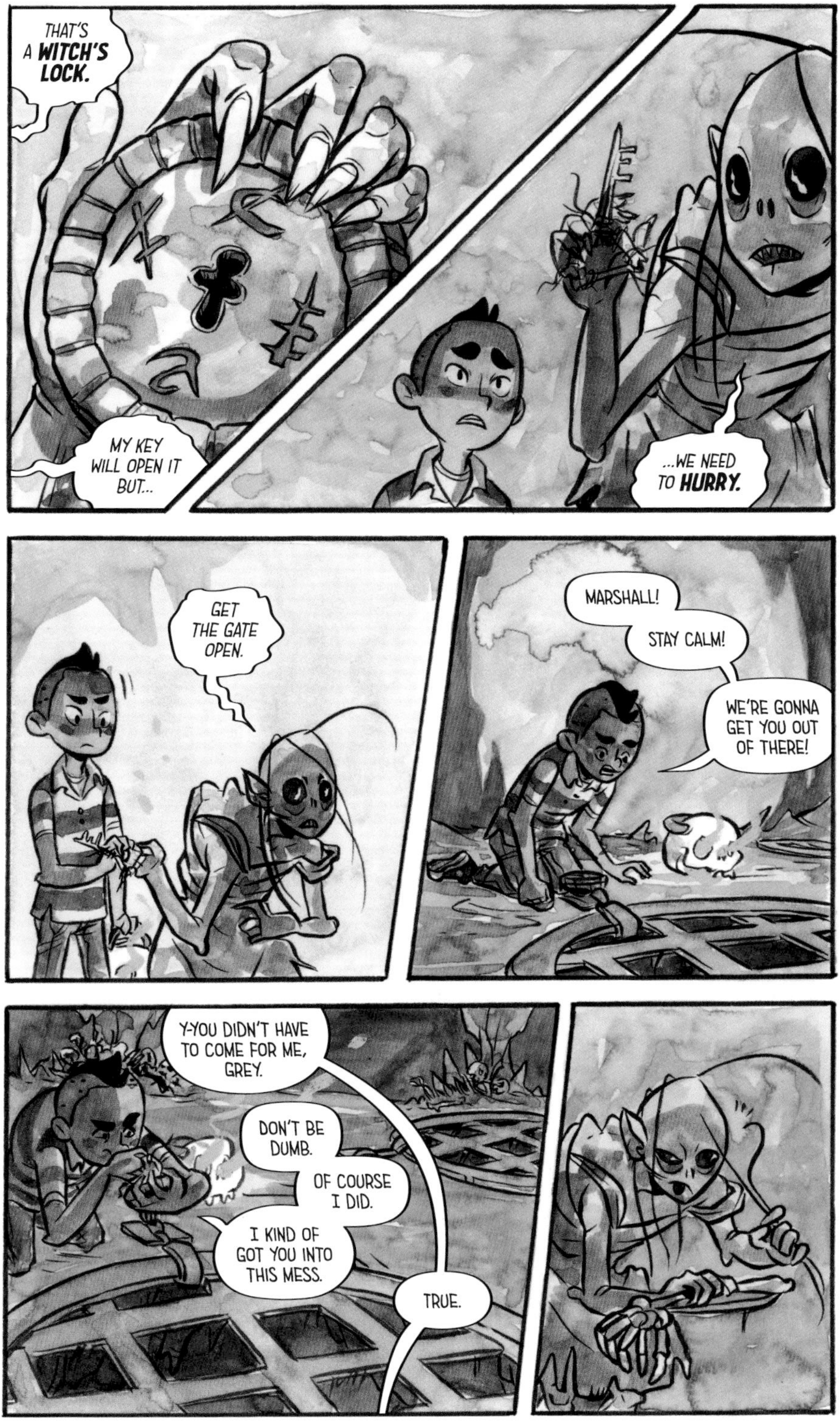
THAT'S A **WITCH'S LOCK.**
MY KEY WILL OPEN IT BUT...
...WE NEED TO **HURRY.**
GET THE GATE OPEN.
MARSHALL!
STAY CALM!
WE'RE GONNA GET YOU OUT OF THERE!
Y-YOU DIDN'T HAVE TO COME FOR ME, GREY.
DON'T BE DUMB.
OF COURSE I DID.
I KIND OF GOT YOU INTO THIS MESS.
TRUE.

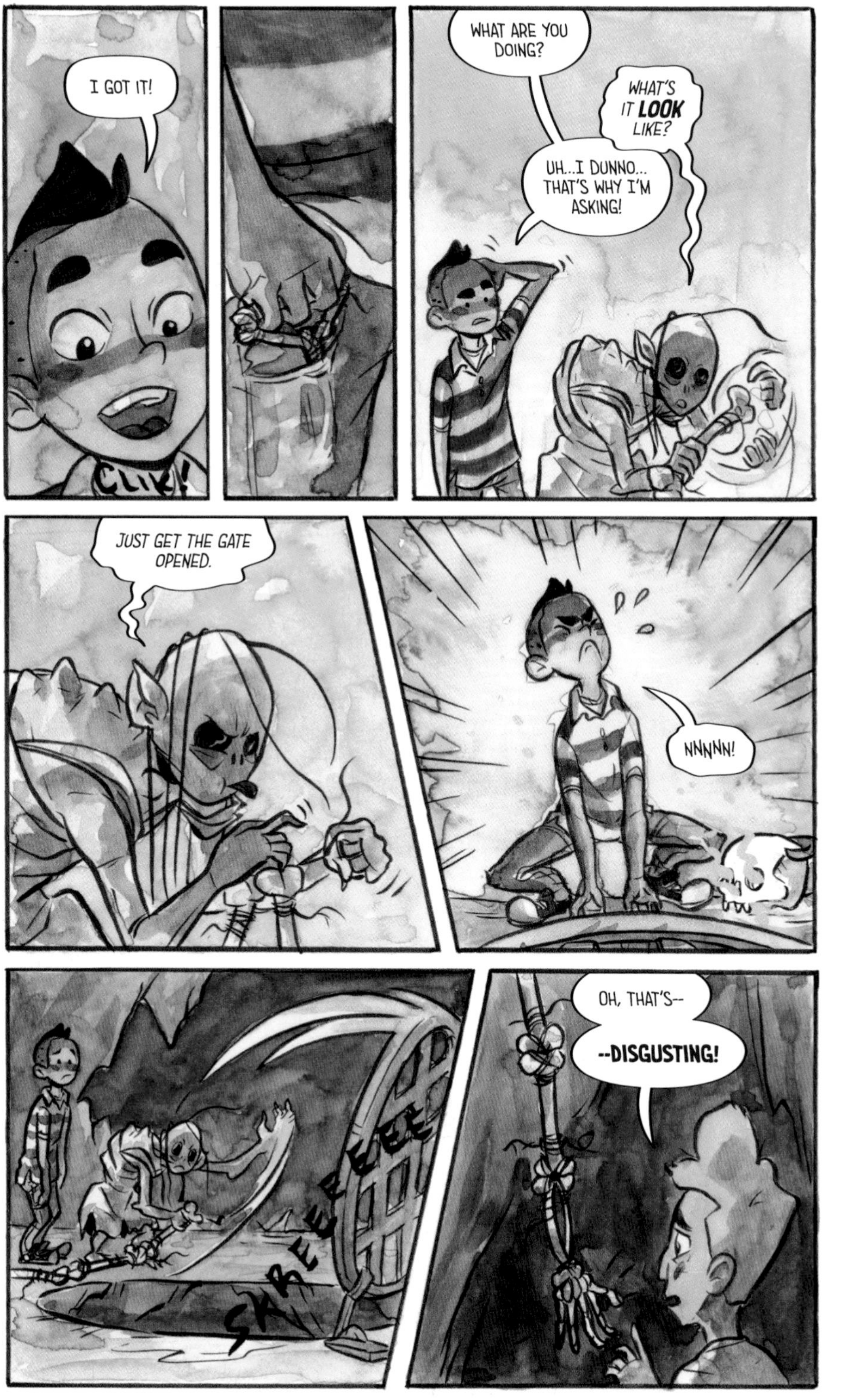
I GOT IT!
CLIK!
WHAT ARE YOU DOING?
WHAT'S IT LOOK LIKE?
UH...I DUNNO... THAT'S WHY I'M ASKING!
JUST GET THE GATE OPENED.
NNNNN!
SKREEEEEE
OH, THAT'S--
--DISGUSTING!

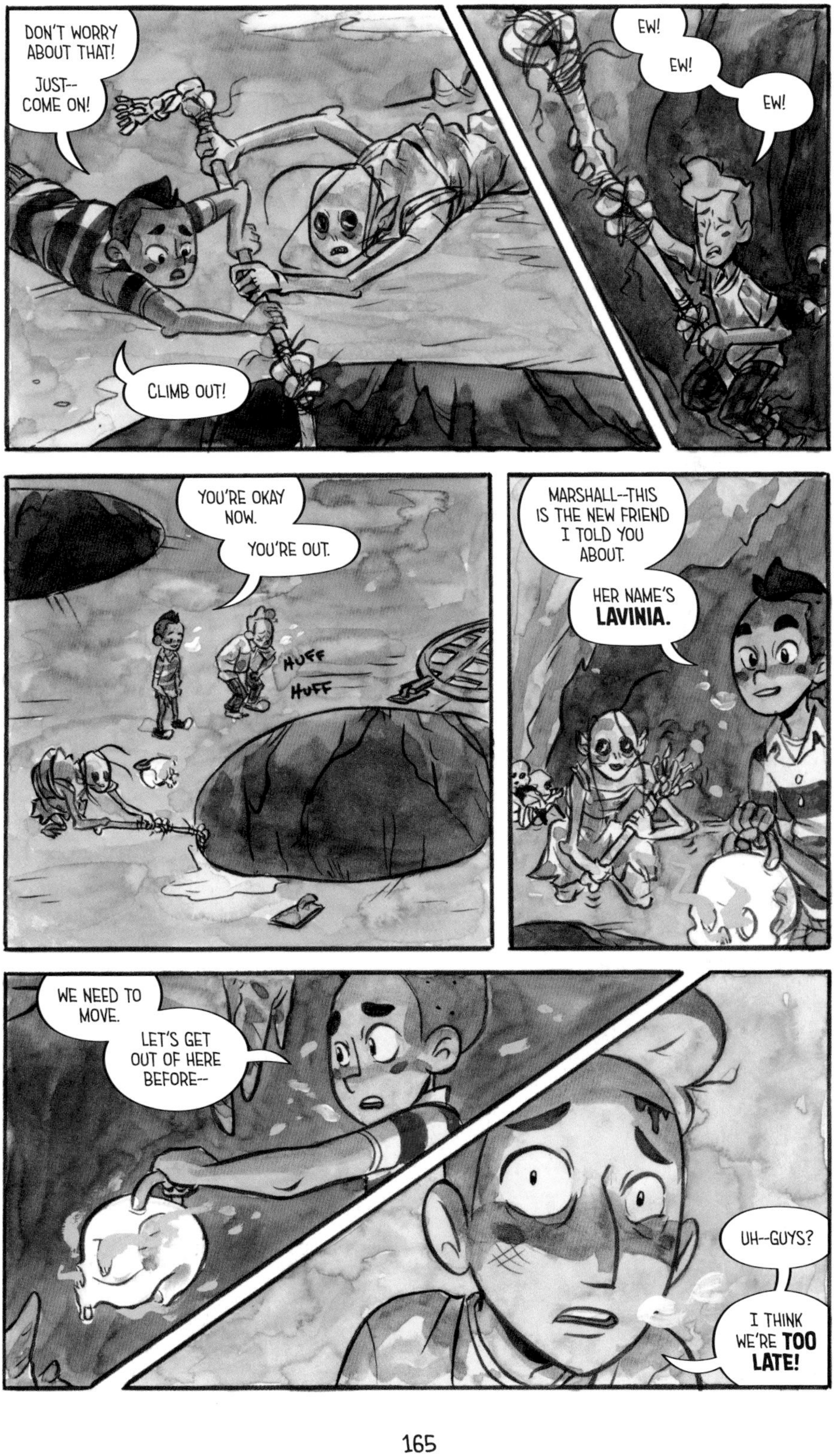
DON'T WORRY ABOUT THAT!
JUST-- COME ON!
CLIMB OUT!
EW!
EW!
EW!
YOU'RE OKAY NOW.
YOU'RE OUT.
HUFF
HUFF
MARSHALL--THIS IS THE NEW FRIEND I TOLD YOU ABOUT.
HER NAME'S **LAVINIA.**
WE NEED TO MOVE.
LET'S GET OUT OF HERE BEFORE--
UH--GUYS?
I THINK WE'RE **TOO LATE!**

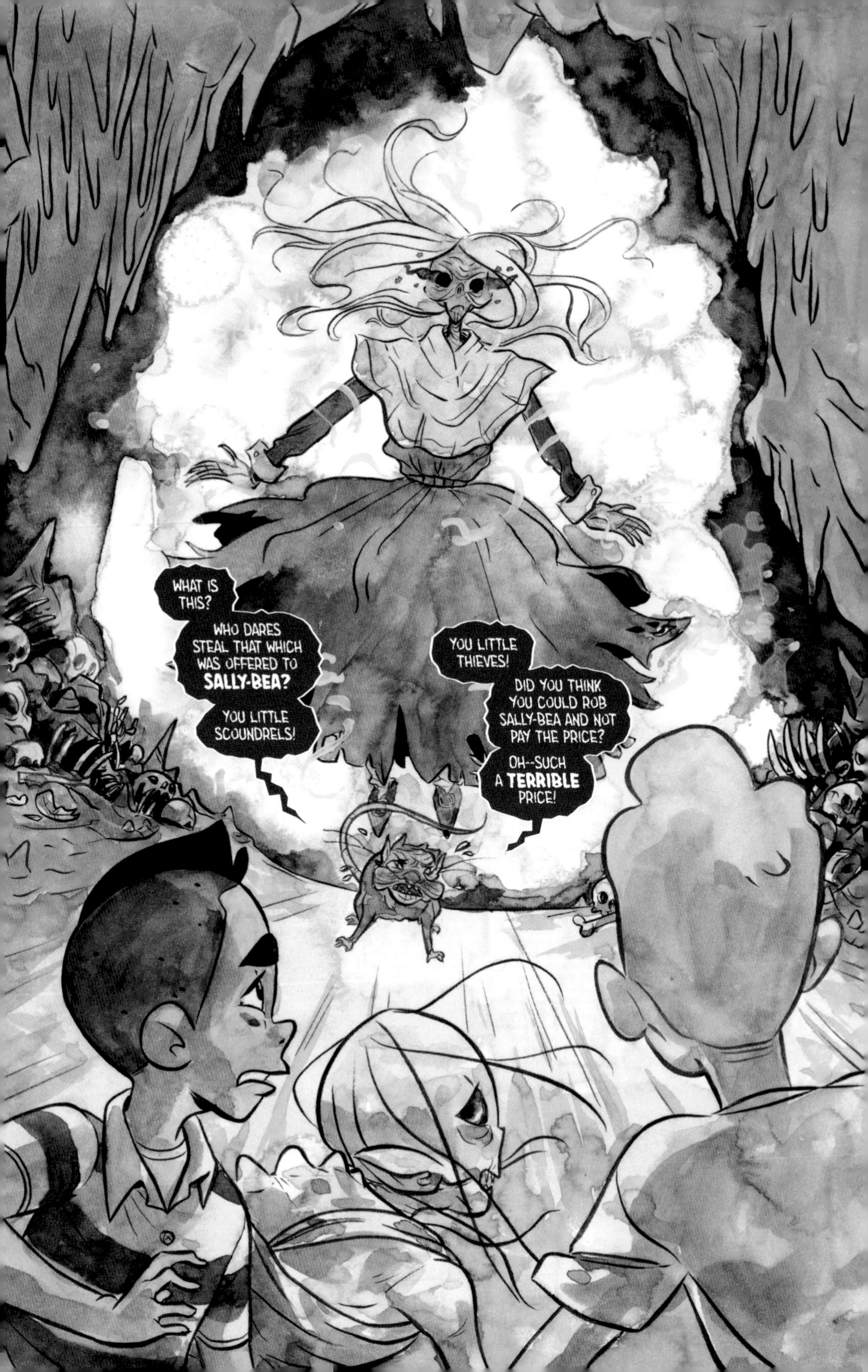
WHAT IS THIS?
WHO DARES STEAL THAT WHICH WAS OFFERED TO **SALLY-BEA?**
YOU LITTLE SCOUNDRELS!
YOU LITTLE THIEVES!
DID YOU THINK YOU COULD ROB SALLY-BEA AND NOT PAY THE PRICE?
OH--SUCH A **TERRIBLE** PRICE!

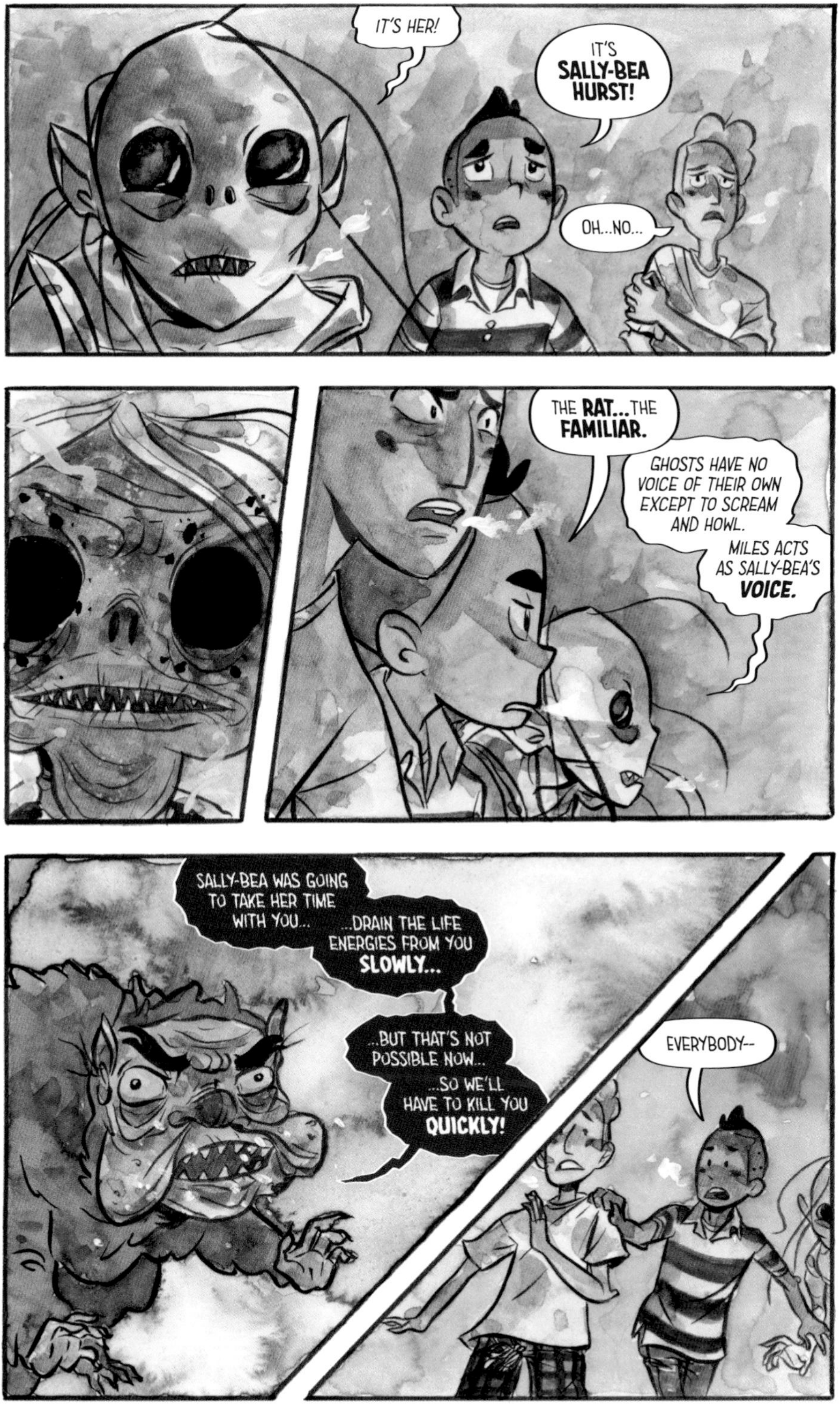
IT'S HER!
IT'S SALLY-BEA HURST!
OH...NO...
THE RAT...THE FAMILIAR.
GHOSTS HAVE NO VOICE OF THEIR OWN EXCEPT TO SCREAM AND HOWL.
MILES ACTS AS SALLY-BEA'S VOICE.
SALLY-BEA WAS GOING TO TAKE HER TIME WITH YOU...
...DRAIN THE LIFE ENERGIES FROM YOU SLOWLY...
...BUT THAT'S NOT POSSIBLE NOW...
...SO WE'LL HAVE TO KILL YOU QUICKLY!
EVERYBODY--

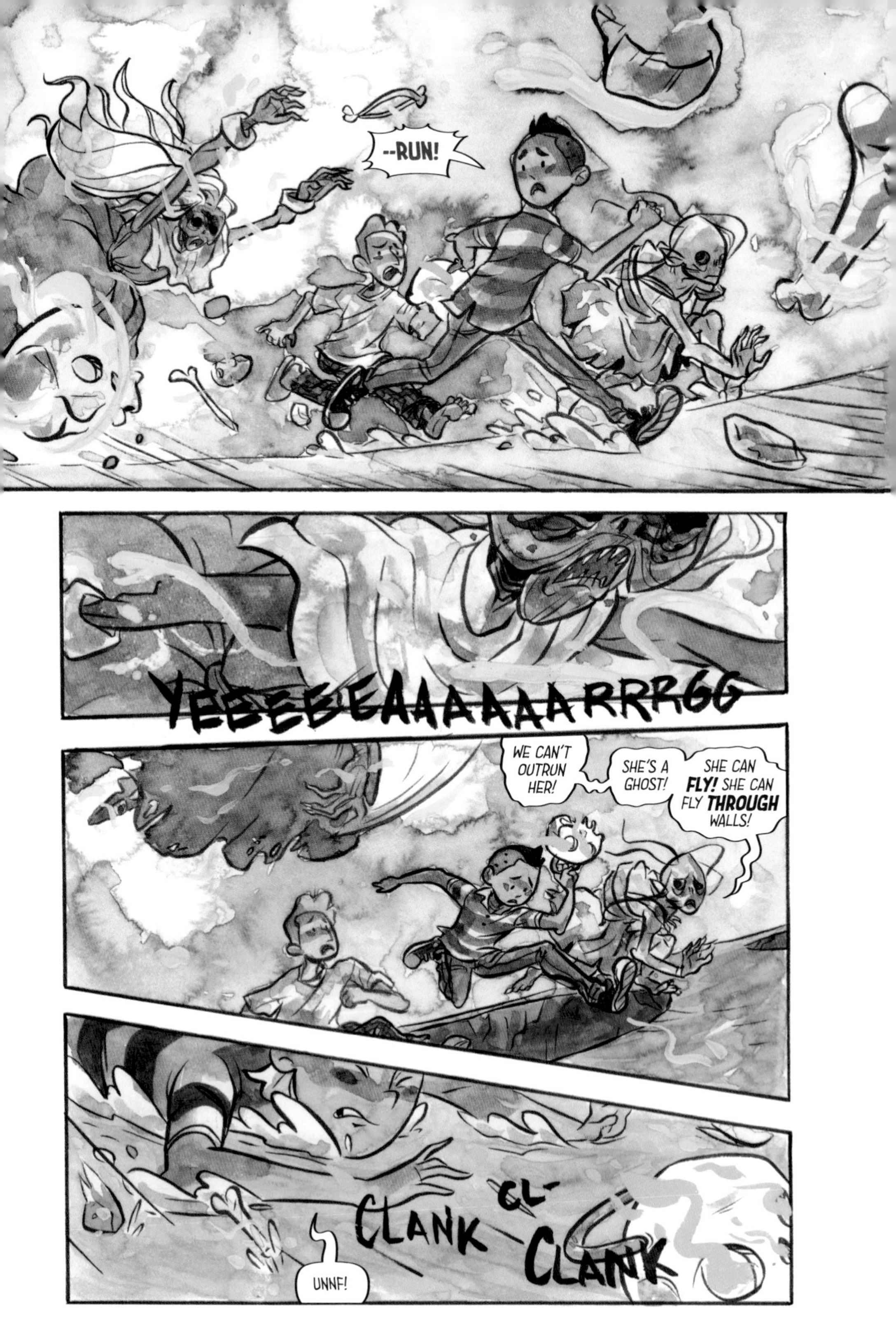

--RUN!
YEEEEEEAAAAAAARRRGG
WE CAN'T OUTRUN HER!
SHE'S A GHOST!
SHE CAN **FLY!** SHE CAN FLY **THROUGH** WALLS!
CLANK
CL-
CLANK
UNNF!

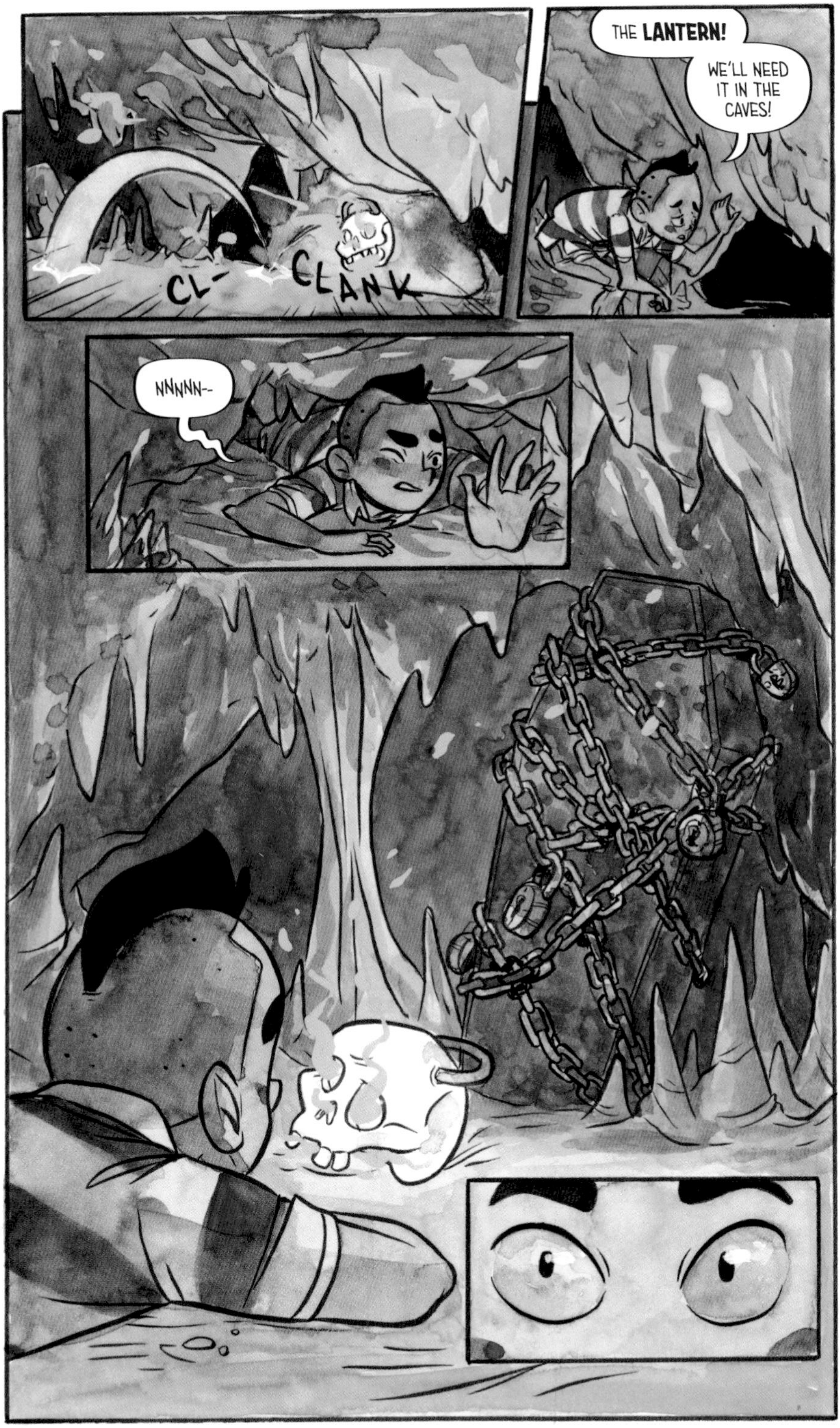
CL- CLANK
THE LANTERN!
WE'LL NEED IT IN THE CAVES!
NNNNN--

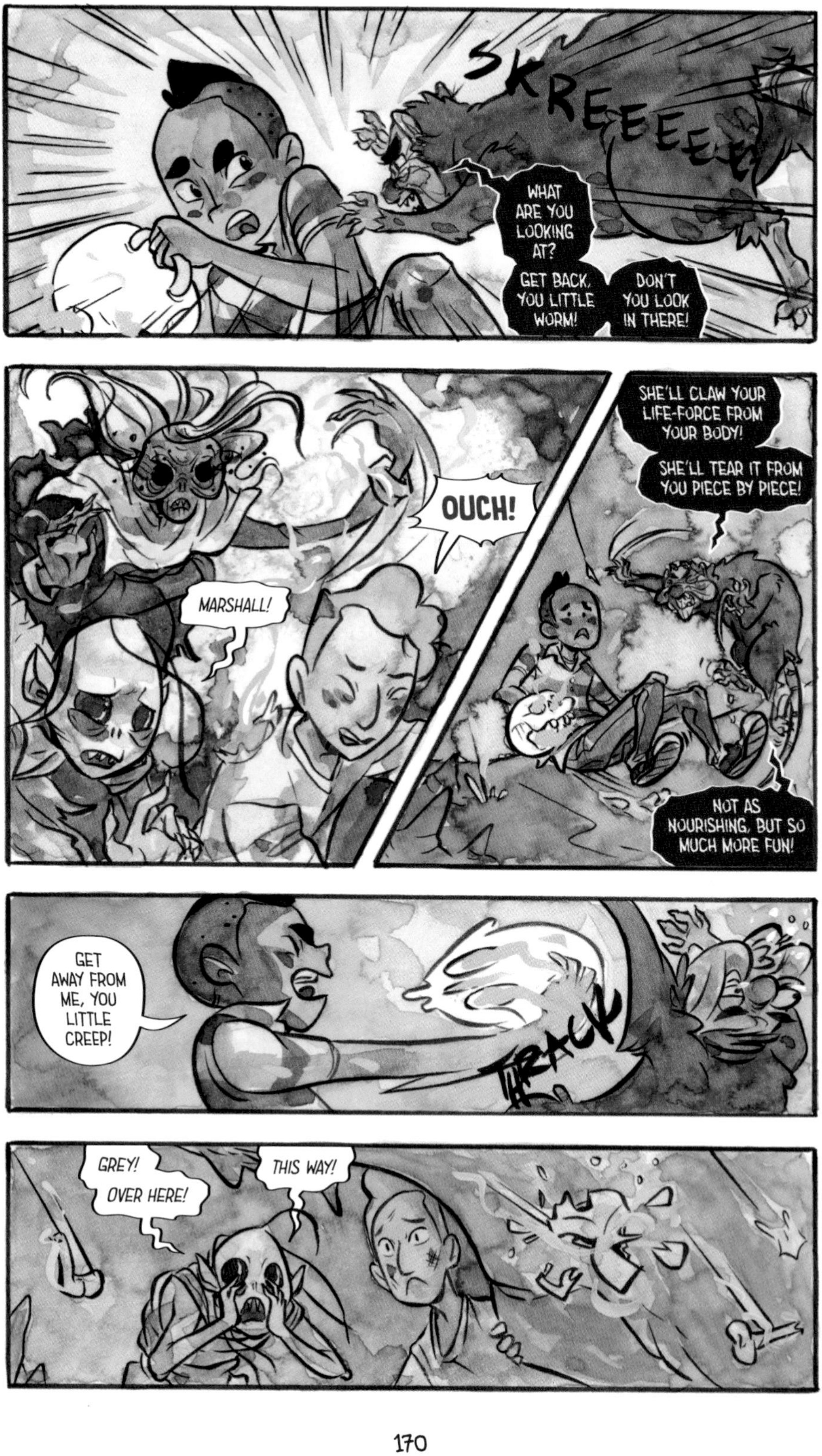
SKREEEEEE
WHAT ARE YOU LOOKING AT?
GET BACK, YOU LITTLE WORM!
DON'T YOU LOOK IN THERE!
OUCH!
MARSHALL!
SHE'LL CLAW YOUR LIFE-FORCE FROM YOUR BODY!
SHE'LL TEAR IT FROM YOU PIECE BY PIECE!
NOT AS NOURISHING, BUT SO MUCH MORE FUN!
GET AWAY FROM ME, YOU LITTLE CREEP!
THRACK
GREY!
OVER HERE!
THIS WAY!

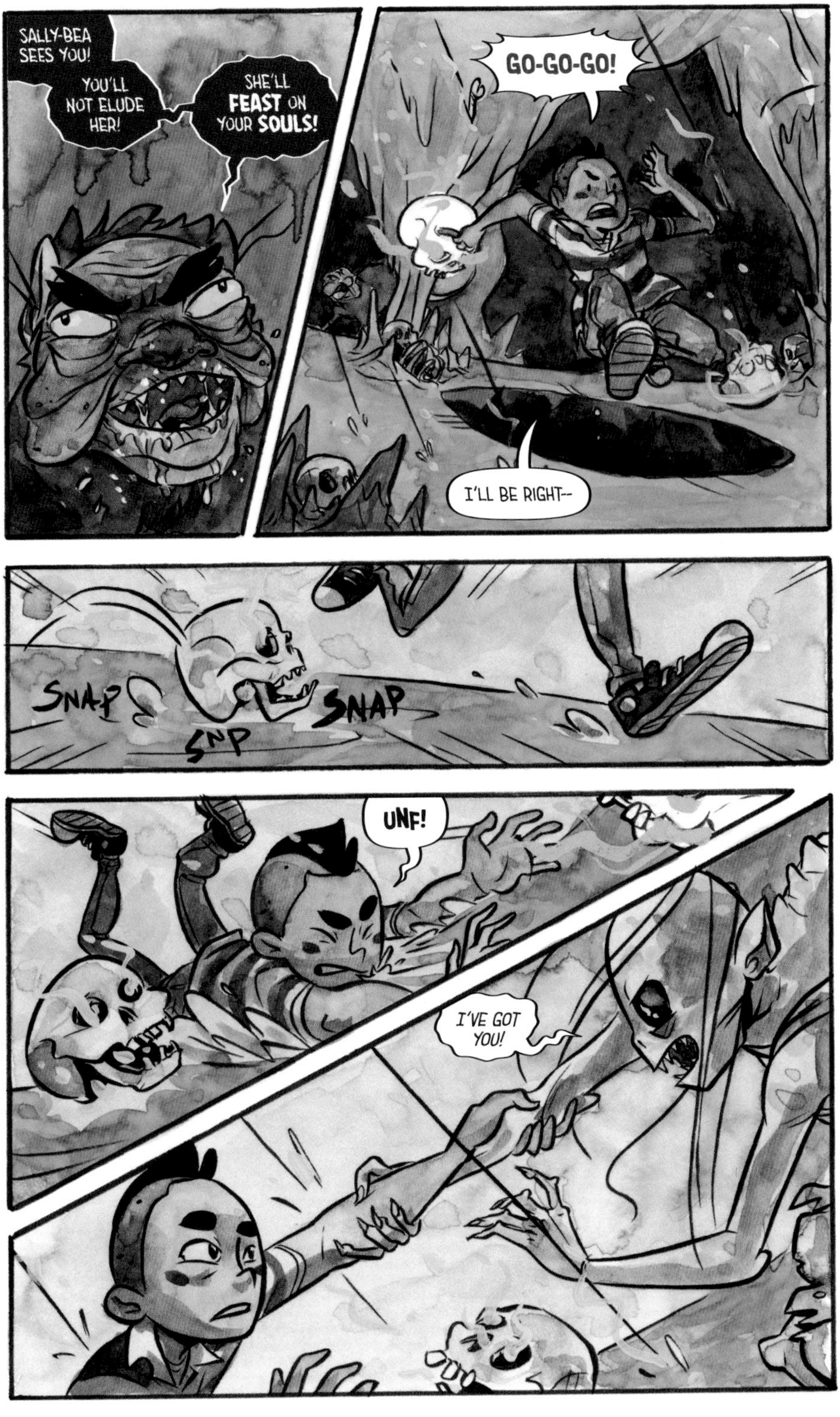

SALLY-BEA SEES YOU!
YOU'LL NOT ELUDE HER!
SHE'LL FEAST ON YOUR SOULS!
GO-GO-GO!
I'LL BE RIGHT--
SNAP
SNP
SNAP
UNF!
I'VE GOT YOU!

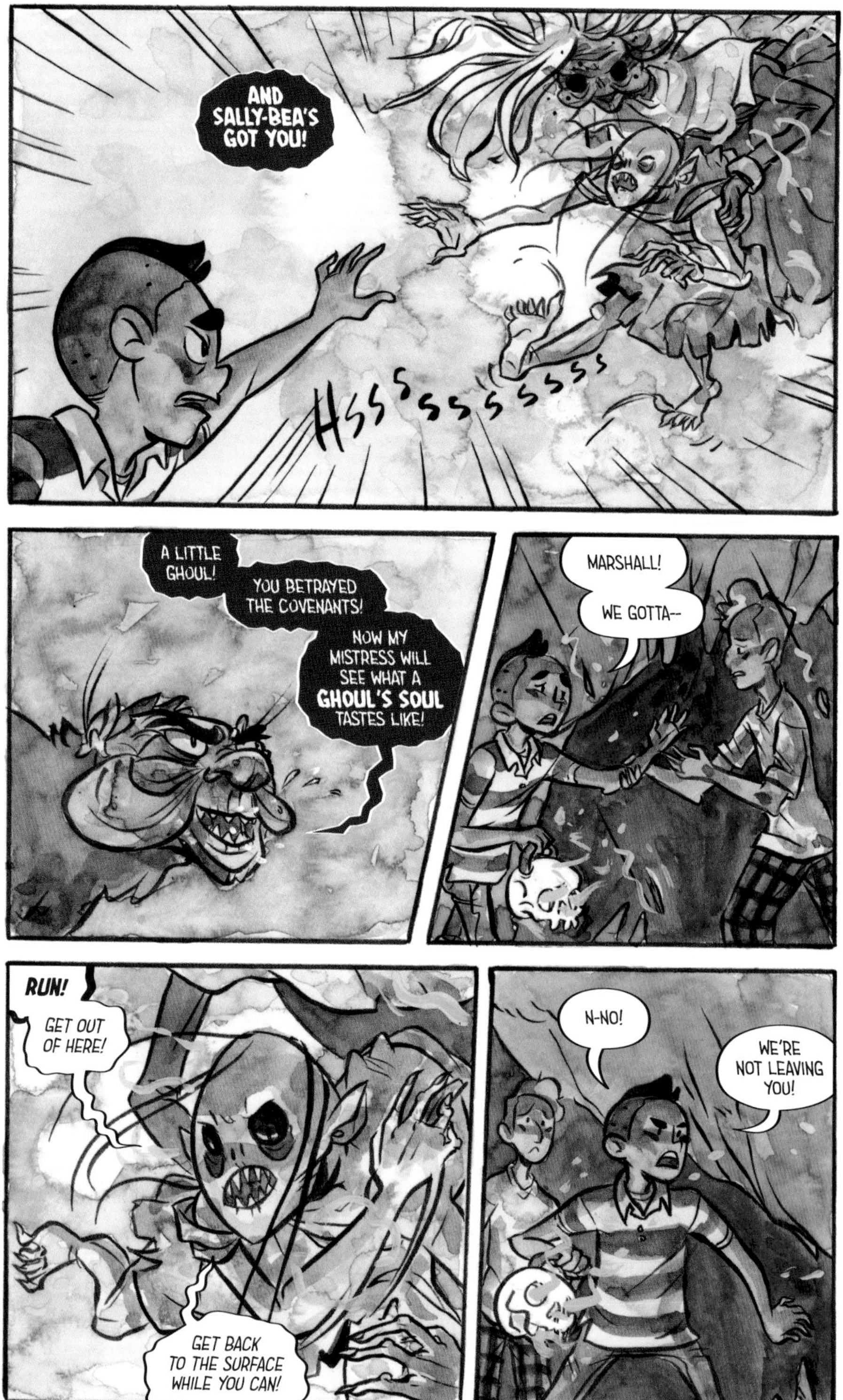
AND SALLY-BEA'S GOT YOU!
HSSSSSSSSSSSSS
A LITTLE GHOUL!
YOU BETRAYED THE COVENANTS!
NOW MY MISTRESS WILL SEE WHAT A **GHOUL'S SOUL** TASTES LIKE!
MARSHALL!
WE GOTTA--
RUN!
GET OUT OF HERE!
GET BACK TO THE SURFACE WHILE YOU CAN!
N-NO!
WE'RE NOT LEAVING YOU!

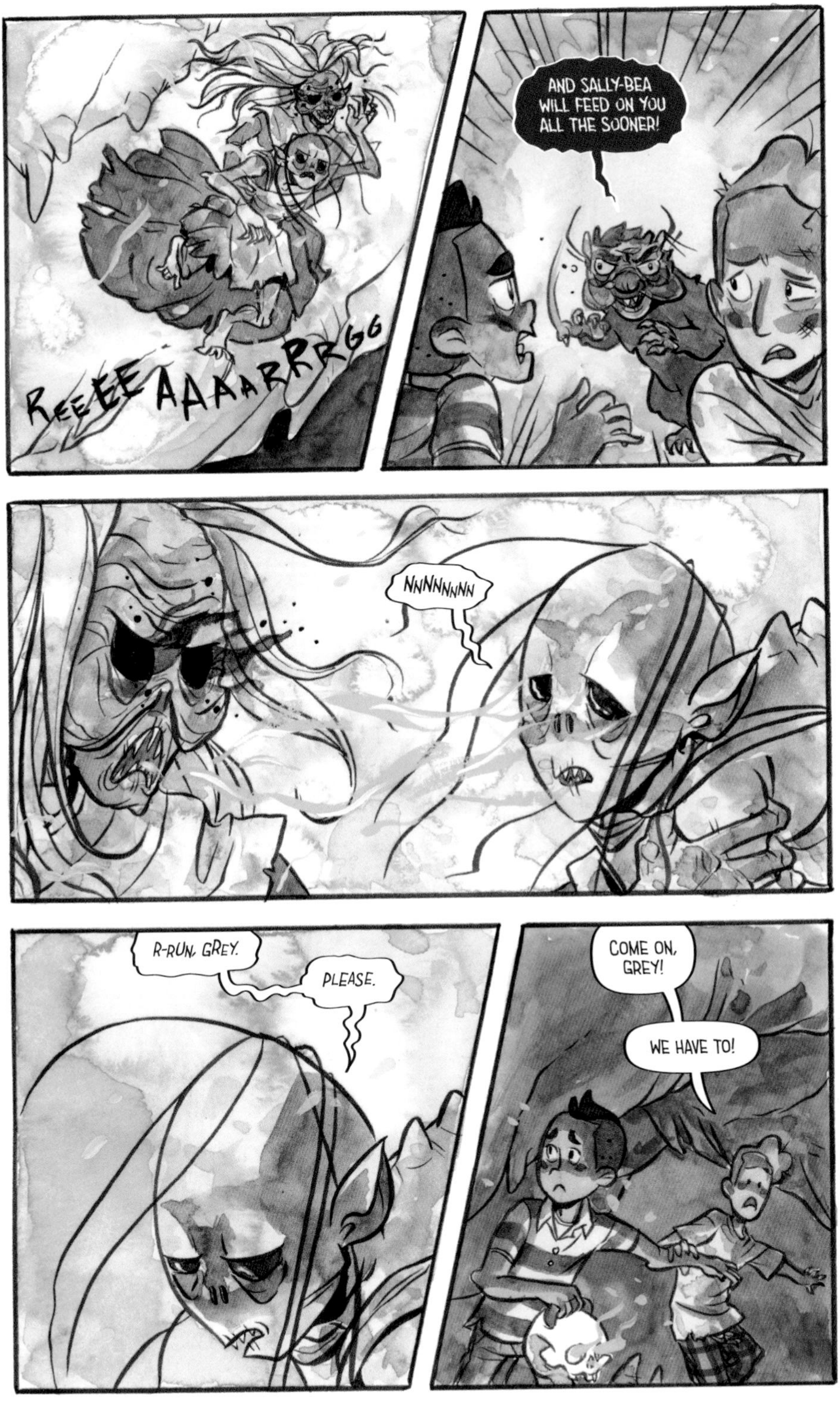
REEEEAAAARRRGG
AND SALLY-BEA WILL FEED ON YOU ALL THE SOONER!
NNNNNNNN
R-RUN, GREY.
PLEASE.
COME ON, GREY!
WE HAVE TO!

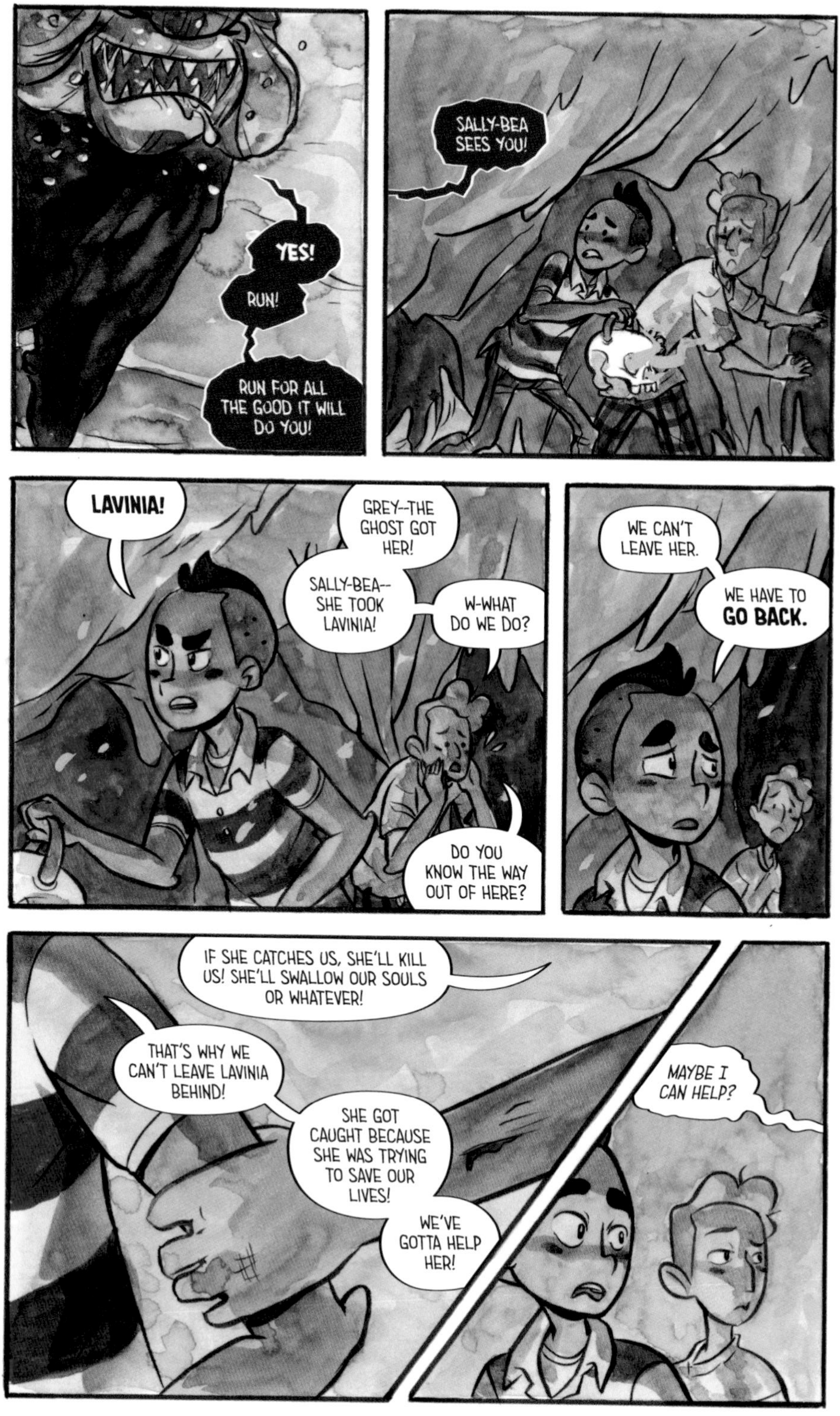

YES!
RUN!
RUN FOR ALL THE GOOD IT WILL DO YOU!
SALLY-BEA SEES YOU!
LAVINIA!
GREY--THE GHOST GOT HER!
SALLY-BEA--SHE TOOK LAVINIA!
W-WHAT DO WE DO?
DO YOU KNOW THE WAY OUT OF HERE?
WE CAN'T LEAVE HER.
WE HAVE TO GO BACK.
IF SHE CATCHES US, SHE'LL KILL US! SHE'LL SWALLOW OUR SOULS OR WHATEVER!
THAT'S WHY WE CAN'T LEAVE LAVINIA BEHIND!
SHE GOT CAUGHT BECAUSE SHE WAS TRYING TO SAVE OUR LIVES!
WE'VE GOTTA HELP HER!
MAYBE I CAN HELP?

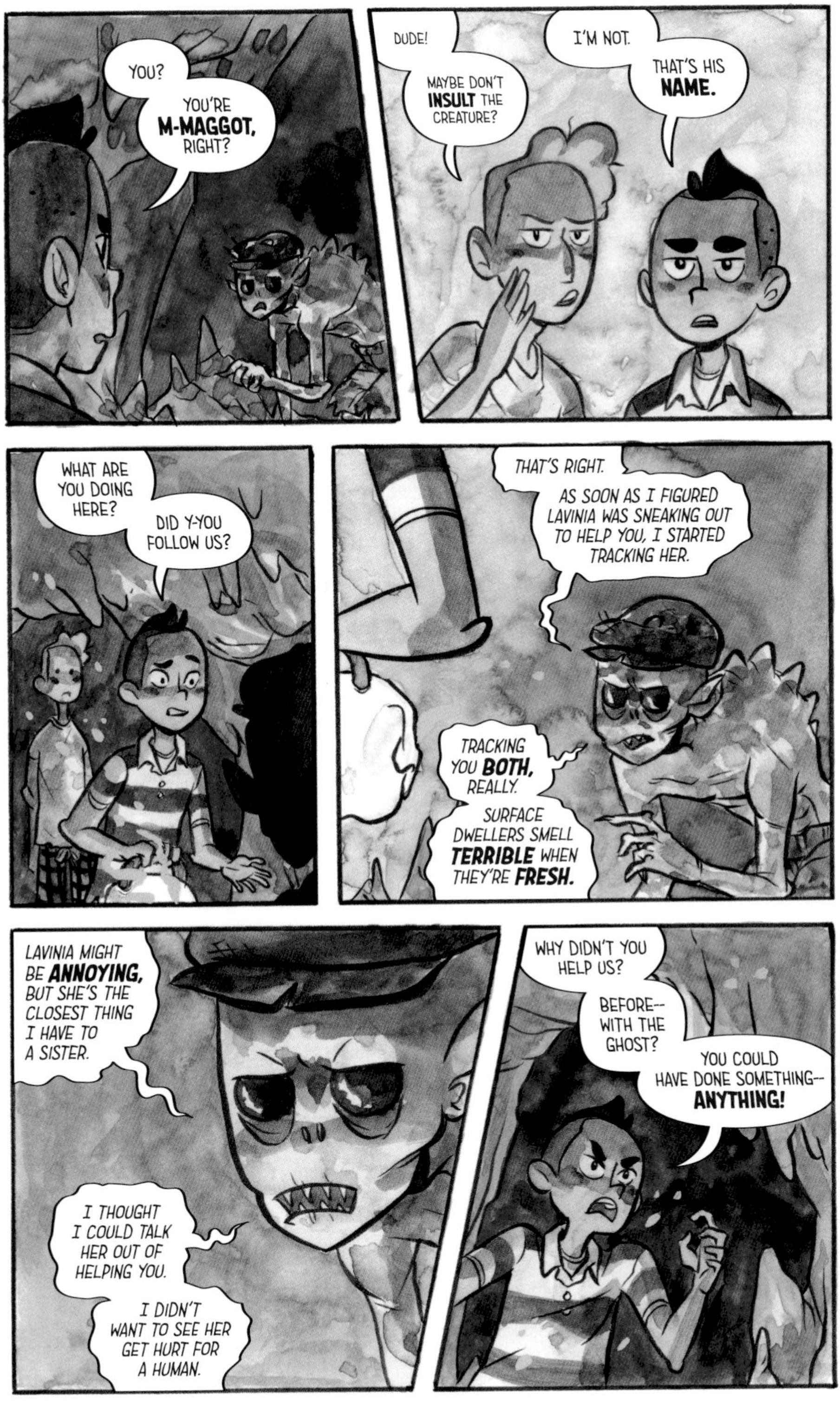
YOU?
YOU'RE M-MAGGOT, RIGHT?
DUDE!
MAYBE DON'T INSULT THE CREATURE?
I'M NOT.
THAT'S HIS NAME.
WHAT ARE YOU DOING HERE?
DID Y-YOU FOLLOW US?
THAT'S RIGHT.
AS SOON AS I FIGURED LAVINIA WAS SNEAKING OUT TO HELP YOU, I STARTED TRACKING HER.
TRACKING YOU BOTH, REALLY.
SURFACE DWELLERS SMELL TERRIBLE WHEN THEY'RE FRESH.
LAVINIA MIGHT BE ANNOYING, BUT SHE'S THE CLOSEST THING I HAVE TO A SISTER.
I THOUGHT I COULD TALK HER OUT OF HELPING YOU.
I DIDN'T WANT TO SEE HER GET HURT FOR A HUMAN.
WHY DIDN'T YOU HELP US?
BEFORE-- WITH THE GHOST?
YOU COULD HAVE DONE SOMETHING-- ANYTHING!

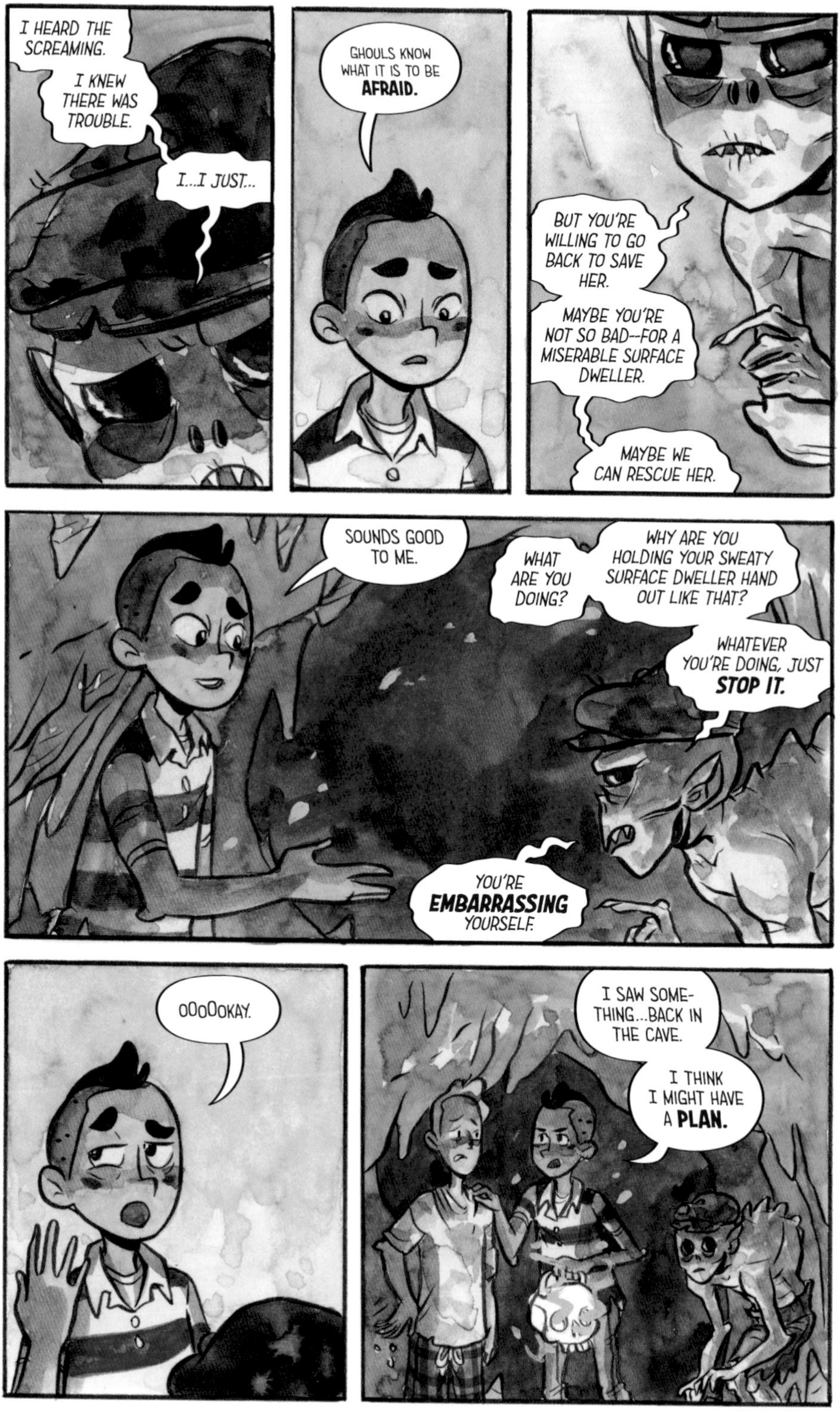
I HEARD THE SCREAMING.
I KNEW THERE WAS TROUBLE.
I...I JUST...
GHOULS KNOW WHAT IT IS TO BE **AFRAID.**
BUT YOU'RE WILLING TO GO BACK TO SAVE HER.
MAYBE YOU'RE NOT SO BAD--FOR A MISERABLE SURFACE DWELLER.
MAYBE WE CAN RESCUE HER.
SOUNDS GOOD TO ME.
WHAT ARE YOU DOING?
WHY ARE YOU HOLDING YOUR SWEATY SURFACE DWELLER HAND OUT LIKE THAT?
WHATEVER YOU'RE DOING, JUST **STOP IT.**
YOU'RE **EMBARRASSING** YOURSELF.
OOOOOKAY.
I SAW SOME-THING...BACK IN THE CAVE.
I THINK I MIGHT HAVE A **PLAN.**

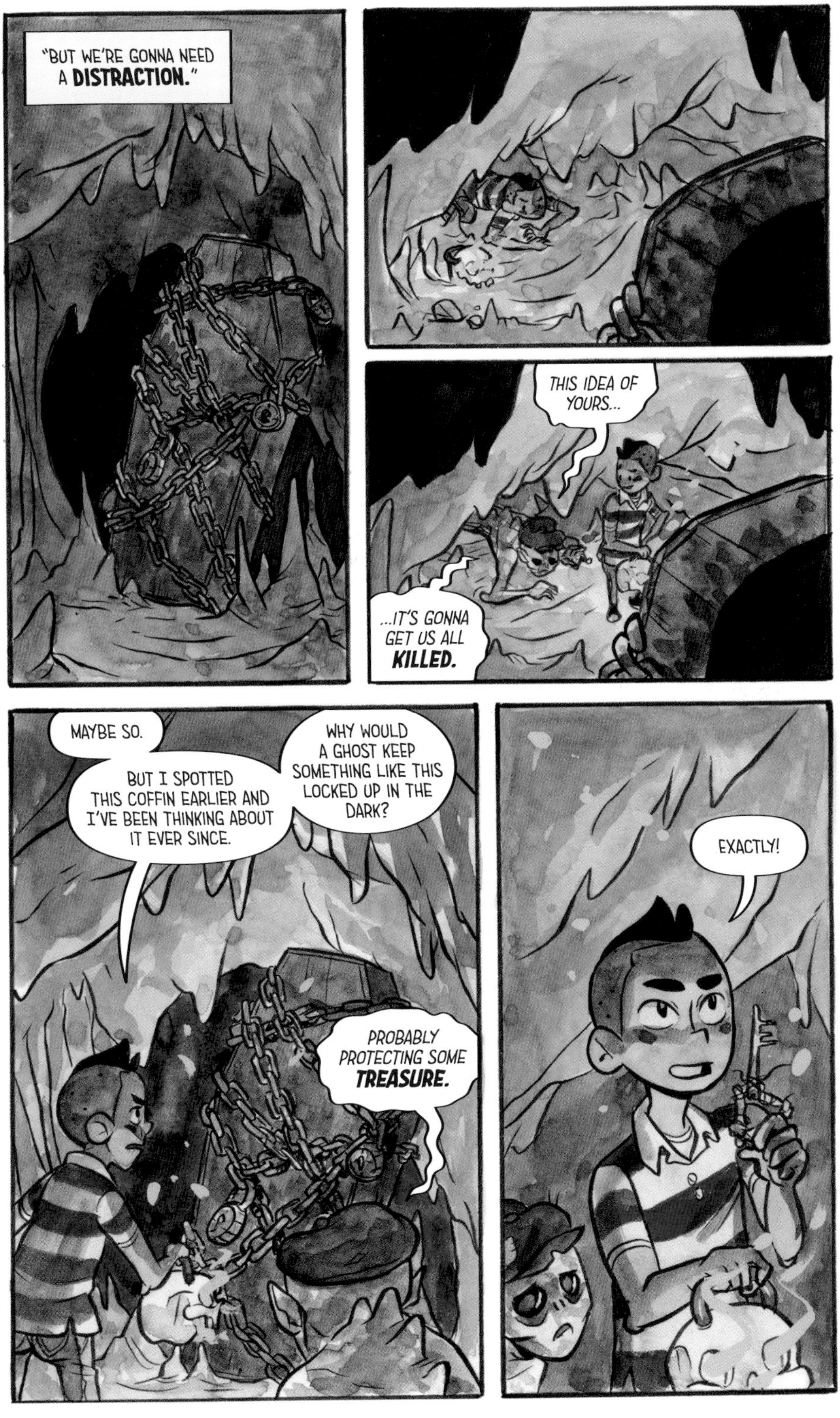
"BUT WE'RE GONNA NEED A **DISTRACTION.**"
THIS IDEA OF YOURS...
...IT'S GONNA GET US ALL **KILLED.**
MAYBE SO.
BUT I SPOTTED THIS COFFIN EARLIER AND I'VE BEEN THINKING ABOUT IT EVER SINCE.
WHY WOULD A GHOST KEEP SOMETHING LIKE THIS LOCKED UP IN THE DARK?
PROBABLY PROTECTING SOME **TREASURE.**
EXACTLY!

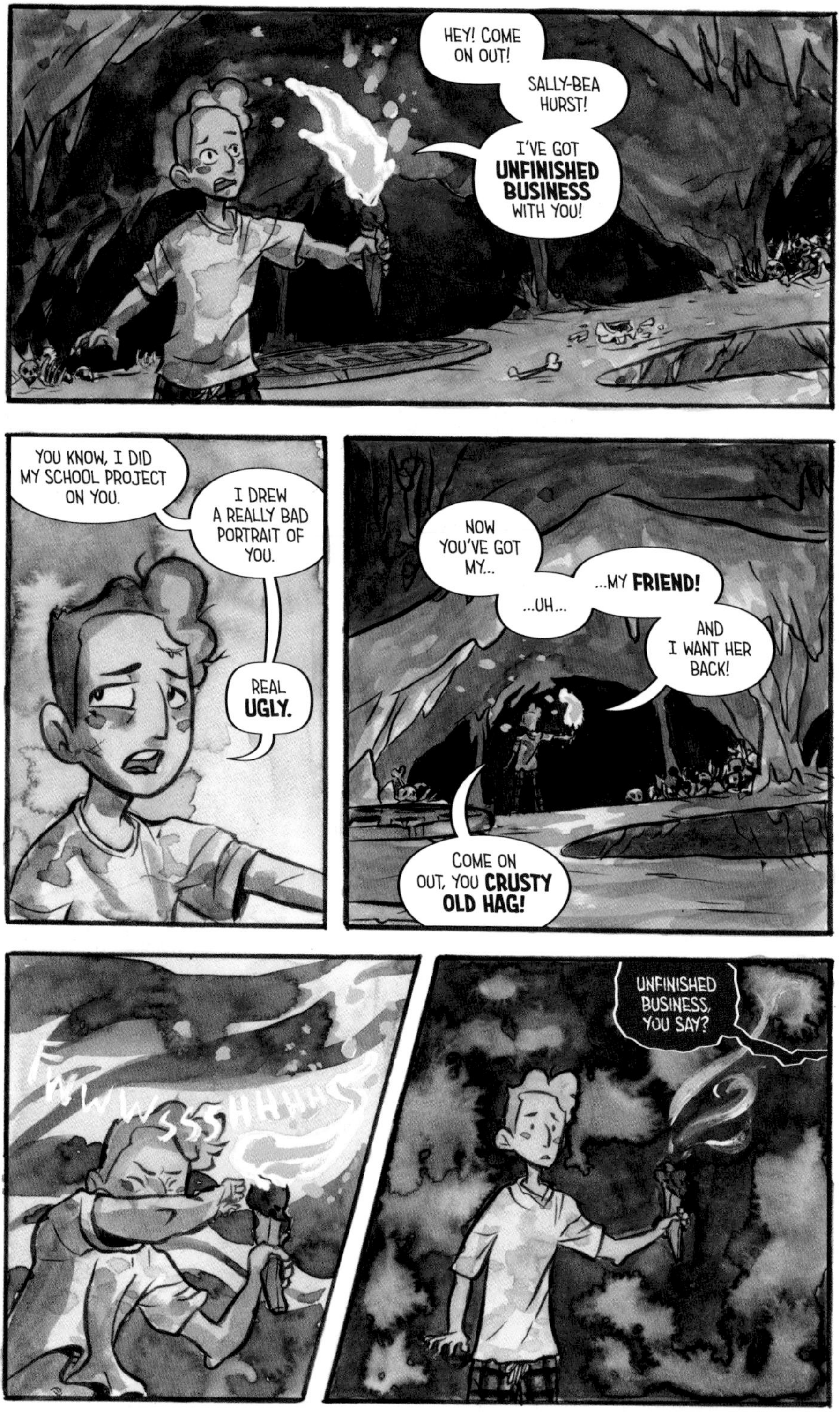
HEY! COME ON OUT!
SALLY-BEA HURST!
I'VE GOT **UNFINISHED BUSINESS** WITH YOU!
YOU KNOW, I DID MY SCHOOL PROJECT ON YOU.
I DREW A REALLY BAD PORTRAIT OF YOU.
REAL **UGLY.**
NOW YOU'VE GOT MY...
...UH...
...MY **FRIEND!**
AND I WANT HER BACK!
COME ON OUT, YOU **CRUSTY OLD HAG!**
FWWWSSSHHHHS
UNFINISHED BUSINESS, YOU SAY?

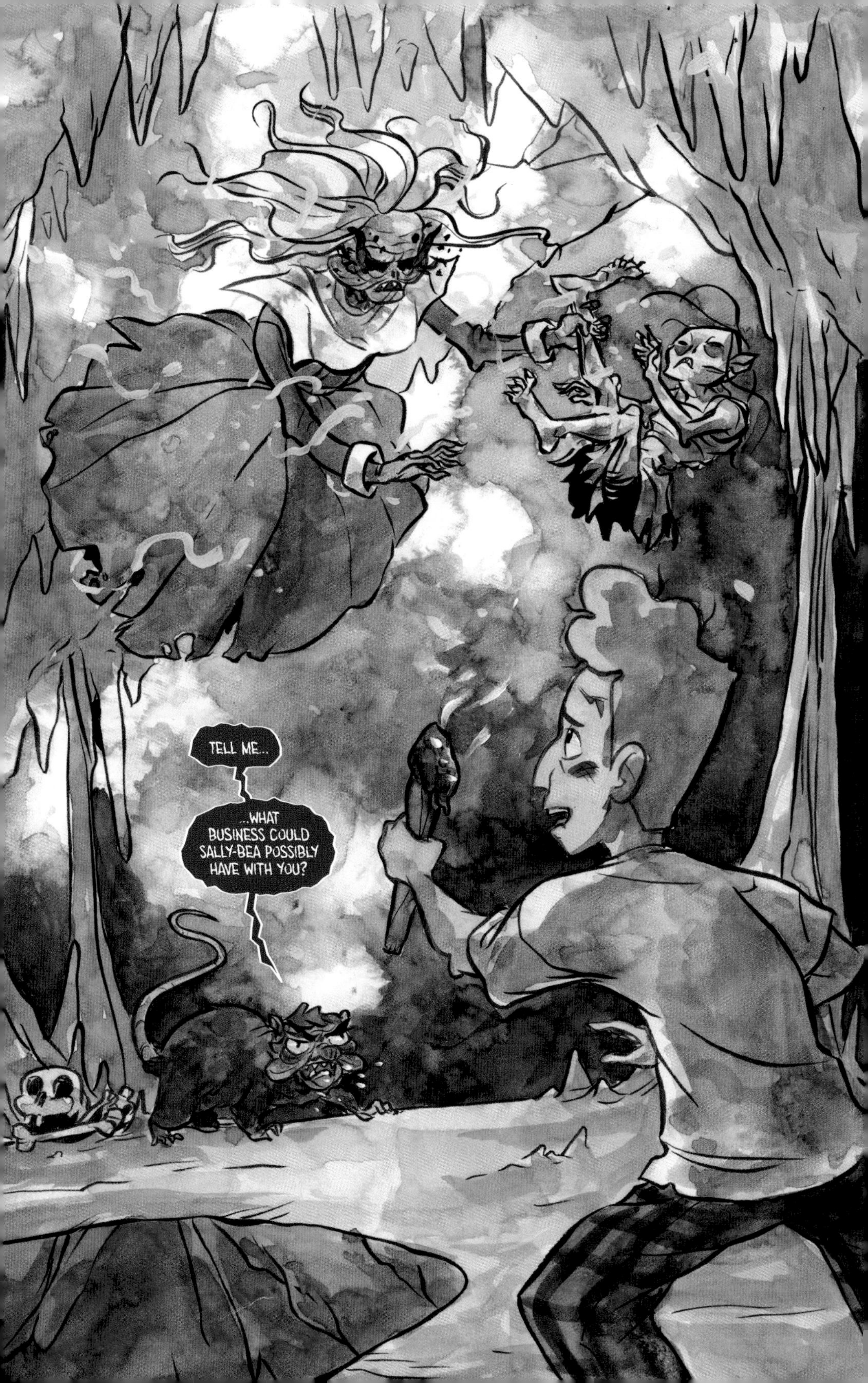
TELL ME...
...WHAT BUSINESS COULD SALLY-BEA POSSIBLY HAVE WITH YOU?

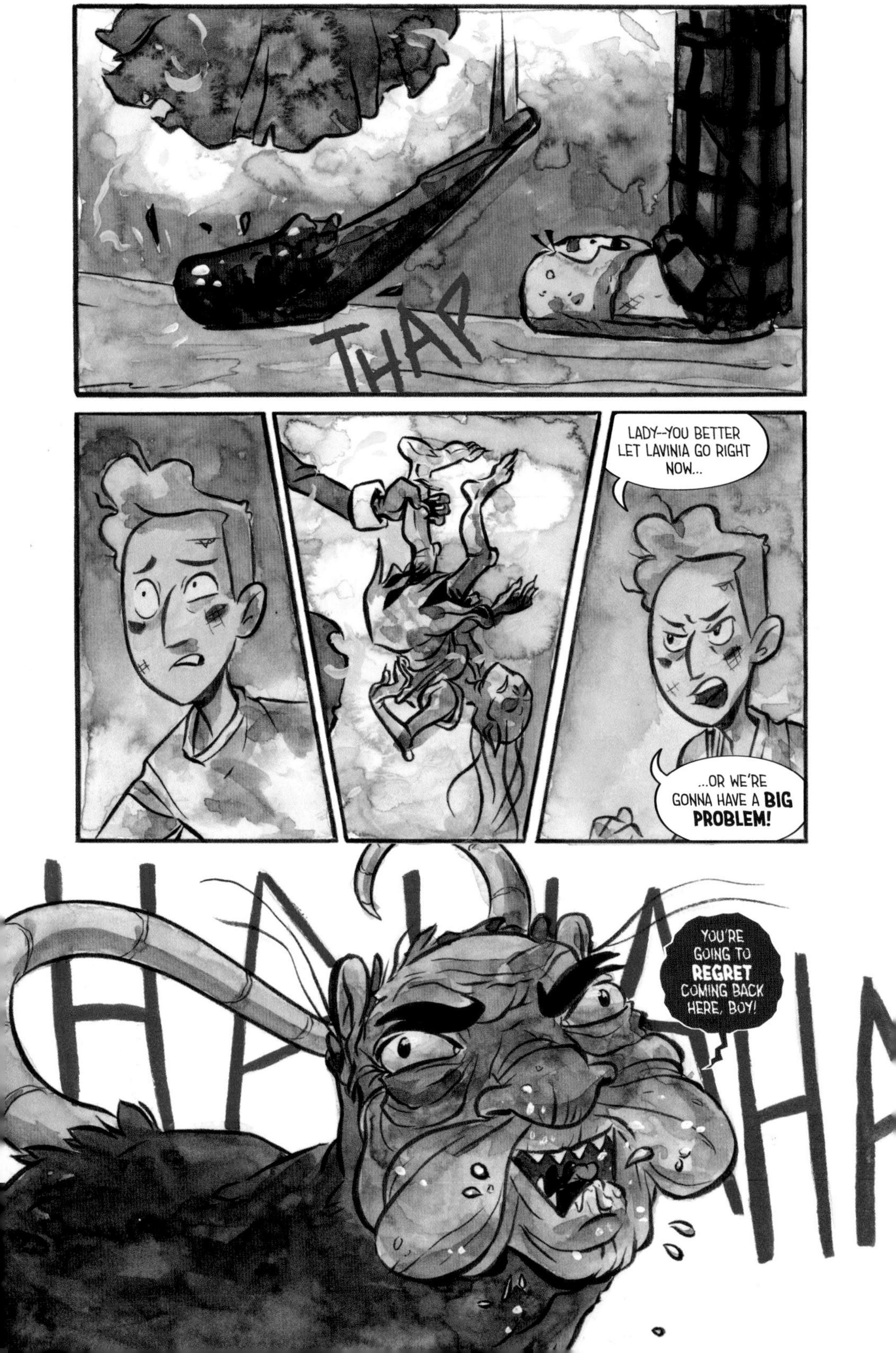
THAP
LADY--YOU BETTER LET LAVINIA GO RIGHT NOW...
...OR WE'RE GONNA HAVE A **BIG PROBLEM!**
YOU'RE GOING TO **REGRET** COMING BACK HERE, BOY!

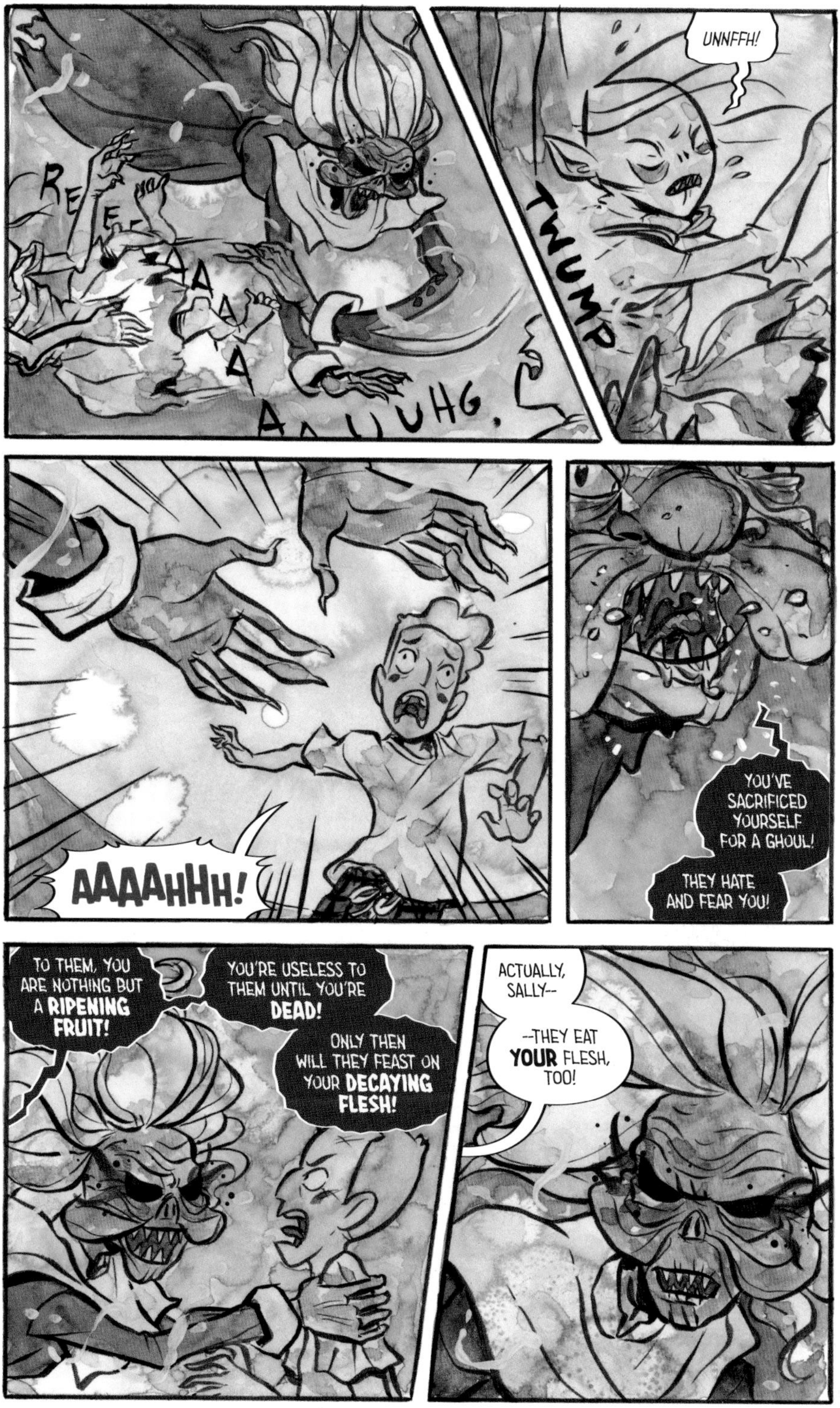
REEEAAAAAAAUUHG
TWUMP
UNNFFH!
AAAAHHH!
YOU'VE SACRIFICED YOURSELF FOR A GHOUL!
THEY HATE AND FEAR YOU!
TO THEM, YOU ARE NOTHING BUT A RIPENING FRUIT!
YOU'RE USELESS TO THEM UNTIL YOU'RE DEAD!
ONLY THEN WILL THEY FEAST ON YOUR DECAYING FLESH!
ACTUALLY, SALLY--
--THEY EAT YOUR FLESH, TOO!

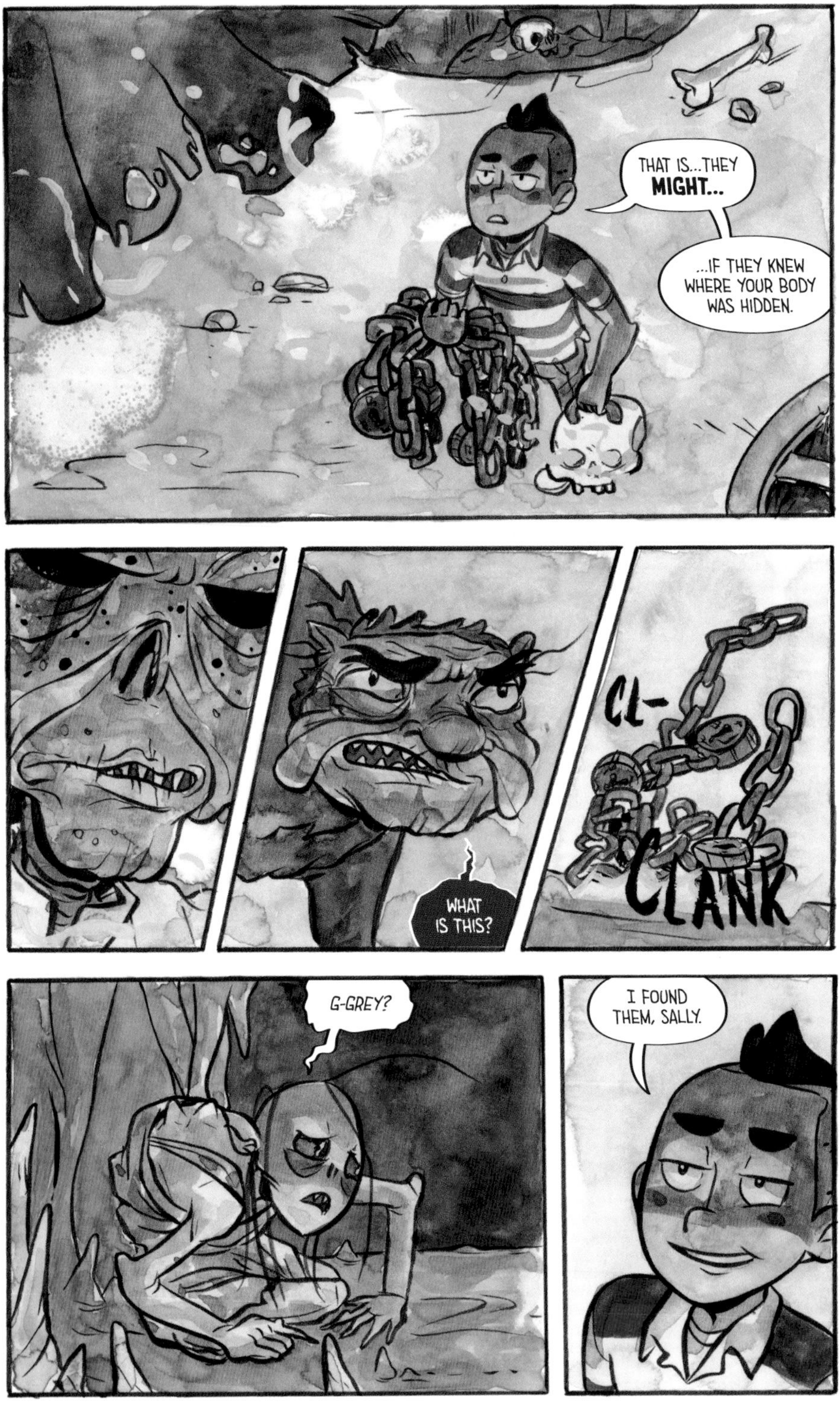
THAT IS...THEY **MIGHT...**
...IF THEY KNEW WHERE YOUR BODY WAS HIDDEN.
WHAT IS THIS?
CL-
CLANK
G-GREY?
I FOUND THEM, SALLY.

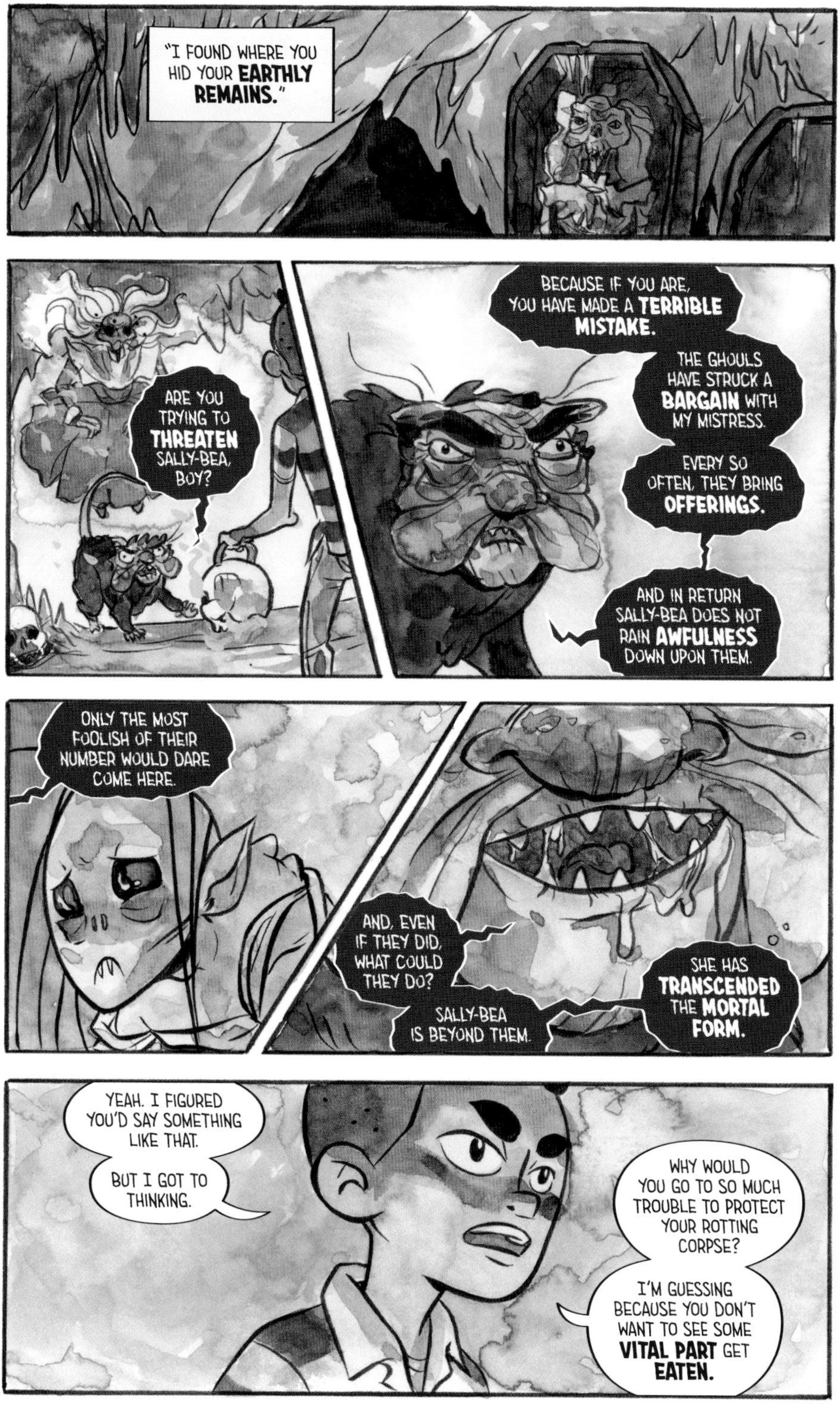
"I FOUND WHERE YOU HID YOUR EARTHLY REMAINS."
ARE YOU TRYING TO THREATEN SALLY-BEA, BOY?
BECAUSE IF YOU ARE, YOU HAVE MADE A TERRIBLE MISTAKE.
THE GHOULS HAVE STRUCK A BARGAIN WITH MY MISTRESS.
EVERY SO OFTEN, THEY BRING OFFERINGS.
AND IN RETURN SALLY-BEA DOES NOT RAIN AWFULNESS DOWN UPON THEM.
ONLY THE MOST FOOLISH OF THEIR NUMBER WOULD DARE COME HERE.
AND, EVEN IF THEY DID, WHAT COULD THEY DO?
SALLY-BEA IS BEYOND THEM.
SHE HAS TRANSCENDED THE MORTAL FORM.
YEAH. I FIGURED YOU'D SAY SOMETHING LIKE THAT.
BUT I GOT TO THINKING.
WHY WOULD YOU GO TO SO MUCH TROUBLE TO PROTECT YOUR ROTTING CORPSE?
I'M GUESSING BECAUSE YOU DON'T WANT TO SEE SOME VITAL PART GET EATEN.

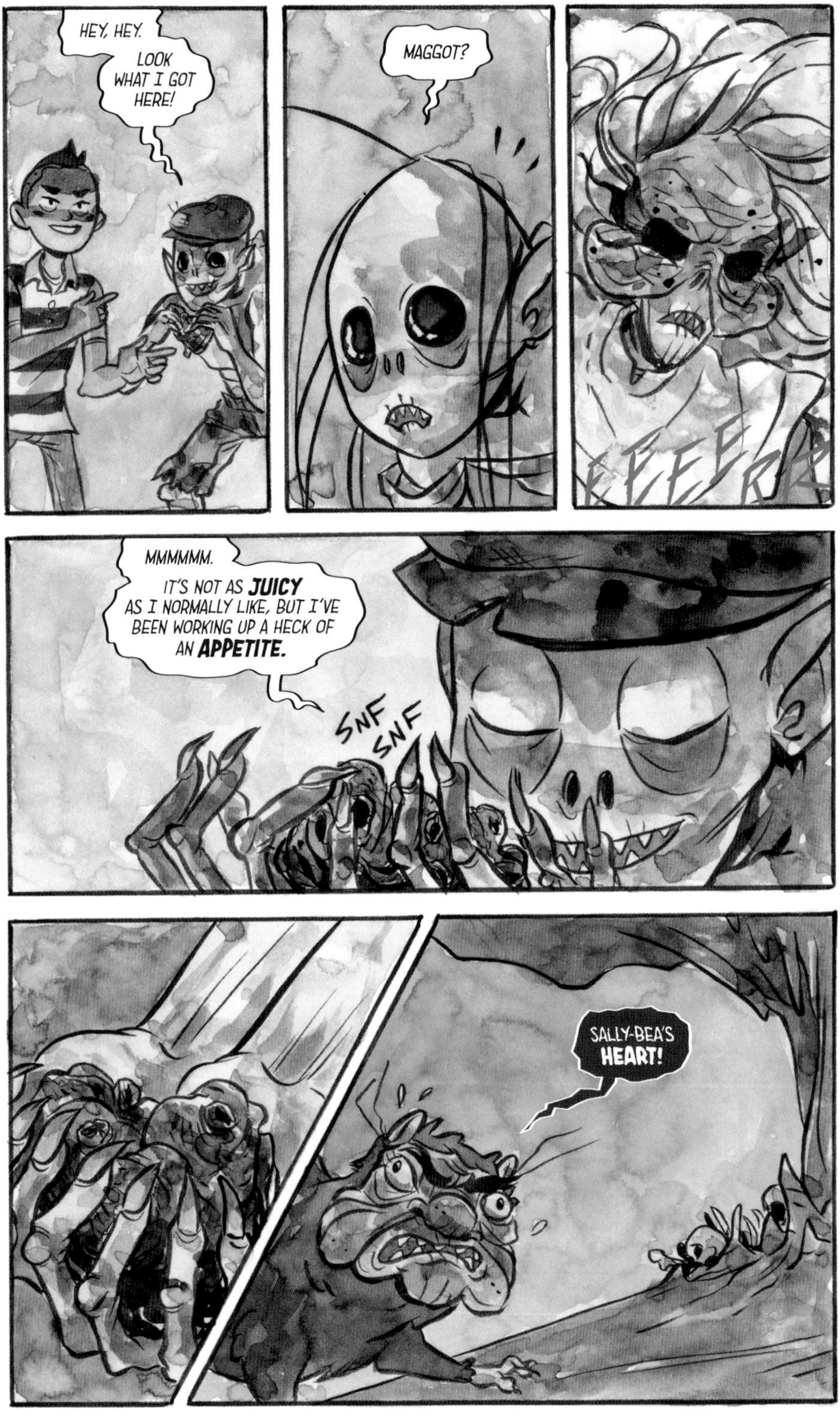
HEY, HEY.
LOOK WHAT I GOT HERE!
MAGGOT?
EEEERR
MMMMMM.
IT'S NOT AS JUICY AS I NORMALLY LIKE, BUT I'VE BEEN WORKING UP A HECK OF AN APPETITE.
SNF SNF
SALLY-BEA'S HEART!

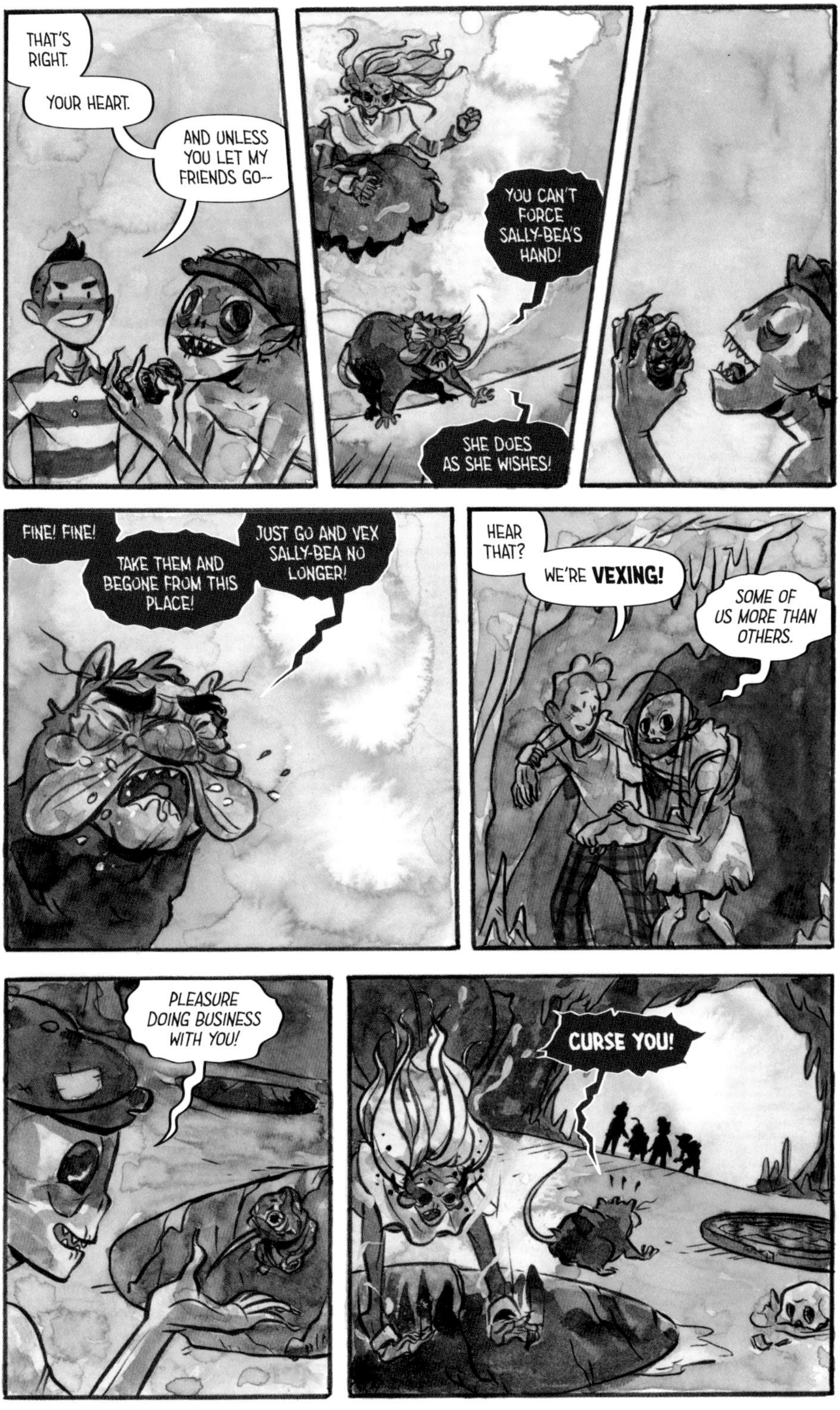
THAT'S RIGHT.
YOUR HEART.
AND UNLESS YOU LET MY FRIENDS GO--
YOU CAN'T FORCE SALLY-BEA'S HAND!
SHE DOES AS SHE WISHES!
FINE! FINE!
TAKE THEM AND BEGONE FROM THIS PLACE!
JUST GO AND VEX SALLY-BEA NO LONGER!
HEAR THAT?
WE'RE **VEXING!**
SOME OF US MORE THAN OTHERS.
PLEASURE DOING BUSINESS WITH YOU!
CURSE YOU!

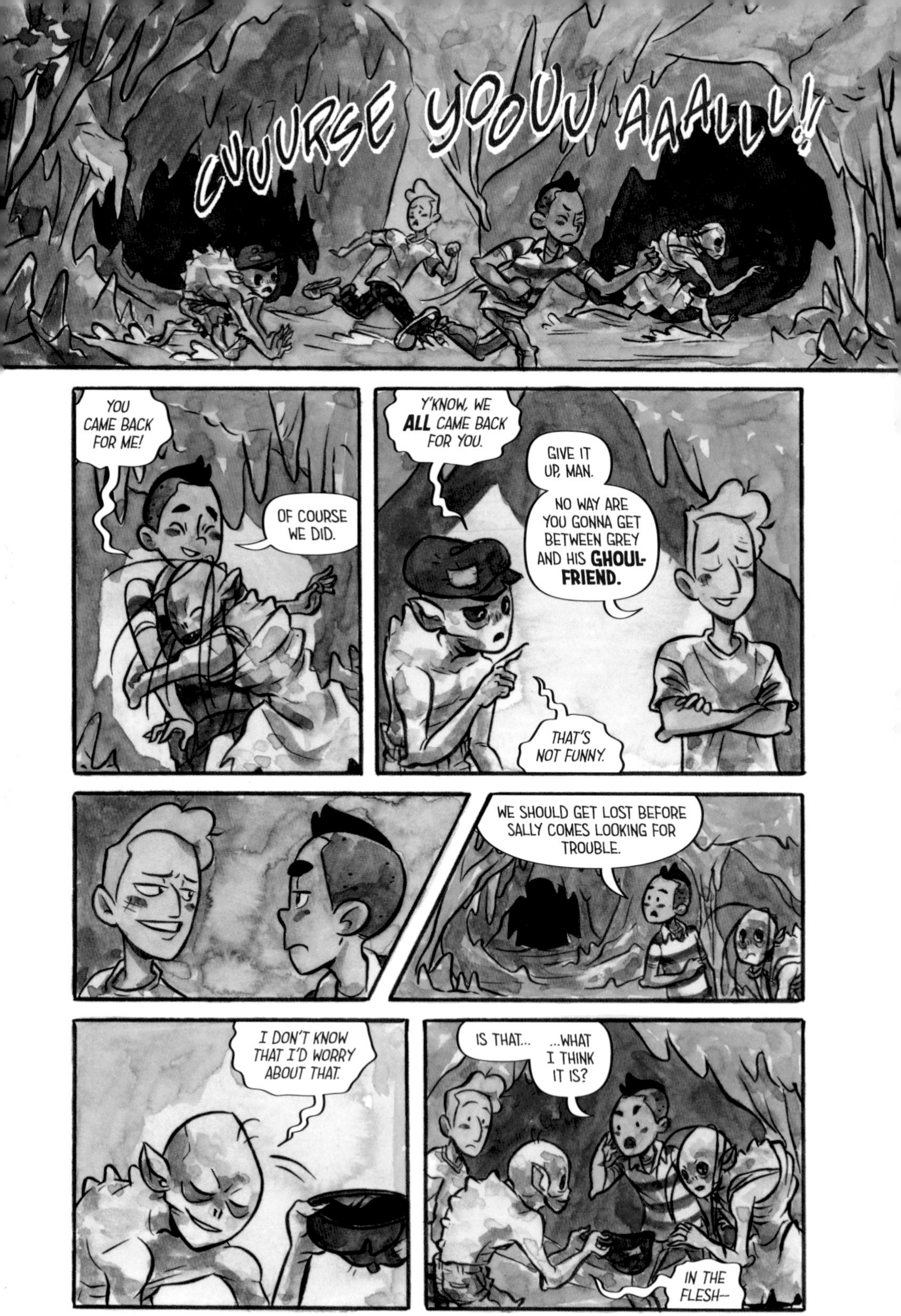
CUUURSE YOOUU AAALLL!!
YOU CAME BACK FOR ME!
OF COURSE WE DID.
Y'KNOW, WE ALL CAME BACK FOR YOU.
GIVE IT UP, MAN.
NO WAY ARE YOU GONNA GET BETWEEN GREY AND HIS GHOUL-FRIEND.
THAT'S NOT FUNNY.
WE SHOULD GET LOST BEFORE SALLY COMES LOOKING FOR TROUBLE.
I DON'T KNOW THAT I'D WORRY ABOUT THAT.
IS THAT...
...WHAT I THINK IT IS?
IN THE FLESH--

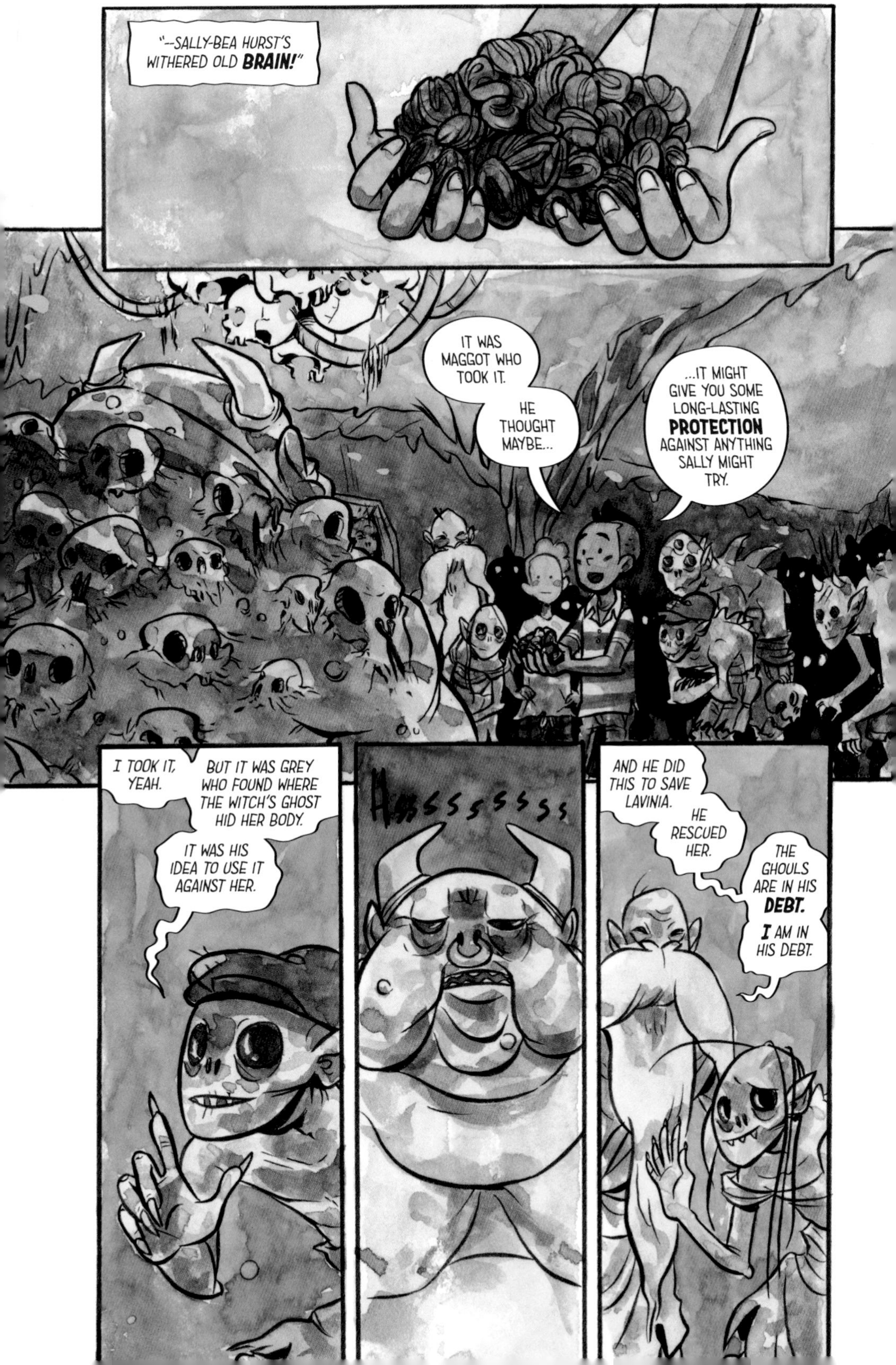
"--SALLY-BEA HURST'S WITHERED OLD **BRAIN!**"
IT WAS MAGGOT WHO TOOK IT.
HE THOUGHT MAYBE...
...IT MIGHT GIVE YOU SOME LONG-LASTING **PROTECTION** AGAINST ANYTHING SALLY MIGHT TRY.
I TOOK IT, YEAH.
BUT IT WAS GREY WHO FOUND WHERE THE WITCH'S GHOST HID HER BODY.
IT WAS HIS IDEA TO USE IT AGAINST HER.
HSSSSSSSSS
AND HE DID THIS TO SAVE LAVINIA.
HE RESCUED HER.
THE GHOULS ARE IN HIS **DEBT.**
I AM IN HIS DEBT.

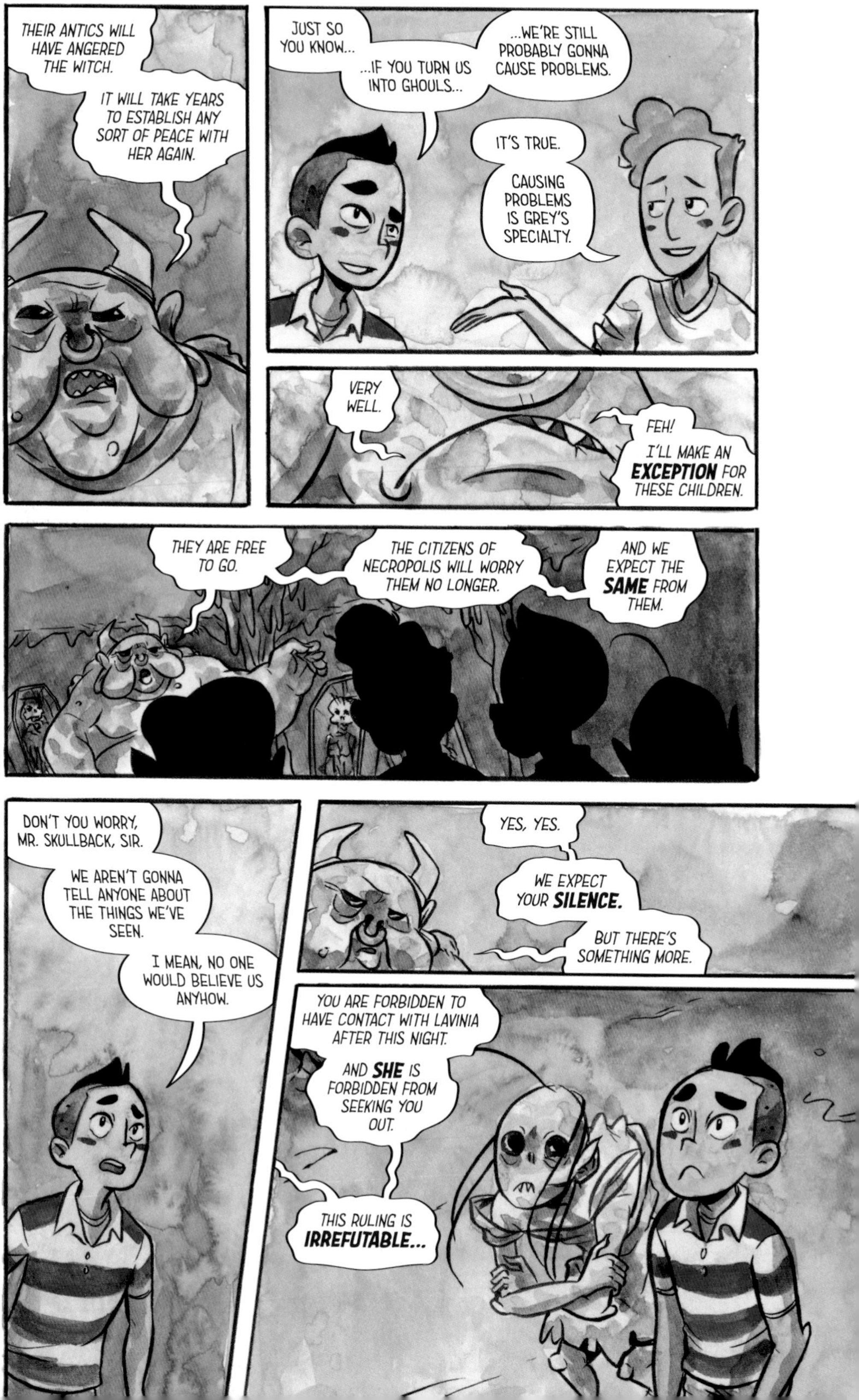
THEIR ANTICS WILL HAVE ANGERED THE WITCH.
IT WILL TAKE YEARS TO ESTABLISH ANY SORT OF PEACE WITH HER AGAIN.
JUST SO YOU KNOW...
...IF YOU TURN US INTO GHOULS...
...WE'RE STILL PROBABLY GONNA CAUSE PROBLEMS.
IT'S TRUE.
CAUSING PROBLEMS IS GREY'S SPECIALTY.
VERY WELL.
FEH!
I'LL MAKE AN **EXCEPTION** FOR THESE CHILDREN.
THEY ARE FREE TO GO.
THE CITIZENS OF NECROPOLIS WILL WORRY THEM NO LONGER.
AND WE EXPECT THE **SAME** FROM THEM.
DON'T YOU WORRY, MR. SKULLBACK, SIR.
WE AREN'T GONNA TELL ANYONE ABOUT THE THINGS WE'VE SEEN.
I MEAN, NO ONE WOULD BELIEVE US ANYHOW.
YES, YES.
WE EXPECT YOUR **SILENCE.**
BUT THERE'S SOMETHING MORE.
YOU ARE FORBIDDEN TO HAVE CONTACT WITH LAVINIA AFTER THIS NIGHT.
AND **SHE** IS FORBIDDEN FROM SEEKING YOU OUT.
THIS RULING IS **IRREFUTABLE...**

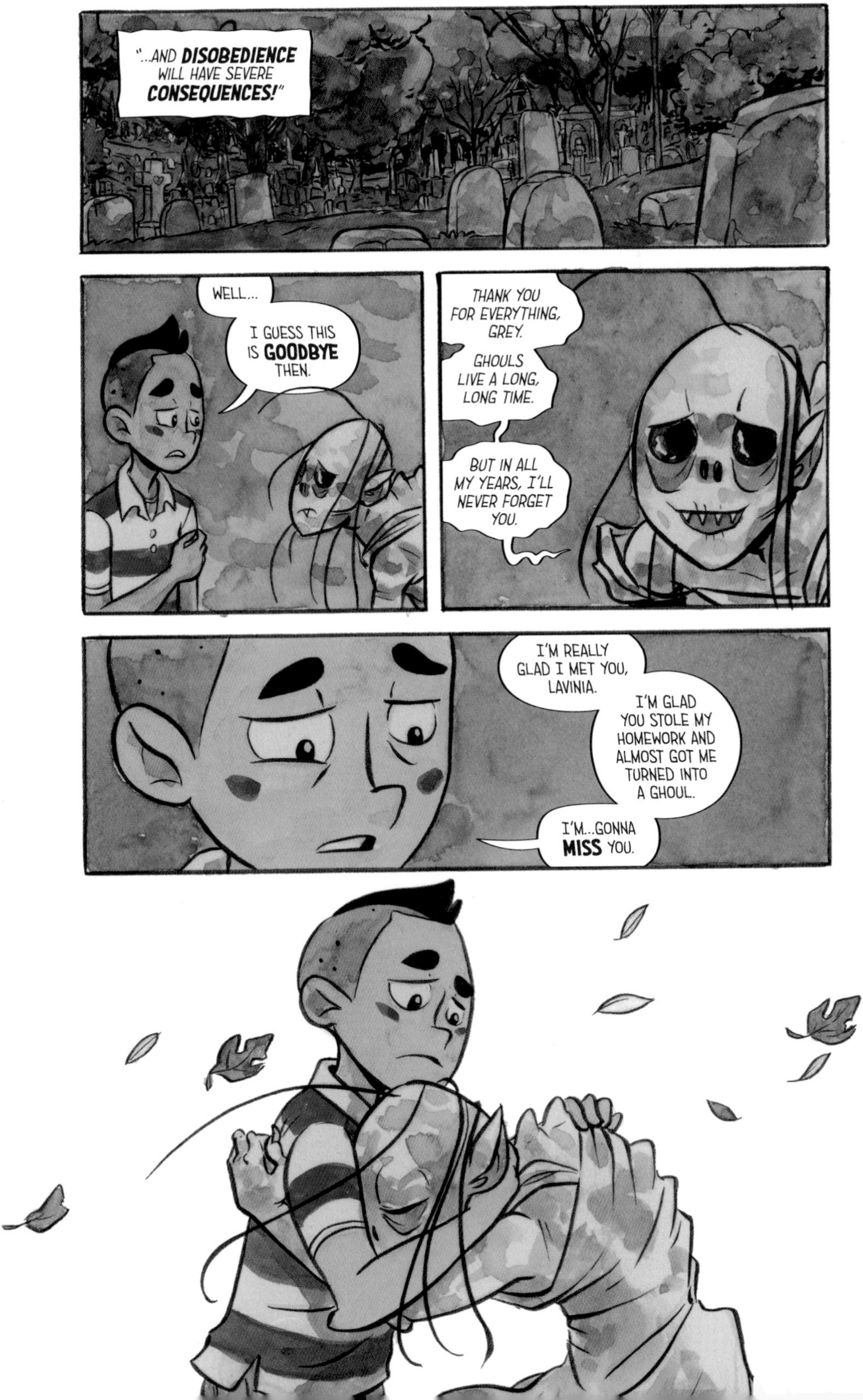
"...AND DISOBEDIENCE WILL HAVE SEVERE CONSEQUENCES!"
WELL...
I GUESS THIS IS GOODBYE THEN.
THANK YOU FOR EVERYTHING, GREY.
GHOULS LIVE A LONG, LONG TIME.
BUT IN ALL MY YEARS, I'LL NEVER FORGET YOU.
I'M REALLY GLAD I MET YOU, LAVINIA.
I'M GLAD YOU STOLE MY HOMEWORK AND ALMOST GOT ME TURNED INTO A GHOUL.
I'M...GONNA MISS YOU.

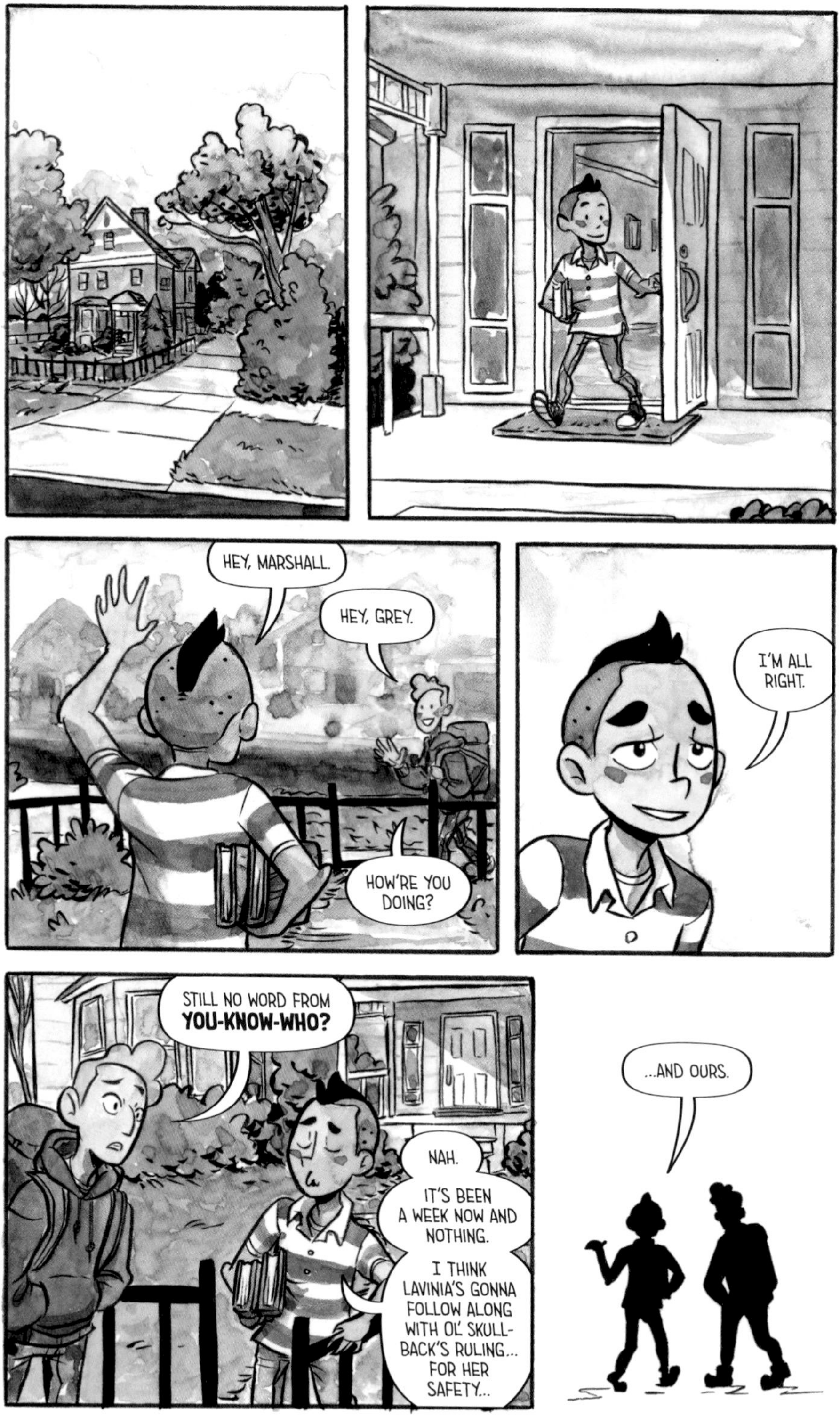

HEY, MARSHALL.
HEY, GREY.
HOW'RE YOU DOING?
I'M ALL RIGHT.
STILL NO WORD FROM **YOU-KNOW-WHO?**
NAH.
IT'S BEEN A WEEK NOW AND NOTHING.
I THINK LAVINIA'S GONNA FOLLOW ALONG WITH OL' SKULL-BACK'S RULING... FOR HER SAFETY...
...AND OURS.

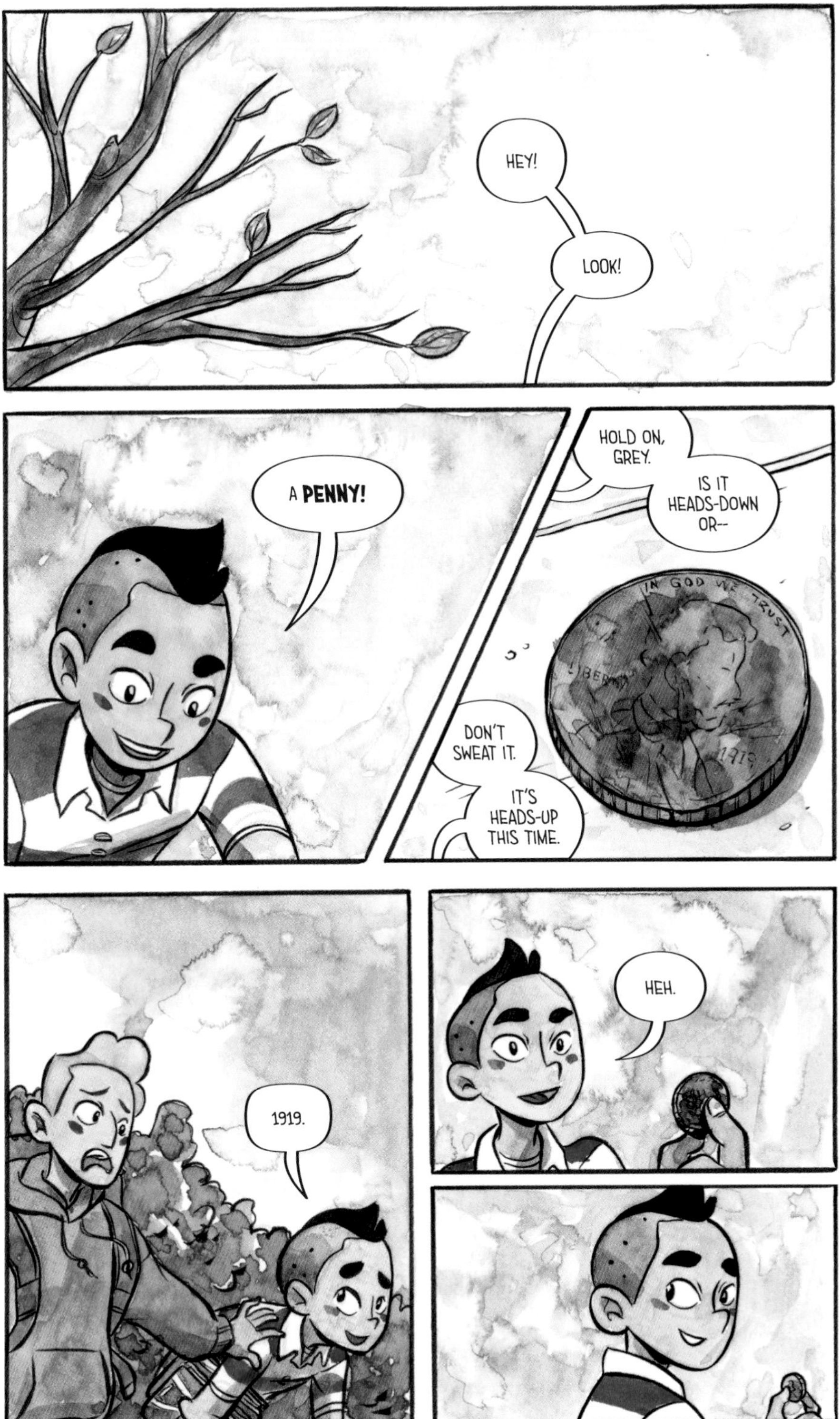
HEY!
LOOK!
A PENNY!
HOLD ON, GREY.
IS IT HEADS-DOWN OR--
IN GOD WE TRUST
LIBERTY
1919
DON'T SWEAT IT.
IT'S HEADS-UP THIS TIME.
1919.
HEH.

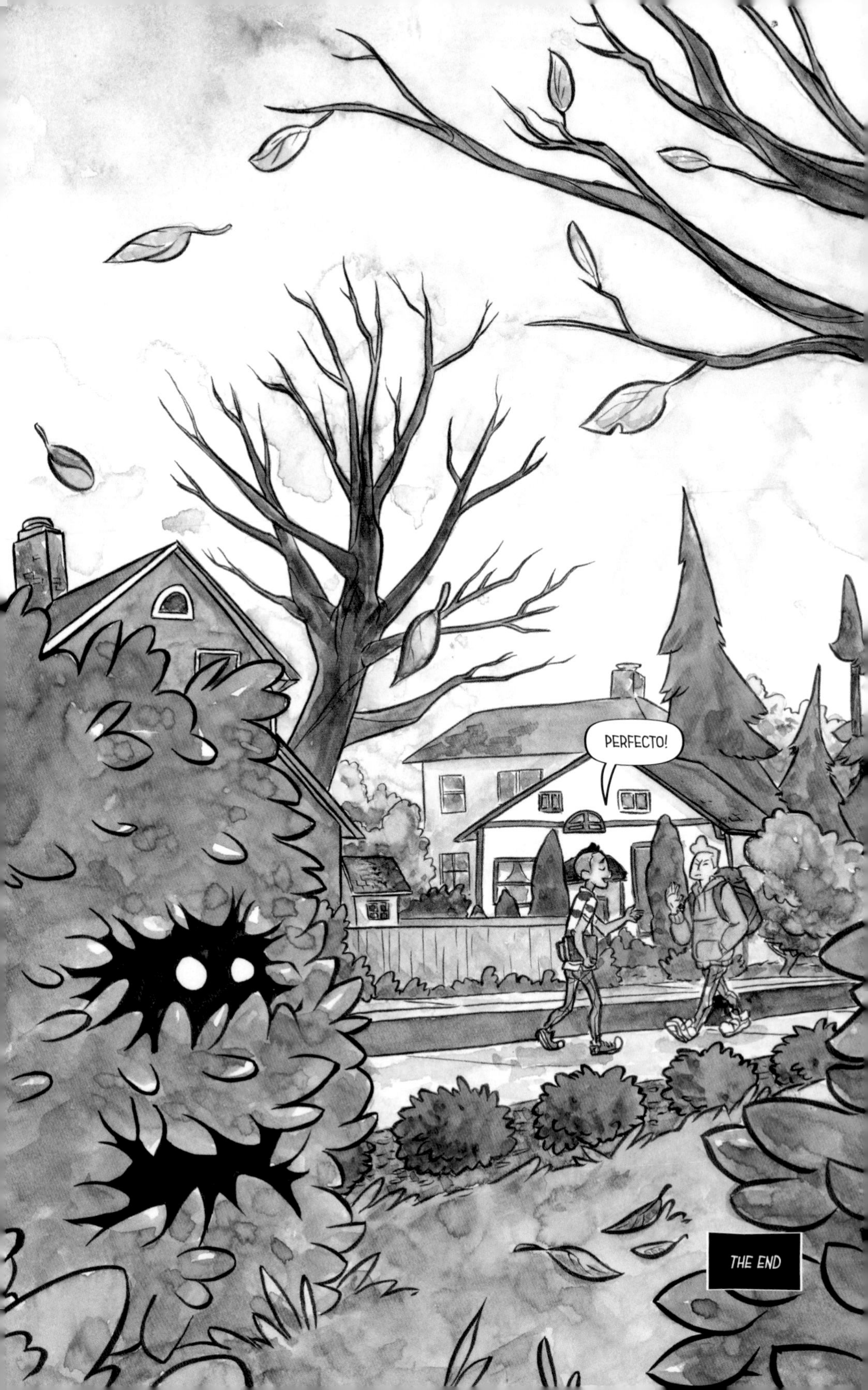
PERFECTO!
THE END

ACKNOWLEDGMENTS

Stories like this exist because of the great people who help you along the way. My sincere thanks to Cat Farris for bringing this book to life and to Charlie Olsen for helping us come together as a creative team in the first place; to our editor Clarissa Wong for making the book better every step of the way; to Aditya Bidikar for his skill in the underappreciated art of lettering; to Anton Kromoff, Josh Roberts, and Scott Adams for listening to me rattle on about dreams of ghoulish underground kingdoms; to Brian Hurtt for the encouragement and feedback along the way; to the Bunnheads for all the support over the years; to my son Jackson for reminding me that I'm still in the "cool zone" in his opinion; and to my wife Cindy for believing in me and helping me make my dreams happen.

—Cullen Bunn

With extreme gratitude to Charlie Olsen for making this happen, Cullen Bunn for writing me a dream script, Aditya Bidikar for jumping in to give this book the letters it deserves, my Helioscope studio mates, the red room crew for always cheering me on, Schmincke watercolor, Tyler Crook, Terri Nelson, Clarissa Wong for being the most excellent editor, my parents, Sally, and my husband, Ron, for helping me go championship rounds with this thing!

—Cat Farris